CW00706234

LENZIE
MILNGAVIE
WESTER

776

2000

00

2002

WINTER ROSES

Recent Titles by Harriet Hudson

INTO THE SUNLIGHT *

NOT IN OUR STARS *

writing as Alice Carr

THE LAST SUMMER
DARK HARVEST

* *available from Severn House*

WINTER ROSES

Harriet Hudson

severn
House

This first world edition published in Great Britain 1999 by
SEVERN HOUSE PUBLISHERS LTD of
9–15 High Street, Sutton, Surrey SM1 1DF.
This first world edition published in the U.S.A. 1999 by
SEVERN HOUSE PUBLISHERS INC of
595 Madison Avenue, New York, N.Y. 10022.

British Library Cataloguing in Publication Data

Hudson,   Harriet
      Winter roses
      1.   World War, 1914-1918 - Social aspects - England - Sussex
          -   Fiction
      2.   Country life - England - Sussex - Fiction
      3.   Domestic fiction
      I.   Title
      823.9'14 [F]

      ISBN 0-7278-2275-6

Typeset by Hewer Text Ltd
Edinburgh, Scotland.
Printed and bound in Great Britain by
MPG Books Ltd, Bodmin, Cornwall.

378789

Acknowledgements

I am grateful to Sara Short and Neville Gomes of Severn House for their enthusiasm and careful work on this novel, and as always to my agent, Dorothy Lumley of Dorian Literary Agency, for her gentle steering of its passage. My thanks are also due to Jane Wood for her editorial advice and push-start to the Ashden Rectory series, which includces *Winter Roses*. I am also grateful for help received from Marian Anderson, Norman Franks, Martin Kender, Mary Lewis, the Imperial War Museum, and among written sources Christopher Andrew's *Secret Service*, and Captain Henry Landau's *Spreading the Spy Net* and *All's Fair*.

One

C ould anything be more satisfying on a Saturday afternoon in June than the sound of a tennis racket hitting a ball? The rhythmic pit-pat, punctuated by distant shouts, was as comforting as the tick of the Rectory clock.

Caroline basked in contentment, ignoring a niggle of heartache that still obstinately lingered. Their yearly tennis match in the Rectory gardens was proving a peaceful haven from the storms of war. Even donning her white tennis skirt, which she had painstakingly taken apart and turned especially for today, had helped. Clapping the old straw boater on her head had seemed a further gesture of defiance.

The cost of food and its shortages had been bravely disregarded by her parents, who had decreed a breadless week at the Rectory in order to provide the ritual cucumber sandwiches, jellies, cakes and ices. Even Mrs Dibble, their housekeeper, wore a smile on her face – what more could one ask? By concentrating very hard, Caroline decided as she emerged from the kitchen with a refilled teapot, she could even command the Rectory garden walls to keep all talk of war at bay for the afternoon. This week the mood had been particularly sombre. The death of Lord Kitchener, the Secretary of State for War, when the cruiser *Hampshire* was lost to a mine, was not only mourned in itself, but seemed an omen for the war he had come to symbolise. In this summer of 1916, it had been raging nearly two years and there was still no sign of its end.

"It's my belief," Mrs Dibble had announced cryptically this

1

morning, as Caroline patiently buttered and margarined mounds of bread, "that he isn't dead at all. They just want them Germans to think he's dead."

"Whatever for?" Caroline had been amused at this political acumen.

"He's working behind the lines, Russia or one of them places. Joe says that's what the top brass think." Joe was her elder son serving in the 5th Royal Sussex Pioneer Battalion and at present on leave.

Top brass or not, the theory seemed improbable to Caroline, as, having done her duty by the teapot, she strolled over to flop on the grass with those of her friends still left in Ashden. Even the smell of the roses wafting over from the red-brick garden walls, could not shut out war completely, for the dozen or so convalescent patients from Ashden Manor hospital, some in invalid chairs, others in the motley collection of seating brought over from the house, provided a stark reminder.

And then there were the Hunneys, another painful recollection of war if Caroline cared to dwell on it. Which she didn't. Lady Hunney was here, her married daughter Eleanor was here, Daniel, her younger son seriously wounded at Mons, was here. Reggie, her elder son, was not. A captain in the 2nd Royal Sussex, he, too, was at home on leave, but he had chosen not to come. Caroline tried to suppress her disappointment, aware she was being ridiculous, for she no longer loved Reggie – at least, not as she had done once. Their engagement had been broken last August. War had driven them apart, and that had to be that.

She had been pleased to see Daniel, however, quite confident now with his artificial leg, and joking with a friend whom she had briefly met in April. Henri Willaerts was able to walk for brief periods on crutches with his two artificial legs. With them was the same Belgian army captain who had been with them then, Captain Yves Rosier, although he now wore khaki, not the traditional Belgian army uniform with shako as he had in April. She had been equally pleased to see him for despite a slight limp he was able-bodied. An eleventh-hour rescue was at hand.

"Thank goodness." She smiled at him in relief. "We badly need another man. I'd just told Janie – Miss Marden – that I'd have to co-opt her to play opposite her brother."

He had seemed taken aback, almost offended. "*Je regrette*, Miss Lilley, that I do not play."

Amazed at the sharp reply and not entirely convinced that the abrupt words were solely due to the fact that English was not his native language, she tried her most winning manner. "It doesn't matter if you're an awful player. We're all rotten, but it's still fun."

It failed to win him, to her annoyance. "My apologies, but I came today merely to drive Captain Willaerts."

"He is *un homme très serieux*," Henri butted in, grinning. "It would do you good to hit a ball around, Yves."

"*Merci, Henri*," a gentler note in the captain's voice, "but I prefer to walk down to the forest." (Ashdown Forest lay less than a mile away down the track called Pook's Way.)

It had felt like a slap in the face, whether intended or not, and, irritated, Caroline made a grimace at Henri as Yves Rosier bowed and strolled off. His limp and the scar on his cheek suggested he had probably met Henri in hospital. She wondered fleetingly what his story was, recalling her first shock reaction on meeting him in April, and then decided to waste no more time on such a prickly guest. Instead, she went in search of Janie.

"You're a man," she informed her cheerfully. "You're doomed."

Janie grimaced. "If I get pole-axed by one of Tim's aces, I bequeath you my thanks."

Since universal conscription had been introduced in May, the manpower both from the village and from among her friends elsewhere had steadily thinned. Many had already enlisted long before conscription became law, but now every man from eighteen to forty-one was vanishing, married and unmarried

3

alike. And, it seemed, indiscriminately. Those who objected to fighting on moral grounds could face a military tribunal to hear their case, though they were greatly disapproved of. There were others not even as fortunate. Men like Fred, who had received his papers, and whose plight lay outside the range of exemptions covered by the tribunals. The Dibbles' younger son, childlike in mind and life, ambled through his days in the Rectory performing one or two small jobs. To his pride, these had expanded in wartime to taking Nanny Oates's spare eggs into Tunbridge Wells for sale. Eggs were a luxury food now and poor Fred had been clumsy with them, until Caroline had had the bright idea of telling him that eggs were like tiny birds to be cherished. After that there had not been a single breakage. Dr Marden and her father had both appealed to the War Office asking for exemption for Fred, and since no more had been heard Mrs Dibble's fears had been allayed.

Caroline, playing with the schoolmaster, Philip Ryde, had quickly been knocked out of the first round of the grandly named 'tournament' this afternoon – hardly to her surprise, for she did not pride herself on being a good player and Philip certainly wasn't. In fact, she was delighted, for it meant she could enjoy the rest of the afternoon without having to display her lack of talent on the court yet again. She left that to the brighter stars such as her friend Penelope Banning, home from Serbia and as yet undecided what to do next, and Ellen, her friend from Dover where they had both been VADs. Under Caroline's haphazard tutelage Ellen had picked up the game remarkably quickly, and her small quicksilver figure darted around the court, returning even the most impossible-looking shots.

Ellen was partnering George, Caroline's seventeen-year-old brother. Having beaten – to everyone's surprise – Beatrice Ryde, Philip's formidable sister, and Joe Dibble who compensated in heftiness for what his game lacked in skill, they would be competing in the one-set final after tea. Agnes, the parlourmaid, and Mrs Dibble were beginning to clear tea away, and

4

Caroline jumped up to help them since it was obvious George couldn't wait to get started.

"We'll win, Ellen," he yelled confidently, as he strode like W.G. Grace towards his wicket, although it was merely the Rectory tennis court with its worn grass and wobbly chalk lines painted by Percy Dibble. Hadn't George cried out something like that two years ago, when he'd been partnering dear Aunt Tilly, much to his initial disgust? Caroline felt a sharp jab of pain as she thought of what else had happened on that glorious day, but instantly fought it. Some kind of new life must surely lie ahead. She did not yet know what it was, but in the meantime she had plenty to occupy her.

Her role on the East Grinstead Women's War Agricultural Committee, which reported to Whitehall's Board of Agriculture, combined with her duties in Ashden meant little or no spare time to mourn a lost love. With her mother's help on the paperwork, she coaxed and coerced village women into volunteering their paid services to farmers to dig, muck out, saw, paint, clean and whatever else was needed. With fewer and fewer local labourers available, and the Government calling for more and more food production, the women were increasingly necessary, and her rotas now came under the auspices of the WWAC. It was not too difficult to find volunteers, for money was sorely needed with prices soaring and menfolk away.

The Ashden hop gardens were Caroline's biggest headache at present. Frank Eliot, the manager, had been called up, and the owner William Swinford-Browne, interested only in his munitions factory at East Grinstead, was letting them go to rack and ruin. Lizzie Dibble (or Stein, as she was legally) at Hop Cottage was doing her best in Frank's absence, but she was expecting their first child in late August and without wages to pay men or women it was a losing battle. Meanwhile the huge hop gardens were virtually untended. The sets had been planted last autumn, and the poles and stringing done, but little dressing, hoeing or nidgeting had followed.

"Game, set, match."

It was Dr Beth Parry's triumphant cry this time. Dr Marden's assistant, who because of her sex was winning only reluctant acceptance from the village, was playing with Charles Pickering, Father's curate, who had applied to be a forces padre but was still awaiting call-up. He was a most serious young man – even more serious than Captain Rosier, and not nearly so interesting, in Caroline's view. However, he and Beth had won, and George and Ellen lost – much to George's obvious disgust.

Did it matter who won the tennis match? It had been all-important two years ago, but what had happened? They hadn't won anything, for war had cheated them out of the rewards of summer. Today everyone had settled down into a stoical acceptance of the continued existence of war, and the days of peace were a distant dream. Life then had seemed for their taking but it had been snatched away. More fronts had opened up, the fighting was intensifying and *everyone* was involved, not just the services. Civilians were suffering in the occupied countries, and here in England they suffered not only from bereavements, hardship and deprivations, but the ever-present menace of Zeppelin raids, which had increased in number this spring.

"Make way for the punchbowl!"

Caroline's mother was clearing a path through the spectators for Percy Dibble who, flushed with pride, was bearing the huge bowl that had belonged to Elizabeth's grandmother. The basis of the recipe was Percy's home-made wine, fortified with brandy, lemonade, fruit and a closely guarded secret ingredient. Alas, the brandy had all been used last year, except for a half-bottle kept for medicinal purposes, and as it was now not so much unaffordable as unobtainable, it would not be enriching this year's brew.

Nevertheless, Caroline saw that her father, who had emerged from the fastnesses of his study – where he had been holding his daily surgery, Rector's Hour – was ladling the punch into glasses with great aplomb. To her dismay, Caroline also noticed that Lady Hunney and the redoubtable Lady Buckford, Father's mother, who had come to blight their lives at the Rectory last November, were *both* majestically moving towards Father for the honour of making the customary loyal toast to His Majesty. How did Grandmother know about that? She must have hidden sources of information, for her arch-enemy Mrs Dibble would never have told her. Phoebe? George? Isabel? Whichever of the family it was, Grandmother failed to benefit, for Lady Hunney arrived first to commandeer the special glass set aside for the toast.

"A mistake!" Caroline nudged Penelope, sprawling on the rug at her side.

Lady Hunney rarely put one of her daintily shod feet wrong, but today she had. This was the Rectory, and to rout Grandmother so publicly did not bode well. Already their private armies were gathering around them. The Ashden Manor patients seemed to be supporting Lady Buckford, despite the fact that the Manor belonged to Sir John and Lady Hunney. Caroline had a suspicion that their choice was not due to her grandmother's winning ways, but to the weekly singsongs at the Rectory, over which Grandmother's unexpectedly talented maid, Miss Lewis, presided at the piano. The Rectory resounded to the sound of 'Goodbye-ee', 'Tipperary', or in rarer, quieter mood, 'Where are the Lads of the Village Tonight?'

The villagers, on the other hand, were on Lady Hunney's side. Again, this could hardly be due to her benevolence; self-preservation was more likely to be the reason. The rivalry between their two ladyships since Grandmother's arrival had become a game of chess, with the two queens slogging it out in defence of their kingdoms. In Lady Hunney's case, the kingdom was Ashden; in Grandmother's, it was power. So much for unity in wartime.

As Caroline sipped her punch, finding herself momentarily alone as Penelope abandoned her to talk to Eleanor, Daniel

7

Hunney seized the opportunity to take her place, plomping himself down heavily on the ground and dropping his stick.

"At last, I've been waiting for a chance to talk to you privately."

"Sounds exciting."

"It is for me. I've found a job." Daniel's constant spells in hospital had put paid to any idea of his working even at a desk job with the army – which, with his father in the War Office, would have been easy to arrange, had he wanted it.

"Daniel, that's wonderful. Travelling?"

"Not yet."

"Oxford?"

Daniel's dream before the war had been to travel from one archaeological site to another, and when balked of that he switched to the idea of returning to university life.

"If you'll calm down, Caroline, I'll tell you," he said patiently. "Not Oxford."

"Here? Or London?"

"London, but before you ask, no, my papa did not find a job for his little wounded son to make him feel a big man again."

"I wouldn't expect him to. Tell me, Daniel, *tell* me."

"It's through a chap I met before the war. He was at Mons too, a major in the Gordon Highlanders."

Caroline hadn't seen Daniel so excited for years. His good-looking face with its mane of dark hair glowed with pleasure.

"It's hush-hush," he continued, lowering his voice even more. "Priest-hole rules." These were even more stringent than the Defence of the Realm or Official Secrets Acts. They stemmed from the Rectory hiding place, in which as children the Lilleys and the Hunneys secreted themselves. "It's a small group which he wants to build up with university chaps like me. MI16 we're called. It's a military code-breaking unit. Just imagine, Caroline. I'll be making a positive contribution to the war by cracking German codes and discovering their plans."

"Real Richard Hannay stuff, Daniel. Right out of *The Thirty-Nine Steps.*"

"You jest, young woman. I'll have you know that's exactly what my job will be."

"What does your mother say?"

Daniel grimaced. For all her drawbacks, he was devoted to his mother. "She put on her Roman matron act: return with your shield or on it, my son. Figuratively speaking, of course," he added hastily, since both of them were only too well aware that Reggie would be returning to the Front in a few days' time. "She pretends to be delighted for me, but life will be bleak for her with Father away so much, and Eleanor . . ."

"Is still unforgiven for marrying a vet?" she finished for him.

"Yes, though as you see they're on speaking terms. Talking of Mother, I'd better get back to her, before she goes over the top and attacks your grandmother with a bayonet."

"I think Grandmother is capable of defending herself."

Daniel laughed. "Help me up, will you?"

It was the first time he had ever asked for help unselfconsciously, and to Caroline it was another sign of how good it would be for him to work in London. Even as she congratulated him again, however, she was aware that for her it would mean another stalwart prop of Ashden life removed. The steady routine of pre-1914 had given way to continuous change. When the war ended – it had to end *sometime* – would that still be so? She had argued this over and over again with her father who still maintained that life would revert to 'normal'. Whatever that was. She disagreed, for her generation at least was beginning to find change normal. New horizons were opening up both for men and women, and the old ones, however much loved, might impose unacceptable limitations.

She jumped up, and by the time Daniel was on his feet, her elder sister Isabel had rushed up to talk to him, linking her arm into his in her usual possessive way. She seemed to assume, married though she was, that every man was basically only interested in her, Caroline reflected crossly.

Daniel turned round awkwardly, as Isabel marched him away. "Tell Felicia, will you?" he jerked out.

Felicia, who at twenty was the third of them in age, was in the Ypres sector in Belgium, nursing at a front-line post set up by her and father's militant suffragette sister, Aunt Tilly. Legally her aunt was Lady Matilda Buckford, but she had long since shaken off not only the dust of Buckford House but also her title – and her mother.

"Tell her yourself," Caroline called back. *That* would be a test. To her puzzlement, Daniel seemed to have rigidly refrained from initiating any direct contact with Felicia since her departure to Belgium over a year ago, although there could be no doubt of the strength of feeling that still existed between them.

A soldier in one of the nearby invalid chairs, whom she had noticed had been listening with interest, called out: "Is that Nurse Felicia Lilley, by any chance. One of the two Lilies of the Field?"

"Yes, she's one of my sisters," Caroline replied.

Felicia and Aunt Tilly had been awarded a medal last year from King Albert of the Belgians, and she and Daniel knew, though Father and Mother did not, that it was for bravery under fire. They fondly imagined Felicia was operating safely well behind the lines, like most VADs, and it was on the Ypres Salient that the Germans had launched an all-out attack at the beginning of the month. Although the ground they won had been quickly regained, she had not heard since from Felicia.

"I know her," the soldier announced, looking highly pleased. Daniel stopped and turned to look at him, and Caroline saw his face darken.

"Have you any news of her?" she asked instantly, though it was a foolish question since he'd clearly been here for some weeks. Daniel was listening for his reply too, and surprisingly the soldier did have news.

10

"I made enquiries after last week's fun and games and was told she was heavily involved at the Front but unharmed."

"Thank you." Her relief was clearly shared by Daniel for, his back rigid, he limped away with Isabel. Uneasily Caroline turned back to the soldier, one leg and arm both swathed in plaster, and his head bandaged over one eye. He was no Daniel. He wasn't so tall and what she could see of his face was nondescript. His large mouth had a quirky grin to it which was appealing though, and there was a lot of intelligence stored up behind the one visible grey-blue eye.

"I'd be up with the angels if it wasn't for your sister and your aunt," he explained. "They dragged me in from no man's land in April. The stretcher-bearers don't have time to assess priorities, but Lissy took one look at me, grabbed one, insisted I was taken straight to the Lilley pad, and stemmed my precious lifeblood which was set on fertilising a foreign field."

Lissy? Caroline was flabbergasted. No one, but no one had ever abbreviated Felicia's name, and here was some soldier out of the blue calling her Lissy.

He interpreted her silence correctly. "She didn't like me calling her that at first, but she came round to it."

"You must have a magic way with you."

"No." The grin on the angular bony face disappeared. "It's she has that. Besides, I explained to her why I called her Lissy."

"And what was the reason?"

"I will tell you when we know each other better, Miss Lilley, not now."

"You seem very certain of yourself." Caroline began to laugh, for there was something about him that was engaging, taking any sting from the rebuff. "Do I want to know you better?"

"You'll be forced to when I marry your sister."

"*What* did you say?"

His turn to laugh. "She doesn't know it yet, but I do. You'll see."

11

"But—" Caroline broke off, stunned, partly by his audacity, but mostly by the thought of Felicia marrying anyone but Daniel. Still, it wasn't her place to interfere in Felicia's life or to dash this wounded soldier's hopes – convictions might be the more accurate word. Moreover, Felicia might be younger than her, but she had proved beyond doubt that she knew her own mind.

"Do you have a name?" she asked instead. "If we're to be related, perhaps I should know it."

"My apologies. Luke Dequessy, Captain in His Majesty's Artists' Rifles. I'd bow if I could get out of this chair."

"I'll bow to you instead," she generously offered, and promptly did so. She decided she liked Luke. "Are you French, Captain Dequessy?" Despite the unusual name, he certainly didn't look it; his height, hair and a way of enthusiastic jerking in his movements of his free arm and leg reminded her of an appealing marionette.

"Once upon a time. The family originated in the Quercy district in south-west France, but came to England so many years ago we count ourselves true-blue British. My mother's American though. I hope that doesn't disbar me from membership of your family."

"We're unprejudiced in the Rectory." Caroline waved a gracious hand, and shortly afterwards excused herself, seeing empty glasses and Percy, lost in admiration of his own handiwork, only slowly cutting up another apple. With a sinking heart, she noticed one of the empty glasses belonged to Lady Hunney. She looked round quickly for aid from Agnes or Myrtle, the general housemaid, but neither was to be seen. She would have to approach the Gorgon herself; though contrary to mythological lore, *this* Gorgon was best confronted head-on.

Her ladyship proved amicable, as Gorgons go. No wonder, Caroline thought uncharitably, having broken up Reggie's and my engagement, she considers me no longer a problem to her.

So it appeared, for having accepted a second glass of punch, Lady Hunney bestowed one of her sweetest social smiles on her.

"Reginald deeply regrets that owing to an engagement in London he is unable to be present today."

"Of course." Caroline's lips were stiff. "I trust he is well."

"Tired, Caroline, as are we all, but physically recovered from last autumn's injury."

Why, oh why, whenever she congratulated herself that her heart was recovering, did some kind person decide to prod the wound again? Caroline fumed at her inability to conquer her own defensiveness when faced with her ladyship, and was annoyed to find her steps taking her towards the orchard after she had (somewhat speedily) left the Gorgon. How ridiculous. Did she hope that the magic of two years ago might be recreated there? Did she imagine that, against the odds, Reggie himself might be there? Even if he were, she reasoned, could she blot out what had happened; the differences that had arisen between them, or the sight of Reggie and Isabel together? No, there was no going back in life. Very well, so why didn't her heart even now quite accept that fact? Perhaps it merely clung to the familiar for fear of the unknown. With this somewhat consoling thought, she determined to forget Reggie – and his mother.

Despite this good resolution, however, her footsteps still drew her towards the orchard like a magnet; it reminded her of childhood days when with the flickering candle for light in her bedroom she would peer beneath the bed to see whether wicked witches lurked there. This time, at least she was confident the wicked witch was behind, not in front of her.

Ahab bounded along at her heels, or perhaps snuffled was a better word. Dignified aged English sheepdogs did not bound unless there was some real inducement in the form of bones. *He* wasn't worried about witches. Yet if there were no such creatures, she asked herself, as she walked through the wicket gate into the orchard, why was her heart pounding like Mrs Dibble kneading oatmeal bread?

At once she found the answer. Because there *was* someone there. Someone in uniform—

"Reggie!"

Her cry rang out even as, realising her mistake, she halted her headlong rush towards him. The uniform was khaki and looked British but it was not, and the officer was not Reggie. As he turned round, she saw it was the Belgian captain, Yves Rosier, who had obviously just entered through the gate from Pook's Way. He was about the same height as Reggie, about five foot ten or eleven, but otherwise there was no resemblance. In place of Reggie's classical handsome looks and light-brown hair, this man, who looked in his early thirties, had a sturdier build, darker hair and an uneven, almost craggy face with that noticeable scar and bitter grey eyes. Smiles, she guessed, did not – or did no longer – come readily to him. How could she possibly have confused the two men?

"I'm sorry," she stammered, feeling foolish, "I thought you were someone else," and when he did not reply, she added inanely: "You missed the arrival of the punchbowl, Captain Rosier."

This time he did reply. "I apologise again, mademoiselle. I am sure the punch was excellent, but I enjoyed my walk in the Forest."

"You like forests?"

"They remind me of my homeland."

Caroline immediately felt conscience-stricken for her lack of understanding. Everyone knew what appalling suffering the Belgian civilians were enduring with most of their country occupied by an increasingly harsh regime. Acute food shortages were causing riots, and the crackdown was swift and brutal. On the Belgian front, its army was on the River Yser line between the British and the sea, protecting the last corner of its territory from occupation. In the early days of the war, thousands of refugees from Belgium had flooded into Britain and were now established in hostels and enclaves trying to build a new life, even, if, as they hoped, it would be a temporary one.

"Is it wise," she asked him impulsively, "always to remind yourself of home? Wouldn't it be better to escape for an afternoon?"

"There is no escape," he replied after a moment. "No escape by playing tennis, no escape in these gardens, no escape by shutting one's eyes to what lies outside. The temptation is great," he added, perhaps to soften his words, "but no. Not before the fight is won."

"You are very sure of yourself." Caroline's sympathy vanished in defensive irritation. "I believe that afternoons such as this help: even the worst of battles is better fought with snatches of rest beforehand."

"I cannot share your view. I came here only to assist my friend, Captain—"

"Is that why you wouldn't play tennis when we needed you?" Caroline interrupted, as the thought suddenly occurred to her. "Because it's an escape?"

He flushed. "I am sorry if that offended you."

"It seemed a small thing to ask."

"To a refugee even the smallest thing can prove an insurmountable obstacle." He stated it as a fact, not as a plea for understanding. Had it been the latter, she would have replied less sharply.

"Refugee? But you are in the Army."

"Yes, but my country is occupied."

"What are you doing in this country?" Curiosity made her speak without thinking. "You speak excellent English." Although his accent was heavy, his grasp of the language was admirable.

There was another pause. "I am in liaison between the Belgian army and British Headquarters."

"Daniel told me liaison was handled at GHQ in France. Isn't—" Caroline broke off, aware there must be more to this. Did she care? On the whole, not very much. On the other hand, she did care about more punch, and that would provide an excellent excuse to leave. She was prevented from doing so when he came closer, stretching out a hand as if to lay it on her arm. He did not do so, but for a moment it felt as though he had.

"I have offended you, Miss Lilley, through my unsocial behaviour. Also," he added, "because I am not this Reggie whom you seek."

He smiled for the first time, and it changed his whole face. For a moment the bitterness vanished, and his eyes seemed fully focused on her, not on some inner concern of his own.

"It was stupid of me to call out his name."

"Why?"

"Because the past is the past, Captain Rosier, and unlike you I *do* believe in escape."

His eyes gleamed in appreciation of her retort. "Tell me of yourself, Mademoiselle Lilley. Daniel has said very little."

"Quite right too. Reggie," she choked slightly, "is his brother."

"Tell me about *yourself*, not about this Reggie. Daniel mentions you are working in the cause of women helping the war effort here."

Did she want to talk to him? Wouldn't she much rather return to her friends and family? Eventually politeness decided the question. To remain silent any longer would put her in the wrong. "That cause is nearly won now that Lloyd George is on our side. If only he were Prime Minister *full* utilisation of womanpower would happen even more quickly. Meanwhile—" She went on to describe what she was doing in Ashden, and on the Women's War Agricultural Committee in East Grinstead. "The food shortage is worsening, Captain Rosier, and now farms are strained to their limit. I believe there is only one answer and so did Lord Milner in the War Cabinet, when he reported to the Government last year. More land. Every scrap of waste or unused land will have to be ploughed up."

"You're doing valuable work, Miss Lilley," he said, yet it had the effect of making her suddenly conscious she had been talking for a long time about something in which he could have little personal interest. She consoled herself that he had nevertheless been listening attentively.

"Thank you." It was her turn to feel awkward.

"However, you could work more directly for the war effort, if you wished to leave Ashden."

"You mean go to the Front like Felicia, and nurse." Her opinion of him promptly sank again. "That's not—"

"No," he interrupted, "you are not like your sister. I have met Miss Felicia, and you are right, that life is not for you. Your heart is too warm and your discipline insufficient for her work."

Caroline could not believe her ears; she was outraged at this familiarity. "You seem to know a great deal about me, Captain Rosier, from our two brief meetings," she replied acidly.

"Three."

With mixed feelings, she realised he too had thought in April that that had not been their first meeting. She had convinced herself she had been mistaken, yet here he was, about to tell her that there had been no such mistake.

"Perhaps I should not remind you," he continued hesitantly, "of that evening when the Zeppelin bombs fell by the Gaiety Theatre. I was on my way to the home for Belgian refugees in the Aldwych when the first one fell. I turned back, otherwise probably I should not be here now. You must have been caught in the blast but you were helping the wounded. You needed a pair of hands to assist you that dark night and I offered mine. You did not take any notice of me. Why should you? But I watched your face, Miss Lilley, as I obeyed your commands. You were eager to help, and it did not seem to occur to you what danger you might be in had the Zeppelin returned to drop more bombs, or should the gas mains explode, as indeed one later did. I thought your face familiar when we met briefly in

April. Only afterwards did I remember where I had seen it before."

"The refugee hostel in the Aldwych was badly hit," Caroline managed to blurt out. He was right. She didn't want to be reminded yet again of that terrible experience which still brought nightmares in its wake.

"Yes, and many friends of mine died there. War pursues us Belgians from our homeland and seeks us out in every sanctuary – perhaps even in this idyllic place." He nodded towards the Rectory. "You are fighting a brave defensive battle here, but if you ever wish to join the offensive, I could offer you a job."

"Thank you." Shock was replaced with fury at his presumption. "Here in Ashden we *do* see our work as part of the offensive, Captain Rosier. Perhaps you could see your way now to accepting a glass of punch – before you leave."

"Thank you. I should like that." He did not seem discomposed by her snub, as he walked back with her across the gardens to join the rest of the party. Perhaps he did not recognise it as such, and she began to feel ashamed at her curtness. Nevertheless, she parted from him with relief, as her mother came hurrying up to her.

"Where have you been, Caroline? It's not like you to leave me in the thick of battle." She was half serious, half joking. "Their two ladyships have declared war."

Caroline laughed, glad of the diversion from her irritating encounter with Captain Rosier. "It will deflect Grandmother from annoying us. What started this off?" She was making a determined attempt to reach the punchbowl, but her mother seemed equally determined to stop her, for she drew her aside from the crowd of people at the table.

"The fact that Lady Hunney, being a generation younger than Grandmother, is always fashionably dressed," Elizabeth replied dolefully.

"Grandmother is too."

"Well dressed. Expensively dressed, but not fashionably."

"There *is* no fashion now, except to look like everyone else. Lady Hunney dresses simply, military style, no frills and bows."

"There is the matter of length, Caroline." Her mother's voice was heavy with meaning.

"Ah." Caroline understood immediately. The older the lady, the nearer her skirts remained to the ground. Even her mother had moved her hemline up a few inches. Lady Hunney had raised her skirts to reveal her booted ankles, if not yet her lower calf. Grandmother had so far not budged them an inch.

"Today she realised her mistake. By choosing to remain in full-length skirts, which is a declaration of age, she has removed herself from competition with Lady Hunney for the position of Queen of the Village. She has just commanded the presence of the village dressmaker – not even by name, though she must know it perfectly well. I told her to walk over and make an appointment like everyone else."

Caroline was both fascinated and impatient with such trivialities. Fascination won. Mrs Hazel, unassuming as she was, went to no one unless they were unable to leave the house. Lady Hunney patronised a London dressmaker, but Grandmother was in no position to follow suit. Nor was she housebound, fortunately for the Rectory. She sighed, wistfully eyeing glasses of punch all round her. Even Captain Rosier seemed to be enjoying one, deep in conversation with Daniel. Talking about code-breaking and army matters, no doubt, not stuck with skirt lengths and battling matrons. "I don't see what you're upset about then."

"You will. Your grandmother has just heard about the flower festival, and her failure over Mrs Hazel has sharpened her claws in that direction."

Caroline understood her mother's concern immediately, and in Ashden terms it was no laughing matter. The home front too had its battles. Lady Hunney had always presented the prizes and helped to judge the festival, which this year was to take place on 29th July. A bid to change that far overranked

Grandmother's attempts to break into the tight-knit committees in charge of war relief.

She had a brainwave. "I'll tell Grandmother there won't be one this year, because it's unpatriotic to grow flowers, not vegetables. I'm sure Father would agree."

Elizabeth looked at her sadly. "I'm very much afraid your Grandmother suggested to your father half an hour ago that the flower show be expanded to cover vegetables and fruit. On the pretext of its being a different show, she intends to be queen of the proceedings. You see?"

Caroline did. "Then Father must change his mind."

"It's too late, Caroline. Your grandmother immediately sent Parker down to the village to inform Mr Bertram *and* told Beatrice Ryde." The sacristan, a keen gardener, was in practical charge of the Flower Show, and Beatrice was the formidable chief organiser.

"Then let Lady Hunney judge the flowers and Grandmother the fruit and veg."

"That's like asking the Kaiser to share his spoils fifty-fifty with the doddery old Habsburg Emperor Franz Joseph . . . whatever's that?"

Caroline broke off, whirling round as a loud scream attracted everyone's attention. This was not merely a plate of sandwiches dropped on the kitchen floor, but some emergency. Mrs Dibble was running across the lawn, waving her arms, screaming out for the Rector. Fire? Accident? Was Agnes's little girl hurt? Myrtle?

Caroline and her mother rushed towards her, colliding with her father as they reached the distraught woman. It was he she turned to, clutching his lapels in terror: "Rector, Rector, do something! They've come for Fred."

"Who?"

"The military police. They've come to take him away to die in them trenches."

Two

"*O God, our help in ages past—*"
Margaret Dibble's less than fine alto voice came to a halt. For the first time He had failed her badly, and all the Sussex pudding in the Weald could not compensate. The Rectory had to go on eating, and the dust wouldn't stop settling just because she and Percy had troubles, but somehow these thoughts failed to rally her. You knew where you were in the old days. None of this 'macon' rubbish. Bacon was bacon then, not made from mutton. Furthermore, if this war hadn't come, her Lizzie wouldn't be in the family way thanks to a man she wasn't married to and who had smartly marched off to the wars. She would still be in her little Hartfield cottage, safely married to that nice Rudolf, and Mrs Stein instead of Lizzie Dibble as she now called herself for her own protection. Of course, she'd still be married to a German and now that everyone knew just what Germans were like, Margaret couldn't wish that fate on her Lizzie either. Life was a half-baked cake to which you had to add your own ingredients, even though you couldn't bank on its turning out right.

She looked up belligerently as her kitchen door opened, but it wasn't Lady Blooming Buckford. It was the Rector. It couldn't be good news, or he would have called her into his study, and not trespassed on her domain – not that those old rules applied any more either. Every Tom, Dick and Harry seemed to think they were entitled to stroll into her kitchen any time they pleased. The Rector was different, though,

21

DUNBARTONSHIRE
Council

"Fred?" she asked sharply. She hadn't had a decent night's sleep since that new offensive on the Somme began two weeks ago. They said at first it was a success, but they weren't making such a song and dance about it now, and someone had to go out to fill in the gaps caused by casualties.

"Can you spare a moment or two, Mrs Dibble?" Rector pulled one of the kitchen chairs out for her. So it was going to be bad. Margaret decided she would sit down. "Would you like your husband to join us?"

"You tell me first, Rector. I can't abide waiting, and Percy takes things hard, thank you all the same."

"I've heard from the military authorities, and they tell me that the medical examiner has re-inspected Fred in accordance with the appeal procedure, but have again passed him as fit for service."

Of course they had. Them army doctors would see no reason Fred shouldn't be another blinking Field Marshal Haig, provided he could see further than his nose and hadn't got the plague. It was them couldn't see proper. Dry-eyed, that's what you had to be in these days. "He's not fit to go outside these four walls," Margaret replied flatly.

"I know that, you know that, but the authorities are only interested in physical fitness, and Fred is a strong young man."

"Who's too chuckleheaded to pick up a gun at the right end, let alone fire it. He'll think a bayonet is for picking up dead leaves."

"I shall keep on trying, Mrs Dibble. He's still in this country under training, as you know, so there is still hope."

"Training!" she repeated bitterly. How long would that last? It was no use Rector looking at her in that compassionate way. All the sympathy in the world hadn't brought Fred safe home, nor all the prayers either.

"I thought you would like to know that Dr Marden has been to see Fred."

Her head jerked up. "How was he?" It was the middle of

July, over a month since he'd been taken and she had still not received a word. Hardly surprising, since he couldn't write.

"A little bewildered, but physically he seems to be coping well enough."

"It's not like you to nuddle about with the truth, Rector."

"Very well," the Rector replied evenly. "Dr Marden insisted on seeing the training-camp commanding officer. Fred is, as you feared, being teased by his fellow soldiers, but we know Fred never minded that too much. He takes it in good part."

"Put that way, it's what I'll tell Percy." Briskness was best. "I understand what you're trying to tell me, Rector, or not tell me. What about His Majesty?"

"I beg your pardon?"

"His Majesty wouldn't want poor Fred to go through all this."

"Try everything, Mrs Dibble. It can do no harm. If I can help—"

"But it'll do no good either." She rose to her feet. "And if you'll excuse me, Rector, thanks for all you're doing, but I'll get on with luncheon or you'll all go hungry. And don't you get bothering Mrs Lilley to pop in to see I'm all right. She's enough worries of her own."

From the Rector's face she knew that's just what he had been thinking, but to her relief he left her alone. She wanted a good cry, before she pulled herself together and went to tell Percy. Three kids, one of them out somewhere on the Front digging trenches, one of them having a bastard, and the other feeble-minded and dragged probably to his death from the shelter of his home. Once Ashden could shelter its weakling chicks; now no one and nowhere could, even though we were supposed to be fighting for a better world.

The Lord sent rain as well as sun, but why did He have to send all the storms altogether? If the Kaiser invaded, at least Fred would come home, and Joe would be safe with Muriel and his little ones, and life—

23

Margaret Dibble, what are you saying? She was horrified at herself. This was treason, and her Joe had told her all about what happened to traitors. His battalion had been on guard duty at the Tower of London when that evil German spy Hans Lody was executed at the end of 1914, so he could speak with authority on the subject. She, Margaret Dibble, might be rowed up to Traitors' Gate just like Sir Walter Raleigh, poor gentleman.

She began to cut the neglected boiled pudding into slices to pop under the roast mutton. This was the Lord's work, and the Lord couldn't have a very high opinion of Mrs Margaret Dibble at the moment. She hastened to make amends, guiltily aware that because of her dallying there would be no vanilla custard with the tart today.

"*Time, like an ever-rolling stream . . .*" Her voice rose up in defiance of everything and everyone who dared attack the citadel which Margaret Dibble had built for her family within the sheltering walls of the Rectory.

Caroline, running up the garden path, heard it and was reassured. If Mrs Dibble was still singing hymns, then even the calamity she had to impart to Mother might be surmounted. She found her mother in the glory-hole, the outbuilding she had taken over in order to work as far away as possible from Grandmother. Here, with a small paraffin stove for warmth in the winter, Mother presided over her office, helping Caroline with the farm rotas, and packing endless parcels of books, old clothes, cooking utensils and blankets for the village war relief committees. The Rectory was a collection point. Seeing the box in the entrance hall, parishioners at the daily Rector's Hour were reminded that there were people far worse off in the world than they were, and a surprising amount of material, despite the continuous call for it in the last two years, was donated.

"Mother, have you heard what Grandmother has done?"

Elizabeth promptly dropped the burning sealing wax as

Caroline burst in, and they scrabbled on the floor to retrieve it, banging their heads together in the process.

"What now?" her mother asked wearily, as she extinguished the flame. "I thought she was being too quiet."

Grandmother had lost the battle for the flower festival. Lady Hunney had graciously intimated to her that the idea of extending the festival to vegetables and fruit was a most patriotic one, and that she had spoken (she could strike like a snake when she wished) to the organisers. Two new silver cups, engraved with the Ashden Manor crest, were to be presented to the winners of the vegetables and fruit by herself and the judge was to be a friend of her husband's from the Board of Agriculture.

Grandmother had been sensible enough to realise she was beaten, and since then she had been very quiet indeed. A sign of trouble, Caroline thought ruefully, if only they had taken note of it earlier. As it was, the festival was only just over two weeks away at the end of July, and nothing could be done. At least, she amended crossly, not by anyone other than Grandmother.

"It's too awful. She's—"

"Arranged for Lady Hunney to break her leg?" Elizabeth enquired.

"If only it were so simple," Caroline grimaced. "She's stepped in to organise the Sunday School treat. Goodness knows how she's wangled it, but she's paying for everyone to go to the seaside in motor charabancs for the day with luncheon and tea paid for too."

"What's wrong about that?"

"It's for the same day as the flower festival, Saturday the 29th."

"What?" her mother screeched. "You must be mistaken, Caroline. Even she wouldn't—"

"I wish I was, but Mr Bertram told me. He should know, he's the organiser of the festival, and Mrs Bertram is the head of the Sunday School. What's worse," Caroline added gloomily, "he said Rector had agreed."

25

"Laurence has agreed?" Elizabeth repeated faintly. "Has he gone mad?"

"I don't know, but if not there'll be civil war in Ashden." It was all so petty in the midst of a real war raging over a large part of the world. Surely everyone's attention should be focused on what was happening at the Somme, not on a battle over flowers.

Her mother must have read her thoughts, for she said: "I suppose people don't change in times of trouble."

"But they could win a few medals for *trying*. After all, even the Mutter and Thorn volcano has quietened down." The generations-old village feud had not erupted for months.

"I suspect dear Lady B convinces herself this is her contribution to the war effort," Elizabeth fumed. "So many people will go on the treat, with all the children, their parents and the teachers, it will be tantamount to a boycott of the flower festival. Not that I personally mind. How dare Lady Hunney ignore our work for agriculture here by going above our heads? Nevertheless, I suppose peace in Ashden comes first, and so I propose we seek an audience with the War Minister right away," his wife suggested grimly.

They found Laurence in his study, thankfully settling down for an hour's paperwork before setting off on his morning calls, none too pleased at being interrupted. For once, Caroline had no compunction about doing so, even though Father's annoyance merely changed to surprise as she explained why they were there.

"Certainly I agreed to my mother's plan. Why not? The Sunday School treat was to be scaled down to a picnic in the forest this year, but when my mother offered to pay, I saw no reason to object, and still don't."

"You *agreed*?" Elizabeth was even more horrified. "Knowing she was planning it for the same day as the flower festival? Apart from anything else, you have to attend both functions, Laurence."

"The same day?"

With guilty pleasure, Caroline watched the conflicting emotions battling in her father's face, as he realised he had been outmanoeuvred by his mother, and tried to find the way out. He didn't succeed.

"I didn't know that was the day she planned," he confessed at last. "I assumed it was the same day as we had agreed for the picnic, in August."

"Never assume anything with your mother, Laurence," Elizabeth said crossly.

"I'm afraid she's outwitted you this time, Father."

It was the best thing Caroline could have said, for Laurence had much of his mother's stubbornness in him, which was why until last year, when her house was bombed, they had seen little of Grandmother save for one annual visit to Dover. It was a visit made by Father, herself and her sisters and brother only, since Grandmother had refused to receive her mother in her house, or even to meet her, until forced to do so last year. The relationship remained strained, to put it politely.

"Leave it with me. Say nothing to *anyone*, and I will deal with it," Laurence told them firmly.

"You'll cancel the Sunday School outing?"

"No. I think our Lord is prepared to assist us on this occasion." He glanced out at the warm sunshine outside, donned his jacket, and strode out in masterly fashion into combat.

"What's he going to do, do you think?" Caroline asked her mother, fascinated.

"Puncture the charabanc tyres, I hope. How did your grandmother organise motorised transport and petrol for the treat in these days – or has she rustled up horses?"

"You make her sound like Buffalo Bill."

"Annie Oakley. Dead-shot bullseye every time."

Her mother returned to the glory-hole, and Caroline, unwillingly, was able to return to her own next problem. She'd almost rather have Grandmother to deal with. However, onward it was for this Christian soldier. She donned her business boater and set out for The Towers, resisting the temptation to go the long way round past the hop gardens to put off the ordeal as long as possible.

There had still been no progress on the question of the hop garden's future. Lizzie had little more than a month to go before her baby was born, but even if she were able to organise the harvest, it would be impossible without William Swinford-Browne's agreement. So far he had turned a blind eye to what they were doing, through lack of interest. She had managed to persuade him that a minimum of labour should be employed to hoe, dress and train the plants, but the hop-picking was a different matter. There would be pickers to pay, before such money could be reimbursed from the sale of the hops, now he no longer had a brewery of his own.

Caroline hated The Towers. She hated the dark, gloomy pretentiousness of the building, and she hated William Swinford-Browne, though his wife Edith was more bearable. Unfortunately Isabel was married to their son Robert, now away training for the Royal Flying Corps, and lived only a few hundred yards away at Hop House. Polite relations therefore had to be maintained.

Isabel spent much of her time at the Rectory, although Caroline suspected this was partly to avoid giving Lizzie a hand in the hop gardens. She made no secret of the fact that she didn't like the girl, considering she was responsible for her own predicament, and anyway, she had informed Caroline that she, Isabel, was not suited for field work. It did not surprise her. Isabel of all of them had not adapted to the war, or to the need to contribute to it. She seemed to think being married absolved her from everything, even developing her own life. Although she paid lip-service to the war effort by helping both her mother-in-law and Lady Hunney with their committee work, Caroline couldn't help noticing that Isabel's duties did not seem to weigh heavily on her.

Her dislike of William Swinford-Browne seethed within her as she walked up the drive, and she had to battle to keep it under control. She was here as a minor representative of the Board of Agriculture. The good of England was at stake, she informed herself solemnly, as she rang the bell. She remembered coming to Isabel's engagement dance here with Aunt Tilly and Felicia; she had been so jealous then because Reggie had been escorting Penelope Banning. How rapidly that had changed – and then changed again.

No, she *would* not think of Reggie. She would think of Swinford-Browne and how best to save the hop gardens. She must play on his concentration on munitions. He would not want to be bothered by repercussions from the Board of Agriculture (heavy hint) if he wasted food. And hops were a sort of food. She would praise him for the valuable asset his cinema provided in the village; it was called 'the horror house' because of its gothic ugliness, although now their eyes were accustomed to it it had become an affectionate name. Even her father acknowledged its usefulness as an escape from war, though he had been in the vanguard of opposition to it when it was erected on Bankside, almost opposite the Rectory, just under two years ago.

She was marched by the butler across the chilly, dark entrance hall into the study, a large room with a desk at the far end. She had to remind herself very firmly that she was a spokeswoman for England.

"Well, Caroline, what can I do for you?"

'Nothing, you horrible man,' she longed to retort to His Imperial Complacency replacing his plump form pudgily in the large chair behind his desk, after a perfunctory rise at her entrance. Instead, seated in the leather armchair, she managed to explain her mission in a most businesslike tone, concluding: "We want your authorisation to organise as many of the usual pickers from London as we can, and to call in soldiers from the local camps if necessary. Time is getting short." Soldiers from the Ashdown forest camp, King's Standing, and Crowborough Warren (where her sister Phoebe worked in the YMCA canteen) could be used only under strict conditions, and provided local labour was insufficient. As women came cheaper than soldiers, most farmers were inclined to overlook their misgivings about female labour and so in Ashden soldiers were called in only for the corn harvest and hop-picking.

"I told you before, Caroline, I have no interest in the gardens." He wagged his finger at her. He really did. Caroline had never actually seen a finger wagged before, and it gave her an insane desire to giggle. She resisted both this and the instant resentment she felt at being so patronised.

"You don't know what it involves," he continued smugly. "Capital for a start – to get those huts habitable, as well as pay the tallies. Now, if I'd had Tallow Field to build new huts . . . but there, we won't go into that."

Though you'll mention it whenever it suits you, Caroline fumed. Her father had recently won a victory over Swinford-Browne in reclaiming the field for his new churchyard. "You'll get your money back when you sell the hops."

He gave a short laugh, and she realised that she had played into his hands. "With the price hops are fetching now? You haven't been reading the newspapers, young lady. Ever heard of the No Treating Order and curtailed drinking hours? Haven't you read about the Carlisle experiment this month? The Government's planning to buy up all the breweries, pubs and licensed hotels. No more advertising drink, fewer licences, no licences to grocers, nobody under eighteen to be served, ban on spirits—"

"The shortage of spirits is good for beer." She was sorry she had said that, for he did not like open disagreement.

"It'll never move further than Carlisle, but the writing's on the wall. Munitions are what this country needs to win the war quickly. You can take your spades elsewhere." The William pear adopted his growling bear approach. "I can't expect you ladies to understand economics. If I can't build a new factory here – and your father scotched that – I'll build elsewhere and the hops can rot. Not worth all the trouble those pickers cause."

"And what of your duty to Ashden? You do live here." Steady, Caroline, steady!

"Not much longer. We're leaving."

Leaving? What a wonderful world this suddenly was. Caroline struggled not to burst out into a grin of joy. "What about the cinema, Hop House, and your estates here?" She couldn't be hypocritical enough to express regret.

"The Army has been after this house for years. Now they're taking it over compulsorily. I won't share it, and that's that."

"But where's Isabel going to live?"

"She's coming with us. I've told Robert." As Caroline gasped, he continued offhandedly, "It's all arranged. Everything's finished here. Hop House, the hop gardens and farmlands are going to the Army, and I'm closing the cinema."

"Closing?" This was bad news too. "But why?"

"Tim Thorne's had his call-up papers, and there's no other manager I can find. Again more trouble than it's worth."

Life gave with one hand and took with the other. Caroline was stunned. Welcome though the news was that the Swinford-Brownes would be leaving, the ramifications for Ashden were many, especially for the Rectory. For all Isabel's foibles, Caroline would miss her greatly. So would her parents who, she suspected, worried more about Isabel than any of the rest of them. Except perhaps George. She knew how much they feared the day he must depart, because in the last year or so they seemed to find it hard to talk to him, and he to them.

Caroline thought quickly. She could do nothing about the cinema, but she could about the land. "Although Lord Selborne has resigned as President of the Board of Agriculture, it's still pushing its 'Speed the Plough' policy. They're already worried about the prospects of the harvest this year, and it's quite likely to become illegal to waste arable land. I'm now on

the County War Agricultural Committee, and active interven-
tion is our policy."

"Are you threatening me, young woman? You've done that
once too often."

"I'm telling you what will happen if this war continues much
longer, and food shortages worsen."

To give Swinford-Browne his due, he listened. "Get the hops
picked, and I'll pay. You'll have to do all the organising. So far
as I'm concerned, it's the last season, and I doubt if the Army
will encourage hops when it takes over." He gave a bark of
satisfied laughter.

She decided to put that problem aside in favour of the more
personal one, and went straight to see if Isabel was at Hop
House. Surely her sister could not know about the move? She
would have been howling down the Rectory walls, if so. Yet
Swinford-Browne seemed very sure of himself, and Caroline
felt uneasy.

Isabel was there, and even came to the door herself, so
Caroline was spared Ordeal by Carpet-Slippered Baggy Ankled
Mrs Bugle.

"Is it true you're going with them?" she burst out before
Isabel could say a word.

"Going where? And who's they? I'm glad you've come. I
wanted your advice on this skirt . . ." Isabel marched off into
her drawing-room, leaving Caroline to shout after her, as she
followed in her wake.

"With the Swinford-Brownes when they leave Ashden."

Isabel stopped and turned to stare at her. "I don't know what
you're talking about. Are they going on holiday?"

"He said he's selling up and you're going with them, as
arranged with Robert."

Isabel laughed, and threw herself on the sofa. "That's nonsense. He was threatening you, Caroline. I expect you were
nagging him about those wretched hops again."

"He was quite specific, Isabel." Caroline remained patient.

"He said he's leaving The Towers and the Army is taking it over. That's why he's given way over the hops."

Isabel was still unperturbed. "He likes to appear straightforward, but he isn't, Caroline. He's cunning. I know him even better than Edith does. I'm sure you'll find this is one of his tricks. I'll mention it to Robert though when I write."

"How is he?" Caroline decided she might as well change the subject. If Isabel wasn't worried, why should she be? And yet . . .

"Not very happy. He's got his ticket, whatever that is. It means he can fly an aeroplane anyway. But he's suddenly forgotten how to land it – after some crash or other. So he might have to be an observer instead," she finished crossly.

"That's not so risky, is it?" It was meant to comfort, but it didn't.

"*Just* as risky. But without the glory."

"There's no glory in war."

Isabel glared. "Don't you start your sanctimonious lecturing. Whatever I want to do, or even what I think, is forbidden because it's unpatriotic. I'm sick of it. Nothing but shortages, no one can afford to give parties any longer or if they do all you get is weak tea and home-made biscuits."

"It depends what it is you want to do." She was unable to disguise her irritation completely. Weak tea seemed a small hardship compared with what was going on at the Somme.

"Because I don't want to work on the land like you, you feel superior. But I wouldn't be any good at it, just as I'm no use at running a house. Not without servants, anyway."

"At least you're honest," Caroline said drily.

Isabel looked pleased. "I am, aren't I. Reggie said—" She stopped, genuinely appalled at her tactlessness at mentioning what had come between them last year. "Oh Caroline, I'm sorry. That slipped out. But it's all over, truly it is."

"And for me too," Caroline struggled to say. "But all the

same, Isabel, I shouldn't talk too much about your friendships with other men, whoever they are. Robert might not like it."

Margaret Dibble spoke more sharply than she meant to, through worry about everything. Mid-August now, and there was no news of Fred, there was Lizzie to worry about, *and* the Rectory. "You mind what you're doing with that blacklead, Myrtle. Haven't you learnt anything after all your training?"

Myrtle, well used to such criticism, bristled, which was unusual for her. "I answer to Mrs Thorn about my cleaning, thank you, Mrs Dibble."

"And to me. You're the tweeny here, not the housemaid."

"I may not be that much longer."

Margaret stared at her in amazement. Myrtle was slow, clumsy, but good-hearted. And most of all, she was part of the Rectory. As well expect the Rector to say he was leaving.

"I've been meaning to tell you," Myrtle continued with pride. "I'm thinking of giving in my notice."

"You?"

Myrtle took umbrage at this patent disbelief that anyone else would want her. "Harriet said I should go into munitions like her. The pay and hours are so much better."

"And the work so much more dangerous, my girl."

"Not at East Grinstead, it isn't. Mr Swinford-Browne takes every precaution, that's what Harriet says."

"You watch what you're doing, Myrtle." Margaret was alarmed for the girl's sake, as well as the Rectory's. "Don't be led by the nose by that Harriet Mutter. You think twice before you give up a nice safe job here, with the Rectory and Mrs Lilley, to go to work in a dirty factory."

"The hours aren't so long, Mrs Dibble." Already Myrtle's will was beginning to crack under the onslaught from old Dibble Dabble.

"You young people are afraid of hard work, that's your problem. You take my advice, Myrtle, and stay where you are."

"And that's what I'll be doing all my life, if I don't take this opportunity." Myrtle's courage had returned, and she marched out carrying the blacklead.

To Margaret's way of thinking, she was set for disaster. What was the world coming to with tweenies talking above themselves? The Rectory had always been good to Myrtle. It had given her a roof over her head, and she had a room to herself; in her parent's cottage she shared one with her four sisters, and the work was a lot worse there than the Rectory. Of course housework was hard; no one said it wasn't. But it was rewarding. You could look at a scrubbed oak table and say, 'I did that. I made it clean.' Margaret could look in her stillroom, full of bottled plums, and say: 'They wouldn't be there but for me'. *And* no need for the Government to keep telling her how important it was to preserve food. She had been doing it all her life, and she was hardly likely to stop now.

She forgot about Myrtle and the Government as she was promptly recalled to her family problems. The tradesmen's door was flung open and Lizzie came in, panting heavily from the exertion.

"Well I never did. It's Lizzie," her mother said unnecessarily. "You look all in. Sit down. I'll put the kettle on."

"I'm all right." But she sat down all the same.

"You're doing too much. It's bad for the little 'un."

What was all this about, Margaret wondered? Lizzie hadn't been here in a month of Sundays. It had been left to her and Percy to pop up to Hop Cottage. Mrs Lilley had suggested she come here to be confined but no, Madam Lizzie wouldn't have it. She'd be all right at home with Mrs Hay the midwife – and her mother, if she could spare the time. Margaret, greatly hurt, had not committed herself.

"Don't fuss, Ma," Lizzie snapped, as a cushion was put between the chair and her daughter's back. "It's another two weeks yet. I can count."

She and Lizzie had never got on like mother and daughter

should. Somehow, however much she tried, Margaret could never understand the girl. Nevertheless, she made an effort. "Why don't you come here, Lizzie, like Mrs Lilley said, and have a bit of home comfort?"

"I am home at Hop Cottage. Anyway, this is a rectory and I'm an adulteress."

Margaret swallowed, sensing Lizzie was deliberately challenging her. "You're in need, that's all I know, and that's all Mrs Lilley cares about. After all, Agnes Thorn had her baby here, and she weren't wed when the babe was started."

"That's different. Me being married to a German, and then living with Frank. It would lose the Rector respect in the village."

Margaret sat down after giving Lizzie a nice strong cup of tea. She had to take this carefully. "There was a time when I'd have agreed with you, Lizzie, but that time's gone now. Fred's gone, Joe's gone, your Frank's gone. I don't think folk look like they used to on these things. We're all beginning to settle down and get on with our lives and problems instead of minding everyone else's. Joe says even them Germans are just like us really, young and scared most of them." She summoned her strength for a last assault. "Why don't you come here, Lizzie? You can take the baby back to the cottage when you're ready."

"If it's still there."

"What *do* you mean, Lizzie Dibble?" What was this? Margaret watched her daughter, stirring her tea a little too carefully. For a start, there was no sugar in it, not even consip, the nasty stuff they gave you instead.

"Now old Swinford-Browne is leaving Ashden, he's letting the hop gardens go. Miss Caroline says that he'll pay for the pickers for one last season, and then they'll be under the Army, and sold when the war ends. Mayhap there'll be no job for Frank to come home to, and perhaps no cottage. We've no rights."

Margaret saw to the heart of the problem, and spoke right

36

out. "You don't know which of them to choose, do you, Lizzie? Rudolf or Frank. You want 'em both."

"Oh, Ma." Lizzie's eyes filled with tears like they hadn't done since she was a child in short pinafores.

"You can't have 'em both, love, but if you're thinking that Frank might ever let you down, I'll say this for him, I don't think he will. He'll be back for you." Margaret paused. "Trouble is, so will Rudolf. Best be prepared."

"All right, Mum, I'll come." Lizzie glared just to show she wasn't entirely convinced.

"Come?" Margaret's imagination was now busy defending Lizzie against two men with rights over her.

"Here to have the baby," Lizzie patiently amplified.

Margaret managed to hide her pleasure. "You'll have to mind your p's and q's, my girl."

"Can't promise that." Lizzie giggled.

When she had gone, Margaret sat down again to recover from the shock of having had a mother-daughter talk at last. And a baby in the house again. Fred would have liked that. That brought unhappy thoughts rushing back, which usually only troubled her during the long nights when she woke up at three or four in the morning. It was like having a continuous tooth being pulled out. Perhaps if Myrtle left, Lizzie could even be persuaded to stay on and . . . no, she couldn't ask that of Mrs Lilley. They had one child in the house already, running about everywhere now she was over a year old. Elizabeth Agnes was a good baby, but even good babies had to be watched. At any hint of trouble, she knew Agnes would suggest she went back to live with Mrs Thorn while the war was on, but Margaret knew how much she'd hate it, and couldn't blame her. Living with them Thorns was a fate she wouldn't wish on nobody.

It suddenly occurred to her that Lizzie had never said exactly what she'd visited for this morning. Could it be that accepting Mrs Lilley's offer was in her mind all the time? Her Lizzie was an obstinate little thing, and would want to be talked into it. Margaret was momentarily incensed, and then she thought what Percy would say – he always did: 'She's a chip off the old block, Daisy.' That was his pet name for her, not that it was used much now. He'd use it when she told him the grand news, though. A baby in the house. *Their* baby. She laughed with pleasure. Then she resumed mincing the meat with renewed zest. "*Ye belong to Jesus, Children of the Lord.*"

Her voice bawled out in triumph over the gardens, and she bustled happily around her domain until the late afternoon when she suddenly remembered that Master George would shortly be back from school and was bringing one of his chums back to tea. She supposed she ought to stop thinking of him as Master George now he was becoming famous for his cartoons. The Rectory saw little of him, for at weekends he was off taking flying lessons at Brooklands, paid for by Sir John Hunney. What a rumpus there'd been about that. Master George had been so keen to join the Royal Flying Corps as soon as he was old enough at seventeen, but luckily they put the age limit up to eighteen. That would be in December, and meanwhile Miss Caroline had told her Sir John was keeping a close eye to make sure George didn't jump the gun by telling a fib about his age. Death came quick enough to those in the clouds, so Joe said, and there was no need to bring grief to Mr and Mrs Lilley sooner than it might otherwise. That magazine *Punch* had taken several of his cartoons now, and Master George was as proud as anything when he talked about it – which wasn't often, because he knew his father didn't altogether approve – and a lot of his cartoons had been made into postcards. Master George never could wait to get good news off his chest, and, to her pride, he often popped into the kitchen to tell her first.

"You're the only one really interested," he had said ruefully to her one day, and she'd swelled with pride. "Caroline and Mother are too busy with their blessed farmers. Father's out all

38

the time, Phoebe isn't interested, and Isabel – well, who'd want
to talk to Mrs Misabel?"

"Now, now, Master George," she'd said, "you speak respectfully of your sister."

Though why he should, when she herself found it hard to talk
respectfully of Mrs Isabel, goodness only knows. In Margaret's
opinion, she was nothing more than a scrounger. Right from a
little girl, she could twist you round her little finger, and didn't
she know it? She had been spoiled owing to Mrs Lilley having
lost a baby in infancy. Marriage hadn't changed Mrs Isabel.
Even a big house of her own, and money didn't satisfy her; she
wanted parties and excitement, and the fact that her parents
couldn't afford it didn't seem to enter her head. Luckily Miss
Caroline had her head screwed on right and kept her in her
place – most of the time. Poor Miss Caroline, she worked so
hard, and what that girl had been through. That Mr Reggie was
nice enough, but he was never worthy of her, and sooner or
later she'd discover that for herself.

Her speedy preparations for George's tea were interrupted by
the bell on the tradesmen's door, and she sighed heavily,
annoyed that scones must take second place to anyone who
happened to be passing. In this case it was probably only the
evening post. Now if only Fred were here. He used to enjoy
opening the door, she reflected wistfully.

None of that, Margaret Dibble. Briskly she dried her hands
and hurried to the door. To her surprise, it wasn't the postman;
it was Miss Phoebe.

"I've brought your post." Phoebe's hand shot out from
behind her back with a bunch of letters.

"Thank you, Miss Phoebe. That lazy lummocks Jim Curtis
lost the use of his legs, has he?"

"He's been called up. He left yesterday."

"One of your jokes, is it?" Even as she was speaking,
Margaret noticed Phoebe's armband and hat crammed over
the mop of dark hair. She'd taken it for some kind of uniform in

connection with her army canteen work at first. "Miss Phoebe, what are you playing at now?"

Phoebe laughed delightedly. "I'm the new village postman. Isn't it splendid?"

"You don't mean you're delivering the post round the village like . . . like—" Words failed her and this was rare.

"Why not? I didn't want to be serving tea all my life, and the YMCA people wanted to send me to a new camp, so I left. I thought about going into the new Women's Army Forage Corps, but I decided I'd prefer to do this for a while."

"Well I never did." Margaret sat down to absorb the true horror of it all. "What's your father going to say?"

"I don't know." Phoebe suddenly lost her grin. "But it's war work, isn't it? And," she grew excited again, "I get sixpence an hour *and* a small weekly war bonus."

"There's war work and war work, Miss Phoebe," was the only reply that came readily to her lips. In any case, she realised thankfully, this was not a problem she had to solve. It was up to the Rector. To her mind, young ladies should be young ladies, postmen were postmen, and farmers were farmers, Kaiser or no Kaiser.

"I suppose," Phoebe said less happily, "I should go and tell Father now."

"That you should." Whatever next? This place was like the picture palace films, full of Keystone Cops, what with everyone tumbling in with news. Not that she'd ever been to the cinema, but she heard enough about it from Myrtle and Agnes. Even Lizzie had been, and didn't come to no harm. Thinking of Lizzie made her remember she hadn't told Percy the good news yet. He'd been out this morning, and then it had slipped her mind. She found him down at his blessed hives.

"You got something to tell them bees, Percy. Our Lizzie's coming to have the baby."

"When?" Percy wasn't one to waste words.

40

She hadn't asked, but she wasn't going to tell Percy that. "Just you wait, Percy," she said loftily.

In fact, Lizzie didn't waste much time. She was down with her bags the next morning, almost before Myrtle had her room ready – the 'confinement room' Agnes had joked, for it was the one she had had when Elizabeth Agnes was born, on the far side of the house, so the noise didn't travel so much.

"You can give me a hand with servants' luncheon, Lizzie, now you're here," Margaret told her once she'd dumped her baggage. She wasn't going to let her have any ideas about her being here for a holiday.

Lizzie grinned. "I'd like that, Ma," she said, and was down half an hour later to take her turn at the vegetables. She was just delivering the peas to her mother when the kitchen door opened and Mrs Isabel sauntered in.

"Mrs Dibble—" She stopped short as she saw Lizzie, and Margaret saw her face change. "This is an odd time to visit," Mrs Isabel said sharply.

"I'm moving in," Lizzie replied levelly. "Mrs Lilley says I can have the baby here. Isn't that kind of her?"

Mrs Isabel didn't reply. She just stared at Lizzie as if she had something against her, then turned round, went straight out, and slammed the door.

"Well, I never." Margaret was taken aback. "What's wrong with her high and mighty ladyship *now*?"

"How could Mother do it?" Isabel screamed.

"What's wrong?" Caroline asked crossly. Isabel had transgressed the rules of the house which included a privacy law that if one's bedroom door was closed, one wished to be alone. Caroline's had been closed. She'd already had to cope with Phoebe bouncing in in triumph having unexpectedly met with Father's approval for her latest venture. The idea of Phoebe getting up at five o'clock to be at the post office at six for sorting was incredible to Caroline, but she didn't want to spoil

Phoebe's own blind confidence in her abilities. It would be one in the eye for Lady Hunney, and she suggested Phoebe deliver the post to her personally in order to see how she took the idea of the Rector's daughter being a postwoman. Now she had Isabel on her hands.

"Lizzie Dibble coming *here* to have her baby. It's not fair on Father."

"He agreed immediately, in fact," Caroline told her briskly. "And anyway, she's not coming for ever, only a few weeks."

"Upsetting the household. Really, I think it's too bad of Mother."

"I think it's too *good* of her. Why are you so upset? You're not usually so – concerned." She'd nearly said selfish. "Lizzie won't be in your way." There *was* something between her and Lizzie. She'd been right.

"I don't approve of babies out of wedlock."

"Nor do Mother and Father, but it doesn't stop them having compassion."

Isabel fumed. "I shall go back to Hop House immediately."

Was that meant to be a threat? Caroline wondered. If so, it failed, for the house ran a lot more smoothly without Isabel's tantrums, and they both knew that her days in Hop House were numbered. However, Isabel still clung to the belief that Robert would never have agreed to her going to East Grinstead with his parents. His silence in answer to her queries proved her point, she said; the very idea of it was ludicrous. In any case, she seemed to be in the Rectory all the time now. Last year—

Last year, Caroline suddenly remembered, the Rectory hadn't seen so much of Isabel. She had spent most of her time at Hop House until she began to get friendly with Reggie. What had been the attraction there without her husband? Not housekeeping, that was obvious, and Hop House was awfully near Hop Cottage, where Frank Eliot had lived alone until Lizzie moved in as his housekeeper. She tried hard to dismiss the logical conclusion of her line of thinking, horrified when she recalled her fleeting suspicion last year. Had Reggie had a predecessor?

By servants' dinnertime, Margaret had recovered her good spirits. Lizzie was coming, maybe no news was good news so far as Fred was concerned, and the Rectory was running much more smoothly now her ladyship had had her nose put out of joint. The Rector had arranged for the flower festival to be pulled forward a week without telling her ladyship until the day it happened. Margaret had the whole story from Mr Bertram. Lady Hunney did all the presentations – as was only right, her being from Ashden Manor – and Lady Buckford had stayed in her rooms all day, eating nothing. You couldn't have pleased her with smoked salmon and oysters, Miss Lewis said, she was that annoyed. Wicked waste of food in Margaret's opinion. Just when they were supposed to be saving all the food they could in this Voluntary Ration Campaign.

Lady Buckford, so Miss Lewis said, wanted to cancel the Sunday School treat then, but the Rector wouldn't let her. He had a few plain words to say to her, and it was all Mrs Lilley could do to keep a straight face. So they all went on the treat, and her ladyship had to sit on the ground and pretend she was enjoying herself drinking lemonade in the rain.

Margaret remained good-humoured until Myrtle came in, looking extremely pleased with herself. Her heart sank. How could she have forgotten? "Given in your notice to Rector, Myrtle?" she asked sharply.

"Lizzie says there's going to be a baby in the house."

"End of August. Looking forward to escaping the hard work it'll mean, are you?" Margaret was a little ashamed of herself for speaking so forthrightly.

"Oh no. I couldn't leave while there's a *baby* here." Myrtle beamed with pleasure.

Three

I t seemed strange to be back in the Norland Square house.
Caroline had only left it in April of this year, five months
ago, yet it felt like a different life. It was the London home of
Lord Banning, where Caroline had lived while she was working
in London for the WSPU, the pre-war suffragette movement,
now heavily engaged in the cause of war work for women. Tired
of endless negative discussion over use of funds, Caroline had
returned to Ashden to take up the reins of her work there again.
Back in London, if only for the weekend, Caroline vividly
recalled the good times she had enjoyed here. Unfortunately
memories of the bad ones came trooping after them, like the
night she and Simon Banning had been caught in the Zeppelin
bomb attack. To banish them, she concentrated hard on the
evening ahead.

This promised to be memorable indeed, and not even the dull
rainy day could dampen her spirits. Nine days ago, on 31st
August *Chu Chin Chow* had opened at His Majesty's Theatre,
Sir Herbert Beerbohm Tree's famous theatre in the Haymarket,
and Simon had managed to acquire tickets for this Saturday
evening in the dress circle. His daughter Penelope had telephoned her in great excitement and Caroline had leapt at the
chance to come. The reviews for this new musical play had been
ecstatic. Sir Herbert was abroad, but the present actor-man-
ager's earlier production *Kismet* had ensured a warm welcome
for this one, which was also set in the East. In essence it was a
pantomime based on the *Arabian Nights* story of Ali Baba and

the Forty Thieves. But what a pantomime! Not only *Kismet*, but Diaghilev's Ballet Russe had created a craze for the Oriental, with music halls enthusiastically presenting Chinese conjurers and Japanese jugglers. Caroline's own contribution to the fashion was a snake bracelet, bought somewhat guiltily in these days of austerity, especially since she was by no means sure she liked it, à la mode or not. *Chu Chin Chow* had reaped the benefit of the craze – perhaps because the more exotic the setting, the greater the escape. Caroline had not changed her views on the need for *that* during this war, despite Captain Rosier's sermonising, which still rankled.

What could be more fun than a real family outing? Simon had been prompted to arrange the evening because Aunt Tilly and Felicia were home for two weeks' rest. Fighting was now concentrated on the Somme, not Ypres, but reluctantly they had been dissuaded from moving their base south in favour of rebuilding their strength. By happy chance, Robert was also on leave, and had booked a hotel room in London for himself and Isabel so that they too could come to the play. On the strength of that, Simon had invited Phoebe and George too, both only too eager for a weekend in London. George had even rushed back early from his Brooklands flying lesson.

No Zeps would have the nerve to attack London tonight, Caroline thought happily, whisking round to the mirror to admire herself in the blue Empire line evening gown. Once upon a time full evening dress would have been essential. Now anything that looked reasonably smart passed, partly because of the prevailing feeling that ostentation in dress was unpatriotic and partly because many of the audience were in uniform anyway. That made it all the more exciting to be able to don her long lace gloves, new button-bar shoes, and wear a *décolleté* gown once more, even if thin chiffon chastely covered the exposed flesh. Not tonight, she informed the Kaiser's airship commanders. I've other plans.

They wouldn't dare come again so soon, though George was

ever hopeful of a repeat performance. On Saturday, 2nd September, seven days ago, the Zeppelins had at long last been given their marching orders by the Royal Flying Corps. They had had their own way for far too long, and the Royal Flying Corps and anti-aircraft defences had seemed powerless to stop them roaming the skies and bombing at will.

"You should have seen it, Caroline." She wished she had. It would have stopped George talking endlessly about it during the week. By chance, he had been staying at Norland Square after his Brooklands flying lesson last week, and from his graphic descriptions you'd have thought he'd been in the cockpit with Leefe Robinson. He had been the pilot of the aeroplane that brought down the first Zep to be destroyed on British soil.

"Masses of fighters were after it," George's words tumbled over each other, "and everyone was out in the streets watching the searchlights, and then when he chased the Zep from London over Hertfordshire – well, you could see the red glow. Crikey, we all knew then what had happened. You wouldn't get that glow from an aeroplane. Buses were stopping to spread the news, taxis – everyone. Oh, you should have been there. Everyone starting singing 'God Save the King'. It was spiffing."

George had telephoned the Rectory from London to say he was going down to Cuffley to see the remains of the Zep on the Sunday, much to Father's disapproval. Caroline had borne the brunt.

"It was history," George had pointed out, much aggrieved when she tackled him. "I had to be there. It wasn't just me going, you know. There were whole armies of sightseers on the trains from King's Cross, and everyone was looking for souvenirs for miles around."

"Like the dead bodies of the crew?" Caroline had asked quietly.

George had had the grace to blush. "They'd been taken away

to the local church," he muttered. "Don't be such a wet blanket, Caroline. This is important. It means something. Think of all the bombs they'd dropped before we got them."

We, Caroline noted. He was right, of course. The shooting down of SL11 had been a rally call. Since then everyone had been more hopeful that the Zeps could be beaten and one day the Kaiser overcome. All the increasingly bad news from the Somme battlefields needed an antidote to lift morale, and this had been it.

Chu Chin Chow was her antidote. As they entered the vestibule of His Majesty's, Caroline was intrigued to see a familiar face. Captain Luke Dequessy came come forward to greet them, and it was obvious he was to be in the party; she noticed a distinct flush on Felicia's normally pale cheeks. He was still limping, and was clearly not fully recovered yet.

"I believe you've met Captain Dequessy, Caroline," Felicia said levelly.

"Indeed, we have met." Caroline bowed, as Luke grinned cheerfully at her, and followed suit.

"Before you ask," Felicia hissed crossly, as Luke went to chat with Aunt Tilly, "no, I'm not going to marry him just because he's coming to the theatre with us. If you must know, Daniel was invited and backed out at the last moment, when he realised I would be coming."

"Oh." It wasn't much of a response, but Caroline could think of nothing positive to say. "Perhaps he is self-conscious about his leg," she ventured.

"He's not, and you know it. He doesn't want to see me."

"He loves you, I'm sure of it."

Felicia immediately whisked round and marched towards the ladies' retiring room, and uncertain of her welcome, Caroline followed. Once there, Felicia turned on her. "You don't understand, Caroline, that's the trouble. *No* one does. Daniel is stubborn, and can't see I want him on *any* terms, because my life without him has no purpose."

"So why Luke?" Might as well be bold, Caroline decided.

Felicia hesitated. "He says he still wants to see me, although I've told him I love someone else. The ridiculous thing is that he seems as obstinate about me as I am about Daniel, but I can't see why."

Can't you? thought Caroline, looking at her sister's madonna-like face. All the rough life on the Front could not obscure or harden Felicia's beauty. Indeed, indications of her hard life, etched on by experience, seemed to intensify it, and the old black evening gown that Caroline had seen countless times before, set it off. Only her uncared-for hands and sunburned arms betrayed how gruelling her work was. Or so she thought until she saw Felicia pull off her old-fashioned tulle cap, in order to conduct a painstaking examination of her hair in the mirror.

"What are you doing?" she asked, astonished.

"Lice." Felicia peered even more closely. "Life at the Front presents hygienic surprises that even Mrs Dibble's powers can't solve. Especially for women."

"How do you manage?" Caroline asked curiously, since the subject had been raised.

"Tilly brings back supplies of these new disposable ones and I burn them when I can. If I can't, I bury them. Don't look so horrified, Caroline. That's the least of my problems. It's war and war is my job at present, not Daniel. Love has to be a luxury. Now, tell me about Fred."

Felicia had always had an affinity with Fred, often preferring to help him in his workshed than to join in the boisterousness of the Rectory. Caroline obliged with the latest news. Father kept in regular touch with the station commander, and though Fred was not due for leave, it was arranged that Mrs Dibble and Percy would be able to visit him. The idea of the Dibbles travelling as far as Hertfordshire when Tunbridge Wells was a great adventure was hard to entertain, but they were going to do it, as soon as Lizzie's baby – now ten days late – was born and she was back on her feet. Agnes, Mrs Dibble reluctantly agreed, would be able to cope with managing the Rectory.

"*There* you are." Aunt Tilly pounced as they returned to the group. Unlike Felicia, her face did display what they were enduring on the western front. The Aunt Tilly of her childhood had always looked so meek and mild, and in the selfishness of youth Caroline had never observed the underlying strength in her aunt's face. That strength, which had seen her through several terms of imprisonment for her suffragette militancy, now supported her in France, and shone over the weather-beaten complexion and deep lines. She looked more fulfilled and content than Caroline had ever seen her.

Simon, who pursued a so far fruitless courtship of her stubborn aunt, obviously agreed, for the moment she moved away to speak to Caroline, he followed. Tilly opened her mouth to protest but he forestalled her:

"No use, Tilly. I don't see enough of you to be generous nowadays."

Caroline laughed. "You told me you were over there at Divisional HQ two weeks ago."

"That was work, not pleasure."

Tilly eyed him grimly. "The Foreign Office seems to have a great deal of business in the Ypres sector at present."

"It does." Simon smiled.

Isabel and Robert had arrived by the time they took their seats, and for once Isabel seemed to regain her old animation, her face alive and sparkling with pleasure, whether at being reunited with Robert for a brief while or at being out for the evening in London. No mention was made of the Swinford-Browne move to East Grinstead, with or without Isabel, and Caroline was certainly not going to risk spoiling the evening with questions.

Sitting next to Felicia, and with Aunt Tilly on her other side, Caroline felt she would burst with pleasure. What could compare with the anticipation before the cherry-red velvet curtain rose on an entertainment which one knew would be enjoyable? As the curtain rose to reveal the exotic eastern palace of Kasim Baba, as his servants prepared the feast to welcome the great Chu Chin Chow, colour hit her immediately, not the subtle tones of English decoration, but a blazing stark colour against the white of the palace. She felt almost scorched by the desert sun. From the first burst of song in 'Here be oysters' to the unforgettable first appearance of Lily Brayton bursting upon the stage as the sensuous desert woman Zahrat, right through to the Robbers' March which Caroline immediately recognised from hearing it whistled in the streets, she was entranced.

By the time the performance ended, his sister was amused to see George was almost speechless with wonder, though Caroline thought this was more likely due to the numbers of apparently naked young ladies on stage who plunged in and out of baths, rather than a tribute to the acting of Lily Brayton.

On the whole it was as well Father hadn't come, Caroline reflected. Had it not been Sunday on the morrow, she was sure he would have done, for he had once had a hankering to go on the stage himself. She tried to imagine him cavorting around in a musical such as this and failed. He had services to take tomorrow, and on Monday she too would be back on duty. She wasn't looking forward to it, for the hop-pickers from London (far fewer nowadays) had arrived a week ago, and she was exhausted from the extra time and organisation it took to oversee them, let alone the soldiers too.

She had hoped Phoebe would be helping her, but Phoebe claimed she was too busy now she was working as a post-woman. Caroline suspected that Phoebe, after the death of her young soldier sweetheart, could not adjust to the company of other soldiers. She had returned to her previous job at the Crowborough army camp canteen, but had seized the first opportunity of leaving, even though this had meant helping Caroline again. Agriculture and Phoebe did not mix well, even

in wartime, and at Caroline's first mention of soldiers to bring
in the hops, she had rushed off to take another job. How long
would that last, and what would be next? Caroline dreaded to
think. Father had remarked rather sadly to Caroline that times
were not only changing, but if his post was to be delivered by his
own daughter, they were metamorphosing into something
unrecognisable.

"I had hoped to play Horatius," he had said to her, "stem-
ming the rush across the bridge of time, but instead I find
myself playing King Canute, demonstrating that the tide of
time can't be held back. You were right, Caroline." A rare
admission indeed.

"Where now, Simon?" Tilly asked, after they had made their
way out after the dazzling finale. "The Carlton?" Simon's
addiction to its restaurant was a standing joke.

"No. We're taking a few rickshaws up west."

"Just as well," Tilly retorted drily. "It looks rather unwel-
coming over here."

Looking upwards, Caroline could see the sky criss-crossed
with searchlights some way away.

For a moment Simon's eyes met Caroline's, both thinking of
last October. "We must go," he said lightly. "The chow mein
will be getting cold. I've booked at one of these new Chinese
restaurants."

"Good," Caroline said immediately. "Here be oysters," and
all humming the chorus from the show, they turned their backs
on the war. Their confidence worked, for no Zeps came that
night.

The next day Felicia and Tilly elected to go down to Ashden
immediately, George and Phoebe went off on their own, and
Caroline decided to take a walk with Penelope in Kensington
Gardens, of which she had always been fond. Her plans,
however, were disrupted when Isabel arrived, just as she was
setting out. Unfortunately Robert was not with her, and this
was an Isabel she recognised of old.

"Oh, Caroline, it's terrible." She flung herself into her sister's arms.

"What is, Isabel? Robert? Bad news?" She was instantly sympathetic, for something terrible must have happened to cause this outburst on Robert's short leave.

"No," she sobbed. "*Me.*"

Of course.

"Oh, Caroline," Isabel wept on, "you were right after all. Robert says I've got to go to East Grinstead. We had the most frightful row this morning. I've come straight here, I knew you'd understand."

"You can't leave poor Robert alone on his leave, Isabel, whatever's happened." Caroline was horrified.

"You don't understand. He says there's no alternative. The Army are taking over The Towers and Hop House from the end of hop-picking. That means in less than a *month*. Oh, Caroline, I shall die, I know I shall."

Caroline tried to comfort her, even while battling with her own mixed reactions to this news. "East Grinstead isn't so far away. We can travel to see you by train, and you can come to see us."

"It's the end of the earth," Isabel moaned. "And how can I be expected to live with Edith and William? That's another thing. I'm supposed to call them Mother and Father. I won't. They're not my father and mother, and Robert is being perfectly beastly about the whole thing."

"Why? He's not usually so dogmatic."

"He says he doesn't want me living on my own again. You don't think – oh, Caroline, last year, you didn't say anything to him about that misunderstanding over Reggie and me?"

Caroline blenched. "No. It's hardly something I'd boast about, is it?"

"I suppose not."

Dear Isabel. Her tactlessness restored Caroline's good humour. "What do you want to do if you don't go to East

Grinstead? They can't press-gang you. There's no conscription for women."

"Don't joke. It's not funny. I want to come home, but I can't while that awful woman is there."

"Grandmother?"

"No, Lizzie Dibble, the trollop," Isabel said viciously.

"She's a nice girl. I like her. Rough and ready, but—"

"I can't stand her and I won't live in the same house with her."

"Then don't come." Caroline's patience snapped. It was beginning to be obvious she had been right about Isabel and Frank Eliot. And Robert wasn't slow-witted either.

"I'm not being turned out of my home by Lizzie Dibble," Isabel shouted.

"What *do* you want then? For heaven's sake, make your mind up."

"Oh, Caroline." Isabel's famous piteous look appeared. "I just want everything to be all right again."

This time Caroline failed to sympathise. Didn't she herself long for everything to be all right again? If only it could be, if only you could crawl back through time to safety. Well, you couldn't. You had to fight your way through to the next safety point. If you were Isabel though, she conceded, it was hard.

"Robert would let you come back to the Rectory," she soothed, "and Lizzie will be gone soon. You'll see."

Isabel shook her head miserably. "He won't. I've already asked him."

"Why is Robert being so stubborn? Anyway, although it would upset him, he couldn't prevent it."

"Yes, he could. He says he'll stop my allowance."

Caroline bit back a laugh. "Yes, I see that would be a problem," she tried to say seriously. "I suppose you're not having a baby, by any chance? That would be reason enough for you to come home."

"A baby? In this war? No, thank you. He did say," this came

out a trifle unwillingly, "that if I were working seriously for the war effort like you and Phoebe, that would be different. But he knows I'm not strong enough to work on the land, even if I wanted to."

Isabel was as strong as a horse, in Caroline's view, for all her fragile fair looks. "It seems vindictive, even for our William, to walk away from Ashden quite so offhandedly," she commented. "Good agricultural land going to waste; cinema closing because it hasn't got a manager, dragging you away. I suppose," Caroline added fairly, "he can't feel all that well disposed towards the village, what with Aunt Tilly humiliating him and then Father getting the better of him – what's the matter?" She suddenly realised Isabel was looking distinctly more cheerful.

"Nothing. I've just had an idea, that's all. Now, what were you saying?"

"Don't bother," Caroline said resignedly. "I doubt if it was important."

"Good," said Isabel absent-mindedly.

Ashden station meant home and Caroline felt a rush of affection for the old red-brick building, although like the Rectory, its beauty was in the eye of the beholder.

As she strolled down Station Road, autumn was sharply evident, after the damp weather. The hedgerows were full of blackberries, and the air of the smells of September. She loved this month, she loved the mellow colour of its sun, and the sense of peace about the countryside before it settled down to winter. Winter had already come to the war. Absent now were the first brave words about the success of the Great Somme Offensive, there was nothing but news of reverses and ever longer casualty lists, which could not be hidden by stories of the bravery of its warriors. Everyone knew how brave they were but it didn't stop them getting slaughtered by the German machine-guns, and it didn't stop them dying in their thousands, driven on route marches like those by their Arab captors after the Siege of Kut, without food, boots or sanitation.

Sometimes, Father had said in his sermon last Sunday after the Zep had been shot down, it took only one small event to turn the tide. Certainly the changed mood had been obvious from listening to people talking, on her truncated walk in Kensington Gardens this afternoon,

The front door of the Rectory opened as if by magic the moment she arrived. Percy had seen her coming, but it was Mrs Dibble who pushed him aside to break the news.

"My Lizzie's just had a fine baby boy." She looked as proud as if she'd produced it herself.

Margaret decided she could do with a nice cup of tea herself, after taking Lizzie one. She'd forgotten how exhausting it could be running up and down stairs all the time, although she'd done it not so long ago for Agnes. If it wasn't for Myrtle and Agnes, she couldn't cope, and that was the truth of it, and goodness knows how long Myrtle would stay once the baby had gone. No stamina these girls. She'd only been here three years.

Agnes came into the kitchen after lighting the morning-room fire, for it was on the chilly side for September. "How's Lizzie, Mrs Dibble?"

Margaret sniffed. "Says she's going to get up tomorrow. After two days. Not if I have anything to do with it."

"It might not do any harm, Mrs D. Better than staying in bed all day fretting—"

"Fretting?" Margaret picked up sharply.

"About what she's going to do. Hop Cottage is going to the Army along with the rest of the estate. That Swinford-Browne wrote to tell her. Fancy giving her less than a month to clear the place when she's just had a baby."

"She'll have to go back to Hartfield where she came from," Margaret said dismally. She'd expected it, but now it had happened it hit her all over again.

"She can't do that." Agnes looked worried. "They know she's Mrs Stein there, and they know Rudolf. If she goes back with a baby, everyone will know exactly what the situation is. People aren't kind, as you know, Mrs Dibble."

Margaret was uncomfortably aware there was a time when she hadn't been kind, and though Agnes seemed to have forgotten it, she hadn't. "She might want to stay here."

"Lizzie isn't cut out for housework," replied Agnes gently. "Besides, there's all Mr Eliot's possessions to think of."

Margaret fastened on the latter problem. "He can come home. Compassionate leave they call it."

"I doubt it. He's out east, Lizzie says. And even if he does, Lizzie would still need a home. I suppose," Agnes hesitated, "if I left I could find another position. Lady Hunney wants someone and—"

Margaret interrupted her. "That's good of you, Agnes, but you're right. Even then Lizzie wouldn't stay. There's no need to upset yourself too."

"No, she's an outside girl," Agnes agreed, looking much relieved.

"She can't live outside. She's not a gypsy." Margaret returned to fighting form.

"You know what I mean. I wonder now—"

But the bell rang then, so she never did hear what Agnes had been going to say. It was her ladyship's bell. Unusual. It was Miss Lewis's opinion that Lady Buckford had been quiet recently only because she was thinking how to get her own back. So what was up now? It was against the rules for her to ring for the Rectory staff instead of her own.

"Who's going, Agnes, you or Myrtle?"

"I'll go. It's not fair on Myrtle."

"No, I will," Margaret suddenly decided. She felt in the mood for battle. "You serve luncheon to the family."

Lady Buckford, ensconced in the wing armchair of her

57

sitting-room, registered no surprise. "Good afternoon, Mrs Dibble. I am glad to see you, and not Agnes."

This was a turnabout, and no mistake, and Margaret proposed to treat it very cautiously indeed. "Thank you, madam." She made her voice as wooden as a forest oak.

"I am concerned that the Rectory is not providing the lead it should to the village in times of warfare."

She knew it. There was trouble coming, though this sounded as if it were heading for Mrs Lilley and the Rector, not her. Her blood began to boil nicely on their behalf, but she managed to trap it behind tightly closed lips.

"There is, as you must be aware, a Voluntary Ration Campaign, and the Government warns of more shortages to come," her ladyship graciously informed her, as though she never read a newspaper.

The tide of trouble was turning in her direction now, and Margaret waited with foreboding.

"I am constantly told by Mrs Lilley," Lady Buckford continued, as though her daughter-in-law were in some distant land, "how well you manage on a limited budget in the kitchen. Indeed, I see it for myself."

Worse and worse. Flattery? Beware the snake that comes with forked tongue.

"I therefore propose to organise cookery demonstrations and talks in the Rectory in order to instruct the village women in how to meet a budget."

Margaret didn't take it in at first, nor at second, neither. Then she appreciated the full implications of Lady Buckford's preposterous suggestion. Margaret's mind rarely boggled, but it boggled now. She wanted to shout that village women had been managing their budgets for hundreds of years without any help from her ladyship, but with those black gimlet eyes staring at her the words wouldn't come. Instead: "Who's going to do the cooking?" the Sussex oak in her asked. "You, madam?"

"Naturally not. I assumed that you would wish to retain the

prerogative of cooking in your own kitchen, and to undertake the task for patriotic reasons."

"In *my* kitchen?" Margaret was felled at a stroke, having overlooked the obvious. "I couldn't do that, madam, I've enough to do as it is."

"Yes, I understand – and indeed hear – that your new grandson is in the house. If you feel the work is too much for you, then you must say so."

This time the implication did not escape her. Margaret, her mind totally confused, took refuge in the only defence left to her, the one that never let her down. "I'll have to speak to the mistress, madam."

Lady Buckford smiled. "Of course. However, my son can hardly object, since it is in our nation's interests, and therefore his wife must agree too. Even the dear Queen is making sacrifices in her kitchens. Where she leads, we must follow."

Margaret spent the rest of the afternoon in a daze, waiting to see Mrs Lilley who had been closeted in the Rector's study ever since she came in half an hour ago. When Agnes came back from her afternoon off, looking very pleased with herself, she was still waiting.

"I think I've solved Lizzie's problem, Mrs Dibble."

"Problem?" For once her mind was not on her family troubles.

"Where to live," Agnes explained, surprised. "Farmer Lake's. He has a cottage free on the farm." She didn't remind Mrs Dibble it belonged to a lad who had been reported missing at Loos a year ago and was now assumed dead. "If Lizzie likes to help out on the farm when she's able, she can have it, and Mrs Lake will look after the baby."

"Look after baby Frank? *My* grandson?"

"It's for the best," Agnes pointed out. "You haven't the time. And one child," she added bravely, "is enough in the Rectory permanently. I could still go, if you prefer, and take Elizabeth Agnes—"

59

"No," Margaret was suddenly quite sure. "I don't know what I'd do without you, Agnes, and that's a fact."

Agnes looked gratified. "Thank you, Mrs Dibble. Shall I tell Lizzie about it, then? You look rather tired."

"No, I'll—" Margaret changed her mind. "Yes, please, Agnes, if you'd be so kind."

For the first time in her twenty and more years at the Rectory, she had to admit she couldn't manage everything, and she listened to Agnes's footsteps marching up the servants' stairs like the knell of destiny, proclaiming the end of her invincibility. "Nonsense," she told herself, taking a few gulps of tea. "Nonsense." It didn't work its usual magic, so she tried a burst of song since at the moment Our Lord seemed far away: "*Fight the good fight . . .*"

That didn't work either. Then she heard Miss Caroline's voice in the hall, laughing at something or someone. Miss Caroline – *she* would cheer her up, if she could think of an excuse to beard her. It occurred to her she could tell her about Farmer Lake, since it would affect her rotas for agricultural work.

Margaret hurried to open the kitchen door. As she did so, however, the Rector emerged from the study further up the passage and called out to his daughter.

"Caroline, I need to talk to you. Could you come in here for a moment?"

As she returned disconsolately to her tea, it briefly crossed Margaret's mind to wonder what the Rector wanted to talk to Miss Caroline about. And why he had been talking quite so long to Mrs Lilley, who was still in the study with them. But she forgot both these things, as she remembered it was almost her time to bath baby Frank.

Four

W hy were *both* her parents here? Caroline, trying to subdue a sudden jolt of fear, followed her father's suggestion that she sit down in the comfortable armchair at the side of his study desk. This only increased her apprehension, however, and she found herself on her feet again. Felicia? Aunt Tilly? Isabel? No, if this were a mere matter of where Isabel was to live, there would be no need for both Father and Mother to be here. She began to feel slightly sick.

"It's Reggie, isn't it?"

"Yes, my darling." It was her father who answered, and both he and her mother rushed to put their arms around her. Father reached her first. "I'm sorry, darling." He hugged her. "I know how much you care for him even though—"

"Yes." She knew what he was going to say. Just because her engagement had been broken, it didn't mean that love had entirely vanished. How could it? There had been a lifetime of Reggie and a few months without him. Love had merely been defeated.

She knew she should say something, for her parents wore that concerned look that close friends and family have when no words seem adequate and silence has to speak for them. Even her father, so soothing and comforting to bereaved parishioners, was dumb. As was she, for there was nothing but numbness in her mind.

"Is it in the newspaper?" she managed at last.

"Not yet, my love. Sir John heard this morning and came

61

down immediately with Daniel to break the news to his wife; then he telephoned us. He particularly asked me to tell you first, Caroline.''

''That was good of him.'' Was this her, responding with such apparent normality? Perhaps, but the real Caroline was curled up in a ball inside her, conscious that if a last flicker of hope for a life married to Reggie had been lingering inside her, then it had been snuffed out for ever. ''After all, I'm not engaged to Reggie any more.''

''He has a high opinion of you, and they too need support.''

Support? With a mighty effort, Caroline forced herself to think of the Hunneys. Tragedy had hit their family another mighty blow. Three years ago they had two healthy sons, both with brilliant futures before them. Now, one was dead and the other maimed for life, even though by his own efforts he was struggling to resurrect his former hopes. Many families had no such comfort. The newspapers were full of stories of those who had lost their complete families; she had read of one widow who had lost seven sons.

''Poor Lady Hunney,'' Caroline jerked out in compassion, recalling how she had looked a year ago when she had told Caroline that the offensive at Loos had begun that day. Lady Hunney had known that the 1st Division, which included the 2nd Royal Sussex, was engaged in it, and for the first time Caroline had seen her as a woman and not as an enemy to be conquered. Reggie had survived Loos, however, although he had been wounded, and over the intervening months Lady Hunney had reacquired her former monstrous image in Caroline's mind. It was gone for ever.

''Where did he die, Father?'' Did she want to know? It didn't matter. Nothing did, but if she knew now, she might not agonise over unanswered questions in future.

''Have you read of High Wood?'' Her father was obviously trying to judge whether or not she really wished to hear the whole terrible story. She was sure now that she did, whatever the pain. Reggie's death was part of Reggie.

"Yes." Newspaper reports of the Somme offensive were still seizing on each minor success, to counteract the appalling casualty lists, which told their own story of disaster, not gains. The battle to clear the way to this wood had begun in the mid-July, and now that Delville Wood had been captured, High Wood had become the focal point. Daniel had told her last week that the British were trying out a new weapon of war there. Camouflaged tanks, which were like huge metal armoured vans, were being used in advance of the infantry, and casualties would be vastly reduced. Well, so far Caroline had read little sign of that. The first major influx of recruits of Kitchener's armies were now being poured into battle, as if sheer numbers could overwhelm the Germans. That policy had never worked in the past, but tactics never seemed to change, even when, Daniel had confided, bombardments destined for enemy trenches sometimes shelled our own lines.

"Sir John told me," her father continued, "Reggie's battalion was holding a front-line trench on the eastern corner of High Wood ready to attack a track called Wood Lane. The Germans have their best troops there, and all the trees had already been destroyed. So little cover was left that the advance was mown down by shells and machine-gun fire. Even when they went into the fight, the battalion had only four or five officers and 150 experienced men. All the rest had been killed, and the reserves rushed up to reinforce them were new and inexperienced."

"Does that matter in this kind of warfare?" Caroline asked bitterly. "Do you have to be experienced to die?"

"It matters whether you go forward or retreat. It matters that the regiment has leaders like Reggie, and he knew that. When he died, he was, as you would expect, at the head of his men."

A line from one of Reggie's letters came back to her. 'All is quiet, leaving me too much time to contemplate whether in action one might fail to do one's Hunneybest . . .' Well, you haven't, Reggie, you did it, and now you're dead. A wave of bitterness overwhelmed her.

"His body was at the nearest point to Wood Lane that the battalion reached," her mother put in quietly.

"But he's *dead*, Mother," Caroline cried out. She had wanted to know, but now that she did she found it of no comfort. It was waste, pure waste. "So are thousands of others. All for a few tree stumps."

"And God may seem dead too," her father replied steadily. "You may not feel He is near, but He is among those tree stumps and He is in Ashden Rectory. Sooner or later you'll bump into Him again."

"I know you're right, Father, but at the moment it means nothing." Caroline knew she had to go before she collapsed, and all the loving sympathy in the world was not going to help. She went blindly towards the door, and then remembered the one question she had not yet asked.

"When was it, Father?"

"Early on Saturday evening."

She had been at the *theatre*. How could she have been enjoying a play when Reggie was dying? Somehow, surely, she should have known, and guilt was added to the pain of loss. However much Caroline struggled to assert logic over heartbreak, she came back to the same point: she had failed Reggie. The Rectory seemed for once claustrophobic, not comforting. She needed not the companionship of her four bedroom walls, but fresh air, where her brain might lose this fog, and she went out into the gardens. If Reggie is anywhere, he will be in the orchard, she told herself. In June she had gone there hoping to see him, and had found no one but Captain Rosier. This time at least she would be alone with Reggie.

It was sentimentally foolish, she told herself; it was sense, came her answer. What did it matter if she cried, for how could she suppress Reggie's death as something irrelevant to her life?

Reggie deserved a mourning. It was there in the orchard they had first realised they were in love; there the love had flowered and now had reached a bitter harvest.

As soon as she opened the wicket gate to enter the orchard, she knew she had been right to come. The orchard was full of the rich smells of ripening apples and damp grass, and of a sense of someone or something waiting for her. Whether it was God or Reggie or both, she did not know, but she felt that here she could attempt to face the agony inside her. 'I'm sorry, Reggie,' she whispered. 'How could I not have known that you were dying?' It was useless telling herself that Reggie would forgive her one evening of escape, for she would not forgive herself. There was no escape while this war raged on. She, like everyone else, must do whatever lay within her power to help end it. She could almost sense Reggie nodding his head in approval, and had a sneaking suspicion he was suggesting to her the first thing she should do. It wasn't a welcome suggestion, but she would act upon it, in accordance with the rules of their childhood game. The whirling dervish would obey the orders of the great Lord Kitchener.

Next morning, she took the familiar route down Silly Lane, through the side gate and across the Ashden Manor park. Instead of turning towards the Manor, as she had done for so many years, she took the path to the Dower House. If Lady Hunney did not wish to see her, she would sympathise but her ladyship would at least know she had called.

She rang the bell and the butler moved aside to let her in, the first time that had ever happened in their hostile relationship. Normally they went through a ridiculous charade of 'What name shall I say?'

"I don't want to disturb her ladyship if she does not feel—" Caroline began, but she got no further. Lady Hunney herself, clad in deep mourning, came out of the Dower House morning-room. She was dry-eyed, and her Marcel-waved hair was as impeccable as ever, but today that could not deceive Caroline.

"Oh, Lady Hunney," she cried impulsively. To her later amazement she ran forward and threw her arms around her ladyship, feeling a tremor of emotion in her enemy's rigid figure. After a few moments, Lady Hunney disengaged herself, but Caroline could have sworn there were tears in her eyes, or maybe that was because there were so many in her own.

She laid a hand on Caroline's arm. "Dear child." Surely she only imagined she heard that, for in a moment she had become Lady Hunney again. "Will you take coffee, Caroline?"

"There is no need," Caroline said awkwardly. "You should be with your family."

"I should be pleased if you would."

Pleased? In a daze, Caroline found herself taking coffee in the morning-room. Lady Hunney smiled slightly as she handed Caroline the sugar, as if she understood Caroline's bewilderment. "One's son, one's husband, are a support, but a woman who understands is a comfort."

"But you know so many ladies, and I—"

"Whom do I know, Caroline? Whom does any of us know?" Lady Hunney interrupted. Her voice was almost gentle. "All that matters today is that we both loved Reggie."

By the time Caroline returned to the Rectory for luncheon, it was obvious that Isabel had heard the news, for she came running towards her as soon as she walked up the path. Caroline had been dreading this moment, fearful that the dragons of last Christmas were not dead after all, but might be resurrected by what Isabel might see as a common bond. In the event, the meeting proved simple, for Isabel just hugged her.

"Oh Caroline, I know how you must feel. All empty and achy, and sick and not sick."

"Something like that," she replied guardedly. How did she feel? She could not even decide that. The distance between her and everyday life seemed an enormous void. Only Lady Hunney had understood.

Isabel hesitated. "Can I say something?"

"No." Caroline dreaded what she might say, and she could not bear it.

"I'm going to anyway. Reggie never loved me, whatever you may have thought. It was all my fault. He was lonely and upset because of you, because he *loved* you, he really did and never stopped."

"Don't," moaned Caroline, "*please*, Isabel. Let's just say we both grieve for him, and that it should bring us closer together, not separate us like last year."

Isabel burst into tears. "I'm *not* going to leave you, I'm *not* going to horrid East Grinstead whatever Robert says. Somehow or other I'm going to stay here. You *need* me."

The pastry mix became blurred, and Margaret Dibble was surprised to find herself crying. It wasn't for Fred this time, but for poor Mr Reggie and Miss Caroline. It was a weary old world. Even Lizzie was leaving her as soon as she was churched. She'd said that Peck was spying on her, and Margaret could believe it too. She had no time for him. A regular Uriah Heep to her ladyship, yes, ma'am, no, ma'am, but a Mr Jack-in-Big-Boots to everyone else. Lizzie was looking forward to going to the new cottage and Percy had been fixing it up nicely for her in his spare time. After she'd gone, she and Percy would go to Hertford to see Fred. She had had a vague idea that Hertford must lie within easy reach of the front line, otherwise why send soldiers to train up there? The Rector said not, however, when he'd come in with some wonderful news that morning. He didn't even stop to knock, just burst in as excited as Master George over his aeroplanes, waving a letter.

"Mrs Dibble, at last I've heard from the medical officer. He's assigned Fred for home-service duties only. He won't go to France."

She couldn't believe it. The milk boiled over and she didn't even notice while she was taking it in. She'd gone to tell Percy straight away, and when she got back the saucepan had boiled dry, and Myrtle was looking at it as if she'd never seen a burned pan before.

"I'll do it, Myrtle," she'd said, and Myrtle looked at her as though pigs were flying all round the kitchen.

In all the fuss, good and bad, she'd almost forgotten about Lady Buckford's plans, and it was a shock when Mrs Lilley came in to apologise for not having been able to speak to the Rector about the problem.

"The idea's not practical, ma'am." Margaret decided to mince her words for once, for there was no point upsetting Mrs Lilley by revealing the true strength of her feelings. "There's not enough room and time in the Rectory to have cookery lessons. What's more, the Rector wouldn't get no peace and the village would think I was giving myself airs."

"Why don't we think of something between us to satisfy her ladyship? If we cook up a good plan, I'm sure my husband would accept it."

"I'll put my thinking cap on, ma'am."

Mrs Lilley clearly had something else to say, because she had that look which said: "You're not going to like this, but I have to say it."

"There's one other matter, Mrs Dibble. Mrs Isabel told me yesterday she's planning to move back into the Rectory when her parents-in-law move to East Grinstead."

"Indeed, madam." Margaret gauged her reaction to this news, in the midst of all her other problems, and decided it was the least of them. Mrs Isabel was here most of the time anyway, so formally moving back in might be easier all round. She wasn't going to admit this right away, however. "And Mr Robert?"

"When he's on leave, of course, he is welcome here. I must admit I feel rather worried about it, since Mr Robert wants her to go with his parents. However, my daughter tells me she is getting a job that will keep her in Ashden."

"A *job*?" Margaret was so surprised, she didn't guard her voice like she usually did.

Luckily Mrs Lilley laughed. "Apparently so. She wouldn't say what it was though."

The day Mrs Isabel turned her hand to hard work, she'd eat her hat, Margaret reflected when Mrs Lilley had gone. Idleness is the rust of the mind, so her mother used to say and if so, Mrs Isabel was very rusty indeed. Then she returned to her own problems before getting the servants' dinner ready. Her thinking cap was going to have to work hard, if Lady Buckford was to be checkmated, but the Lord today seemed to have left Margaret Dibble to her own devices, since He wasn't rushing to come up with ideas for her.

He continued to take His time for the next week, at the end of which Lizzie insisted on moving into her new cottage. Without the delights of baby Frank, and once she had done all that could be done to see Lizzie was 'provided for' – in other words, that she wouldn't starve for lack of a full larder – Margaret decided to face the problem of Lady Buckford. She discovered that events had taken a surprising turn. The Lord might be intervening on her behalf after all.

The day after the memorial service for Mr Reggie in St Nicholas, Lady Buckford had walked over to the Dower House, without even demanding the use of Dr Marden's pony and trap. She had paid a visit to Lady Hunney. No one knew what had passed between the two women, but Margaret gathered it was generally felt in the Rectory that the feud was at least temporarily at an end. Perhaps that might mean an end to this nonsense of cookery lessons. On the other hand it might not, for her ladyship wouldn't be satisfied without meddling in something, and the newspapers were increasingly full of sombre warnings about worsening food shortages, what with all the ships being sunk. There was even talk of the need for a Food Controller, and everyone knew what that meant. Rations of some sort or soaring prices or both. It was clear she needed to lay in her stores before it was too late. Unpatriotic, Mrs Lilley would say; but then, what she didn't know about couldn't worry her.

Caroline's numbness gradually cleared leaving sharp pain in its wake. Even the memorial service had seemed to be about some stranger, not about the Reggie she had loved. Late that evening, she and Father had gone to the oak tree on Bankside, on one side of which the initials of all those who had fallen in the war were carved, and on the other those that had volunteered before conscription. Reggie's name – and those of many others – was now on both sides. She had expected to carve it quietly in the twilight of the autumn evening, but people had quickly gathered, and by the time it was finished a large crowd was silently watching them. One of them had been Lady Hunney.

In the Rectory her mother watched her anxiously, but it was easy to avoid notice at the moment, for Isabel was in the process of moving her personal possessions from Hop House and packing Robert's for East Grinstead, and continually coming and going. Her sister still had not expanded on her original statement that she had a job in Ashden and, egged on by her mother, Caroline decided to tackle her.

"What's all this about your getting a job, Isabel? Why haven't you told us about it?"

"I've been busy, that's all." Isabel put on her airy look. So she was biding her time to tell them something they might not approve of.

Everyone had their own interpretation of the word busy, and packing up one small house with the help of the entire staff of The Towers did not, in Caroline's opinion, compare with getting in the harvest. The latter was taking all her own time at the moment, and she was grateful, because while she was arguing with farmers over pay, sorting out hop-pickers' disputes, and trying to plan for winter ploughing, she could not be aching for Reggie.

"Come on, Isabel, what *is* this job?"

Isabel gave in. "Promise you won't tell Father before I've actually started, but I'm going to manage the cinema."

"*What?* The Gothic Horror? You can't mean it. *You?*" Caroline burst into laughter, regardless of the offended expression on Isabel's face.

"I believe it to be a most worthwhile means of fighting the war," Isabel announced loftily.

"So that you don't have to go to East Grinstead?"

"Not at all. I see it as my duty to provide a means of escape for those tortured by war and its problems."

If there was one thing worse than Isabel in tears, it was Isabel being pretentious. Isabel had rehearsed these laudable opinions, Caroline suspected, in order to try them out on her before breaking the news to Father. True, he had come to accept the existence of the picture palace, since although there was still virulent discussion in the newspapers as to cinema's disastrous effect on the morals of the young, Father had judged by results. Apart from increased noise on Bankside at night and custom in the Norville Arms, the morals of Ashden did not seem to have deteriorated – or if they had, the change could not be attributed to the cinema. Ruth Horner, who showed patrons to their seats, wielded her torch very efficiently. Nevertheless, that didn't mean Father was going to approve of his daughter working there.

"How will you cope? You're useless at figures and know nothing about business," Caroline asked with genuine interest.

"Thank you for your confidence in me," Isabel retorted crossly. "I don't remember ever asking you how you manage to drum up women for your rotas, with your noticeable lack of patience." Caroline blushed. "Managing isn't about adding up columns of figures anyway," Isabel added. "It's about organising other people to do it."

Now there she had a point, Caroline conceded. If anyone could persuade others into doing boring jobs for her, Isabel could.

"I'm looking forward to it," Isabel continued defiantly. "I've already thought about which films I'll choose. It's had far too many gangster and Red Indian films up to now; we want something for the older folk to draw them in. I'll have Father sitting there roaring his head off with laughter before too long."

"I'll believe that when I see it. How on earth did you persuade our William to let you do it?"

"I told him what I've told you." Large innocent eyes held Caroline's. "It's a service to the village, it takes people's minds off war, and keeps Ashden on the map – and the name of Swinford-Browne."

"Now tell me the *real* reason he agreed."

Isabel gave a reluctant grin. "If you must know, I threatened to tell Edith all about Ruth Horner if he didn't let me run the cinema."

"Isabel! Is that wise?"

"It's not really blackmail."

"It's not the ethics that worry me. It's trying it on William."

"I won." Isabel shrugged.

This round perhaps, thought Caroline anxiously. Isabel was all too apt to think a problem solved when it was merely resting. Edith was still, they believed, in blissful ignorance of the now commonly accepted fact that her husband was the father of Ruth Horner's illegitimate baby. Somehow he must have managed to persuade his wife that any gossip was ill-founded, but if Isabel came out with the truth, Edith would believe it. She had a flattering notion that the Rectory bred only saints, who could never lie.

"Do you know, I'm looking forward to this job." Isabel seemed slightly amazed at herself. "I'm even getting a small salary. That helped too, because Father-in-law saw a chance of paying me less than he would a man. He always responds to a bargain. I'm getting one pound a week. *And* Robert can hardly stop my allowance now, so I shall be quite well off."

The thought of Isabel demeaning herself in the service of the village was so captivating that Caroline was diverted for a while from grief, but once alone in her room again, listening to George chatting excitedly to Phoebe on the stairs outside, it soon returned. How could life in the Rectory continue normally, when hers had so radically changed? Irrational guilt over Reggie's death tore at her, and she had long talks with her father, hoping to find an answer. Though he provided consolation, he had gently pointed out that answers could come only from within herself. But how? She seemed incapable of thought, let alone decisions.

She had tried to talk to Phoebe, since she had suffered similarly. It had been nearly a year now since Harry Darling died and Phoebe never mentioned him. It took courage on Caroline's part to raise the subject, for Phoebe seemed almost back to her old buoyant self, so much was she enjoying her job as postwoman.

"Did you feel guilt over Harry's death?" she had asked her one evening when they found themselves alone in the drawing-room.

"Guilt?" Phoebe fiddled with a loose button, pulling the thread until it came off in her hand. "No. I was angry. I still am. It just isn't fair, young men having to die."

Angry? Did she feel angry about Reggie? No. Reggie had volunteered like Harry, but he was years older, and trained for war. Harry had been a mere boy when he signed up.

"But the closeness between you – did you *know* he had died, without being told?"

"It was different. If you remember, I was with him in hospital. Look, Caroline, do you mind if we don't talk about this? I can't help; I wish I could, but no one can. Not really. You just have to live through it."

Phoebe was right of course, but *that* didn't help either. If only Felicia were here. She immersed herself in work, spending as much time as she could outside the Rectory. Her parents' attention was not all centred on her, to her relief, for she was sharing it with George. Everyone was aware that in a little over two months George would be eighteen, and next week he was going solo to try for his ticket, his pilot's licence.

"What do you plan to do then, George?" Caroline asked him.

"Sign up for the RFC," he announced gleefully.

"What about Father?"

"He doesn't want to join the RFC."

She laughed at that. "Don't be silly, George. You know what I mean. He might try to stop you."

"No. I'll be eighteen in December, and that's that. Even Father can't stop me now." He suddenly looked anxious though. "It's the chance of my life."

"That's exactly what it is," Caroline pointed out. "If you went into the Army, as he wants, the war might be over by the time you'd trained."

"I'm sorry, Caroline. Reggie and all that. But chaps see things differently to girls. I can fly a plane now, and I jolly well want to have my shot at the enemy. Come on, Caroline, you know there's no talking me out of it."

"I'm not sure I want to."

He looked taken aback. "You're changing your tune quickly."

"One does, with this war. We cheer a destroyed Zeppelin, the Germans cheer at the numbers they've mown down in High Wood. They cheer Reggie's death. Can you blame either side? No. Tell me, George, when you and Phoebe went to see the wreckage of that Zeppelin at Cuffley, did it change your determination to get into the RFC?"

"You know it didn't."

"Not even seeing the dead crew?"

"They were inside the church." George hesitated. "I'll tell you this, Caroline, and you won't like it. The church was locked and there were police guards on the coffins in case the crowds broke the doors down to get at the corpses. Inside, the police were playing football with one of the helmets."

"I know it's not pretty," he continued, seeing her instant look of revulsion, "but if we want to come through this war we've got to blinker ourselves to everything save the need to win it."

"No matter what the cost?"

"Yes." George thought for a moment. "Seeing that downed Zep did affect Phoebe though. She thought she was going to be cheering and dancing in triumph; the Zep crew's lives for her blessed Harry. But she told me afterwards it wasn't like that. It made her think of Harry all the more, in case someone had done that to his body. Interesting, isn't it?"

It was. Only two years ago George and Phoebe were children, now they seemed to know their own minds more than she did, and moreover Phoebe could talk to George but not to her. Was that her fault too? Had she been so busy in her job and so bound up in her grief over Reggie, first with the broken engagement and now his death, that she had let her own family drift away from her? Caroline made a further effort. "So what you're saying is that there's no escape from the war till it's over?"

"I suppose I am."

No escape. Just as that Belgian captain had said in June. Was it enough that all Caroline's energies were being used in her work in Ashden? Increasing submarine warfare and the poor wheat harvest in America were forcing the shilly-shallying Asquith government ever nearer to direct action in food production. By next year, agricultural labour would surely be nationally organised, and proud though she was of what she had achieved, it would soon be out of her hands. Once hop-picking was over, and the future of the gardens and the rest of the Swinford-Browne estate settled with the Army, her current responsibilities would be over, and she could leave the winter rotas to her mother to organise. She had at last come to a decision.

With the advent of October, at the traditional last-night hop-picking party, which she managed to persuade Swinford-

Browne to pay for (though with some difficulty), she had a sense of finality. It was evening, a time to say goodbye. Soon this land would in all likelihood hold hops no longer. Isabel had moved into the Rectory two days ago, Lizzie was safely installed in Farmer Lake's cottage. The Swinford-Brownes, having ostentatiously hired a removal carrier not from Ashden, but from East Grinstead, had paid a stiff and formal visit to the Rectory one evening to celebrate their parting (though that wasn't the word used in front of them). Everything was ending. Everything was beginning.

The next day Caroline took the train for London, and went to the address she had been given and asked for the person she wished to see. Five minutes later he came down the stairs into the entrance lobby where she waited.

"Good morning, Miss Lilley." He bowed as she rose from the chair to greet him.

"Good morning, Captain Rosier. You told me to come to you if I wanted to take a job to help the war effort more directly. I am here."

Five

Margaret Dibble's back was straight. She intended these swish people in the carriage, who were looking down their London noses at her, to know she was well used to travelling, thank you very much. She supposed she was, now she'd been all the way up to Hertford and back with Percy. Even she didn't quite know how she'd managed it. Worry over Fred must have been what made the journey there pass in a flash; coming back seemed to be taking much longer. You had time to brood, and she couldn't very well burst into 'Praise my soul, the King of Heaven' in this solemn railway carriage. The tensions of London were only just beginning to subside. She seldom went to big towns, and when she did, she didn't usually have to find her way on strange buses and underground railways clutching a suitcase. Percy was no help; he was more bewildered than she was. 'Here,' he'd said, 'let me carry those,' but what she needed was a help carrying burdens other than luggage. Ones you were weighed down by inside. But there, that's what women were for, to carry on uncomplaining.

The Rector had fixed up a nice place for them to stay in Hertford, with an elderly vicar and his wife. The Reverend Jones had some funny illness which meant he couldn't be a vicar any more; usually those called by God had to go on in His service until they were called up higher still, owing to them not having enough money to live on otherwise. Margaret knew all about that from the Rectory.

The Reverend Jones and his wife were Welsh, of all things.

77

Naturally she was a little wary of them at first, but they turned out to be no different from anyone and they enjoyed a good sing-song just like her. When they sang that song about Wales, it brought tears to her eyes, for all they were singing in Welsh. She could hear it now, '*Gwlad, gwlad . . .*' They told her in English it meant: 'Wales, Wales, O but my heart is with you.'

She felt her eyes pricking all over again, not for Wales, but for Fred, and had to stare out of the window as if she was ever so interested in East Grinstead railway station. She couldn't wait to get back to her kitchen and be surrounded by her own pots and pans, and be able to shout at Myrtle. On second thoughts, she wouldn't do that, in case Myrtle changed her mind now the baby had gone, and decided to go to the munitions factory after all. Myrtle wasn't what she would call ideal, but there was no such thing as an ideal tweeny to be had with the Kaiser still up to his tricks.

Once she was home, she'd be able to wipe the sight of Fred standing in that hut from her mind and think of him again back in his workshop; he'd be mending wounded animals there, not training to kill Germans, as even on home service he'd have to if the Kaiser broke through and invaded. First though she'd have a strong cup of tea and a good cry. She couldn't share her troubles with Percy; he had just retreated into himself and was pretending nothing was wrong.

She had hardly recognised Fred when he came into the Adjutant's hut. Short hair, uniform – she felt quite proud of him. Then she took in the fact he was limping and his puffy bruised face. There'd been trouble.

"Hallo, Fred," she'd said, trying to be natural.

But he'd just looked at her blankly. The horror had hit her: *he didn't know who she was.*

It was Percy who had saved the situation then. She couldn't do or say anything she was so shocked, but Percy just strolled up to Fred and shook his hand. "Hallo, son." Fred had looked at him, then looked at her, but still said nothing.

"What have they done to your hair, love?" She had found she could speak at last, but it wasn't the hair she was thinking about; it was the bruises. "How did this happen?" Fear made her voice rise, but still he looked at her with that blank stare. Then, to her relief, he grinned, though he still said nothing.

"Right, Percy." She had nerved herself up to march up to that stuffed shirt Adjutant and demand to see the doctor; she informed him she'd see anyone if he wasn't around, but she wasn't going away without asking a few questions. In Ashden she'd never have the nerve to demand to speak to Dr Marden, but then in Ashden Fred wouldn't be black and blue.

"Just a bit of horseplay," the doctor said when at last a reluctant Adjutant had collared him. He sounded surprised that anyone would make a fuss about a black eye. "Lads will be lads."

"Fred won't," his mother had replied. "Why isn't he speaking?"

"Private Dibble has his own little ways, you know."

"I do know," she replied grimly. "What I also want to know is what little ways you've used to make him like this."

Fred was standing by with a silly smile on his face all the time, and never said a word.

"He was off duty, at a public house, and the other lads have got it into their heads he's an army-dodger since he's been categorised home service only." The Adjutant had clearly decided honesty would get rid of trouble more quickly. He was wrong.

"A public house!" she'd shrieked. "Fred never had a drink in a public house in his life. We're loyal abstainers like His Majesty."

"Your son is an adult, Mrs Dibble."

"He's a child, and you know it. Are you going to send him back home? He's no use to you."

The Adjutant lost his temper. "This is the Army," he roared. "My job's to make a man of him, one way or another."

She'd fixed him with a look. "God didn't make a man of him. How do you expect to?"

She had marched out, head held high. Her outbursts did no good, but it relieved her mind. So did the familiarity of the lush countryside, now they were back in Sussex. When the train stopped at Hartfield, she could have wept for pleasure. Home was still there, waiting like a cocoon to swallow her up. Back at the Rectory she'd have support, she'd ask the Rector to intervene to get Fred released. Quickly, in case he got beaten up again in just a bit of horseplay.

Nevertheless, as they got out at Ashden Station she put on her most forbidding face, just in case her pleasure at being home showed too much. "Good morning, Mr Chappell."

"Morning, Mrs Dibble. How's our Fred then?"

"Doing splendidly, thank you very much."

Even the Rector couldn't achieve miracles, it appeared. "Once the medical examiner has passed him, and the appeal procedures have failed, there's no legal way to obtain his release," he explained, after listening compassionately.

"He'll be dead without going to France at this rate." Margaret could see from the Rector's face, the way he was looking at her so gently, that there was no hope.

"I shall go on trying, Mrs Dibble. If I kick up enough fuss they may relent. I can also ask Sir John Hunney if he can get a release for him. But don't pin your hopes on it; Sir John is not in the right department of the War Office to authorise it."

"I'm pinning my hopes elsewhere, Rector."

"On our Lord, Mrs Dibble?"

"On His Majesty. I'm writing to him to let him know what kind of army is fighting for him."

Margaret marched back to the kitchen where *she* was queen, and only the King of Heaven had precedence over her. It was time to re-establish that fact, and not a moment too soon. "What have you been doing here in my absence, Mrs Thorn?"

she demanded of Agnes, having stalked straight in to inspect her larder and stillroom. "There's no flour left."

"Mrs Lettice is delivering today. There's been a delay."

"It must have run out a couple of days ago. However did you manage with the cooking, if I may ask?"

"I enjoyed it," Agnes replied peaceably, "and we didn't run out till yesterday."

Margaret sniffed suspiciously, observing that Agnes looked uncommonly happy. "What are you looking so cheerful about? Think you're going to take over my place, do you?"

"No." Agnes laughed. "You know that would be impossible. I'm not a real cook like you. I'm cheerful because Jamie's home. He came yesterday on an unexpected week's leave."

"God bless us, where is he staying?" Already she was calculating whether there were enough eggs or whether she should run over to Nanny Oates to see if the hens were laying.

"With me upstairs. I hope you've no objection, Mrs Dibble. Mrs Lilley said it would be all right, and I'll make sure it doesn't give you extra work."

"What about those Thorns? Doesn't he want to take you to stay with them?"

"He says he prefers it here. His mother was upset. Now Len's had to go into the Army, she's lonely, but ever since there was all that trouble over Ruth Horner, Jamie's been funny about going home. I don't try to persuade him too hard; they don't like me, and I don't like them, but he ought to take Elizabeth Agnes to see them."

"Where's his lordship now?"

"He's in Fred's workshop. Oh, Mrs Dibble, I'm worried for all I'm glad to see him. He just sits there. He's polite enough, and talks at meals here, and talks to the Rector, but it's all yes sir, no sir. He doesn't really *talk*. Not even to me."

"Finds it strange being home, I expect," Margaret said knowledgeably. She remembered poor Miss Caroline pouring her heart out about this problem once. "He's just getting his bearings, don't you worry, Agnes."

"But he's not my Jamie. He hasn't been like this before."

Margaret could see her point. The last leave Jamie had come strutting in fuller of himself than a turkey-cock. On the whole she liked Jamie Thorn, but he had been getting too big for his army boots. Even Mrs Lilley had remarked on it, and Percy had been disgusted the way he sat lazing around with those boots on her precious stool with the tapestry rose she'd worked before she was wed. So if he was quiet, she was inclined to think this was all to the good. In any case, she had other things to worry about. Rectory dinner for instance. Would the flour be here in time for pastry? She'd better get Percy to fetch it. The potato store was low. You never knew where you were nowadays. First it was 'eat more potatoes', then it was 'you can do without potatoes, there aren't enough to go round'. Ah well, time to be thinking of winter. Lucky she got her bottling over early this year.

Margaret began to relax. She was home again.

After yet another meal at which Jamie said nothing more than he had to, Agnes summoned up her courage. She'd asked him twice to pass the potatoes to Mrs Dibble, and he had glanced at her as though she was a stranger, instead of his Agnes. He even ignored Elizabeth Agnes, and that was hard enough the racket she was making.

After she'd helped Myrtle clear up, and laid the drawing-room fire for this evening, she walked over to Fred's workshop. It seemed ominous to her that though the sun was shining, the air full of autumn smells, and Michaelmas daisies, nasturtiums and chrysanthemums making the gardens as colourful as in the summer, there was a nip in the air as if to say: Agnes Thorn, you watch out. Winter is coming.

She could see Jamie through the window as she walked by it, so taking a deep breath, she lifted the latch and went in. He was hunched up in his khaki, sitting at Fred's bench, staring at nothing. It was odd to see him there with Fred's carved animals all around the shelves, and the bench all higgledy-piggledy like Fred always had things. It looked as if Fred had just popped out for a few minutes.

Jamie looked up warily. "Teatime, is it?" She sensed he was trying to be jolly.

"No. I want to know what's wrong, Jamie."

"Nothing."

"Oh, yes it is. I'm your wife. You've got to tell me. Wounded, are you? Shell-shocked?" She'd heard of such things, even seen one or two at Ashden Manor Hospital, men with vacant eyes, and no visible wounds. They were never the same again, so it was said.

"No."

"What then?" That was one relief anyway.

"Nothing, I tell you," he shouted at her in sudden rage. Then he looked abashed. "Sorry, Agnes, I don't want to talk. It's bottled up."

"Like Mrs Dibble's plums?"

He managed a weak grin. "Worse."

"You've only got to break the seal, Jamie," she encouraged him. So there *was* something, and she tried not to show her alarm. She needed to keep calm, if she was to help.

"There's no point. I don't know where to begin. It's this effing war."

"Jamie Thorn!"

"You see?" he said bitterly. "You don't understand. Out there there's more swear words than the other kind, so how can I talk to you if you behave like the blessed Salvation Army?"

"You're right, Jamie, and I do want to understand. But what am I to think? You won't go to see your parents, you won't talk to me, or even to the Rector. Why not?"

"No one understands, that's why. While I'm here I've got to see my mum and dad, but I don't know how, or what to say to them."

"Seems to me you'd better talk, Jamie, if we're ever to understand each other again. Remember," she said bravely, "what happened before when you wouldn't tell me the truth, and we were nearly parted?"

His eyes took on a look of cautious hope. "All right, I'll try. You remember the trouble two years ago. Well, my mum in particular didn't believe me over you know what." He avoided looking at her now, both of them aware that Agnes herself had wavered at one time, until she came to her senses. "So I told her I'd never come back till I got a medal to show for it."

"That was daft, Jamie. It's you we all want. Not a medal."

"But I've got one, Agnes." His voice went very quiet.

"You what?" She almost screamed in her surprise. "Jamie Thorn, why didn't you tell me I was married to a hero? Why—"

"It's not like that," he interrupted. "I couldn't tell you. You see, they were recommending me for a Distinguished Conduct Medal, and now it's been approved, that's why I've got leave."

Agnes's mouth dropped open. She'd always wondered why they said shock had that effect, but they were right. Hers really did, and it was her turn to go quiet. "A DCM, Jamie. I've heard of them. You *are* a hero. You'll be famous, and I'm married to you." Medals weren't all for field marshals and officers; ordinary men like Jamie could win them too, for outstanding courage beyond the call of duty. It was a great honour. Her mind whirled as she tried to take it in, and excitement began to well up inside her. Perhaps they'd go to the palace and meet the King. Her Jamie and a parlourmaid, at the palace. This would show Ashden. She felt quite dizzy with the shock of it all, until she came to her senses: "Then what's wrong, sweetheart? Why aren't you as proud as punch? You must have done something really special and brave."

To her horror his face crumpled, and he hid his face in his hands, his shoulders sagging with misery. Her Jamie was crying. Terror replaced jubilance, as she threw herself at his side and put her arms round him. "Tell me, my lover, tell me what's wrong."

"I can't."

"You can. Tell me."

"All right. I don't deserve the flaming DCM," he yelled, sitting upright and staring at her like he thought she would spit on him.

"They decide that, Jamie, not you."

"But I *know* I don't, Agnes. It looked as if I did, but I didn't, and they won't believe me. They think I'm being modest. Christ, if it were only that. I wanted any old campaign medal, just to show them, not a fucking DCM I didn't win fair and square."

This time Agnes ignored the bad words. "*Why* don't you think you deserve it?"

"The Somme," he muttered in despair. "The bloody, bloody, *bloody* Somme. Oh, this was going to win us the war, this was the big offensive we'd all been waiting for. A couple of days and the Kaiser would be screaming for mercy. And what happened? We all got massacred. Just capture Ovillers they said. It sounded so blooming simple. Our brigade wasn't even in the first assault; we were held back, 35th and 37th could capture it easy. A couple of villages on the German line that bulged out towards us, one of them only fifty yards away, and between them were two valleys we called Sausage and Mash. That's a laugh. It was us was the sausage and mash. Mincemeat, that's what they made of us. The 35th and 37th didn't get Ovillers so they sent in the Sussex. The Germans would be softened up by now, they said. Not bloody likely. They'd had their appetite whetted. Must have been a big joke seeing all our shells falling short, exploding too soon, and hitting us. The CO told us afterwards eighty per cent of us were stiffs in ten minutes, what with that and the machine-gun fire. Sausages? We were trapped like rats. Our company lost all our officers to the machine-guns. After that no one knew where we were going. Some platoons got lost, so the story went later. Without the officers, you're done for in the blue. Then I saw there *was* one officer left, who seemed to be going in the right direction at any rate, so I led the rest of my platoon as fast as I could after him."

"That was brave of you, Jamie. You could have gone back."

"No, it ain't brave. You don't have time to think or you wouldn't do anything so daft. You'd drop where you were, hide in a shell-hole and no one could blame you for that."

"And that's what's been worrying you?" Oh, the relief.

"No. It's what I had to do to go on, and you'll see why I ain't so brave. My mate, Joe – we've been together since training days – copped it from one of those shells that fell short. One minute he was running at my side, the next he disappeared, and I was knocked sideways face down in the mud. I got up and there was Joe. He was still alive, Agnes. He . . . I'm not going to tell you."

"Yes, you are." She steeled herself.

"His leg was blown off, and half his face gone, and his guts spilling out, but he was living, and he knew me. I could have got him back to the lines, but I bloody well went on and became a bloody hero. Now do you see?"

Agnes thought rapidly. His eyes were beseeching as though his whole life depended on what she said next. "No, Jamie, I don't see. War is like that. You have to do what seems best at the time."

"But I was a f—, a blinking coward, not a hero. Suppose I was scared of him dying on me? Suppose I was scared it would take so long a bullet with my name on it would get me easy? I was panicking, not thinking."

"What happened to Joe, Jamie?"

"He died later."

"And what happened to you and the men you were leading?"

"We got as far as we could, then they stopped the attack. It took another couple of weeks and more to get that bloody village."

"How many of those men you led died, Jamie?"

"Two or three. Most of us got back to the lines."

"And who recommended you for the DCM? The officer?"

"Yes, and the chaps backed him up. They didn't know, you see—"

"Oh yes they did," Agnes interrupted calmly. "They knew that you led them through hell and back and that they were still alive, instead of having been mown down by the next barrage. They lived, thanks to you."

"You think so?" Jamie began to sob in relief.

"Now, Jamie, I want you to go straight in to tell the Rector you won the DCM. *Not* about Joe, for he's nothing to do with the medal. He's your private loss."

"I can't."

"You can." Agnes paused. "You have to, because now I'm going to tell Mrs Dibble about it. *Then* we can go to tell your mother."

"A medal?" Margaret almost screeched. "Well, I never did. You'll both be too high and mighty for the Rectory kitchen now."

"I won't," replied Agnes laughing. "It's Jamie has won it, not me."

"Rector's grandfather won a medal in the Crimean War, but you'd expect that, wouldn't you, his being a lordship? Fancy your Jamie getting one. It just shows. We're all alike really."

Margaret tried hard to assimilate this news. Perhaps Agnes and Jamie would go to the palace and could have had a word with His Majesty about Fred. No, she would write her letter now, not that she had much hope. After all, His Majesty was spending a lot of his time encouraging the troops and was in uniform himself. It was the Queen who realised they were fighting a war here too, bless her. Perhaps she should write to Queen Mary, not King George.

She was still pondering this dilemma when Mrs Lilley

knocked and came in. "Mrs Isabel and I cooked up a wonderful idea while you were away, Mrs Dibble."

Margaret treated this with caution. Other people's wonderful ideas tended to result in more work for her. Normally she didn't mind, but life seemed to be steamrollering over her and it was time she looked out for herself. She immediately began to bristle. "I can't do it, Mrs Lilley, and that's flat."

"I realise that. However, Mrs Isabel is the new manager at the cinema, and she has suggested that during the mornings the cinema could be used for the cookery lectures and demonstrations. It would provide a better venue than the Village Institute, since that has no stage."

"And who's to give them?"

"Mrs Isabel said she could ask her housekeeper, Mrs Bugle."

Margaret nearly exploded. "Mrs Bugle, madam, as you know full well, couldn't cook a boiled egg, even if we had any eggs to boil, which we don't." Mrs Bugle had elected not to go to East Grinstead but to remain to 'look after the army'. "What's wrong with my cooking, Mrs Lilley, if I might ask?"

"Nothing. You would be ideal." Mrs Lilley had a look of surprise on her face. "Naturally we thought you would be too busy."

"I'm never too busy to do my bit for England," Margaret replied severely. "You can tell her ladyship that, and you can tell Mrs Isabel too. Percy can take that old portable stove over to the cinema right away while I have a good think about it."

After Mrs Lilley had gone, it briefly occurred to her that Mrs Lilley might not have been serious about asking Mrs Bugle, but the thought vanished; even if she wasn't, she couldn't take the risk. After all, it was only patriotic for the Rectory to take the lead in such matters, even if it meant showing a lot of flibberty-gibbet young wenches how to cook good honest Sussex food.

She could even make a start now, getting out her recipe book which she had inherited from her mother and painstakingly kept up. The days of 'take a dozen eggs' – meant for large families and times when the word 'shortage' would never be heard in a kitchen – were gone. Still, it might give her some ideas for wartime recipes. Her mother had been a great one for God's gifts. The good Lord provided a lot of food in his meadows and hedgerows to eke out the produce from the Rectory garden. Percy was growing more and more, so perhaps she should ask him to give talks on growing your own vegetables, using not only every available inch of the garden, but any old tub or box on a windowsill as well. Mustard and cress would grow a treat there. Miss Caroline had even told Percy he'd have to dig up the lawn soon, and she was only half joking in Margaret's opinion.

She could instruct her ladies on how to make things go further; no selling unwanted bones or fat at the kitchen door to the fat-collectors without boiling them up first. Even tiny strips of fat could be boiled in water and reduced to a nice solid cake for frying. She could tell them how old bits of celery could be dried in a slow oven, and used weeks later in soups and stews. And how God provided not only mushrooms but dandelion leaves, chestnuts, wild garlic, nasturtium seeds . . . Didn't she have a recipe in her book for Sussex chestnut soup?

Margaret found herself getting quite excited at the idea of her forthcoming demonstrations. She'd even put up with her blooming ladyship's presence if she had to. She browsed through the book so long that she didn't notice the time. When at last she did, it dawned on her that Myrtle was taking a very long time to come back with the bicarb. It wasn't like her to run out of this essential ingredient, and especially with the sugar shortage getting worse. Bicarb cut the need for sugar in stewing acidy fruits and she didn't want to be reduced to her mother's old trick of a piece of bread in the pan.

She looked up sharply as Myrtle shot through the door. She'd give her a piece of her tongue – no shortage of that at least.

"I forgot," was Myrtle's only defence.

"You *forgot*? Now—" she broke off, aware of the girl's white face. "Whatever's wrong, Myrtle?"

Myrtle promptly burst into sobs. "They were all talking about it at the General Stores. That's why I forgot it."

"I daresay a bit of bicarb isn't the end of the world." Margaret was quite surprised that Myrtle was still taking her job so seriously. Maybe she had been a bit sharp.

"It's the factory. It's blown up."

"What factory?"

"There was an accident and some shell cases exploded and caught others, and, oh, Mrs Dibble, she's *dead*."

"Who? Where, girl?"

"Harriet. In the munitions factory. And lots of others too, the girls mostly, dead. Terrible accident it was."

Margaret tried hard to assimilate this new tragedy, one which affected the Rectory too. Harriet Mutter had been housemaid here, and gone off to make good. The canaries, that's what they called the munitions girls, because of the yellow colour of their faces from the stuff they packed in the shells. '. . . and cockle shells, and pretty maids all in a row.' Only they weren't pretty any more, they were dead, and no amount of hymns would help change that.

"It seems to me, my girl," she said heavily, "we're fighting on the Sussex front here, just as our lads are on the western front. What with Zeppelins and deaths, and now this . . ." She made Myrtle a cup of tea. The girl had had a shock, and they were all in this together.

Later that evening Percy returned from mending Nanny Oates's mincing machine (via the Norville Arms, if she guessed aright, only for once she didn't care). He had the full story. Harriet and six other girls had been killed, two of them from Ashden. Thirty had been badly injured. The Rector had been out all evening with the Mutters and the parents of the other two girls, and Mrs Lilley had gone with him. They were bringing the bodies back from East Grinstead tomorrow, and Harriet's uncle,

George Mutter, was taking over the coffins. Bert Wilson of Lovel's Mill, home on leave and sweet on Harriet for many a long year, for all she'd hardly give him the time of day recently, was said to be sobbing his heart out, poor lad.

"Is the whole factory gone, Percy?"

"They say old Swinford-Browne is opening up what's still standing tomorrow. Patriotic, he calls it. I calls it greed. Folks have got no respect nowadays."

"At least he won't show his fat face back here wanting to build nasty factories. If I'm going to be blown up, I'd rather it was by a soldier than that Swinford-Browne."

With this melancholy thought, only cheered by the fact that she'd be seeing Lizzie and the baby tomorrow, Margaret went to bed, so sick at heart that she forgot to read her passage from the Good Book – her nightly ritual, each chosen at random in the hope that the Lord might in this way be sending her a personal message.

When she arrived in the kitchen next morning, it seemed He must be punishing her, for yet another problem for the Rectory family (in which she included herself) emerged an hour or two later. Miss Phoebe, instead of being out delivering post, had still been abed. She crept shamefacedly into the kitchen for something to eat when her parents were safely out of the way. She had a face as long as a jumping-pole.

"Whatever are you doing here, Miss Phoebe? Aren't you well?"

"They don't want me any longer at the post office." Phoebe tried to sound offhand, but failed.

"Why not?" To her way of thinking it was a good thing, however upset Miss Phoebe was.

"I was late too often, and then yesterday the bag was so heavy I had to leave some of it in the hedge while I delivered down Silly Lane. You know it's impossible to ride a cycle down there. That beastly old Farmer Lake reported me and old Ma Jasper gave me a lecture about the sanctity of the Royal Mail,

91

and said she'd manage without me. It's not fair. It was perfectly safe."

"Deserve success and you shall command it," Margaret announced cryptically. "That's what my father said."

Phoebe kicked the table leg crossly. "I *did* deserve it."

"What are you going to do now? Help your ma with the farm rotas?"

"I'm sick of rotas."

"We're all sick of a lot of things, but we have to do them."

"The worst about being a Rector's daughter is that other people nag you all the time." Phoebe was aggrieved. "I'm boffled, as you say. Yet look at how I stuck to the canteen job, until they wanted to move me. I was never late."

"Because you enjoyed it. So what *are* you going to do?"

"I'll think of something, don't you worry." Phoebe marched out of the kitchen like a martyred saint, and that she wasn't.

Miss Phoebe broody and doing nothing, Mrs Isabel doing well at the cinema. Who'd have thought that would happen? Good things as well as bad were coming out of this war. Miss Felicia nursing at the Front, and Miss Caroline off again. How she missed her. The Rectory wasn't the same without Miss Caroline, and that was a fact. She had said she was doing some new job, for the Government. But it couldn't be a very important one, because it wasn't in London. It was in Folkestone. Margaret was mystified. What kind of war job could she have at the seaside?

Six

F olkestone? Caroline felt as though she had just jumped through the Looking Glass. This was a town she thought she had known all her life. On her family's annual visit to Grandmother Buckford in Dover, they would occasionally drive out in stately fashion in Uncle Charles's Daimler to take tea, or to listen to the band on the Leas. It had been a fashionable, restful resort, whose elegantly clad visitors were indistinguishable from residents, and whose small harbour held fishing boats and ferries.

The town had been transformed, submerged by foreign accents and uniforms even more noticeably than in London. Thousands of khaki-clad Tommies on their way to France thronged the streets and seafront, and packed into rest camps set up in the centre of the town and on the outskirts. They poured out from the railway stations daily and she was already used to seeing the columns of troops marching down the Slope from the Leas on their way to the transport ships. Her office overlooked the seafront, and sometimes at night she watched the bright lights in the sky over the French coastline and heard the rumble of distant guns.

The enlarged harbour was now a busy military-led working place, though some commercial ferries were still running. Her new work involved the Folkestone–Flushing route, and naval ships were used for communications with GHQ in Montreuil. Each time she saw a ship leave for France, she had a thrill of pride, as though she herself were tucked inside it, *en route* for the war front.

Dover had always been England's main exit to the continent, but it was obvious to her that Folkestone was rapidly overtaking it for troop transport. It too had received a huge influx of Belgian refugees, and many of them had remained in the town. They, the Canadians and Tommies numerically dwarfed the local population. The Belgian community had, however, settled into Folkestone life, and inaugurated their own clubs, restaurants, libraries and church services.

Although she had only been here a few days, Caroline already knew more about wartime Folkestone than its residents. They were aware only that various government agencies – not only British but also Belgian and French – were operating here, in houses donated by industries and private individuals or requisitioned hotels. The average Kentish civilian could have no idea what functions these agencies performed, but Caroline was daily coming to learn more.

Somehow she, Caroline Lilley, Rector's daughter, had become a member (even if a very insignificant member) of His Majesty's Secret Services. Why Folkestone, she had asked at that all-important meeting, disappointed that she was not being sent to France or at least to remain in the centre of war-planning in London.

"War is everywhere, in the trenches, in Folkestone, in people's minds," the captain had replied, and whether or not he had intended a snub, she had felt reproved.

It had all happened so quickly. When she had come to see him in London, Captain Rosier had remained silent for a few moments, as if summing up how serious her intention was. Apparently whatever he saw convinced him, for he took her into a private office in the Whitehall Court building, and talked to her for a while. He said nothing about the job, nor asked why she had come, but merely chatted about the tennis match day, life in London, life in Ashden, until she grew impatient and bewildered. At last he escorted her to the War Office, where she had walked at his side along uninteresting corridors, and her sense of being in Lewis Carroll's confused Looking Glass land had begun. Perhaps the Red Queen would pop up at the end of this trek?

It wasn't the Red Queen, it was the Red King. When at last Captain Rosier knocked and entered one of the offices, Sir John Hunney rose to meet her.

Immediately, Caroline thought she understood the situation. After she had greeted Sir John, she turned to the captain. "So you had already been asked to approach me in June."

He looked embarrassed, and Sir John quickly intervened. "It is true, Caroline, that I told Captain Rosier we needed extra staff and that if he found anyone suitable I should be glad to know. Captain Rosier is not part of our organisation, however, and I did not mention you by name."

"Then perhaps I should leave, Sir John," Caroline replied awkwardly. "You could hardly have expected *me* to arrive, and I would not want to put you in a difficult position." For all her brave words, she was conscious of deep disappointment. Boring these corridors might be, but behind those dull walls the war was being fought, and it was frustrating to be so close, only to be checkmated by fate in the form of the Hunneys once again.

"There is no such difficult position, Caroline. Do please take a seat."

"Because Reggie is dead?" she blurted out before she could stop herself.

"No," Sir John answered quietly. "Both I and my wife have the highest regard for your capabilities, and as regards our past differences, circumstances in Ashden are entirely different from those here. If you would like to work for us, the Service could employ your talents."

She wanted to, oh, how she wanted to, but she still wavered, aware how intensely both men were studying her reactions. Sir John was courteous and seemingly relaxed, while Captain Rosier looked at her with those piercing eyes, and an expression that like Sir John's gave nothing away. Was Sir John being kind because Reggie had died? No, she dismissed this thought as unworthy of him. Of course he would not let private sympathy affect his professional judgement. Both these men must believe she was capable of the job – whatever it was.

"I would like to work for you very much, Sir John."

"Excellent," he replied. "I propose to explain briefly what is involved, and then you can make arrangements to leave. As soon as possible, if you please." The captain rose, about to depart, but Sir John stopped him. "If you can spare the time, Captain Rosier, you might wish to help Miss Lilley with lodgings and so forth."

He hesitated, then replied, "I should be most pleased."

She fancied there was little warmth in his acceptance, however, and tried to convince herself she was being unreasonable in her instant reaction of annoyance. His part was over. Why should he have to do more? She was well able to look after herself. Then she forgot Captain Rosier, who resumed his seat, as Sir John began to explain:

"You must be aware that this country, like most others, has a secret intelligence service."

Her wild guess had proved correct. Scenes from John Buchan's *The Thirty-Nine Steps*, William le Queux's novels, and E. Phillips Oppenheim flashed through her mind. They were based on fact after all, and she was now part of this clandestine world. She could have thrown her arms round Captain Rosier and kissed him, so thrilled was she that he had given her this chance. Not that he was looking very kissable; he was as shuttered away as ever behind that poker face. Closed up for the duration of the war, she decided.

"The details of that particular organisation," Sir John Hunney continued, "need not concern you. Suffice it to say it collects intelligence from agents all over the world. At the turn of the century, the Army decided it needed more specific and concentrated intelligence, and set up its own department.

Although at present the Secret Service is nominally under War Office control, it still pursues its own path. Army intelligence is therefore constantly expanding to meet the current crisis, and is operated from here and from GHQ Montreuil. What it desperately needs is continuous information from occupied Belgium, and northern France, as well as from neutral Holland and Switzerland. Its prime need is information on German troop movements, most of which are now by rail.

"There is, you will appreciate, one major problem. We are not fighting this war alone. The British GHQ is at Montreuil, the French Government at Le Havre, and King Albert of the Belgians is leading his army from La Panne near Dunkirk. Between them and the intelligence on which we all depend, lies the front line, through which information cannot travel. We have therefore to find other methods."

He went on to describe briefly how, where and on what she would be working, and Caroline began to feel dizzy with excitement. She would be back in London again, and this time in the heart of the war effort. When Sir John finished, she turned jubilantly to the captain. His services would not be required. "There is no need to find me lodgings, Captain Rosier. I'm sure I can live in Lord Banning's London home."

"I'm afraid that won't be possible, Caroline," Sir John had said briskly.

And now Secret Agent Caroline Lilley was actually here in Folkestone, working for the British section of the Allied Intelligence Bureau in this seafront house. There was also a Belgian and a French section. Each controlled its own network of couriers and patriotic civilians in Belgium, and after sifting its reports and liaising with the other two bureaux to double-check and pool information, produced a digest to be forwarded to the GHQs. She was to be employed on transcribing reports, the digest, and perhaps helping to check it against those of the other two bureaux.

Captain Rosier had found her lodgings in Sandgate Road, quite close to the office, and seemed to know the town well. So whom did he work for, she wondered? She did not dare ask him – yet. Not only was there the Official Secrets Act, by which she was now bound, but she didn't want one of Dame Dora's officious taps on the shoulder. The Defence of the Realm Act seemed to govern everything now from accidental chinks of light to innocently sketching a harbour scene.

On the difficult journey down, on which he insisted on accompanying her, she had asked him, since they were alone in the first-class carriage, to tell her more about the work she would be doing. If he were merely doing his duty in escorting her, she would at least pump him for information in compensation.

"It seems very cumbrous," she ventured to say, "getting intelligence reports smuggled from Belgium into Holland, then back to England, down to Folkestone and back to France again. It could get very out of date."

She held her breath in case this prickly man took this as a criticism, but to her surprise he seemed prepared to discuss it with her.

"This is true, but it takes several days to transport a whole division, and many more for enough new divisions for an offensive, so it is not as bad as it could be. But pigeons are quicker."

"*Pigeons?*" She was so surprised she laughed.

He did not. "In Belgium and France pigeons have long played their part in war. Belgium has more carrier pigeons than any other nation, taking messages out and faithfully returning to their homes, and we tried smuggling baskets of birds in as well. But the Germans issued an edict forbidding carrier pigeons, and are shooting any they see."

"Could they not be dropped by aeroplane?" Caroline suggested.

He looked at her in some surprise. "You should be at British

GHQ, Miss Lilley. That's exactly what they did, but now the Royal Flying Corps are all occupied in fighting German aeroplanes, so we are back to drugging the birds and smuggling them over the border."

"Which border?"

"The Belgian frontier with neutral Holland." Captain Rosier paused. "Miss Edith Cavell was part of an organisation that took wounded and stranded Allied soldiers after Mons over the border, which at that time was guarded relatively lightly. It also took young Belgian men who wished to join the Belgian army. Now the Germans have doubled their barbed-wire barricades and the number of guards. It grows more difficult."

She had arrived for work on the following day, eager to plunge into the unknown. Readers of William le Queux would have been disappointed at the very ordinariness of the offices. Papers everywhere, shabby desks, two typewriters, cupboards for storage, heavy blackout curtains at the windows now drawn back, and a few late and wilting chrysanthemums in a vase. Besides herself, there were six clerks: two girls in their twenties, as she was, and four young men, two or three disabled with war wounds. All the young men had been at Oxford or Cambridge, and the two girls had been teachers. The first day had been bewildering, which made the surprise on the second day even more pleasant.

Of Captain Cameron, the head of the British section, there was no sign, and she had been told to expect to see very little of him as he was usually closeted away on an upper floor, or at meetings with his French and Belgian counterparts. However, her immediate boss bore a familiar face.

"Captain Dequessy," she cried in delight, "are you part of this too? Captain Rosier seems to have had quite a haul from our tennis party."

He grinned. "You can't blame him for landing you with me. I was highly envious of Daniel Hunney's disappearing into the vaults of the government work, and thought what could be better? If you have to sit behind a desk in the Army, make it an interesting one, say I. I badgered Daniel, until to get rid of me he recommended me to Sir John. This is the next best thing to being at the Front."

Near Felicia, was her immediate thought, and he continued as though she had spoken it aloud. "Odd world, isn't it? There's Lissy out in the front line, and here's me skulking at Folkestone."

"You're not skulking," she declared. The home front was vital now. It was no longer just a question of keeping the home fires burning till the boys could come home, but of brandishing their own torch of defiance at the enemy.

The work made little sense to her at first but, subduing panic, she told herself this was natural at first. There had, she gathered, been a complete blackout in the last few months, with no information coming through at all from Belgium, after the steamer *Brussels* had been sunk, and secret service agents betrayed by compromising documents picked up by the enemy. Since for much longer than that none had been coming from occupied northern France either, the section had been quiet.

Now links had been re-established with Belgium at least, and there was a hotchpotch of reports for her attention. Many were written by mapping pen in Indian ink on tissue paper, which could be tucked into hat-bands, or sewn into buttons to escape detection at the border. Some arrived by a variety of other means – old bus tickets with simply the date, time, reference number for the train watching post, and 1 v of, 10 w s, 3 w ch, etc, meaning one artillery unit of one passenger coach for officers, ten flat trucks for soldiers, three for horses, etc. If she was lucky, a translation was supplied by one of her colleagues. Those in code normally came to her already decoded. If not, she had to appeal to Luke. From one agent, the report came in the form of darned socks. Captain Dequessy gave it to her as a joke, for there was no transcription with it, and then explained it was a genuine agent's report, and the message, in a code of different darning stitches, was of top importance; one identification of a German division in Belgium could point the way to German intentions. In this case it most certainly did, for this particular crack division had been on the Verdun front and after recent French successes there, it suggested Ludendorff, the German Commander-in-Chief, had decided to halt his offensive there.

"Or it might mean they needed a rest?" she said, inspired.

"It might," Luke returned sweetly. "So that's where you come in, Miss Lilley. The three C's we call them: co-ordination, corroboration – and concentration. Fortunately for us, John Charteris, Field Marshal Haig's intelligence chief, deals with what it all means, so you won't have to decide on where the next offensive will be."

"Here," she declared, dangling her sock, "I'll start on it now."

The fog of war, it seemed to her, was nothing compared with the fog of government agencies, which from her brief experience all seemed intent on doing what someone else was doing, only better. In addition to the Secret Service, there was another organisation, working from London, which also reported to GHQ Montreuil, and which operated in much the same areas as the Folkestone section, causing much inter-service friction. She couldn't help feeling Mrs Dibble could have sorted this confusion out in a moment.

Her head soon began to whirl with references to regiments and places she had never heard of, and she often had to ask for access to Luke's copy of the Brown Book, which was a carefully compiled guide to the German Army. She also needed to study the Belgian rail systems. *And* brush up her French. A dictionary could take her only so far.

"Ask Yves to take you to the Belgian clubs," Luke suggested. "Your ear will soon get tuned."

"I think he's seen quite enough of me. He didn't exactly leap at the idea of escorting me down to Folkestone."

101

"No?" Luke shrugged. "I'll have a word with him."

"Please don't." She was horrified at the idea.

"Don't you like our gallant captain?"

She considered this. "Yes, I do, but I always feel I'm imposing on him and he has far more valuable things to do with his time."

"Ah." Luke looked pensive. "You could be wrong."

"I'm never wrong," Caroline informed him cheerfully.

"Except about me and Felicia," Luke replied, equally cheerfully. "You don't think she'll marry me. I know she will. And speak to Yves. That's an order."

"I don't know where to find him."

"He'll turn up sometime."

"Like the Cheshire cat," she muttered crossly.

On Sunday the cat did turn up. In the early afternoon as she was reeling from her landlady's best efforts to toughen up a joint of beef for the war effort, Yves Rosier called at the house. As she came down the stairs, summoned by the landlady Mrs Clark, reluctance seemed to be written all over his face. He stood awkwardly in the narrow hallway, twisting his cap round and round in his hands. It was a pity the splendid pre-war Belgian army uniforms with shako and red piping on the navy blue had now been replaced with British khaki cloth – it was not nearly so impressive, in her opinion.

"If you are unengaged this afternoon, Miss Lilley, we might walk on the cliffs, or perhaps listen to the band on the Leas. I do not wish to leave you alone in Folkestone on your first weekend."

Really, this was carrying his duty too far. No wonder he looked so reluctant. She thanked him politely, but could not resist adding: "You sound just like my Grandmother Buckford." However, she would be glad of anyone's company today, so she asked him to wait while she found hat, coat and, she supposed, gloves. The rules of dress had relaxed greatly in two years of war, but mindful of Ashden convention and that this

102

was Sunday, she donned the kid gloves that she had worn to attend church this morning at St Peter's. Everyone else seemed to be in groups, and she had missed the warm familiarity of St Nicholas in Ashden.

As she returned, fully gloved and hatted, she realised she had been churlish; she was glad he had come, and told him so, as they descended the steps and began to walk towards the Leas.

"I told Major-General Hunney I would look after you," was his reply.

"Thank you, Captain Rosier, but I do not need looking after." Caroline's hackles were roused once again; irrationally she was feeling distinctly overpowered as she walked at his side. It was almost a trot, for he strode out as though they were heading for Dover, not the Leas. She was reasonably tall for a woman, but though the captain was about the same height as Reggie, he was more sturdily built than . . . no, she would not think about Reggie.

"You would rather be alone?" He stopped abruptly.

"There is no need for you to give up your afternoon to entertain me."

"In that case, Miss Lilley, I must not impose on your time. Please accept my apologies for troubling you." He removed his hat, bowed stiffly, and strode away.

Dismayed, Caroline watched him go. You are a stupid woman, she told herself. Had he wanted to go, or had she driven him away by hurting his feelings? How difficult it was to know with someone, in a strange land, who, however good his English, could not be expected to understand all the nuances of every situation. The fault was hers. Conscience-stricken, she rushed after him. He had already reached the clifftop of the Leas which was crowded with afternoon walkers from fresh-faced youngsters in khaki to ancient dowagers and toddlers reminding the wartime world that life went on.

"Captain Rosier!"

He turned round at her call.

Face to face with him once more, she found herself unusually bereft of words, and had to force them out. "I would indeed be grateful for your company, if you can spare the time." This comedy of manners made her feel as if she were in a Jane Austen novel.

He hesitated, then said, "Do not think you have offended me, Miss Lilley. I understand—"

Her tongue mercifully came back to her. "It was I who didn't understand. You took one look at me and decided I'd want to eat jellied eels and whelks for tea down by the harbour."

Doubt replaced silence.

"That was a joke," she pointed out hastily.

What had been lines of bitterness transformed themselves into a smile. He was almost good looking in a strange kind of way, she thought, as he replied, "I might like jellied eels."

"But I prefer tea, so perhaps we should have both."

In the end they had neither. They listened to the band until the October sun grew chilly, and then strolled down to the seafront. It was only as the sun began to sink from sight that she realised they had been talking most of the afternoon – and she still knew little about him. Or had they been talking? How strange. She couldn't remember. Perhaps silence had replaced words without her noticing and without its mattering. All the same, it was a good time to ask a few questions.

"Do you live in Folkestone too, Captain Rosier, working for the Belgian section? Or can't you tell me that?"

He smiled. "As an officially approved member of Captain Cameron's staff you are bound under the Official Secrets Act not to reveal such important information to our enemy as that Captain Rosier does not live in Folkestone, so I will tell you that he does not. Nor does he work for the Belgian section."

"So you escorted me to Folkestone because Sir John asked you to?"

"Again at the risk of offending, Miss Lilley, no. I have many friends here in the Belgian community, and I constantly visit not only yours but the Belgian and French sections too, because of my job."

"Why are you in Belgian khaki uniform, if you work for the War Office?"

Dress was varied in her office. She herself hadn't known what to wear and compromised with her old blue costume suit. The men in the office wore uniforms, but the women did not, though Luke had told her this might change if women were formally incorporated into the services. If only Asquith would go, and Lloyd George take over the premiership, this would almost certainly happen.

"Because I don't work for it. I am a serving officer in the Belgian army," he replied. "My role as yours is in intelligence; I am a liaison officer reporting directly to King Albert in La Panne on the situation in occupied Belgium, from my own digest of the digests from British GHQ of your digests from Folkestone, as digested with those of the French and Belgian sections, the Wallinger intelligence service in London, and from French GHQ, and from the British Secret Service. I then regurgitate these for His Majesty." He delivered all this without a glimmer of a smile.

Caroline did not dare assume he saw the funny side of this, though she suspected he did, so with equally grave face, she commented: "I know I've only been working here a few days, but I keep wondering, if there's so much intelligence around, why haven't we won the war?"

"If you sent twenty people to watch a rainbow, Miss Lilley, you would have twenty different reports, and some would contradict the others."

"And some would only see the fairies' pot of gold said to be buried at its foot."

"Dreams, Miss Lilley. Those reports too have their place, provided one knows that until the gold is found, they are only dreams."

"You're thinking of Belgium, aren't you?"

"I always think of Belgium."

"Captain Rosier," she began impulsively, wanting to break just a little of the barrier.

"Miss Lilley?"

"I have enjoyed this afternoon. Thank you."

"*Moi aussi, Miss Lilley. Je vous remercie.*" He gave one of his quaint little bows.

"I see you've been ordered by Captain Dequessy to improve my French."

"No, but would you wish me to do that, Miss Lilley?"

She was taken aback at her light comment being taken seriously, but then considered the suggestion. Why not? Her French certainly needed it, and the slight differences between French and Belgian would be all to the good since the majority of her work came from Belgium.

"I would, very much. Thank you."

He actually looked pleased; and, slightly surprised at herself for agreeing so quickly to more of the still formidable captain's company, she arranged a meeting in the coming week.

As they walked back along the Leas they saw crowds of Tommies, many with a girl on their arms, coming towards them, and she was aware they were being overtaken by similar crowds coming from the opposite direction. Yet more crowds were gathered down below on the seafront road.

"Where are they all going?" she asked idly.

"To the Leas Shelter. It is built into the cliffside. If you look down you can see the decks as they are called, outside each level of the theatre. It is a pleasant sight, just the glow of torches as the crowds congregate in the dark. Every Sunday evening at six-thirty there is a free concert there for soldiers. Also at the town hall, but this one is the more popular. Perhaps because it is small and crowded," he added matter-of-factly. "And it has a little magic."

"Shall we go?" she asked impulsively, watching the soldiers entering, each with their torch for light, and the orchestra already in place.

"This evening, I regret that I cannot, and it can be rough. No place for—"

"A Rector's daughter?" she finished for him. "In war that hardly matters, Captain Rosier. If bombs hit everyone, then music can help everyone."

"That is true. I think I said to you in London that war is everywhere, we must carry it in our hearts and minds; it has to be fought in the West, in the East, in Africa, and one day in America too, as they will realise. It is fought in the trenches, it is fought in villages as peaceful as Ashden." He paused, then asked: "Why did you come to me to ask for this job, Miss Lilley? I was sorry to hear from Sir John of your fiancé's death. Is that the reason?"

"No." Caroline was quite sure of that. "I did not come to escape from grief, if that is what you are thinking, Captain Rosier. I came because Reggie's death made me realise that what you had said when we met at the Rectory was correct. There *is* no escape, not even on June afternoons."

As they walked up towards Sandgate Road, they heard the first sounds of the orchestra. He was right about that too, she thought. It did have a little magic.

She was glad she had so readily accepted the chance to improve her French. Even though many of the reports were already translated, she was immersed in the language every day, and was relieved she didn't have to cope with digesting the Flemish reports too. There was a young soldier, a 2nd lieutenant, at work on that, who had a Flemish mother and English father, and did the translation too. As a Flemish speaker, James Swan had been removed from the front line much to his indignation coupled, he confessed, with a little shamefaced relief.

"What we're doing here is just as valuable," she pointed out.

"Maybe. But it's not what I want to do, and don't preach at me that that's not important. I know it isn't, and it doesn't help at all. If a chance comes up of replacing me, even with a woman—" He broke off in some confusion as Caroline jumped up and dropped a mock curtsy.

"Thank you kindly, sir."

"I didn't mean you. You're jolly efficient. Oh, Jiminy," he stopped, as he realised what he'd said now.

As the days passed, Caroline still didn't feel efficient; she felt like a pole stuck in the garden supporting a line of washing which was constantly being changed without any help from her. There was a constant movement of people through the offices. Sometimes they wore British uniforms, sometimes they wore civilian clothes, some had several days' stubble on their chins and spoke in guttural Flemish or rapid French far beyond her level, and sometimes they wore French or Belgian army uniforms like Captain Rosier. She had gathered from Luke that the couriers collected the reports from a letterbox system in the occupied territory, and smuggled them across the frontier by one of their *tuyaux*, secret passages through. They had even been hidden under priests' robes, and in schoolboys' satchels, but it was dangerous and even these methods had been discovered by the Germans. This was the reason some agents preferred to pass their information on by less damning evidence, such as the socks.

Caroline used a typewriter, first to type the reports, then to précis them. She was reasonably efficient on the machine having taught herself during her time at the WSPU Suffragette headquarters, but there were typewriters and typewriters. This one, apparently all the British Government could afford, was a venerable machine with a strong dislike of the letter 'e'. It refused to type it, even though everyone in the office had had a go at bending the spoke back and forth, cleaning the machine, brushing it, and alternately cursing and wooing it. All that resulted was that the spoke condescended to place a slight smudge on the page which might or might not be an 'e'. As 'e' was the most frequently used letter in the English language, this gave her digests an interesting appearance.

108

"Using code, I see," Luke remarked, leaning over her shoulder one day.

"How about a new typewriter?" she asked savagely.

"Sorry. Only Belgian refugees get new typewriters."

"I *am* a refugee," she muttered. "I'm being driven out of my mind."

And not only at the office. Her lodgings were hardly a home from home. Her landlady, Mrs Clark, was thin and anxious, with a husband away at the Front, and her mind seemingly always there with him. When she caught sight of any of her four lodgers, she invariably looked slightly surprised as though wondering what these people were doing in her house. It was a strange life, and mealtimes tended to be like Mad Hatters' tea parties, with Caroline presiding as Alice. There was an elderly lady who had lodged here for years, who like the dormouse said very little and that in a whisper; a middle-aged railway worker from somewhere in the north of England; and the Mad Hatter, who had worked for a tailor and wore a mental top hat all the time. It usually fell to Caroline to initiate any conversation, but sometimes she was too tired to discuss anything but the weather.

It took a week before her first post arrived, and there – oh wonderful – was a letter from home. She remembered how much that had meant to her when she was in Dover. Eagerly she tore it open.

'Dearest Caroline'. Her mother's large sprawling handwriting leapt out at her. 'How we miss you. Especially me. Mrs Dibble's face is even longer since you left. I shouldn't say that, with the terrible news about Fred (though she doesn't know about it yet), and indeed she seems to be doing her best to co-operate over these cooking lectures. She even said your Grandmother would be welcome to introduce the first one . . .'

Terrible news? What was it? Mother must have forgotten that she had had no way of hearing such things. She would have to plead with Luke to let her use the section's telephone. Oh *bother*. She crammed on her hat, and half ran, half walked to the section office. If she was there before Luke he wouldn't know . . . She gasped out a quick prayer for forgiveness, but He couldn't be listening for Luke *was* there, and she had to explain to him just why it was so important. He picked up the receiver and handed it to her without a murmur (had he heard from Felicia?) and in a few moments she was speaking to her mother.

"What was wrong?" Luke asked as she put the telephone receiver back in its cradle, distressed at what she had heard.

"The authorities have gone back on their undertaking to keep our housekeeper's son Fred on home-service duties. Father hasn't broken the bad news to Mrs Dibble yet. He's making one final appeal through Sir John, but has very little hope of its succeeding. They need every man they can get for the Front, and Fred's one of them."

Seven

Margaret felt as if she were off to serve in the trenches herself, as she set forth with Percy to give her first cookery talk. She had decided to call it 'Fighting the Food War', and she bore a suitably militant expression on her face, but that was no help when she was all too well aware that inside she was quaking like a two-year-old. She might be queen in the Rectory, but now she had to capture unknown territory, and, worse, she would have the Lord High Executioner with her. Lady Blooming Buckford would be sitting on the platform, watching every move she made. A pound of pluck is worth a ton of luck, Margaret encouraged herself, but it didn't help.

She had been in a quandary over the cooking. One small portable stove hardly seemed enough, and it was no good showing these women how to prepare food if you couldn't show them the finished result. Only God was privileged not to do that when He offered us the Kingdom of Heaven. Stews were another matter. It was no use expecting them to cook in under three hours, and her audience would still be there when Mrs Isabel began to show her Charlie Chaplin films. Margaret had agonised over this dilemma for some days, until even Percy noticed something was wrong: "Fred?" he had asked.

"My stewed cow heel," she had replied gloomily. No news was good news as far as Fred was concerned.

"Now look, Daisy," Percy had obviously decided for once in his married life to assert himself, "it's no use your getting all het up about this. You could do it standing on your head."

She'd been so surprised at this unusual support that she had told him what was bothering her.

"Take two of them," was his answer.

"Pardon?"

"Prepare one there, but take one already cooked."

She stared at him as though this were some stranger she had suddenly found herself married to. "Percy Dibble, maybe you're not so chuckleheaded, after all."

Percy had almost burst with pride, and then excelled himself even further. "Why don't you cook one here, then pop one in the haybox to finish off, and I'll take it over. You're always saying there's nothing to beat the old haybox." There was a new note of authority in his voice, of which Margaret didn't altogether approve, although for once it was welcome.

Clothes proved her next worry. She was representing England's best interests and must dress the part. As is the cook, so is the kitchen, she reminded herself, so if she wanted her work respected, she had to think about what she should wear, even if her pinny covered the lot. She had held out for some time against adopting the shorter length of skirt, but when even she could ignore no longer the patriotic need to save material, Margaret's ankles had slowly and cautiously appeared, reluctantly followed by an inch or two of calf. She had to admit it made life easier. Today she had put on her best, a navy-blue costume she'd made before the war and shortened. A nice pouched blouse with it, and her grandmother's gold brooch, and her old wide-brimmed hat with the headband, and she was all set. Ten-thirty to eleven-thirty was the time she'd arranged, so it didn't interfere too much with her Rectory routine – if such a thing as routine could be said to exist now that daily life was all over the place.

A new worry came into her mind as she crossed the road to Bankside. What if no one came? She'd be the laughing stock of Ashden.

"They will," Percy declared with his new-found assertiveness. "You'll see."

She didn't see anything of the kind. As they walked in, her worst forebodings appeared fulfilled. The audience was as sparse as currants in a wartime cake.

"It's only ten o'clock," Percy pointed out. "You don't begin till half past."

Margaret sniffed, unconvinced, but decided to turn her mind to yet another worry. Would Agnes be able to cope with Rectory luncheon? The girl meant well, but Margaret had had to turn her eyes away when she saw her peeling the carrots so thick. And what about stage fright? She'd heard of such things. You opened your mouth and no words came out. Suppose Mrs Coombs from the Dower House was there, or Dr Marden's housekeeper? Or even – a new horror loomed up – that Dr Parry, who was interested in diet from a professional point of view.

In her mind, all these dragons sat waiting in the front row, to sink their fangs into Margaret Dibble's reputation, while from behind her on the stage Lady Buckford had a dagger ready to plunge in her back. Her hand trembled a little as she laid out her knives and bowls on the table, setting up her own little kingdom. The haybox, with the stew finishing off inside, sat on the floor in front of the red screen curtains, and the portable spirit stove was behaving itself.

She felt a little more confident as she unpacked her ingredients, and the hall began to fill up, until the thought flashed through her mind that they were all coming to see Margaret Dibble made a fool of, not to learn how to bottle plums. Then she saw Lady Buckford walking majestically up the aisle with Mrs Isabel, which, oddly enough, served to settle her down nicely. There was one good thing about an old enemy: you knew where you were with them.

By the time ten-thirty came, you couldn't have squeezed another person in, not if it was Lady Hunney herself, which it wasn't. Margaret didn't hear a word of Lady Buckford's speech, she was in too much of a bivver. All she could think

113

of was the moment she had to rise from her chair, look at all those faces out there, and open her mouth.

Clocks never ran backwards, and when Lady Buckford sat down, Margaret found herself on her feet, instead of glued to her chair as she'd feared. She swayed slightly at the sea of faces raised to hers, and terror seized hold of her. Then a voice inside her head told her: Margaret Dibble, you can do it. She glared at her audience.

"It's no use you thinking there'll be strong liquor in my food. There won't be; we need all the wits we was born with to fight the Kaiser, and I'm here to show you how to fight on the Sussex front.

"I'm going to start with a few words about what the Good Lord has provided free in His fields and hedgerows in the way of weapons, and there won't be no nettle beer either. You can find your own recipes for alcoholic beverages. You won't hear from my lips about anything other than the good wholesome food we're ignoring, and how to make our food stretch further. After that, I'm going to show you how to cook a nice cow heel with parsley sauce, and if it's good enough for the Rector, it's good enough for you . . ."

She was back. Agnes hadn't made too much of a pig's dinner of family luncheon. The fish pie was quite tasty. Margaret beamed approval at the table in the grandly named servants' hall. She deserved the treat of not cooking this meal herself; everyone had seemed really interested in her talk and crowded round the stage as she did her demonstration. The stew had popped out of the haybox just lovely and she gave it to poor Mrs Hubble who had a hard time of it now Timothy was gone. Margaret congratulated herself she was a village personality now, and then hastily told herself not to pat herself on the back. She'd done it for England, not herself.

After dinner, the Rector asked her to pop into his study, and she wasn't surprised. He must have heard from his mother how well she'd done.

It wasn't about that, though; it was about Fred, and she came out feeling as if she'd got a half-cooked suet pudding inside her. Some of it was in her stomach, but most was in her heart. Rector had said he was being sent home on leave, but what was the use of that now? She made a great effort to move the leaden weight by reminding herself that others were suffering too.

Miss Caroline was learning French, so Mrs Lilley said, which sounded bad. Miss Felicia and Miss Tilly were over in France; surely they couldn't take Miss Caroline too? It would just about break Mrs Lilley's heart, like it would any mother's. While they remained within the boundary of England's shores, it felt as if they could be home any day. Over there was a long way away. And once you were there, over there you stayed.

Like Fred. That's what this leave was for. Come and kiss me quick, mother, because I'm going over there.

Margaret decided to prepare her next talk. A week went quickly, and it was only five days away now. Besides, it took her mind off what was happening elsewhere. Before this war, you knew where you were. The Rectory came first, but you were all part of the family; your own kith and kin just got along with life as best they could without much worry from you. Now it was all different, everyone was going their own way, so you had to worry about everybody. Percy had gone up to London to meet Fred off the Hertford train. Fred wouldn't know how to cross London to Victoria if he wasn't met; he'd just sit on the platform till it was time to go back, his happy old grin on his face, bless him. But he wouldn't be going back. Not for long, anyway.

No wonder her letter to King George had had no answer save a printed acknowledgement. Young Jamie hadn't gone to the Palace to get his medal personally, so she'd had to send her letter by post. It was nice the Rector had made a point of Jamie's medal in his morning service, so the whole village knew he was a hero. Agnes had been so proud, and even little Elizabeth Agnes had sat quiet for once while her daddy was being praised.

She would concentrate on fruits of the field in the next demonstration and maybe plum-heavies. Fred liked them. Margaret pulled herself up. No thinking of Fred. How about thinking of Mrs Isabel? She had not, as Margaret had predicted to Percy, given up her cinema job in a few days; she was carrying on like a trouper. Who'd have thought that? There'd been a few wails and tears at first, and Mrs Lilley had had her work cut out calming her down, and had even gone across to the picture palace with her one day.

As far as Margaret could piece together, Norman Mutter the projectionist, who had a weak chest and couldn't join up, Mrs Taylor who took the money in the grandly named box office, and Ruth Horner, who showed people to their seats and flashed torches on those who might be doing what they shouldn't be doing till they was wed (not that she could talk), joined forces against her. They turned themselves into a quartet with old Miss Spenser who played the piano, usually several minutes behind the action, so that she banged out ragtime or the 'Ride of the Valkyries' in the middle of Douglas Fairbanks kissing Mary Pickford.

Together they had set out to make life difficult for Mrs Isabel, seeing her just as another of them Swinford-Brownes. He might still pay their wages, but now he had moved away he was no threat. Mrs Lilley's presence that day had reminded them that Mrs Isabel was also the Rector's daughter, and that Rector *hadn't* moved away.

After that, life was easier, and Mrs Isabel had even come to seek the servants' opinion on what to screen. That showed times were changing. Before the war, Mrs Isabel didn't think servants *had* opinions.

"I'm going to obtain the film the Government has made about the Somme battle," Mrs Isabel had told her, full of her own importance. "Then all of us can see what our menfolk are achieving, and in a little way share their hardships with them."

"They're achieving precious little, in my opinion," Margaret

116

had answered. "And what about those who've had enough of war? How about *Birth of a Nation*?" She was no picture-goer, but even she knew from Miss Caroline how good this new D. W. Griffith film was, even though it was American, and lasted longer than her stews took to cook. "Then you've got war *and* stories of people."

"Yes." Mrs Isabel seemed doubtful. "It would cost too much money though."

"Worth it."

"I could ask, I suppose. But I still think Ashden should see what's going on in France for themselves. We could show the Somme film on our anniversary in November."

"You was married in August."

"The *cinema's* anniversary. It's been open two years."

"I shouldn't remind that father-in-law of yours." The opening day of the cinema had not covered William Swinford-Browne in glory.

Mrs Isabel laughed. "Even he couldn't object to a grand showing of *The Battle of the Somme.*"

Out she went in a flurry of skirts, letting the door bang behind her as usual.

"*Battle of the Somme*," Margaret muttered. Fancy that, and fancy Mrs Isabel even coming to talk to her.

Meanwhile she had the Rectory to run, as well her cinema lessons, and there was planning to be done for the spring. There was tomorrow to think of too. They'd let Fred get accustomed to home again, and then they'd have a bit of a party. Muriel, Joe's wife, said she'd get the 10.12 train from Hartfield with the little ones, Sunday service or not, and Lizzie would bring the new baby – Fred would enjoy that. That's if he remembered who everyone was. She shivered at the thought she might see the same lack of recognition in his face as she had at Hertford. It was all very well to wear a bright smile on your face, but sometimes it was all she could do to keep it there.

She'd think of food: that never let you down. She could spare a bit of sugar for a cake surely. Cravenly, she decided Mrs Lilley need never know. Those sugarless cakes didn't taste right and she had a fair bit of sugar stored up for Christmas. The Lettices knew which side their bread was buttered on. She supposed she should say fatted on, for no one spoke of butter, or margarine, or oil. It was just 'fats'. Fred liked fairy cakes too; she might be able to dab a bit of icing on some for him. She used to put animals on the icing before this war. At least the Kaiser wasn't sinking jelly supplies. She could make a nice milk one. And there had to be one of her special trifles. And cinnamon sandwiches. When was she going to get all this done? The Lord ought to provide for a few more hours in the day during wartime.

There was a quick knock on the kitchen door and Mrs Lilley popped her head in. "I forgot to say, Mrs Dibble, that you must take time to bake a cake for Fred's return. And use what sugar you need."

"Thank you, madam," Margaret shamefacedly muttered. She often forgot that Mrs Lilley had a habit of thinking along the same lines as herself.

Percy Dibble found himself almost as bewildered as Fred at St Pancras without Daisy to help him sort things out. It seemed to him the whole world was coming home on leave the way soldiers were pouring off the train. How could he find Fred in this mob? He'd have to wait till everyone else had gone so that Fred would be left alone. Unless the white slavers got him, or he had followed someone else. Anxiety after anxiety shot through Percy's normally placid mind. War had a lot to answer for. Invasion-watching for example. They were asking for volunteers to man a watch tower at Gibraltar Farm in Hartfield and when no one spoke up from Ashden, Rector said he'd go. He couldn't let the Rector do that, so Percy went in his place. But Hartfield was a long way to travel by bicycle in the dark, and anyway, after he'd done it once or twice they said they could manage without him, to his surprise.

118

Now that Margaret was doing something for England he felt left out, so he had joined the local guard, keeping a watch on the railway line and the bridge. What for, he wasn't too sure. If those Germans invaded, they'd hardly come by train from Tunbridge Wells.

He'd asked Master George what it was all about, because at the beginning of the war, when Master George was in the scouts he had done this job. As usual he knew the answer. "We're like *francs-tireurs*," he'd said.

"Frank who?" Percy had never heard of the chap.

"It's French for armed civilians. If they invade and blow up the bridge, we'll stop them."

"Why would they blow up the bridge?" Percy asked blankly. "Just to stop us getting to Hartfield?"

Master George had thought this very funny. "The more panic the Germans can instill into villages like Ashden the quicker they'll win the war, or so they think. Anyway, the trains are used by our troops."

Percy had thought this over. "No one's going to blow up anything in this village while I'm around."

"Good for you, Mr Dibble."

Percy hoped someone like him was guarding St Pancras railway station, because he felt uncomfortable enough already without adding more problems. Then he cheered up for there was Fred, ambling along the platform for all the world as though he were at the seaside. He liked the seashore, did Fred. Only not the one he'd be seeing soon, he remembered. Percy was more of an optimist than Daisy, and still hoped Rector could stop that happening.

"Hallo, son." Percy hurried towards him and shook his hand, relieved to see he wasn't limping any more, and there were no fresh bruises – not that he could see at any rate. Percy took his pack from him, but Fred made a grab for it. "Mine."

At least he was speaking now, even if he didn't seem too sure who Percy was.

"You carry it, old chap," Percy said heartily, not knowing

what else to say. "Fancy a nice cup of tea before we go?" Without waiting for an answer he headed nervously for the café, which was packed with soldiers, until he realised Fred was no longer at his side, and hastily returned.

"No tea."

Percy hadn't heard Fred be so definite for a long time, and he was looking upset. What was wrong with a cup of tea? Could it be the Tommies and their noise? Surely he'd be used to that by now? He'd just travelled here with half the British army.

"Want to go to France," Fred said suddenly.

Percy was terrified. "We're going back home, Fred, *then* you'll go to France." They'd have to keep telling him that or he'd think he was coming home for good. What was he going to tell Daisy if he came home without Fred? "Come on, Fred, have some tea and then we'll go."

"Mess."

"What's that you say?" Percy was indignant on behalf of his wife and the Rectory. Daisy kept a clean kitchen.

"Don't like."

Percy followed the direction of his eyes; he was watching a group of sergeants walking into the café. He realised poor old Fred was confused, thinking the café was the sergeants' mess, and camp was probably home. He swallowed and took courage.

"What about the Rectory, lad? See your workshop again? Animals and birds, just like these pigeons?"

To his relief Fred broke into one of his beaming smiles, but Percy didn't relax completely until they had squeezed onto the East Grinstead and Tunbridge Wells train and it was steaming out of the station. In one hour and forty-seven minutes they'd be at Ashden, they'd walk down Station Road and then they'd be home. Never had he wanted to see Daisy so much in his life. Still, there was nothing more to worry about now.

"Ma, sit down," Lizzie commanded. "You're pacing around like old Lake counting his corn bales."

Farmer Lake, invalided out with the loss of his arm after the first battle of Ypres, was not an easy man to work for, even though it was nominally his wife who was in charge now.

"Suppose—"

"Suppose you walk up to the train to meet them, Ma? You're doing less than a scarecrow for a blind crow here. I'll peel the blessed potatoes for you. It makes a change from digging them up."

"You mind you peel 'em thin, my girl." It was an automatic response and there was no malice in her mother's voice. Margaret was grateful, for it might help to walk up to meet them. She put on her coat quickly, for the train they'd be on should have got in a few minutes ago. She crammed her hat on her head, the one with the feather Fred had given her from one of his wounded birds, and went out, hoping the drizzle had stopped. It hadn't quite, but she was too anxious to go back for an umbrella. Besides, Percy hadn't mended that spoke yet. She must have a few words with him.

She hurried across the road, waving to Nanny Oates who was sitting outside her door on Bankside selling eggs. Whoever would have thought before war came that she'd be greeting her old foe? It just showed you, war could bring you together as well as separate . . . No, don't think of that. But she found she was almost running in her anxiety as she turned into Station Road. Mrs Lettice stopped to talk, but Margaret just said what a nice day it was for the time of year and carried on. In the distance she could see people walking towards her, and her eyes searched for Percy's tall figure and a Tommy at his side.

She thought she saw them, and was quite sure about it as she drew nearer, but they weren't alone; there was a large woman with them, whose shape she didn't recognise. Was she a nurse sent with Fred to look after him? No, she'd be in uniform and, besides, the Army didn't run to nurses. It was a stranger, not too old either, despite her shape. What was Percy playing at? Then she forgot about the stranger as she felt tears of relief pricking at her eyes because Fred was home again, and even

121

though it was only for a short leave, he was still alive. She closed her mind to the future. We are safe in the Lord's hands, is what the Rector would say. She didn't mind that, it was being in Field Marshal Haig's hands she worried about.

As she grew close, she could see the relief on Percy's face as he caught sight of her. She knew that look; it meant Percy was out of his depth. Why was he bothering to make conversation with this girl? She was a country girl, that was clear from her red cheeks and healthy look, but she wore a funny kind of wooden shoe on her feet.

However, Fred was all she cared about, and she primly kissed him.

"Hallo, Ma."

He had recognised her, and almost sobbing with relief she felt she could take anything now.

"This is Miss Katie Burrows, Margaret. She's from York-shire." Percy couldn't wait to hand over responsibility.

Yorkshire was in the north, wasn't it? That was the other side of England, almost Scotland really. "How do you do?" she said shortly, annoyed at this intrusion on her reunion with Fred. She found her hand being pumped up and down like a washing dolly. The girl grinned, and let off a stream of unintelligible words.

"That French, is it?" she asked.

"Yorkshire, Margaret," Percy said nervously.

"Oh. Where are you staying, miss?"

It was Percy answered. "The Rectory, Margaret." He didn't dare look at her and no wonder.

It didn't just rain, it stormed. What was this new calamity? "Mrs Lilley didn't say."

The grin on the girl's face faded. She rummaged in her bag and produced a letter, headed National Land Service Corps. She flourished it under Margaret's nose, and the only words she took in were: "You will be lodged at the Rectory, Ashden in Sussex."

Margaret left Agnes making everyone a cup of tea, and immediately marched in to tackle Mrs Lilley in her glory-hole, deep in a precious moment of free time to sort out 'The Heap'. It was Miss Caroline who had given it that name; onto this pile was thrown every article of clothing or household equipment not yet specifically designated for a particular relief fund.

"You mean she's come to stay with you?" Elizabeth looked puzzled.

"It doesn't say, madam. It merely states the Rectory. I thought being a Land Corps lady it might be to do with you."

"I must come and talk to her . . . oh, my goodness!" Elizabeth sat down again. "I've just remembered. When Caroline resigned from the Agricultural Committee, their representative came to see me to ensure someone would be continuing her work here. I said I'd need a helper. I was thinking of Phoebe or someone local of course – but she was an officious kind of woman. I wonder if she's sent someone from outside the area. It was a mistake, Mrs Dibble. I know we have the room, but it's the work—"

'And the Rector' lay unspokenly between them. The Rector believed in people coming in need but going as quickly as possible.

"And this weekend, when Fred is home," Mrs Lilley lamented. "I'm so sorry."

Margaret was disposed to be gracious at the look of consternation on Mrs Lilley's face. "You leave her to me, ma'am. I'll put her up in the room next to Miss Lewis."

"Oh dear. How difficult. If she's helping me, I'm afraid she'll have to be treated like those awful Belgians who came here. As a guest."

"Very well, ma'am. If you say so. She'll be dining with you, then." Margaret's voice was wooden, to disguise her relief.

"I suppose she will," Elizabeth agreed unhappily. "My husband won't like this at all."

Miss Burrows, to Margaret's satisfaction, was swept from the kitchen and installed in the small bedroom next to Tilly's, a room rarely used now. Agnes quickly made it up for her – trust Myrtle to choose today for a day off. Still, Myrtle had been as

123

good as gold since that munitions affair, or as near gold as she was capable of. Five-thirty rising or not, she had at last appreciated when she was well off.

How the Rectory took the news of the stranger amongst them and whether they understood a single word she said, Margaret neither knew nor cared for once. It was *her* day off on Sunday, and Fred was home. *Her* family, not – for the first time ever – the Rectory's.

It was nice to have a party. Fred seemed bewildered at first, but by the Sunday morning he seemed to know where he was. She had a fright, not finding him in his room, but then thought of looking in his workshop and there he was. There he stayed too, and had to be persuaded in to meet everyone. He was very pleased to see the cake, at first. Then he said: "No candles."

"Fancy you remembering you have candles for your birthday, Fred. But it's not your birthday, love," Margaret said fondly.

"We'll have a special one for that," Lizzie chimed in. "I'll bake it."

Fred laughed. He'd obviously remembered what everyone knew – that Lizzie's cakes were like cannon-balls. But where would Fred be on his birthday, with his big smile and empty head?

"Absent loved ones," Lizzie said quietly, toasting with a glass of Percy's home-made wine. Margaret didn't mind. It was a special occasion, after all. It even crossed her mind she'd have a sip, but then she thought of King George. He'd signed the pledge and she was quite sure he wasn't taking a nip on the side.

"Absent loved ones," she echoed, with her glass of elder-flower cordial. There was Lizzie's Frank, sent out east some-where, now he was trained, and Rudolf goodness knows where. And there was Joe, pioneering away on the western front.

Muriel was shedding a tear or two. Although Joe wasn't in a fighting battalion, he took just as many of the risks. Margaret sighed. She'd like to think that one day, when – God willing – those absent today would be back, it would be like old times again. Only it wouldn't for the old times were gone for good.

Eight

M rs Dibble would have her worst suspicions confirmed if she could see these teacakes. Caroline could almost hear her saying: 'Potato teacakes with sultanas and dripping? Not in my kitchen, whatever the Kaiser says.' Her landlady had been so proud of them too. Apparently her grandmother used to make them in the Isle of Wight. 'Isle of Wight?' Mrs Dibble would say scornfully. 'English cooking's good enough for me.'

Caroline sought for something to break the silence in the stultifying atmosphere of Mrs Clark's private parlour, otherwise she might giggle at the stoical expression on Captain Rosier's face as he bravely ploughed his way through 'tea'. Her landlady had graciously allowed Caroline to use the parlour for her lessons, with a cryptic addendum that she did so only because Miss Lilley was a lady. It took some time before it dawned on Caroline that Mrs Clark still clung to the belief that entertaining a gentleman in private could lead to only one conclusion. Tea, provided unasked, was an attempt to protect her lodger's virtue. The days of uncorseted ladies in flimsy floating tea-gowns entertaining their lovers to tea – and whatever they hoped might follow afterwards – were over, however; an ancient blue serge costume and potato cakes following a tired piece of ham and – as a treat – half a hard-boiled egg, did not provide the same ambience, even in the dark gloom of the parlour.

This too was a relic of the past, crowded with souvenir china of visits to Margate with the absent Mr Clark, several framed photographs of Mr Clark, Mrs Clark and Master Clark (now married himself), a china plate commemorating General Gordon at Khartoum, a picture of the King and Queen, and a print of a Gainsborough lady. In front of the window on its own spindly support stood an aspidistra which looked as if it were bravely resisting every effort to kill it.

"Custer's last stand." She broke the silence at last as she saw Captain Rosier gazing at the plant, then realised he could not possibly understand what she meant. To her surprise, a quick nod of the head showed he did, and moreover it encouraged him to speak:

"It need not fear. I have no tomahawk." He hesitated, then asked politely: "If you please, Miss Lilley, what is this meal I am eating? Supper?"

"No. The famous British institution: high tea. That means it is more than afternoon tea, and has pretensions to being an evening meal."

"*More* than tea?" He looked at the sparse table.

"In summer it would have a lettuce leaf with it. And shouldn't we be speaking in French?"

"*Je m'excuse*, Miss Lilley." Conscience-stricken, he began painstakingly discussing the tablecloth, the potato cakes, the appalling trifle, the knives and forks, and then correcting her pronunciation in her replies, until she wondered why on earth she had agreed to this charade. The time had come to speak out.

"I'm very grateful to you, but this isn't the kind of French I need to know."

He immediately began to rise from his chair, consternation on his face since he had obviously assumed he was being dismissed.

"Please don't go," she cried in alarm, appalled at how easily misunderstandings could still arise. "I didn't mean that I don't want to learn French from you. I do. But not about teatables. Or is it this terrible tea that you want to get away from?"

Up until then, his correct manner had made her assume that

he was here only in response to Luke's suggestion. Now, however, his eyes sparked with interest, and for the first time she felt they understood each other. "*Naturellement*," he said, "you need to know how people speak when they are together, and the words they use. I have been selfish in enjoying your company here alone."

Flattery sat oddly on his lips, and so she ignored his last comment. "Could you arrange for me to meet other Belgians, Captain Rosier, or should I ask someone from the section office to introduce me?"

"I will escort you." He seemed a little reluctant however, adding to her annoyance: "Would your parents approve?"

"Whatever have they to do with it? And of course they would approve of you." Really, was he proposing to ask their permission to escort their precious daughter without a chaperone?

"I am honoured, Miss Lilley."

He was trying not to laugh! How dare he – even if it was obvious she had misunderstand what he meant.

"My compatriots, as you know, Miss Lilley," he explained, "meet in the clubs such as the one held in the bathing establishment's hall, and that run by the Catholic Church of Our Lady Help of Christians, and many others. They have their own schools and church services, and their own newspaper, *Le Franco-Belge*, published here in Folkestone. I can give you copies of that, and take you to the clubs, even the *Militaire Cercle Albert* held in the parish hall. However, in the evenings, when lights grow dim and drink flows, some of the language and behaviour can be bad. Not all the Belgians here are interested in literary discussions, many are Belgian soldiers passing through the town and, like the Tommies, they have more basic concerns."

Her annoyance increased, as she realised she had *over*estimated this man. "I'm here to work for the war. How can you believe I am too prim and proper to visit a few rough clubs, where people drink too much in order to forget? If you won't take me, Captain Rosier, then I will go alone."

127

She found herself on her feet. She must get out of this claustrophobic room. He had risen too, however, and seemed to be towering above her, barring her way to the door, although he was only five inches or so taller than her. She couldn't very well rush past him. She would wait and let him speak. Would he grovel in apologies or simply stalk out of the room with his deep hurt eyes? He did neither. He took her hand, and raised it to his lips.

"I will take you wherever you wish, Miss Lilley, and we shall go now"

"And don't call me Miss Lilley." She felt ridiculously like crying.

"Caroline." It emerged as *Caroleen*, which sounded delightfully different to her.

"May I call you Yves?" Did she have to make every move herself?

"I should be honoured."

"Then, Yves, let us hide those two remaining potato cakes in my bag, smuggle them past my landlady's suspicious eye, and when no one is looking feed them to the seagulls. Then you can introduce me to your Belgian friends."

That had been a month ago, and since then she had begun to think she was more Belgian than English. She spent her evenings at Belgian clubs, and she visited the Belgian section bureau run by Major Mage, a first-class intelligence officer, Yves said. She even went to the new Belgian schools. It was difficult at first, for even with Yves present the talk was too quick and too idiomatic, quite apart from the fact that half of the Belgians were Flemish-speaking. She had already picked up some written Flemish through her work, but the spoken guttural sounds seemed to bear little relation to it.

Before the war there had been no love lost, Yves had explained, between the French-speaking Walloons and the Flemish, but war had brought them together in their determination to free Belgium. The German governor of occupied Belgium therefore spared no effort in trying to set one faction against the other again. Caroline gathered that just as a few months ago the Germans had ordered every male of military age in occupied Belgium to register for work, so King Albert had issued an edict for all Belgians to enlist for national service. As boys reached fighting age they would leave Folkestone and other towns where the refugees had settled to join the Belgian army; those in occupied Belgium tried to escape over the border into Holland, to make a roundabout way to the lines via Folkestone.

To her gratification, Caroline found her French was improving rapidly, and she had even mastered the small but important differences between Belgian French and that spoken in France. The Belgians were comfortable people to be with, and she instantly felt at home with them. Literally so, for she could pick out their Ashden counterparts. *There* was a Wally Bertram, if ever she saw one, and she had been charmed when he informed her half in French, half in broken English, that he too was a butcher. And that elderly black-clad Mère Bissart was a Nanny Oates, just as shrewd and just as cantankerous, and also well into her eighties.

Caroline was treated to strange drinks at private gatherings (a practice now forbidden in licensed premises) and wondered how they were obtained in times of war. Smuggled over from Holland, she presumed, for the terrible food shortages in occupied Belgium, particularly Brussels, were an international disgrace. King Albert had appealed to the free world for food supplies to be sent, and although the Germans had the wickedness deliberately to sink some of them, there should have been plenty to satisfy starving Brussels, especially from America, busy salving its conscience for not joining in the war. But there wasn't enough, despite all the Allied International Relief Committee could do.

It seemed all wrong that she could enjoy Belgian cooking here in Folkestone. Mrs Dibble, she felt, would approve of it –

apart from the use of beer. It was even used in stews, to her amazement. Waterzooi would undoubtedly have Mrs Dibble's blessing. And there wasn't a single snail in sight, Caroline wrote triumphantly to the Rectory.

In the evenings they talked movingly of their homeland, produced faded photographs, and sang their own songs. Wherever she was, the evening always ended with 'God Save the King' followed by 'La Brabançonne', the Belgian national anthem, before they went their separate ways to grope their way through the darkness to their temporary homes. They talked of their villages, their homes, their towns, of the burning of lovely Bruges, of Louvain, but seldom of the personal horrors of the war they had experienced, or of the plight of those left behind. She never asked questions, for fear it would reopen wounds, knowing how increasingly harsh life was in their own country. In addition to the food shortages, civilians were being forced to work for the German army, which was against the Hague convention; and more ominous still, in the last month thousands of Belgian civilians had been deported to Germany to work. Bruges and other towns that refused to supply lists of its citizens had paid heavily for their defiance.

"They have ruined our economy with their high taxes, their fines and their seizure of our harvests, and now they leave us to starve," Yves had told her matter-of-factly.

"How can you appear so calm," she asked him impulsively, "when you must be suffering so much?"

He had shrugged. "Like you, Caroline, I have a job to do. What use would I be to His Majesty if the facts I conveyed were clouded by a humble captain's grief?"

He never spoke of his own life in Belgium and, as was her policy, she never asked him, even though she talked to him of the Rectory and its problems. Yves listened with great attention and what seemed genuine concern, offering useful comments. Perhaps it provided him with something to replace what he had left behind in Belgium.

But what *had* he left behind? She was longing to know about King Albert and Queen Elisabeth, both of whom he must know very well through his regular visits, but reluctantly she decided she should ask him nothing at all, not even where he came from or whether he was married or a bachelor. She didn't even like to ask him where he now lived as it wasn't in Folkestone. He appeared, as befitted a Cheshire cat, at intervals, but she supposed he must have a base nearby as well as in London. Did he have a home there? And how did he get that deep scar? The questions would probably remain unanswered because he obviously preferred to put his private life into a temporary limbo. Well, she could understand that. She had done the same in Ashden, because of Reggie's death. Yet perhaps this was wrong, for every experience should provide a lesson.

Now she was getting as sobersided as Yves. And that was unfair. He wasn't sobersided at all once you had a pass permitting entry through the first barrier. Once past that, he had an engaging way of seeing the oddities of life the same way as she did, such as that plant in the parlour, for example, and they tended to laugh at the same things. Perhaps it wasn't mere flattery when he had said he enjoyed her company.

There was plenty of news from the Rectory to talk over with him. Caroline had been both aghast and fascinated to read in her mother's latest letter in the third week of November about the arrival of Miss Burrows. She could guess how her father would react, forever torn between his duty and his love of peace and quiet. He had taken the arrival of Elizabeth Agnes in his stride, but babies were one thing and noisy young women quite another. Miss Burrows did at least provide a constant source of amusement.

'It's unfair to laugh,' her mother wrote, 'but she does do the most extraordinary things. She cannot get used to the fact that we all have our own jobs to do in the Rectory, your father his, Mrs Dibble hers, and Agnes and Myrtle theirs. I even found our Kate polishing the front steps, much to Myrtle's indignation.

And she will keep bursting into Yorkshire songs. She's particularly fond of "On Ilkley Moor b'aht at" and whenever this
breaks out Mrs Dibble redoubles her efforts on "O Lord and
Father of Mankind." Your father wants to turn the old tackle
room next to my glory-hole into a study so that he can work in
peace. I pointed out there's no real heating, but he said grimly a
paraffin heater was infinitely preferable to our Kate. However
she's a star turn with George; he even seems slightly sorry he's
joining the RFC. He's fascinated by her, and has even started
helping me in my work for a chance to be with her. Kate treats
him like a faithful sheepdog. I came across some sketches he
had done of her, all curves and bounces. Maybe he's a budding
Rubens as well as a cartoonist.'

Caroline hoped not. She had an instant vision of Father
walking in on George, paintbrush in hand, painting a nude,
curvy, bouncy lady from Yorkshire, with or without tasteful
drapery, and related this to Yves.

"He is nearly eighteen," he pointed out.

"Yes, but his birthday is on 12th December—" Caroline
broke off. She had been going to say George was young for
his age, then remembered that he already made a name for
himself as a cartoonist and could fly an aeroplane. She read
on.

'Whether we like it or not, George must go into the forces.
However, one does hear such terrible rumours about the speed
with which new pilots are killed, wonderful work though they
are doing, I do wish he'd joined the Army as Father wanted.
However, as soon as he got his aero certificate, he went to
London to sign on and that was that, and he is waiting for his
papers now. Between you and me, Caroline, we were lucky to
keep him so long. Lady Hunney let the cat out of the bag – and
never tell your father: the reason Sir John paid for the flying
lessons is that he caught George trying to enlist a year ago, and
bribed him to change his mind. Laurence's annoyance over the
lessons was misplaced. We owe a lot to Sir John. At least you,

my rock, are still in England, Caroline. And Isabel too of course . . .'

And Isabel too of course. Caroline laughed. She had received only one short scrawled note from her sister, informing her how busy she was running the cinema and all about the imminent great anniversary celebration. She was bursting her buttons with pride at showing *The Battle of the Somme*. Although there was still fighting at the Somme, the film covered the first two months of the battle, and had been rushed out to cinemas and parish halls around the country. It displayed live scenes from the battlefront in order that those at home could appreciate what their loved ones were achieving, and her parents approved of Isabel's choice. But Caroline did not, for she had seen it.

Margaret selected her best felt hat. Mrs Isabel was loaning her the cinema for her cookery talks, so the least she could do in exchange was to attend the anniversary celebration film. Myrtle was looking after Elizabeth Agnes and Lizzie's baby, because Lizzie wanted to see the film too, and so did Agnes. Her Jamie was out at the Somme, and Lizzie felt perhaps where Frank was, out east, might be something like France too. She and Agnes were getting on ever so well, although both of them had their prickly side, as Margaret well knew.

Even the Rector was coming to the cinema this evening, his first ever visit. Mrs Lilley had told him they had to support Mrs Isabel, and Margaret suspected that he'd secretly been longing to see what all the fuss was about, and was only awaiting a suitable picture to do so. Master George was coming and Miss Phoebe. It was a real Rectory family outing. Usually family only mixed with servants in church, and it was a funny old world when picture houses could be compared with the Lord's dwelling.

Percy was coming too, and she had to admit she was glad. She could talk to him, knowing they were both thinking of Fred. He was out in France – suppose he was at this Somme place? It wasn't likely he or Joe would turn into a hero like Jamie, or like the men they'd be bound to show in the film, but seeing soldiers going over the top would remind her all too vividly that Fred was there somewhere. It would be like being at the Front with him.

She marched down the central aisle behind the Rector to the reserved seats. First, Mrs Isabel was going to make a little speech, then there'd be a nice short Charlie Chaplin film to start off with. Then would come *The Battle of the Somme.*

Agnes was so white she had to lean on Lizzie's arm to help her home. Crying too, and no wonder, Margaret sympathised. Jamie Thorn had been through that lot, and even worse was back there now, medal or no medal. A little circle of metal on a ribbon wasn't going to save him from a German shell. She took Agnes's other arm, more to steady herself than the girl. She couldn't deny it had been a shock.

"Don't you worry now, Agnes." Margaret tried hard to find encouraging words, but how could she say those films always showed you the worst of it, when everyone knew the Government thought they was showing the best of it?

Anyway, no words could make them forget what they'd felt like, seeing that film. Wounded soldiers in hospitals wearing nice white bandages were one thing; staggering all over the battlefield with their eyes out and blood running and the bodies lying there dead, was quite another. The worst of it was that film was out to show how much our boys were achieving. *Achieving?* She'd seen precious little sign of it; there was precious little sign of anything, except stumps of trees and holes in the ground they called trenches.

"Oh, Margaret—" Agnes slumped down at the kitchen table. That showed how upset she was. She didn't often dare call her Margaret. "I never knew. Jamie tried to explain, but I never imagined it like that. Them trenches aren't fit to keep a rat in, let alone my Jamie."

The buzz of anticipation as the film started had turned to shock as they saw the wounded staggering through the trenches to get help. Where was the marching off to glory now? Master Reggie had died somewhere like that. Margaret's eyes filled with tears, for Reginald Hunney, for Tim Hubble, for Joe, for Fred, and any mother's son caught up in the hell of war.

"What can I do?" Agnes whispered. "What can we do, now we know?"

Margaret looked up to see the Rector and Mrs Lilley coming through the tradesmen's entrance into the kitchen, and didn't even register at the time this was unheard of. She just said: "I'll make a nice cup of hot milk all round."

The Rector sat down at the kitchen table, and Mrs Lilley came to help Agnes get the cups down. "Are you all right, my dear?" she heard Mrs Lilley ask.

Silly question really, Margaret thought, but Agnes seemed to appreciate it. "Yes, madam."

"No," Rector said quietly. "We're none of us all right, Elizabeth, not after that. I think, Mr Dibble, that Agnes and perhaps all of us are in need of a drop of your medicinal brandy even more than prayer."

Percy went to get the bottle as though this were the most natural thing in the world, but it wasn't, and Margaret knew it. All they had left was three inches in the last bottle of pre-war stock, saved for the Christmas pudding and medical emergencies. Margaret didn't say a word. She poured a cup of hot milk out for everyone, and Percy added a dash of brandy to each one, except hers of course. His wife looked him full in the face.

"I'll take a dash of that brandy, Percy, if you'd be so good."

Next day she wondered whatever had got into her, but then it hadn't been like taking strong liquor, since it was in hot milk, and whether it was the milk or the brandy, she'd slept like a baby and the devil didn't interrupt her dreams in his delight at her wickedness. She didn't dream at all, not even about the film.

Her good night's sleep strengthened her, which was just as

well, for Mrs Isabel was in a rare taking. Mrs Lilley had gone to East Grinstead and it was all Margaret could do to get Mrs Isabel off to work.

"How could I know, Mrs Dibble?" she wailed, still sitting at the breakfast table when Margaret went in to clear the dishes. "I thought they'd be pleased, getting such an up-to-date film."

"So did the Government," Margaret pointed out. "You've nothing to reproach yourself with, Mrs Isabel."

"I kept thinking: what about my husband?"

It was the first time Margaret had ever heard her talk about Mr Robert since he left for the war two years ago. "He'll be all right." Meaningless words, and she knew it. For all her faults, Mrs Isabel had her father's intelligence, and would know them for what they were.

"He's nearly finished his observer's training now. What if he gets sent out there? Aeroplanes get shot down so easily. I don't wonder my parents are so worried about George."

Margaret had no reply, for Mrs Isabel was right.

"No one spoke to me last night," Isabel mourned. 'No one will ever come to the cinema again. Father-in-law will never speak to me again. He's never forgiven me for staying here. He only agreed because Robert put his foot down for once. He'll close the picture palace down and I'll have to go to East Grinstead. And I won't, I *won't*.'

Margaret was vastly relieved at this torrent of woes. That was more like Mrs Isabel, thinking of herself. "He likes that purse, that one, so fill it. Next week show a Charlie Chaplin and a Mary Pickford, Mrs Isabel," she suggested, "and offer half-price seats in the daytime to anyone who has a loved one at the Front. You'll be packed out all day."

"That's a brilliant idea, Mrs Dibble," Mrs Isabel said admiringly. The tears vanished immediately as her enthusiasm returned. "But I can't wait till next week; I'll start tomorrow if I can get the films by then. I shall close the picture palace today."

"No, Mrs Isabel. You keep *The Somme* running till the end of the week. That's my advice."

"But I can't. You saw how appalled the audience was."

"Yes, we've all had a shock, but it's not like it's not happening. We have to face up to it. You mark my words, everyone will be wanting to see it now when they hear about it from their neighbours. They'll be queuing all down Bankside. The newspapers are all too fond of telling us everything's in the garden's lovely; we thought it couldn't be, and now we *know* it isn't."

So much was going on Margaret had forgotten all about what else happened last night. When they got back Myrtle had said the baby was running a temperature, and Lizzie took her home immediately.

'We had another scare too,' Caroline's mother wrote. 'Lizzie Dibble's baby was running a temperature and Dr Marden is worried it might be diptheria. We won't know for a few days, and he's calling in daily. November is the peak month for it, he says. That cottage of hers stuck out in the wilds must be very unhealthy. Percy's going to do some more work on it to keep the damp out, and Lizzie has promised to keep a better fire.'

"A better fire." Caroline finished giving Yves the gist of the letter, as they walked along the seafront towards Sandgate. "Father says he'll take that for his sermon next week. Not just 'keep the home fires burning' but 'keep a *better* fire'." The wind whipped round her legs where the boots ended and the skirt didn't quite begin, a reminder that winter was setting in fast. Unthinkingly, she asked a question. "Do you have texts for sermons like that in Belgium, Yves? Are you a Roman Catholic?"

"Yes"

"I wish you could hear one of my father's, but I suppose you cannot even attend a service in a Church of England."

"It is heavily frowned upon. At one time I would have

thought that important. No longer. I attend many church services in Folkestone, besides those of Our Lady Help of Christians." He seemed very relaxed today, even though there was still a formal twelve-inch space between them. She decided to risk another cautious question, as she skirted round three children leaping around on jumping poles.

"You never talk of your home in Belgium, Yves, and very little about what is going on there."

He replied after a moment: "We often choose not to talk. The Belgian people you meet here are constantly wondering what is happening to their families. What they read in the *Franco-Belge* is terrifying enough. Do you still read it?"

"Of course. I buy it regularly – thanks to you, sir—" she dropped a curtsy to him in the middle of the path to a chorus of approving shouts from a passing group of Tommies. If he wanted to steer the conversation away from himself, she supposed it was his right.

"Then you know about the deportations, the executions, the closure of theatres and restaurants, the lack of food, the constant snuffing out of any resistance. If we celebrate our Independence Day, they forbid it; the girls dress in our national colours, the men wear rosettes, and that is forbidden. We plant red and yellow flowers on our balconies in black-painted pots, and that too is treason."

He said 'we', identifying himself with his fellow citizens. She risked going further.

"I read that Dr Bull was re-arrested and tried, and this time found guilty and imprisoned. Do you know him? He sounds a remarkable man."

"Yes. I knew Miss Cavell, also Philippe Baucq, who died with her, and Louise Thuliez, the Countess of Croye – the entire organisation."

"Is that when you got that scar?"

"Sometime about then," he replied guardedly. "However, unlike them, I am alive and free."

138

"Only physically."

He shot a look at her. "Perhaps. As you too."

She didn't want to think of Reggie, and unfairly resented his intruding into her private domain.

"Do you have links with *La Libre Belge* – that is the main secret newspaper in Brussels, isn't it?"

"Yes." His voice was clipped, and she was illogically pleased to have annoyed him.

"Is that how the *Franco-Belge* published here gets its news of what's happening in Brussels? Do the couriers bring over copies?"

He stopped abruptly. For a moment she thought he was furious with her for overstepping the boundary he had tacitly laid down. To her amazement, however, he was shaking with laughter. He took her gloved hands in his, swinging her round to face him.

"So, Caroline, what is this? Has Governor-General von Bissing found himself a Grand Inquisitor?"

"I am a secret agent," she informed him loftily. "I'm entitled to ask questions."

"Secret agents are solemn gentlemen who walk by night with hats tipped over their eyes to avoid notice. They are not beautiful young Englishwomen with dancing brown eyes and brown curls that will not quite obey their owner."

One of her hands automatically freed itself to push the recalcitrant curl back under the hat, but he captured it again before it reached its destination.

"Please leave it. It is your free spirit, Caroline."

She had wanted the barrier broken, but now that it was, she was tongue-tied. Perhaps he saw this, for he dropped her hand, and partly to her regret, and partly relief, returned to neutral ground. "You are right, Mademoiselle Schwarzteuffel. That, for your information as a secret agent, is the nickname of the hated military inquisitor in Belgium, von Bergam, in charge of the treason trials. *La Libre Belge* publishes news – to the great annoyance of the German Governor-General – about the progress of the war, especially of British or French victories for this raises morale in the city. It moves its location for every issue, and so far the Germans have never caught the editor, though the distributors are often arrested. My friend Philippe Baucq was one of them. It also pokes fun at our unwelcome visitors to Belgium, and that they cannot abide. It is a good method, for he at whom you laugh is already conquered in the mind."

"Yet you do not laugh much, Yves," Caroline pointed out bluntly. "Do you have a family still in Belgium?"

She *had* gone too far, for she saw his lips draw together in a tight line. She thought he would not answer, but eventually he did. "I have my parents; also a brother, serving like me in the Belgian army, but he is on the Belgian front, waiting."

"For what?"

"Like your sister, for the next offensive there. It will come, believe me. King Albert fears it, and has written in the most strong terms to protest for he believes it would ruin Belgium for ever. But His Majesty is not even accorded a seat at the Allied military discussions. It is insupportable. It is known to GHQ and to the governments of America, Britain and France, though not to the public, that His Majesty has not ruled out a negotiated peace with Germany to avoid more slaughter and the ruin of our fair land."

Caroline was horrified. "You don't approve of that, surely?"

"This humble captain believes that Germany would demand Belgium's complete economic dependence on her, which effectively means we would remain occupied in spirit if not physically. He also believes that Field Marshal Haig, this new French commander Nivelle, and perhaps even the bashful President Wilson, who does not show his face in this war, know that Ypres will be the battleground for Armageddon."

She did not comment, for she had her wish. He was speaking about what he felt most deeply and even if she felt with Queen

Victoria that 'she was not a public meeting', she must listen if she wanted to know more about Yves. And she did. A great deal more.

When she returned to her room that evening, she looked out of the window into the street below. Nothing to be seen here, the hum of voices, a faint glow from a dim headlight. Somewhere out there in the dark was Yves. She still did not know where he lived, and yet he had held her hands and told her she was beautiful.

December began without the anticipation of Christmas providing its usual excitement. The village, so her mother had written, was predicting a long hard winter ahead, and late November had brought two new shocks for Caroline. On the 22nd she had read in the newspaper to her horror of the torpedoing in the Aegean of the *Britannic*, which she was almost sure was the hospital ship on which her friend Penelope Banning had been working as a Red Cross nurse. Tired of the constrictions of English life after her time in Serbia, she had volunteered her services yet again. She had immediately telephoned Simon, only to find he was in the dark as to Penelope's fate. There were casualties, there were survivors, but her name did not show on the list. He still did not know.

The other shock had been in the section office. When she walked in one morning, it had been immediately obvious something was wrong. Every single file seemed to be piled up on desks, each pile with someone rapidly going through it, and some of the faces she did not know. Others she did – they were from the French and Belgian sections. Captain Cameron himself was down there, and even Luke's mask of casual *bonhomie* had slipped.

"What's going on?" she asked in alarm, as soon as she could reach him.

"It's bad news, Caroline. The ship was intercepted by German warships from Zeebrugge."

"The Flushing ferry?" Stupid question. Of course it was. Why else would the office present such a scene of pandemonium? In addition to couriers not only from theirs, but from the French and Belgian sections too, it would have been carrying bags of compromising mail.

"All the secret baggage was thrown overboard to prevent the Germans getting it if they boarded, but the devils managed to scoop up at least one of our bags before it sank."

"Is it as serious as the sinking of the *Brussels*?"

"Oh yes, it's serious. It's Baer-le-duc all over again."

Everyone in the Joint Bureau knew about Baer-le-duc. It was a tiny Belgian village completely surrounded by neutral Holland, not far from the Belgian-Dutch border. The Germans could not therefore occupy it, much to their annoyance, and a remarkable number of deceased Belgians near the frontier had, according to their families, expressed that their dying wish was to be buried in unoccupied Belgium. Each funeral procession, including the coffin, was carefully searched by the Germans before it left, and again at the frontier, but nothing was ever discovered. The cemetery at Baer-le-Duc was soon filled to capacity, and three more fields had hastily to be consecrated. At last an extra diligent search disclosed ingenious methods of concealing agents' reports such as a tube inserted down the corpse's throat. Many executions had followed, the frontier checks were strengthened, Baer-le-Duc returned to its normal funeral rate – and the Allied intelligence services began the task of rebuilding shattered networks.

"We have to start again?" she asked Luke.

Luke's normally cheerful face was grey. "Worse. It could well mean the end of this little operation."

Nine

I t had begun to snow again, but it hadn't brought any manna from heaven down with it. Margaret Dibble sniffed, as she inspected the recipe Miss Caroline had sent her for wartime Christmas pudding. Say what you like, a pudding made with raw potato and carrot with only half a cup of dried fruit was not a real pudding, and Christmas was not Christmas without a real pudding. Anyway, even though she'd had the fruit and flour to make one proper pudding, there had been no one to stir it. She'd called Agnes and Myrtle in, and even Percy, though he was a fat lot of use with a spoon, but Myrtle started stirring widdershins, as if they hadn't had enough bad luck. Miss Caroline still wasn't sure if she'd be able to get home for Christmas, and Margaret supposed she couldn't be blamed for that. The war didn't stop just because three wise men and some shepherds once made their way towards Bethlehem.

Christmas was only two weeks away now, but she couldn't muster up the usual sense of excitement. No Fred, no Joe, only Lizzie, and even Muriel was going to her parents in Withyham. Not that the Dibbles were alone in this. There was no Miss Felicia, and Mrs Isabel would only be here part of the time, because Mr Robert was coming home and wanted to spend Christmas with his parents. It was only natural, but Mrs Isabel didn't see it that way. Moaning and groaning, you'd think she had been asked to go to Australia instead of East Grinstead. Miss Phoebe would be here, but she'd been very quiet since Master George had enlisted. It was his birthday today, poor lamb, and he received his papers this very day. He'd be leaving in the new year.

"Ma Dibble!"

Margaret promptly dropped the recipe into the mixing bowl. Whatever had happened? That was Muriel's voice, and sure enough the door burst open and Muriel came in bringing half the snowstorm with her. It must be the children. Or Joe? He was dead, she knew it. Must be for Muriel to have come with the carrier or by train all the way from Hartfield. Muriel was waving a piece of paper too! It must be the yellow telegram, for tears were streaming down Muriel's face. Then Margaret realised the tears weren't of sorrow but of happiness, and her stomach stopped churning up like a mincing machine.

"Joe!" Muriel cried. "He says he's been lucky in the draw for Christmas leave. He's come home, for three whole days, so we'll be coming here on Christmas Day. Oh, Ma." She flung herself into Margaret's arms, most un-Muriel like. "It's going to be a *wonderful* Christmas."

It was going to be a *wonderful* Christmas. Firstly, Penelope was safe. At the last moment, she had been switched from the *Britannic* to land duties. Secondly, Caroline had heard that she would be able to have leave for Christmas even though Luke would also be away. She had been so busy since the ferry incident that she not been able to visit the Rectory as the bureau had been at sixes and sevens, as no one could be sure who or what had been compromised in Belgium. Information was coming in in dribs and drabs, and as the ferry service had been suspended, they had to rely on whatever transport the couriers could find. It was a serious matter now that the bad weather had halted the impetus at the Somme and Verdun. Winter was a friend to peace, Yves said. It had defeated Napoleon; if only it could manage the same trick with the Kaiser.

In addition to the pandemonium caused by the ferry incident, Caroline was also aware that something else was going on, something in which minions were not invited to join. Luke was spending more time than usual with the French and Belgian sections, and when she visited them herself, she noticed an air of suppressed excitement.

Gradually the sea of faces who came to their office had separated itself into distinct personalities. There was Guy, a regular courier from Holland who acted as a post-box near the frontier in Belgium and, when that was too heavily guarded, on the seashore for night-time deliveries from the sea. He was a placid, bespectacled man whom in peacetime one might expect to see behind a bank counter. There was Jean-Claude, a morose fisherman, who brought his boat over once a month, sometimes with verbal or written reports, occasionally with refugees or agents who feared themselves compromised. 'Agents' were seldom like those that enlivened spy novels; they were railway workers, housewives, tradespeople, just ordinary people apparently leading everyday lives. The train-watching agents kept continuous shifts, night and day, and were always at risk. One elderly lady, Madame Stevens, communicated through a code of knitting stitches, rather like the darned sock method, and was able to give them interesting information such as that on the railway line from Liège to Louvain – beneath her window a whole German artillery division had been transported in thirty-one trains, following each other at set intervals.

Caroline had taken a particular fancy to Olivier Fabre, a small ferret-like man with glittering eyes, who had a stream of curses far beyond the scope of her French and spoke virtually no English. Indeed, apart from his curses he rarely spoke at all. So far she had gathered little about his role, since Luke was uncommunicative on the subject. She had not seen him for a month, however. His arrival was especially prized since he was a *passeur*, one of the paid agents who brought reports from the letterboxes and sometimes people from the interior through one of the *tuyaux*, their routes across the frontier, a task that involved india-rubber gloves and shoes and a great deal of courage.

She had not seen Yves recently either, and was delighted when he called in to suggest she accompany him to see *Disraeli* at the cinema that evening.

"I have an even better idea," she said impulsively. "It's my brother's birthday and I can't get home for it, so let me treat you to dinner at the Metropole to celebrate it. They haven't made treating of food illegal – yet."

He hesitated. "I will come with pleasure, but I must—"

"Oh Yves. Let me pay." She laughed. "I've been helping to fight for women's rights for so long, and now I'm earning money. I deserve this victory."

The Metropole on the Leas was a grand hotel in the old style, and dining there reminded her of the treats Aunt Tilly used to give her at the London Carlton on very special occasions. Like all hotels now, the clientele was dominated by uniforms. She had put on her best evening gown, in blue voile and lace, an acquisition of which she was guiltily proud. (After all, what was earning money *for*, but the occasional treat?) She was glad she had done so for most of the other women diners were resplendent in satins and silks. The food revealed there was a war on, however, with the menu abbreviated and uninspiring, but nevertheless it was better than anywhere else.

"I've something else to celebrate too," she told Yves happily, as a rather small trout arrived before her. "I'm going home for Christmas."

Seeing an instant reaction, she was annoyed with herself for her tactlessness. "How selfish of me. What will you do?"

"I am expecting someone from Belgium."

"Oh."

Why did she feel so deflated? She should rejoice for him. She was so used to thinking of Yves as her friend alone, that she forgot he must have many, many friends. And family too. He wasn't married, but perhaps this was a sweetheart who had managed to escape over the frontier, or perhaps worked for Queen Elisabeth, who ran a hospital at Poperinghe. To think she had had the wild idea that if he were on his own he could come with her to the Rectory. Of course he would have plans of his own.

"Will you be in Folkestone?" she asked.

Yves looked embarrassed. "No. Sir John Hunney has invited us to stay at the Dower House, since Daniel has to work and cannot be there."

Caroline's head spun. She began to feel distinctly put out, without any reason whatsoever. "Then as the Hunneys always come to us for Christmas Day after the service, you must come too. Father would understand if you preferred to attend mass in Hartfield. That's the nearest Roman Catholic church."

"You must not feel obliged to entertain me. But I should be honoured to attend St Nicholas, even if His Holiness the Pope excommunicates me. In fact, my friend is a Huguenot Protestant."

"Does she speak English?" Caroline couldn't think of anything else to say. The trout tasted most unappetising.

Yves looked at her in what might have been amusement. "*He* does, Caroline. As you will have guessed, it is one of our couriers."

Oh, what a polite man he was, she thought, as the trout regained its appeal.

"Olivier Fabre is a very special *passeur*," he continued. "He is a puppeteer and takes his marionettes round all the Belgian cities, where he collects reports from the letterboxes. Some come from local puppeteers, who give information by an elaborate code of stories and movements, which he notes down. He even takes his marionettes to the German Governor-General in Brussels and has, as a special favour, obtained a regular pass to neutral Holland signed by von Bissing himself. No india rubber gloves for him. He is presumed to be touring Holland at Christmas, but he will come here for a week before he returns."

"You must bring him to the Rectory too, of course," Caroline said warmly. She had had no idea about Fabre's marionettes, but was not going to reveal her lack of status to Yves.

He still looked doubtful. "He is not—" he stopped.

She knew immediately what he was going to say. "No one at the Rectory will understand his bad language. Not even me."

He smiled. "I would enjoy coming very much, Caroline, if Sir John and Lady Hunney—"

"They will come," Caroline interrupted, eager to remove obstacles, and again following his train of thought. "They have always come and that will not change, although Reggie will no longer be there."

At the end of dinner, he thanked her formally for her hospitality. "In the new year I shall repay you."

"You can repay me now," she instructed him in high glee. "You can't escape yet. I'm longing to dance."

All during the meal the sound of the orchestra in the adjacent ballroom had been luring her. It was hardly the latest jazz band, but it was making a gallant attempt at some ragtime, and to her delight tangos no longer seemed to be frowned upon. Times were indeed changing. She hadn't danced since she left London, save for local informal parties – and nowadays there were precious few of these – and her feet were tapping. She half thought Yves would refuse, but he informed her it would be his privilege. Hardly words of wild enthusiasm, but she would make him repent them.

"It is not too much of an escape?" she asked gravely.

"I have decided," he replied equally gravely, "that since you are a work colleague, you do not come under the category of entertainment or pleasure."

"Captain Rosier," she declared, "you will eat your words."

"Then you will pay for that second dinner also, for I do not dance well."

She was bound to admit he was right, but how she enjoyed it all the same. Dancing to ragtime was a new and bewildering experience for him until he began to get used to the rhythm, but in the waltzes he was more at home. What did he *do* in London? He couldn't work all the time, surely, and these days you could hardly avoid ragtime if you tried. Whereas she now rarely gave a second thought to dancing clasped by men she hardly knew, she became acutely aware of her closeness to Yves. The warmth of the hand on her back was comforting, the excitement of dancing with him making her tingle from head to foot. Perhaps he felt it, for he suddenly looked down at her and smiled.

"You dance well, Caroline. Better than I."

"You're wrong."

And indeed she began to believe it, until he attempted a tango. An over-enthusiastic stride on his part and twist on hers landed them both on the floor, to the disapproval of the matron at whose feet they had landed. That made her giggle even more, but Yves, having picked her up, turned and bowed to the dowager whom Caroline belatedly recognised as a friend of her grandmother's.

"I wish to apologise, madam, for my invasion of your country."

He must have charm for others as well as herself, for the frost on Mrs Carrington's face melted as quickly as if he had held a candle to it.

When at last they emerged into the dark night, clad in galoshes and mackintoshes, the snow was driving fast against them. Perhaps she ought to get herself some puttees, which Felicia said she wore most of the time at the Front.

"No escape from General Winter," Caroline sighed as Yves battled to put up his umbrella.

The Leas, so high and pleasant a spot in summer, had presented a different face in this terrible autumn and winter. Snow and frost had come early, and before that gales lashed the seas at the bottom of the cliffs, and the winds drove over the open grassland of the Leas.

"But I eat my words, Caroline." His voice was almost lost in the wind although he must have been shouting, and he took her arm to support her as a sudden gust of wind sent her staggering back and a blinding flurry of snow in her face.

"Good." She missed her footing as they struggled forward, and she felt her arm dragging his down. "And we agree a little pleasure does no harm."

She thought for one moment he was shouting back 'With you in my arms—' but he couldn't have been, he must have been repeating, "No harm."

"So the Rectory will see you at Christmas? I will not remind you and Olivier too much of work?"

He kissed her hand as he left her at the door of her lodgings. "No, Caroline, you will not do that."

"That's splendid, Mrs Dibble. What good news." Mrs Lilley was delighted to hear about Joe.

What with a Christmas tree or two, and Miss Caroline coming home, and Miss Phoebe and Master George decorating the house, it would be just like old times. Miss Phoebe had been hard at work making paper decorations, as she used to years ago, and Master George had scoured the woods for cones and pinched only a little bit of greenery from Ashdown Forest. They didn't officially have the right to cut it, it being some way away from the gates. Margaret had knitted a nice cardigan for Joe, and one for Fred, though goodness knows whether he would ever get his. The pudding mixture hadn't tasted too bad, and Mrs Lettice had saved her some nice ham and a few extra currants, and what with Percy's efforts in the garden over vegetables they wouldn't starve. Wally Bertram had set aside two geese for her: one for the family and one for the servants' hall.

"There is just one problem," Mrs Lilley continued.

"Yes, madam." Any problems could be solved today. Margaret was overflowing with pleasure at the thought of it all.

"Do you think you could possibly manage seven more for luncheon?"

Margaret couldn't believe her own ears. Before the war, madam would hardly have needed to ask. Now the destination of every currant had to be considered, and here was madam wanting to almost double the numbers just like that.

"Sir John and Lady Hunney, and three guests of theirs are coming. I understand Caroline knows at least one of them, and

Mr Robert is coming, and Miss Burrows is staying after all, I'm afraid."

"What about Miss Eleanor, ma'am? Mrs Eleanor, I should say." Margaret tried to pull herself together. Mrs Lilley looked so apologetic, she would have to do her best.

"Dr Cuss has leave, so they are spending it alone."

And a good job too, in Margaret's view, since Lady Hunney still wouldn't speak to poor Dr Cuss, for having had the impudence to marry her daughter. She battled with her conscience. There was a war on and she should be generous. She also reminded herself that she had a family too and they deserved Christmas, yet she'd never forgive herself if she let herself down by serving an inadequate meal in the Rectory. After all, you could do a lot with a tough chicken, and plenty of folks didn't even have that.

She took a deep breath and spoke. "It just so happens, ma'am, when I went to collect the butcher's last, he told me he'd managed to put two geese aside for me—"

It was worth the sacrifice to see the relief on Mrs Lilley's face. Then she looked horrified as she interrupted: "But what will you eat, Mrs Dibble?"

"Besides the one for me, that is," Margaret lied.

"Sometimes I think the Rectory is becoming a war front all on its own," Laurence said ruefully. "I'm glad you're back, my love; at least I recognise your face and can understand what you say. Unlike our Miss Burrows and – I gather from Sir John – one of his Belgian guests."

Caroline grinned. "It'll be good for your French," she informed him cheerfully. "You'll enjoy it. Look how big a cast you'll have for the Family Coach." This game was the traditional way of passing Christmas afternoon.

"Ah yes." Her father made a face. "I'm afraid that our Lord must have had too much on His plate this year for He has not yet provided me with an inspiration for its theme."

151

"You'll have to hurry up. It's less than twenty-four hours away now." Caroline was alarmed, for usually her father had this planned weeks in advance.

"The midnight service is somewhat more important."

"You can't compare them, Father. You know that perfectly well."

He smiled. "Perhaps. And as half of the western front and a large part of the home front will apparently be breathlessly awaiting my every word tomorrow afternoon, I had better start thinking in earnest."

"You could always repeat last year's."

He looked indignant. "I could not, and you know it, Caroline. That means surrender. I did find my narrator's costume this afternoon buried deep by mistake in your mother's glory-hole, so perhaps an idea will follow in its wake. Incidentally, I wonder if you would keep close to your grandmother at the service this evening?"

"Why?" Caroline asked guardedly.

"I'm afraid the peace that we all assumed now existed between her and Lady Hunney may be about to break down, if it has not already done so. You know how much store Lady Hunney sets on the carol concert, almost as much as the flower festival. I am quite sure it was by pure coincidence, but your grandmother's maid, Miss Lewis, held a sing-song in the village hall on the same night, and the concert at the hospital was very poorly attended."

Caroline sympathised with Lady Hunney. She had always enjoyed the concert, which, if the weather were clement enough, ritually ended in a procession from Ashden Manor round the village and back through St Nicholas carrying candles. Because of the lighting order, the procession could no longer take place, but the concert could. It was an old tradition that Grandmother – and she was quite sure she must have had a hand in it – had no right to disrupt.

"So Tweedledum and Tweedledee are spoiling for a fight

152

again. Don't worry, I'll keep an eye on her," Caroline said confidently, and, as she left the room, failed to see her father suddenly spark with the beginnings of an idea.

It was wonderful to be home. Everyone was so delighted to see her – especially Mrs Dibble. Caroline had gone to the kitchen first of all, to rid herself of the precious burden she had been carrying. No need to fear its going off in this arctic weather. She had hurried in, swinging her trophy by the handles of its covering bag.

"Look what I've got for you," she crowed. "A goose!" She had queued up for an hour to obtain one.

"Oh, Miss Caroline." The way Mrs Dibble looked, her eyes were devouring that goose then and there.

"It seemed only fair," Caroline had explained, "since I'm responsible for two extra people."

"Three," Mrs Dibble corrected her absent-mindedly. "Sir John has three guests." Her eyes were still glued to the goose.

"What's another guest or two at Christmas?" Caroline waved an airy hand and departed, anxious to see her parents.

"Nothing now," Margaret said to herself thankfully as the door closed.

Caroline opened her eyes, realised it was already light, wriggled her toes luxuriously, and looked to see if there was an orange at the end of the bed. Santa Claus had always left this magnificent offering in her childhood. She had never been sure what relationship Santa Claus had to God, and Father could never explain to her satisfaction, so she just accepted Him and His gifts as one of those mysteries of life. This year there was only the still-painful memory of Reggie climbing in her window to greet her on Christmas morning two years ago. No orange, and now no Reggie.

"*Boo!*"

Caroline shrieked, as a head shot up at the end of the bed. Felicia's head. Her sister laughed. "That surprised you, didn't it?" She emerged from her hiding place, as Caroline leapt out of bed to embrace her.

"You might have worn a Christmas stocking on your head with an orange tucked in it," she laughed.

"Stockings are too precious to wear on my legs, let alone on my head."

"What are you doing here? You told us you couldn't get away for Christmas."

"I thought I couldn't. Then Luke arrived and told me he had to be in Ashden for some reason at Christmas, and I was coming too."

"He's not supposed to be at Ypres *or* here, he's supposed to be at GHQ Montreuil," his junior assistant said indignantly.

"You know Luke. He explained to me St Luke was the apostle who told the best Christmas story, and so that gave his namesake the right to arrange other people's Christmases for them. He had it all fixed up with Tilly before I could get a word in—"

"She's here too?" Caroline asked joyfully.

"No. We decided one of us must remain – no Christmas truces now – in case there's an attack on the Salient."

"But surely there won't be an offensive till spring?"

"There doesn't have to be an offensive for us to be busy. If you read in the newspapers that the fighting moved to the Somme, that doesn't mean it stops on the other fronts. There are always skirmishes, always shells, and always attempts at breakthrough. Oh, what am I talking of war for, when it's Christmas and I'm in the Rectory? And before you ask, don't worry about Tilly. Simon's gone out there. She asked him to do so when he still didn't know Penelope's fate, and now she's safe, he refuses to let her back out."

"Simon? But he's in the foreign office, not in uniform."

"He'll think of some reason to get to the Front. He's as determined as Luke. Tilly decided I needed a rest, though I'm strong enough."

Caroline looked at her sister. Her mental stamina was greater than her physical, and her face now looked drained of any colour at all, save a sallow yellowing by the weather. Oddly enough, the lines on the once flawless complexion were increasing her beauty rather than diminishing it, giving it a depth it had not had before.

"And where's Luke? Disguising himself as your Christmas stocking?"

"Caroline! I'm shocked." Felicia laughed. "We only got here an hour ago. He's tucked up in the pink bedroom, small but cheerful."

"Luke is?"

Felicia threw a pillow at her. "The bedroom, idiot."

Caroline longed to ask: what about Daniel, but she would not spoil this unexpected moment of pure happiness. "It seems to me," she laughed, "what with Luke, Sir John, Yves and Monsieur Fabre coming, I might as well have stayed at Folkestone."

"Oh no." Felicia flung her arms round her and kissed her. "This is home. We're back in the Rectory, together."

There used to be twelve places set for Christmas luncheon; sometimes thirteen with Aunt Tilly; now there were sixteen, and some of them were for new faces. Thank goodness Isabel had persuaded Robert to stay here for Christmas Day, although they were leaving for East Grinstead tomorrow morning. At last Caroline would have a chance to talk to the famous Miss Burrows. She had seen what Mother had meant by George's finding her fascinating; he had been sitting next to her at breakfast, torn between talking to Robert and ogling Kate. Her large beaming face was quite unlike that of a Sussex woman, and she looked as if she was well accustomed to working outside with her hands. Mother had told her, however, that Kate had an excellent brain and was far more organised than she was herself. In short, Caroline gathered, Kate was a success even if her bluntness and clumsiness made daily life in the Rectory somewhat hair-raising.

The mystery of the third guest had been solved after morning service. 'The Three Musketeers' George named them promptly, as Yves, a considerably tidier Olivier Fabre than Caroline was accustomed to, and Henri Willaerts appeared with Sir John and Lady Hunney. Henri and Luke? Wasn't that a little odd? However, she forgot this as, glowing with pleasure, and feeling that she had, as her father had predicted, bumped into God once more, she began to relax. Perhaps she had subconsciously feared that Yves would feel out of place here, as he had at the tennis match in the summer. Far from it, he was animatedly talking to Father on the way back to the Rectory and he seemed to have little difficulty with the Church of England service. Perhaps he was getting used to Communion being in English, not Latin. She herself hadn't found the midnight service, which he did not attend, as moving as she usually did. The 'eye' she had been told to keep on Grandmother should have been a ball and chain. Grandmother had not entered the former Norville pew, where she usually sat with Peck and Miss Lewis guarding her like Gog and Magog. Instead she had marched up the aisle to sit at the very front. It seemed innocent enough, but it did mean she would be taking Communion before Lady Hunney.

Yves was surprised and a little embarrassed that among the presents heaped – even in wartime – under the Christmas tree were several tiny parcels for him, Olivier and (hastily wrapped up at the last moment) Henri. For the latter two she had bought English pipes; for Yves, after a little thought, a nicely bound copy of the *Rubáiyát of Omar Khayyám*.

"In Belgium, Christmas morning is only for the children," he told her, crestfallen. "The adults exchange presents on the evening before. Forgive me."

"I prefer our tradition," she said quickly. "I like having everything together."

"Then I see why you chose this poem for me."

"You know it then?"

156

"Yes, but not in English. It is more beautiful, I think, in your language." He looked through it, and read to himself more than her: " 'Ah, Love! Could you and I with Him conspire/To grasp this Sorry Scheme of Things entire/Would not we . . . /Remould it nearer to the Heart's Desire.' "

She wondered what thoughts were running through his mind, but then he briskly changed the subject. "Now, tell me if you please, about this Rectory here. How does it come to be so oddly shaped?"

"You like it?" Caroline was highly pleased.

"Yes, it is a warm house."

"Even with the coal shortage?" she said lightly, deliberately misunderstanding. She decided she would take him on a quick tour of the house before luncheon, so that she could explain how mediaeval, Tudor, Stuart and Victorian owners had all had a hand in the shaping of the Rectory. "The twentieth century has added nothing," she concluded when her tour was complete.

"Every owner adds something, even if it cannot be seen. At my home—" Yves broke off, and reverted to talking about the priest-hole which she had just shown him.

This time she would not let him. "Would you tell me about your home?" she prompted.

"It was somewhat like this; ugly but warm."

She was about to retort that the Rectory was not ugly, when she realised he meant it as a compliment. He said 'was' though, not 'is', and she tried to decide whether this was significant.

"This is the kind of house," he continued, "that says come in and not go away. My home was like this, only rather more Gothic. We too have our tower and gables." So the home did still exist, and there had been no significance in his use of the past tense. Why on earth was it so important anyway? she asked herself impatiently.

At luncheon he sat next to Monsieur Fabre whose conversation was non-existent, partly because of language and partly, she suspected, because he was under strict instructions not to utter profanities. He gave the occasional grunt and that was all. Henri, as usual, made up for him, and seemed bent on charming Grandmother, to Caroline's amusement. Her attention was diverted as the grand procession arrived at the dining-room door.

"The goose!" she cried out. Not *the* goose; to everyone's surprise not only was Agnes bearing a second goose, but behind her Myrtle had another. And, yes, Percy with *another*. How many geese were there? Even her mother looked startled. Perhaps her father had performed some miracle, multiplying geese as Jesus had the loaves and fishes. Then she forgot to wonder about it anymore, as her father said grace, and the meal began.

Conversation was flowing well, with the help of several bottles of wine provided by Sir John, until in one of those odd silences that fall on the best of convivial tables, George's voice suddenly rang out clearly: "That's jolly dangerous, isn't it, Robert?"

"What is?" asked Isabel sharply.

Oblivious of the fact that Robert was desperately trying to shut him up, George replied: "Balloons. Robert says he's going into balloons."

"I was going to tell you, Isabel—" Robert began awkwardly.

"Bal*loons*. What on earth do you mean?" Isabel was staring at him, open-mouthed.

Caroline inwardly groaned. Trouble was on its way. Why at Christmas, and *why* just before when the pudding arrived? she lamented.

There was no stopping it, however, and everyone was listening now. "As I still can't land a kite, I don't want to be an observer or sit behind a desk, I've volunteered for balloons," Robert said defiantly.

"But I don't understand. What balloons? Like the ones George told us he saw flying at Lydd?"

"Yes, but these," Robert swallowed, "are in France."

"They are merely used for observation. There is little danger." Yves intervened to Caroline's deep gratitude.

"Yes there is. The Hun uses them as target practice," George shouted indignantly.

"George!" Laurence yelled in his most formidable voice.

George went scarlet. "Sorry, Isabel. I didn't mean that. It's jolly brave work and not dangerous really."

Isabel was white faced. "Balloons," she cried. "You're going to fly *balloons*." She burst into tears and before her mother, who was nearest, could stop her, she rose from the table and fled from the room.

"She's worried for your safety," Elizabeth said defensively, as Robert rose to his feet less than enthusiastically to follow her. Caroline was not sure she agreed with her mother, but knew she had to reach Isabel before Robert did, or the hopes for a happy Christmas were over.

"I'll go, Robert." She forestalled him at the door, and telling Phoebe to ask Mrs Dibble to hold the pudding procession back for five minutes, she dashed upstairs after her sister.

Robert, having made no attempt to dissuade her, was obviously relieved. "I should have told her earlier. I was putting it off," she heard him say, and Yves' reply: "I think it's most courageous of you, Lieutenant Swinford-Browne."

Torn between anger and concern, Caroline found Isabel lying sprawled across her bed, shoulders heaving piteously. She tried to make her voice steady and reassuring, a hard task with Isabel in a mood. "Everything's dangerous in this war, Isabel." She sat on the bed at her sister's side. "Don't make it worse for Robert than it is already."

Isabel promptly sat up, glaring furiously at her. "I know it must be dangerous. It was such a shock. I thought he wanted to be a fighter pilot like Albert Ball, not play with balloons like a little boy."

The truth was out, and Caroline could have wrung her sister's neck. To have Christmas ruined for the sake of Isabel's pride was too bad! She had thought her so much improved since she took on this cinema job, but here was the same old leopard with the same old spots.

"Can't you think of anyone but yourself just for once, Isabel? What do you think Robert feels like, having failed to become a pilot as he wanted, when George will in all likelihood shortly be flying off to France? Robert's a very brave man, firstly to enlist in the Army as a private when the William Pear was so dead against it, then to endure all the mocking he had there, then to transfer to the RFC where the life expectancy – I'm sorry to say this, Isabel, but it's time you faced up to war like everyone else – is counted in weeks, not months. Now he's volunteered for one of the most dangerous jobs there is."

Isabel's tears stopped abruptly. She began weakly, "You don't understand, Caroline."

"I do understand. And I had thought I understood you well enough. We were so pleased when you started at the cinema, doing something for the war at last. You've been so much more lively and interesting than you were. Now I see you only took the job so that you could stay here and have your decisions made for you by Mother, while Robert is away."

"You're wrong, you are, you *are*," Isabel yelled.

"I'm right, and you know it."

"I might have begun at the cinema for that reason," Isabel conceded, quietening down, "but now I enjoy it. I do. I love choosing films. *Captain Scott*, and the film of *The King at the Front*. It's important, and it's what I want to do, it really is. But Robert never succeeds at anything." She burst into tears, not of anger this time, but real.

Caroline sat with her quietly and let her cry for a few minutes, then asked: "Do you love him at all, Isabel?"

Her sister hesitated. "I think so," she snuffled.

"Then why don't you wipe your face, and come back to the table, and make him believe you do?"

"I can't bear it. Father will never forgive me."

"Father will, and anyway, Robert is more important."

"Lady Hunney—" Isabel began.

"Least of all does it matter what our Maud thinks."

Isabel giggled, sat up, wiped her eyes, and blew her nose. "All right, but you must come with me." A pause. "Caroline, I'm not really as nasty as you said, am I?"

"No." Caroline sighed. That was the problem.

Margaret's moment had almost come. To him that hath, shall be given. Through her own efforts she'd managed to wangle two geese for the Rectory; she had followed her conscience and let Mrs Lilley have them both. Then Miss Caroline bought another one, so the Lord had clearly intended the Dibbles should have their goose. Then just before luncheon the Hunneys' kitchen had sent down two more, already cooked, at Sir John's request. They were rolling in geese; if these were the Middle Ages when folks greased themselves up and sewed themselves into their clothes for the winter, there'd be enough fat to keep a nice cosy blanket round her and Percy.

Now it was time for the pudding and then her own goose would be done. Lucky they still had the old range as well as the gas oven. Some families sang a carol when the goose or turkey came in, like the Boar's Head Carol, but in the Rectory the pudding always called for a song too. Afterwards she could relax, and they would have their own Christmas, even though Peck and Miss Lewis would be with them. Anyway, they were almost the family now, even old Peeper.

Mrs Lilley had come out to the kitchen while Percy was flaming the pudding (the real pudding). Christmas was an exception to Margaret's rules about drink since Miss Caroline had always said that pouring over brandy and setting it alight had religious significance. Nevertheless she liked Mrs Lilley to be at hand, just in case the Lord frowned at seeing Margaret Dibble alone with a bottle, thinking she had forgotten her solemn promise to abstain from alcohol (apart from emergencies like that terrible film).

She emerged bearing the pudding engulfed in blue flames,

and Mrs Lilley bore the next so-called pudding. She could see Miss Caroline and Mrs Isabel were back inside the dining-room, and wondered what that trouble Miss Phoebe mentioned had been. Then she forgot about it in the anxiety of whether the flame would go out before she reached the darkened room. Miss Caroline dashed out to join in the procession and sing in a deeply pontifical voice:

> "Plum pudding as I understand
> Is the finest dish in all the land
> Mrs Dibble is our cook
> Praise the Lord and His Good Book."

Then her voice was drowned by Master George yelling out: "Here it comes!"

The pudding was still flaming blue as she entered, and as Miss Caroline sat down, Margaret saw Mrs Isabel plant a kiss on her husband's cheek.

"Darling, I'm sorry," she said loudly. "You're so brave. I was just upset because you're going to do something so dangerous."

Margaret thought what a sweet lady Mrs Isabel was turning into after all.

Caroline saw from the satisfied look on Father's face when he entered the drawing-room in his narrator's costume complete with jester's hat and bells that inspiration had at last come to him. It was just as well, for he had a large audience, including Grandmother who was clearly determined to stay close to Lady Hunney's side, no matter how tired she was.

"My lords, ladies and gentlemen," Father began, having swept his usual deep bow to the company. "I announce the Family Coach. This year the coach is involved in a most serious investigation, and I must ask you all to do your utmost to take part in it. A fiercesome creature known as the Snark is our quarry, and it is feared that the Snark we seek is a Boojum,

162

leading to the most dire consequences for the finder, who may softly and suddenly vanish away. Nevertheless, it is our mission to find the Snark, with the help, naturally, of the Family Coach."

Oh, clever Father, Caroline thought admiringly, remembering her reference to Lewis Carroll's Tweedledum and Tweedledee yesterday, and wondering if her comment had played any part in Father's choice of his 'Hunting of the Snark'.

"For the purposes of the Hunt, it is not necessary to be acquainted with the story, however, merely to understand one's own part," Father explained

"I'm playing the Wheels," shouted George.

"I'm the little dog," cried Phoebe.

"There isn't a little dog in *The Snark*," Caroline pointed out.

"There is now," Phoebe said. "There's always a little dog in the coach isn't there, Father?"

"That is true, Phoebe. Once you all have your role," he added for the benefit of the newcomers, "you stand up and twirl round whenever you hear your name called; if you forget, you fall out of the game. If the words "Family Coach" are mentioned, you all stand up and twirl round." He demonstrated a fine twirl. "Mother and Henri, you are excused. You can remained seated and wave your arms."

Lady Hunney looked smug that she was not deemed incapacitated, to Caroline's amusement. Before Grandmother came to live here, she had never taken part in the game; now she appeared only too eager to do so.

"This year," Laurence continued, "the coach will be carrying the bellman, the boots, a maker of bonnets and hoods, a barrister, a broker, a billiard maker, a beaver, a baker, a butcher, a banker—"

"But no Snark," Elizabeth finished for him.

"A large coach," observed Henri.

"This one carried people on top," Caroline explained.

"I will be the bellman," said Yves, "and look after the beaver, since Monsieur Fabre does not understand English well."

So Yves knew the poem of the Snark too. What an interesting man he was, Caroline thought. And kind too, for Monsieur Fabre was looking mystified at first, but as Father's story unfolded he began to leap up and twist round when prodded by Yves.

If only Father could write his sermons as quickly as he had this story of the Christmas Snark! Caroline had worried that those who did not know the poem would be utterly baffled but Father was managing to dovetail the Snark and the story of the Family Coach splendidly, and bellman, billiard-maker, butchers and bakers – not to mention the wheels, the doors, the hamper, the cushions, the coachman, the horses – all duly leapt up or waved their arms or failed to do so in the requisite time on cue. With so many people playing, the game took much longer than usual, and Caroline was exhausted both with laughing and with the constant jumping around by the time Father concluded:

"And so the wheels," (*George leapt up*) "of the Family Coach" (*cue for everyone to leap up*) "came to a halt on the ground where the Baker" (*Grandmother waved*) "had met with the Snark. Alas, the Baker" (*Grandmother waved again*) "had 'softly and suddenly vanished away, for the Snark was a Boojum, you see'."

"I," declared Grandmother, "have no intention of vanishing." She looked round grimly, and Caroline realised the impossible was happening – Grandmother was making a joke. She quickly burst into a peal of laughter, and a little belatedly was joined by the rest of the gathering, even Lady Hunney. Grandmother looked pleased.

Father slipped into his usual brief prayer. "Oh Lord, as we rattle forward into this new year, may the Snarks, Jub-Jubs and Boojums of war all vanish away with Thy help, so that our quest be at an end and the baker, the bellman, the butcher and their comrades may return in peace to their loved ones. Amen."

There was a surprise addition to the programme, during what was usually a valiant attempt at a quiet period before the evening game of hide-and-seek began. Yves announced that Monsieur

Fabre would like to thank them all for their hospitality with a marionette show. There was polite, if not rapturous, applause. Phoebe and George were, Caroline could see, looking down mental noses at such childish entertainment, though Sir John, surprisingly, looked very interested. The marionettes' home was in a battered suitcase, but obviously he had brought no portable theatre with him. A substitute was quickly rigged up under Mother's organisation from masking sheets and Grandmother Overton's old table as a stage, and Olivier Fabre began his show.

With memories of Punch and Judy, Caroline wondered which language he would perform in, then inwardly laughed at her own stupidity as he began. It was in a universal language, that of artistry, and that was all the story of Harlequin and Columbine needed.

Quaintly carved and painted puppets played and danced to music played on a small wind-up gramophone. There were only three records with it and Yves had been deputed to play which was most suitable: *Swan Lake*, for Harlequin and Columbine. '*Au près de ma blonde*' for Clown, and 'The Ride of the Valkyries' for Policeman. She wished she could see the hands of the puppeteer, for they must be moving with a grace hard to imagine in someone who looked so down to earth and unimaginative as Olivier. Columbine and Harlequin, with double-jointed legs and arms, slowly danced out their love story. Caroline was entranced. Who needed words as those lovers embraced and parted? Who needed words as Harlequin sobbed his lonely heart out, on his knees, hands shielding his bowed head? Who needed words for the immortal chase of Clown, with his stolen sausages in hand?

The applause at the end was ten times as loud as that at the beginning, and she was amused to see Phoebe and George were leading it.

Full of good goose and pudding, Margaret sat down next to Joe to relax with a cup of tea while Muriel and Lizzie did the washing up. She could hardly believe this strapping son in uniform at her side was real; it had been only six months since she saw him but it seemed much, much longer. Later on they'd all have a sing-song, with Miss Lewis at the piano. The babies would enjoy it too, even little Frank. In the meantime she was going to talk to Joe, but she was forestalled by his following her into the kitchen on the pretext of helping her take back dirty teacups, there being no Agnes or Myrtle today. They'd both gone home at twelve o'clock.

"I saw Fred, Ma."

"You what?" Margaret went quite pale; she had been trying hard not to think of Fred too much even when they toasted absent friends. She didn't want to start crying on Christmas Day.

"I went to see him. "They're in the lines at Booty Wall and Cor."

"How—" Margaret found herself choking "—is he?" She'd never heard of those places, but it didn't matter. Perhaps Joe had got it wrong.

"He's fine, Ma."

"In the trenches?" She'd have to keep on at him. Joe was a dear, but he didn't see much further than the end of his nose sometimes. Like his father.

"No. In the cookhouse when I saw him. Peeling potatoes, he's good at that. He's always there, he says."

Margaret could hardly believe her ears. She ran back to the servants' hall yelling with joy. "Percy, do you hear that? Our Fred's peeling *potatoes*." Tears streamed down her face. "Thank you, God, thank you. No one gets killed peeling potatoes, do they? To potatoes!" She seized the nearest glass, not caring what was in it.

"Let's have a toast." Percy was as relieved as she was. "To spuds!"

"Here's to potatoes," Peck bawled, in a voice that would have won him instant dismissal from her ladyship. He raised his teacup on high.

"And bully beef," Joe added, in an effort to outdo the sensation he'd unwittingly caused.

"Peeling bully beef?" Margaret Dibble screamed with laughter. "Do you hear that, everyone? Our Fred's peeling blooming bully beef!"

They didn't hear. They were still bawling out the toast to spuds. It was Christmas, after all.

"We shall seek it with thimbles," announced Father. "The Snark shall not escape." He gravely handed a thimble to Caroline. "We shall pursue it with forks and hope." A kitchen fork was duly given to Phoebe. "We shall threaten its life with a railway share." An important-looking piece of parchment was entrusted to Felicia. "We shall charm it with smiles and soap." He placed a bar of soap in George's outstretched hand.

They had already drawn lots to play the Snark, and it was Kate who drew the short pipe-cleaner, to her great amusement. She had promptly disappeared, and her heavy footsteps could be heard thundering up the main staircase. Caroline caught her mother's eye and read her thoughts exactly: there would be no difficulty in finding this Snark.

They were wrong, for it took quite a lot of time. Some people, Caroline suspected, were more interested in pursuing their private conversations than in hunting for the Snark. Well, they shouldn't be; it was Christmas. She had bumped into Isabel who was with Robert, and showing no signs of wanting to leave the morning-room in pursuit of any Snarks. In her own bedroom she found Felicia talking by the window with Luke, and felt fiercely protective of the emotions of absent Daniel. She had never seen Felicia so relaxed and forthcoming as she was with Luke, responding to his easy banter as if he was one of the family. Which, of course, he was determined to be.

It was eerie with the house in darkness. There were only the oil lamps turned down low on the ground floor, and one or two very dim torches for them to move round the house. Caroline began to wish she had someone with her to hunt with, since Kate had obviously done a good job in vanishing. The next person she came across was Phoebe.

"Have you seen George?" she asked crossly. "He was with me and he had the torch. Then he just disappeared."

"No," Caroline said, pleased. "You'd better come round with me."

Phoebe decided differently. "No. I'll go and find that nice marionette man."

Monsieur Fabre had remained behind with Henri and the older generation in the drawing-room; much as she liked him, she wouldn't have thought he would appeal to Phoebe.

Caroline was irrationally disappointed to be left alone, especially since she had pressed the torch into Phoebe's hand. She managed to find her way up in the dark to the attic floor where the servants' rooms were out of bounds, but several unoccupied lumber rooms remained to be searched. She opened the door to one of them cautiously, and recognised Yves standing there, lit by the moonlight coming in through the dormer window. She wondered what he was doing here, then saw he was smoking. On seeing her, he promptly extinguished the cigarette in an old candle-holder which stood on the dormer windowsill.

"I am glad to see you, Caroline," he said. "I feared I should rot here forever."

"Like the Man in the Iron Mask?" She laughed, delighted to see him. "Why?"

"I am imprisoned by darkness, and there is no buxom Kate to console me."

It was on the tip of her tongue to say if he found buxom Kate attractive, he *could* rot there for ever, but instead she heard herself saying: "Isn't there a candle stub in that holder? If not, if you take my hand, I can lead you down the stairs. I think your buxom Kate must be outside. I've searched everywhere in the house."

"There is no candle."

He meekly offered her his hand. It was large, warm, and

oddly comforting in the dim light. As she carefully led him step by step down to the ground floor, she found it even more comforting in the dark. As his hands had been once before. Memories of the night of the bomb came rushing back, and she tried once again to concentrate on nothing but these hands in order to dispel the horror.

It took an effort of will for her to whisper in the darkness to break the spell. "She must be in one of the outhouses."

"Who?"

"The Snark of course. Your buxom Kate."

There was a silence. Then: "Shall we seek her? Do you still have your thimble?"

She fished in her pocket, drew it out, and stuck it on his little finger. "There," she said crossly. "That'll help you to find her."

She led him by the hand to a garden door through what was grandly known as the library and out into the darkness. There was still snow underfoot after the heavy falls of a few days ago, and a pile of coats and Wellington boots had been placed in the library for intrepid searchers.

"We'll try here." Caroline shivered and managed to push open the door to the old stables, although the moon had disappeared behind clouds. "It hasn't been used since Poppy died."

"I am sorry – I had not realised. Another sister?"

That restored Caroline's good humour. "No, our old horse. Since she died last year, we have shared one with the doctor. He has a motor car and we can borrow his old horse. He's even older than Poppy, which is why the Army didn't want him. Anyway, it's too cold here." She dragged him out again. "We might try the applety and mother's glory-hole."

The glory-hole was empty, but the applety was not. This was the grand name given to a wooden shed where all the apples from the orchard were stored on an upper floor, and as she opened the door and drew him in, the smell of James Grieve apples was the first thing to greet her. The second was the sound of breathing. There *was* someone here. Yves had left the door open and the pale light from outside revealed a figure. As he drew it to, and her eyes became accustomed to the lack of light, she saw it was two figures closely locked together. It was George embracing Kate. Not even the sudden shaft of dim light over her shoulder disturbed them, and Kate's disarranged clothing revealed this was no light embrace.

In shock, Caroline stepped back accidentally onto Yves' foot, then she tugged at him to pull him out of the applety, slamming the door behind them. She intended to run back to the house, but he would not let her. He opened the door of the glory-hole instead, drawing her inside. There was suddenly a glow of light there too.

"What is wrong, Caroline? Tell me."

"Nothing . . . You've had a torch all the time!" She could see it in his hand.

"Yes. Now tell me what is wrong." He turned the torch out. "It is easier to talk in the dark."

Was it? And why on earth was she crying? For George, her little brother, who was little no longer? Or for herself? She felt Yves' arm round her shoulder, and allowed him to push her gently in her mother's basket chair behind her. "I will stand over here, and you will forget my presence. Then you can talk. Like the confessional." In the dark he backed straight into The Heap, and his yelp of surprise made it easier to talk relatively normally.

"George and Miss Burrows, Kate, they were—"

"Making love. Yes. I saw them. Why does that upset you?" His voice was very gentle. "Because Miss Burrows is who she is and your brother who he is?"

"No." Caroline was horrified at that idea.

"Because he is your little brother and you don't want him to grow up?"

Less certain this time. "I don't know. It was horrible, *horrible*." She surprised herself by her own vehemence. Would she have felt that way if it had been Felicia and Luke?

"To you, perhaps, but for them it was not. Why do you mind so much, Caroline, *why*? Pretend your heart is the front line, and cut a trench along it. Look deep inside and tell me."

When she still could not speak, he tried to help again. "You are twenty-four and the sight of physical love cannot be new to you. Does it repel you?"

"No." She was sure about this too.

"Then it must have struck a chord of memory. Of Reggie, perhaps?"

"Oh!" She jumped, burying her face in her hands. Last year, on Christmas Eve, she had faced both betrayal and loss when she saw Isabel and Reggie together. She had thought the pain long since surmounted, but seeing another incongruous couple in George and Kate had brought it back. As she swayed with the shock, she was hardly aware that he had come to her until she felt his arms round her, and his chest and shoulders against her.

"Tell me, *cara mia*," he said quietly, one hand stroking her hair.

For a year she had tried not to think about it, in order to blot it from her mind, but now the whole wretched story tumbled out. Perhaps the dark did form a confessional, for when it was over she was still trembling, though aware of how ridiculous this must seem to him. She disengaged herself from his arms in embarrassment.

"I'm sorry," she said.

"For what?"

"For standing here, dressed in Father's old coat, a muffler and Wellington boots."

"No, that is not what you are sorry for. Tell me, *cara*."

"George and Kate. It seems so little," she blurted out.

"But it was not little, was it? It was big, because of Isabel and Reggie, but perhaps because you have discovered this, it is not now quite so big."

"It won't vanish though," she said forlornly.

171

"Nothing can make it do so but yourself. You still love your sister, don't you?"

"Yes."

"You understand what made Reggie do it?"

"Yes."

"Then there is only yourself left to understand, Caroline."

She felt his hands cup her face, then his lips gently first on one cheek then the other, then, even more gently, the fleeting touch of his lips on hers before he released her. She could hear him breathing, hear herself breathing, even hear the silence between them.

"Yves?"

"I am here."

"Would you kiss me again?"

This time his lips rested longer on hers and, as he drew her closer into his arms, harder, until the response they aroused turned the darkness into light. Almost as quickly, he released her again.

"And now, we must remember our quest. The thimble has found our Snark for us." He took it off his finger and pressed it into her hand.

She began to laugh shakily, adjusting easily to his change of mood. "Shall we 'softly and suddenly vanish away? For our Snark *was* a Boojum, you see'."

"Yes, let us leave our buxom Kate Snark to her baker, *cara*. If you will take my hand, I will lead you back through the night to the Rectory."

"You have a torch," she pointed out. "You cheated."

"And now I cheat again."

172

Ten

W here was it all going to end? It was all very well her cheering the village ladies on about the wonderful things you could cook out of today's meagre supplies, but somehow Margaret was failing to inspire herself. It was bitterly cold outside; even the heater in the entrance hall failed to distribute its usual warmth round the house, and the continuing coal shortage meant that fires had to be strictly rationed. If this wasn't a rectory, she'd send Percy down to the forest to sneak a bag or two of wood when no one was looking. As it was, they had cold bedrooms, and Jack Frost iced the windows up so thick you hardly needed the black-out curtains. Most of the family had taken to sleeping with their doors open so that what warmth there was penetrated, but up in the servants' quarters they couldn't – not because a little heat didn't find its way there, but because with old Peck the Peeper around the girls didn't feel safe. She and Percy were all right in their quarters, and if old Peck tried his peeping on her, she'd give him what for. At least in the kitchen she had the heat of the range to enjoy. It didn't seem fair on the family somehow, but Mrs Isabel and Miss Phoebe had taken to coming in by the tradesmen's entrance, not the front door, so they could have a warm-up first.

There was another warm spot too. Her achievement with her demonstrations was about to be crowned. Margaret hugged the glory to her. Last week her ladyship had told her that the Board of Agriculture under this new Lloyd George government was going to start training courses for women in economic cookery, because of the food shortage. They had written to Lady Buckford to see if she'd be interested in organising the training in Tunbridge Wells. At last someone up there in London was seeing sense, and saw that the Margaret Dibbles of this world could do their bit. Lady Buckford couldn't do the work herself, so Margaret would be the organiser and give the demonstrations. She was sure she could arrange to visit the Wells one day a week; she'd spoken to Agnes who would take over the Rectory cooking. All she awaited was the official approval of her name from the Board of Agriculture, and then she too would have her national war work. She was a little nervous of lecturing anywhere so grand as Tunbridge Wells, but she couldn't let this opportunity slip by.

It was only January; this winter, like the war, showed no sign of ending. And even when it did, that would only mean another grim time coming. Once spring had brought cheerful things like birds and flowers; now it brought another big attack somewhere or everywhere, and with it the chance that Fred might be taken off his potatoes and Joe off his digging and pioneering work, and both of them sent over the top.

At least Christmas had been a happy time, so that's what she'd think about. Miss Caroline had been full of beans at Christmas, and so had Miss Felicia. Miss Felicia was long since back in France, poor lass, and no doubt it was just as cold there. Margaret wondered what kind of hospital she was working in, and hoped they had plenty of coal to keep warm. That Captain Dequessy seemed very attached to her.

Miss Caroline seemed to have got over Mr Reggie's death too. On the day after Boxing Day she had brought that serious-looking captain into the kitchen, and he was carrying a plucked chicken – from the Dower House, he said. Then Miss Caroline had announced that if Mrs Dibble had no objection the captain was going to cook servants' dinner that day, and the family were going to have cold ham and potatoes. She'd do the potatoes herself.

Naturally, Margaret hadn't taken her seriously at first; but

174

after Miss Caroline had found a spare pinny and put it round the captain's neck, she hadn't been called upon to do anything apart from telling them where the ingredients were. Instead, she'd been ordered to sit down in her own kitchen and make a cup of tea. She'd watched with fascinated foreboding, as vegetables were peeled, and her large braising pan brought down from its hook. There was a spot of bother over something the captain demanded called 'teem', but Miss Caroline guessed what he meant and rushed out to scrape the hard-packed snow off the herb garden to see if she could find any thyme snuggling under it.

Judging by the preparations, Margaret was not impressed by Belgian food. "That's only chicken stew." Margaret didn't sound too scornful about it, because she was relieved that foreigners' recipes produced nothing better than good Sussex fare.

"Ah yes, but for waterzooi we now need a liaison of cream and eggs," the captain had said.

"Not in Sussex we don't."

Caroline laughed. "Just try it, Mrs Dibble. I'm sure you can spare one egg and I know there's cream left over. It can't have gone sour in this weather."

Margaret watched dubiously. She was still shocked at the sight of the captain wearing her pinny. He stirred the mixture into the stew while Miss Caroline burnt her fingers tearing the flesh off the baked chicken. It didn't do, she decided. It was the last time she'd permit any stranger to come walking in and take over her job, Christmas-time or not. When Percy came in, he was flabbergasted at seeing a gentleman stirring a pan on the range, and she had to nod to him that it was all right in case he thought she'd gone off her head. She probably had, but Miss Caroline was laughing just like she used to, and that was worth an upset or two.

"Where did you learn to cook, Monsieur Escoffier?" Miss Caroline asked the captain jokingly.

"My father was in the Belgian army, and he believed in

bringing his sons up to survive anywhere from the Arctic to the jungle. When we were children, he took us out to the forests of the Ardennes to camp. We cooked with an old Soyer portable stove, sometimes for a day, sometimes a week. We hated every moment."

"No wonder, if you had to cook this."

He had smiled at that. "We did not. But much as I disliked the means, I did learn something of the art of cookery."

Art? Margaret had never thought of her daily work like that, but she supposed it was in a way, and felt quite proud.

Miss Caroline and the captain didn't only cook this water-zooi dish; they insisted on serving it to her and Percy, Agnes, Myrtle, Miss Lewis and old Peck in the servants' hall. Even little Elizabeth Agnes was waited on.

Margaret hadn't been able to get used to that idea at all, and kept trying to get up from the table to help. Miss Caroline wouldn't let her, and Myrtle started giggling . . . She'd have to watch her, Margaret decided, in case she got above herself. It was kind of Miss Caroline to think of this treat, and she meant well. It didn't do, however. Margaret preferred the old ways. Miss Caroline seemed to understand her thoughts, though, for she said placatingly:

"It's only because of the war, Mrs Dibble. Everything has to change a little."

Maybe, but it could change back afterwards, and she wouldn't stand for being told how to cook by foreigners, thank you very much. All the same, this captain seemed a nice gentleman, and if he took Miss Caroline's mind off poor Mr Reggie, he could have Margaret's full approval. As had, she was forced to admit, this Waterzooi concoction. Though she still preferred Sussex chicken stew.

Now they were into January, and a bleak old month it was turning out to be. Miss Caroline had gone back to Folkestone, and yesterday Mr George had left home for the Central Flying School at Upavon in Wiltshire. She'd asked him why, if he had passed his flying test, he had to go to another school? He'd said something about having to get his RFC wings, and she'd pointed out he was no angel. She knew why he'd come here. You could always tell when there was a row in progress. The Rector went around with a wounded expression and whenever she took the dishes in to the dining-room there was a nasty silence.

This one seemed worse than usual, however, and she'd caught Agnes and Myrtle talking about it in the servants' hall, when she entered unexpectedly. She knew it by the way they broke off immediately.

"What was that you were saying, Mrs Thorn?" she had enquired politely, but in a tone that brooked no nonsense.

She could hardly accuse Agnes of gossiping, but that's what it sounded like to her. Agnes flushed in embarrassment, but Myrtle piped up. "Mrs Thorn just said Master George seemed sorry to be leaving, and that Mrs Lilley had told her Miss Burrows is going as well tomorrow."

"That's the first I heard of it." Margaret was outraged. She was overall housekeeper here, and it wasn't right for Agnes to know first.

"It is very sudden," Agnes said apologetically. "You were in the village, and Mrs Lilley couldn't find you. She only mentioned it to me because I was about to help Myrtle to change the sheets in Miss Burrows' room."

Margaret had been a little mollified, but it didn't explain the thunder in the Rectory air. When she had gone to see Mrs Lilley in the morning-room, as she did most days, the mistress had told her: "One less for dinner today and two from tomorrow, Mrs Dibble. Mr George has left, and Miss Burrows has suddenly been recalled home."

"Will she be returning, Mrs Lilley?"

"I don't believe so." Mrs Lilley had sighed heavily. "It's a good thing it's winter. I don't know how I'd manage otherwise without her. Miss Phoebe does a little, but her heart isn't in it, and that means her mind isn't either, half the time."

177

"How about Miss Ryde, madam?"

Mrs Lilley had brightened up. "That's a good idea. If I could—"

She broke off, but Margaret had guessed exactly what she was going to say: "If I could put up with her." That Miss Ryde was a tartar, good-hearted but strong-willed. No wonder Mr Philip was so anxious to get married. That had been a surprise too – Dr Parry announcing her engagement to Mr Philip. You could have knocked her over with her own feather duster when the Rector called the banns. They'd be getting married in three weeks' time, and there had already been a lot of conjecture about what Miss Ryde would do. Would Dr Parry move in to the schoolhouse or Mr Ryde move out to Dr Parry's cottage? Or would they all live together? She couldn't see Dr Parry being happy living in the same house as Miss Ryde. There had been much chat in the servants' hall over this, until Dr Parry herself provided the answer when she came to see Elizabeth Agnes yesterday; the little girl had been poorly with a nasty cough she couldn't shake off. Dr Parry would be moving into the school-house, and she would have her very own extension of Dr Marden's telephone line. Marvellous the things they could do nowadays. Miss Ryde had elected to go temporarily to Beth Parry's cottage in Dr Marden's grounds, until she could decide what she wanted to do.

"I'll have a word with her today." Mrs Lilley had shivered, looking at the bleak greyness outside. "There's a heavy ulster among the cast-offs in my glory-hole; I wonder if I dare wear that to see her? I can't remember who sent it in, but I'll just have to hope they don't spot me."

It had snowed heavily later that day, and snug in her kitchen, watching the snow driving against the window panes, Margaret was surprised when Lizzie thrust open the kitchen door, coming in like a snowman with flakes all over her coat, farm trousers and Wellingtons.

"What are you doing out in the dark?" her mother demanded

178

as Lizzie lay down her dimmed torch. "And where's the baby, if I might ask? Nothing wrong, is there?"

"No. I've left him with Mrs Lake. Don't want to bring him out in this weather."

"What are you here for then? Cup of tea and home comforts?"

"Something like that, Ma."

Margaret's antennae were twitching. "Out with it, girl."

Lizzie sat down, wet coat and all, and began to cry. "I've had a letter from Rudolf."

For a moment Margaret thought she meant Frank, who was out east somewhere now, and though he wrote regularly, sometimes weeks would go by with Lizzie hearing nothing at all, and then the letters would all arrive together. Then she realised Lizzie did mean Rudolf.

"What's he got to say for himself?" Margaret asked in trepidation. She had liked Rudolf, everyone had; he was a slow, gentle sort of fellow, or so she'd thought before he went home to fight for the Kaiser. It was no use Lizzie saying he'd have been interned if he stayed here; her mother just wasn't convinced he didn't want to go. There was no doubt Lizzie was going to be in a pickle if he ever came back. Somehow Margaret had got out of the way of thinking about Rudolf, what with Frank and the baby.

"He's been wounded. He's back in Germany until he gets well. The hospital train went through Switzerland and he managed to get this note sent. Oh, Ma," Lizzie wailed. "What am I going to do? He says he'll be back the day this war's over."

Once more Margaret agonised over this dilemma. Once she'd never had a good word to say for the man who seduced her Lizzie – for seduction it must have been despite all Lizzie and Percy maintained – but she had to admit Frank had stood by her. Sent her money regularly through his bank, not that it came to much. She didn't get an allowance because they weren't wed, and so she and Percy were forced to dig into their purses for little extras for Frank.

"Which one do you love, Lizzie?"

"Both of them." Lizzie howled again.

"When there's nothing you can do, do nothing, that's my advice," her mother informed her briskly, unable to speak the words of comfort that her heart was forming. "It's no use asking the Lord what to do—you got yourself into this mess . . . though He might lend a hand," she added consolingly, "since there's baby Frank to consider."

This didn't seem to cheer Lizzie up at all, but suddenly Margaret's heart found its way to her tongue. "Look, Lizzie, girl," she sat down and planted her hands on the table, "there *is* no answer to this. We don't know when this war's going to be over, but it ain't going to be yet. So concentrate on getting through the little worries of the day ahead of you and sooner or later the answer to the big problem will come strolling along."

What was in Margaret's mind, though she didn't hardly dare admit it even to herself, was that with the number of soldiers being killed everywhere now, it was highly likely that either Frank or Rudolf wouldn't be coming back at all. Or perhaps neither of them would. She sent up a brief prayer to please turn a blind ear to what she'd just thought; she'd read in a magazine somewhere that out in foreign parts pagan witchdoctors killed people just by wishing them dead; or was it the victim had to believe they were dying? Whichever it was, she'd better not take any chances, and her knees had best stay down another few minutes tonight.

To take Lizzie's mind off her own troubles, she told her about Miss Burrows leaving so suddenly; Lizzie had got on well with Kate. "It's been a day of it," Margaret said, "what with Master George having gone too."

Lizzie perked up and to her mother's astonishment sniggered.

"What are you laughing at all of a sudden?"

"That's why, ain't it? I bet there's been an almighty row here, hasn't there?"

"Yes."

"I reckon the Rector found them at it."

"At what and who's them, may I ask?" Margaret was affronted. The younger generation were a great deal too forward.

"That Miss Burrows and Master George. Maybe he's put her up the spout."

Margaret gazed puzzled at the old brown teapot before her, until she realised what Lizzie was talking about, and it wasn't teapots. "Lizzie Dibble, that's disgusting. I brought you up to be a lady, and you come out with dirty talk like that."

"Sorry, Ma. It's the farm." Lizzie was giggling outright now. "And anyway, the talk isn't what's important, it's whether they did it, and I reckon they did."

"Master George is a—" She was going to say a young gentleman, but Lizzie interrupted.

"A young *man*, Ma, and she's a young woman with a gleam in her eye and an itch—"

"Lizzie Dibble, that's quite enough!" Her turn to interrupt. Margaret, red cheeked, took a sip of tea, while she pondered whether there was anything in what Lizzie had said. Master George was still a schoolboy – no, he wasn't that any longer; but all the same he was brought up a Christian gentleman and this was a rectory. If Lizzie was right – and she wasn't convinced, mind – it must have been that Miss Burrows who started it. She was just the type. Earthy. Good-natured enough, but . . . Oh, yes, it was her started it.

"She can't be expecting," Margaret maintained stoutly. "The Rector wouldn't turn her out if so, and nor would Mrs Lilley."

"Plenty would."

"But not Ashden Rectory."

Before Miss Burrows left the next day, she popped her head in the kitchen to say goodbye and it was all Margaret could do not to take a covert look at her stomach. Not that she'd be showing yet, she reasoned. She'd lain awake all night, worrying if Miss Kate were expecting and hadn't dare tell the Rector.

"Bye." Miss Kate looked just as cheerful as she always did.

Margaret couldn't stop herself: "Where will you be going, miss?"

"Back home to help dad, and then I'll enlist."

"Enlist?" That was for men, not girls. Maybe she didn't hear right. Miss Burrows had a funny way of talking owing to her coming from Yorkshire.

"I'm in the National Land Service Corps at present," Miss Burrows continued, "but there are rumours we're all going to be co-opted into a new Women's Army to work on the land."

"You're all right, then." Margaret was relieved for the Rector's sake. She couldn't be in the family way if she was enlisting. All the same, she felt aggrieved that she'd lain awake worrying over nothing at all. It had been nothing to do with Mr George. As if he would . . .

Strictly speaking, Elizabeth Agnes was not supposed to be in the main part of the house at this time of day, but she was developing a strong liking for Margaret's honey biscuits, and having realised she was their sole source, the toddler appeared all too frequently in the kitchen. What a pity Fred wasn't here, he could look after her. The thought of Fred made sudden tears come to her eyes and Margaret had to blow her nose firmly.

"By the way, Agnes, Miss Burrows is going back home to Yorkshire. Lizzie thought Master George and she had been doing things they shouldn't, and in case you were thinking the same, I can tell you you're wrong. She's going to sign on for some new government farming army."

Agnes hesitated. "I'm sure you're right, Mrs Dibble."

Mrs Dibble glowed in triumph at this minor victory over the young who always thought the worst.

Myrtle, who had been peeling parsnips in the scullery, had brought the products of her toil through the door and must have overheard. Tact was never her strong point. "No, Mrs

Dibble, I know they have. Master George's bed weren't slept in quite a few nights."

Elizabeth Lilley finished her weekly letter to Caroline almost with reluctance. Writing to her daughter made her seem much nearer, and there were things she could tell Caroline that she couldn't write about to Felicia. Her mother suspected that she was a great deal nearer the front line than she revealed to them. Surrounded by war, broken bodies and shattered lives as Felicia was, Elizabeth could write to her only of the everyday happenings of the Rectory, and of the latest news, good or bad, from Ashden, for all these things would speak to her of home. What she could not write about just in order to relieve her own feelings was the Affair Burrows. To Caroline, however, she could, and she had done so.

If only it had been Elizabeth who had run into George emerging from Miss Burrows' room clad in pyjamas and dressing gown at dawn two days ago, and not his grandmother! She could have dealt with it quietly and without bringing Laurence into it. Lady Buckford had shown no such reticence, and first poor George, then poor Kate, had been hauled into the study for a lecture on behaviour becoming in a gentleman and lady respectively, and conduct proper under a rectory roof. At least Laurence had been firm, and had insisted that he and he alone would deal with it. The lecture had bounced off Kate like water off a duck's back.

'By gum, Rector,' she'd said (Laurence later confessed to her, trying not to laugh, his wife suspected), 'don't you worry about me. I enjoy it.'

When he had suggested tactfully to Kate that she had been at the Rectory long enough, she beamed her thanks for his consideration and said she'd been thinking that way herself, and if he was ever up Yorkshire way, to be sure to call in for a glass of hot whisky and lemon.

George's retribution, however, had been no laughing matter,

and by the time his father had finished with him, they looked like a couple of glaring turkey-cocks. Poor George had departed without even saying goodbye to Laurence, which upset him even more. Indeed, Elizabeth was quite sure that it was tension over George's departure that had led Laurence to such wrath, preventing his displaying his usual ability to have his say and then smooth over the rancour. Now George had gone, and the absence of his noisy cheerfulness left a silence that would be hard to fill, especially with Kate leaving.

At least Elizabeth had, thanks to Mrs Dibble, found the solution for her absence – if it worked out in practice. Beatrice Ryde's face had coloured with pleasure when she'd asked her to help with the rotas. (Once they had got over the embarrassment of the ulster. Too late, Elizabeth remembered who had given it to her.) She was still a little doubtful, for Beatrice lacked the gift of getting on with the villagers; she too often treated them like the schoolchildren they had once been, and coaxing was a verb unknown to her. Elizabeth knew she would have to tread carefully.

Much more of her own time had to be devoted to parishioners, for Charles Pickering, their curate, had at last been called up in November, much to his disgust – not, she guessed, because he was a shirker, but because he was leaving the field for Beth Parry's affections wide open for Philip Ryde. Philip had lost no time, and Elizabeth admitted she was glad of it. Philip deserved a good wife, and Beth Parry, though as resolute as his sister Beatrice, had a great deal more compassion in her manner.

How strange to think it had once seemed possible that Caroline might marry Philip. She could see now it would never have worked, and nor even would marriage to Reggie. War had shone a spotlight onto pre-war Ashden life; it hadn't so much changed people, in Elizabeth's view, but revealed a truth that might otherwise have been years in emerging. Perhaps it might never have done so, but it was too late now. Seeing Caroline with that Belgian officer at Christmas had made that fact glaringly obvious. She grieved for herself, not only because Caroline might never return to the Rectory, but because two of her daughters were walking away to where she could no longer help them.

"Today's problem, Elizabeth," she reminded herself. There was the catering for the wedding to be arranged.

There were so many memorial services, so much bereavement everywhere, that a wedding, even in this cold, hard winter, was to be enjoyed as much as possible. Even baptisms now had an air of sadness about them, for the fathers were often far away in the trenches instead of standing proudly by the font; and confirmations brought the realisation that children were growing up, and if the war did not end soon, they would be called up to fight.

She would ask Caroline to try to come home for the wedding. It was not a good time of year to travel, but oh, how she'd love to have her here. Beth and Philip wanted a small gathering, and Elizabeth had offered the Rectory drawing-room and kitchen services so that Beatrice need not be bothered with the cooking. At first Miss Ryde had indignantly demurred, then at Philip's prompting agreed.

Catering brought a less welcome next task, too, and this one infuriated her, since it was so unnecessary. But then wherever Lady Buckford went, unnecessary trouble followed. No sooner was the matter of George dealt with – if that was the right word – than the Gorgon bobbed up on a different front. And this time, Elizabeth, not Laurence, had no option but to deal with it herself.

Elizabeth hesitated before knocking gently on the kitchen door, hardly bearing to contemplate the hurt she had to inflict, and knowing there was nothing she could do about it. She had already had her say to her ladyship, without any effect whatsoever, and perhaps there was a chance that it would come as a relief to Mrs Dibble.

"Did you manage to get some meat for the weekend, Mrs Dibble?"

"I did, madam, and Wally Bertram says he'll see we're all right even if rationing does come in."

"I don't think—" Elizabeth had started to say she didn't think her husband would approve of that, but changed her mind. Her real mission was, alas, more important. "Lady Buckford spoke to me this morning, Mrs Dibble—" (Of course she did. Of course, the old so-and-so would get someone else to do her dirty work for her.) "She's heard from the Board of Agriculture about the cookery demonstrations in the Great Hall in Tunbridge Wells."

Mrs Dibble's face grew pink. "It'll be a pleasure, Mrs Lilley. We'll show those Wells folk what Ashden can do."

Elizabeth ploughed on as best she could. "However, Lady Buckford was concerned about you. She felt that with all your responsibilities in the Rectory and the demonstrations in Ashden, Tunbridge Wells would be too much for you to cope with." Elizabeth's heart sank as she saw the excitement ebbing away from Mrs Dibble's face.

"I can manage my own responsibilities, thank you, madam. I'm quite capable, please tell her ladyship."

"I'm afraid that with the best of intentions Lady Buckford has replied to the Board that her maid Miss Lewis will be in charge of the Tunbridge Wells course."

Mrs Dibble went very pale. She sat down, a thing she'd never do normally while Elizabeth was here. "She's not a cook," she replied flatly.

"She *can* cook, her ladyship says—"

Mrs Dibble interrupted. "Her ladyship don't know a thing about it. There's more to cooking than following a recipe book. *And* to teaching."

"You can—" Elizabeth stopped, for the unthinkable had happened. Mrs Dibble was crying.

"Just go, madam, if you'd be so kind," came her muffled voice.

Comfort her? Go and tell Lady Buckford what she thought

186

of her? Bring Laurence into it? Mrs Dibble might resent her comfort at a time of such an unusual breakdown. Elizabeth decided she had to tackle Lady Buckford.

"I fail to understand your meaning, Mrs Lilley." Lady Buckford eyed her frostily from the straight-backed armchair in her sitting-room.

"I've made it quite clear," Elizabeth blazed. "As I told you this morning, your action, without even consulting Mrs Dibble who has been wholly responsible for making your scheme a success, was a gross insult to her."

"On the contrary, I had every consideration for your house-keeper, which is why I am sacrificing my own comfort by sending Miss Lewis."

"You are not doing it out of consideration for her, but for your own prestige. I presume you consider Miss Lewis has more social standing than Mrs Dibble."

"She is a gentlewoman, certainly."

"And you think that makes any difference?"

"Would you kindly not bellow at me, Mrs Lilley?"

"I'll bellow all I like," Elizabeth shouted, over a year's bottled feelings released. "It might make you see I'm *here*. I'm Elizabeth, I've been married to your son for nearly thirty years, I'm the mother of your grandchildren, and I am not a serving wench to be—"

"*What* is going on here?" Laurence rushed in, breathless from running up the stairs. "I can hear you shouting from the study."

Elizabeth took a deep breath. "Lady Buckford will tell you, Laurence."

"Your wife appears to have taken offence at my disinterested actions."

Laurence listened to his mother while Elizabeth fumed, then put his finger on the salient point. "Does Mrs Dibble want to do these courses?"

Elizabeth nodded. "Passionately. I'm afraid I hadn't realised how much, or I would not have let this get so far."

"Then, Mother, you should write to the Board of Agriculture and tell them there's been a change in plan."

"I will not do so, Laurence."

"You *will* do so, Mother," he said gently. "You are under our roof and must take note of our wishes."

Elizabeth, weak at the knees, felt guilty that Laurence had been drawn into the argument, but greatly relieved that he was.

"If you insist on this sentimental course of action," Lady Buckford retorted icily, "I will follow your instructions. However, I shall no longer remain in this house. I have a home in Dover."

Down on the ground, thrown, punched out of the game, Elizabeth knew when the game was lost.

"You can't do that, Mother, while there is danger of air raids." Laurence was appalled. "You must go to Wiltshire to Charles's family."

Oh, glory be. Elizabeth could hardly believe it. He was siding with her. Just as he had over their wedding.

"I shall return to Dover."

He tried one last time. "I ask you, Mother, to reflect. Mrs Dibble has done all the work to establish these courses. Miss Lewis would not dispute that she should therefore have priority. It is a small thing I ask of you."

"I never change my mind, Laurence. I shall leave."

Elizabeth felt close to tears. Oh, the obstinacy of some people. Thank goodness Laurence was his mother's son.

"Very well, Mother. Please write to the Board, and I will make arrangements for your departure."

On the stairs, Myrtle was agog with excitement, able to hear every word that was being said. She rushed downstairs to impart the good news to Mrs Dibble.

"You're going to Tunbridge Wells. The old hag is leaving."

"Myrtle, what are you talking about? I told you not to repeat gossip."

"It's not gossip. It's true. She's going. You're going."

Margaret fastened on the one salient point she understood. "She's leaving? Well, I never did." The Good Lord sent some splendid miracles and no mistake.

"She's going back to Dover, because Rector put his foot down about you. He didn't want her to go," Myrtle chattered on, "but she wouldn't change her mind. He was ever so upset."

"Dover? With all them air raids?" Margaret did an unusual thing. She left the egg whites half-whipped, took off her apron, went into the main house and up the stairs to Lady Buckford's sitting-room. The door was open and Rector had gone. Just as well. This was between her and Lady B.

"Begging your pardon, your Ladyship." She knocked on the door.

"Yes, my good woman?"

Margaret swallowed hard. The Rector's mother was like something out of Dickens, all black, clawlike hands on the arms of the wing chair. "I heard as how you were leaving the Rectory."

"How dare you interfere in my personal business?"

Margaret grew bold. "From what I hear it's my business too. I just wanted to say I don't want you to leave over me doing those lectures, I'd rather you stayed, and Miss Lewis did them."

"Why? Don't you want to organise the demonstrations?" The beady eyes fastened on her sharply.

Margaret thought about not answering, but decided the old besom should know just how she felt. "Yes, ma'am, I want to do them very much, but I don't want your blood on my conscience because of them bombs, and I don't want . . ."

"What, may I ask?" Lady Buckford snapped as Margaret halted.

". . . the Rectory upset because of me."

She turned round and marched out, head held high, already

189

planning a half-pay pudding like her mother used to do, for her next demonstration in the picture palace. To make up for the treacle (standing in for sugar) and for the wodge of suet, milk and breadcrumbs unlivened by dried fruit, she'd show them a nice sauce, not just a blob of consip or saccharine jam.

By late January, with the snow and frosts not letting up, and having to battle in person at the shops to establish the Rectory's precedence for food (not that she put it that way to Mrs Lilley), Margaret felt as dispirited as Percy's last brandy bottle. Empty, gone, and when would this gloomy old life produce some more? There'd been another upset in the Rectory. Miss Phoebe had left unexpectedly. She had bounced in, looking happy for the first time for months, to tell her all about it – to get her reaction before telling her father, no doubt. Apparently she'd been learning to drive with that Miss Swinford-Browne in East Grinstead, and having done so she had joined the Women's Legion Motor Transport Section, which she said the Government might turn into a division of the Army, like with Miss Burrows. She was off to London to start training, and three days later she had gone.

Margaret's heart went out to Mrs Lilley, and after the mistress had returned from waving Miss Phoebe off at the station, she went to the morning-room to show her that one thing wasn't changing in the Rectory. Her routine.

"How many for dinner tonight, madam?"

Mrs Lilley looked very, very tired. 'It's just us now, Mrs Dibble. Her ladyship will eat in her rooms as usual, so it's just the Rector and myself.'

"What about Mrs Isabel, madam?" Margaret was startled.

"Oh, yes, Isabel will be here. I don't count her."

Mrs Lilley wasn't herself or she would never had said such a thing, even if she thought it. But it was unfortunate for the mistress could not see, whereas Margaret could, that Mrs Isabel was standing in the doorway and must have heard every word.

Eleven

Caroline's boot slipped on the hard-packed ice, and Luke had to grab her to steady her. Three days earlier, Thursday, 8th February had brought the severest frost for over twenty years, and January had produced never-ending snowstorms. At least the snowstorms had been fun; their aftermath of frost and ice was not. Despite the weather, at long last she was going to a Sunday night concert at the Leas Shelter, although it was not Yves but Luke who was escorting her.

Life was very contrary. She had tried to rediscover her sense of humour at its quirky little ways, but this evening, it seemed lost for ever, good company though Luke was. Even St Anthony couldn't find it for her. Christmas had been a mirage which had lured her into seeing it as a turning point for a happier year ahead. What had seemed quite obvious then, that her love for Yves had not only revealed itself to her but was reciprocated, had been mere self-deception. Their brief coming together had meant a short happiness, not a lifetime's. Her gratitude to Yves for his companionship during the dark days of the autumn had led her to put more significance than she would otherwise have done on two kisses. Yes, that must have been the reason.

She couldn't quite believe it, even now, for this explanation just did not seem to fit the facts. This new love for Yves had nothing to do with any she had had or might still have for Reggie. She had been almost frightened by the response his kisses aroused in her, dizzy with the realisation that life could change in a moment from bleakness to joy, from emptiness to fulfilment. She was in little doubt of her own feelings; what she had done was to misread Yves'. He had been merely comforting her when he kissed her; and it had been she who had asked him to kiss her again – he could hardly have refused – and the strength of her emotions had convinced her he shared them.

So where was he? Why was she clinging to her boss's arm on this Sunday evening instead of to Yves'? She had seen him only once since Christmas – once in over six weeks. And even that had been in the office. He had dropped in to see Luke in the early days of the new year, and stopped at her desk on his way out.

"Caroline, you will forgive me I know, but I must discontinue our French lessons. I have to be away from Folkestone for some time – you understand?" Had it not been for the fact his voice was intimate, that it was the voice of the Yves she had come to know and not that of Captain Rosier, he might have been speaking to any of the office staff, so formal were his words.

She had stumbled out a reply in similar vein, but she had felt her expression, which must have registered her delight at seeing him, stiffen. "Of course, Yves. How long will you be gone?"

"I'm not sure," he replied quickly. Too quickly, and the first doubt had entered her mind – to be angrily dismissed. "There is, as you know, an increasingly large question mark over King Albert's plans."

Caroline did know. If President Wilson continued to hold out against involving America in the war, King Albert might well be tempted to accept the Draconic terms of the Kaiser's offer of peace. If he did, there would no longer be a Belgian army, the German occupying forces would remain, and Germany would maintain control of the transport system and harbours.

At that moment Captain Cameron had come in and whisked Yves back to his private office; later he escorted him to the front door. From the air of suppressed excitement, she had sensed there was some big flap on, which perhaps even Luke did not know about, let alone her humble self, but at the moment she did not care. She could hardly leave her desk and rush after Yves crying: 'What about me?' Instead, staring at her work, her eyes stung with the effort of control.

Since then Caroline had almost convinced herself that with the reports of slave labour drives in Belgium – 90,000 had gone in one week alone in December – as well as the lack of progress on the American front, Yves could well be on an extended visit to King Albert. There would surely be a spring offensive, somewhere – that could be another reason for his absence. He would be discussing it at La Panne, and with British GHQ.

What was worse, their intelligence pointed to Ypres. Olivier Fabre had brought them worrying reports from the Ghent and Cambrai letterboxes that fresh divisions were pouring into Belgium by rail. With the help of the Brown Book, Luke had identified one of the divisions at least as coming from Romania, which meant a German crack division now that the Germans were advancing so rapidly there. Such a concentration of units was a clear sign of a brewing offensive, rather than mere relief of divisions in the line.

While she was at work these explanations of Yves' absence satisfied her, but alone in her room at night (having faced her landlady's inquisitive questions as to why the captain didn't come any more – was it her high tea?) Caroline was forced to face the more likely truth: Yves, for whatever reason, had thought better of continuing what had so inevitably (it now seemed to her) begun at Christmas. So where now, Caroline? she asked herself ruefully. She wasn't the same person who had discovered her love for Reggie in 1914; that was the Caroline who had grown up in Ashden and, had it not been for war, would still be there. Now Ashden could no longer cocoon her for ever – and nor could Reggie's memory. It was this new Caroline who was so attracted to Yves, the one who was vainly telling herself that life was opening up, not closing in darkness around her.

193

As she turned off the gas light (oh, the bliss of that, and yet how she missed the comforting candles and oil lamps of home) and climbed into bed, the huge pit of ache in her stomach cried out: *why?* Was she so dull, so unattractive, so uninteresting? Perhaps she was. She had a spot on her face that refused to go, and one of her back teeth was aching. Yves did not want this horrible lump called Caroline Lilley, she reasoned; very well, somebody, somewhere, surely *must.* But she could not believe it.

That had been over five weeks ago, and Yves had not yet returned to Folkestone. Very well, she had decided in a fit of defiance, this weekend I shall go to the Leas on my own. When Luke suggested she accompany him, however, she agreed with some relief. The building built into the cliff-side had outside 'decks' at different levels leading off the hall, and they were swarming with Tommies, Canadian soldiers, uniforms of all sorts. She felt out of place with her own civilian clothes, though with Luke in uniform she presumed she passed for a soldier's girl, which was almost as patriotic. The audience was jammed shoulder to shoulder, and the chairs of the row in front were right up against her knees; the smell of tobacco and the noise contributed to the atmosphere, and the sense of unity, as they listened to the concert. Tomorrow evening, Caroline thought, she would still be in England but many of these soldiers would be in France, and the memory of this evening precious to them. As she and Luke walked back along the Leas, a group of Tommies all round them were whistling the *Merry Widow* waltz with a fervour that probably masked great fear.

Time was precious for her too, and she could hold back no longer. "Have you heard anything from Yves, Luke?" Even she could hear the slight wobble in the casualness of her voice, and Luke could hardly be blamed for picking it up too.

"He'll be back sometime, Caroline."

There was comfort but little conviction in his voice. In for a penny, in for a pound. "Do you know where he is?"

"I've a fair idea."

"Occupied Belgium?" It had suddenly occurred to her that Yves might have gone to recruit more agents. Was he even now in St Gilles, the prison for political prisoners, undergoing interrogation by Schwarzteufel in the dreaded office in the Central Bureau of Espionage?

"I doubt that, Caroline. Truly."

Relief combined inevitably with the question rearing its painful head again.

Luke put his arm round her in affection. "I expect he's with King Albert. There's not a lot going on here at present. You know that, don't you, Caroline?"

Yes, she did. Intelligence was sparse, and save for Olivier Fabre's, useless. Speedier methods like aerial photographs – despite the loss to aeroplanes – were necessary for GHQ, both in London and Montreuil, and she had a nasty feeling GHQ was well aware of the fact.

Alarmingly, Luke seemed to agree, when she told him this. "My guess, Caroline, is that Yves is deeply involved at La Panne, and that when he returns he'll be relying more on our sister London-run networks than with the bureau here, save for contact with the Belgian section. It could be we're being gently dropped."

"Can't we get more agents ourselves?" Caroline was horrified.

"It takes time for Fabre to find out who is and who is not compromised. Even with the checks we introduced of no one knowing their colleagues' identity, there are so many German stool pigeons moving around, and so many forced to talk by the gentle methods used by the German Secret Police and Field Police that there are all too frequent arrests and executions. And we still don't know the full extent of the damage from the ferry disaster, though Fabre is treating everyone as suspect till proven otherwise."

Caroline tried to concentrate on the problem. At least it took her mind off Yves. "Do the other intelligence organisations have the same problem?"

He shrugged, then slipped on the ice himself, nearly dragging them both down. "How could I know? But I suspect so because we all attract the same odd folks. Those we pay, anyway, not the true patriots."

"All the world is odd excepting you and me and even you're a little strange," she quipped. The old adage had been a favourite of Reggie's. "Is this what you were discussing when you visited GHQ in France at Christmas – or was that just an excuse to bring Felicia home?"

"How would you like to sit down suddenly in an icy snow drift?"

She laughed. "Felicia was happy at Christmas."

"I know."

"You're very confident, aren't you, Luke?"

"I have to be."

"Even though you must know Felicia still hasn't forgotten Daniel?"

She had bravely tackled Felicia once more on the subject before she went back to France, feeling she had a right to do so sine she worked with Luke. Felicia had finally answered: 'I love Daniel, I love Luke. But my love for Daniel is part of me.'

"I don't think, Caroline," Luke replied, seriously for once, "that Lissy will ever marry Daniel. Whether she marries me is another question, but it's a question I have to answer with yes. See?"

Caroline squeezed his arm in reply. She did see.

"It's not a matter of whom one prefers nowadays, Caroline," Luke continued, "war doesn't allow such luxury. In pre-war days one could dance with an Angela or Big Bertha, kiss Catherine, reject Doris. It was all within one's control. Once war came striding in, it declared itself as an arbiter. It decided you weren't going to marry Reggie; I believe it's also going to decide whether Daniel or I marries Lissy. We're controlled by it. The most I can do is to try to nudge it along in the direction I want. I've no idea why Daniel can't make up his mind – that's if he loves her. Maybe he doesn't."

"He does. And I don't know either."

They had arrived at her front door. Luke hugged her, kissed her cold cheeks, and then her lips. "One for Felicia," he told her matter of factly, "one for Yves."

"How did you know—?" she began.

"One can't be in love oneself and not see it in others."

"In Yves?"

He planted a final kiss on her forehead. "I'm not war, Caroline. It must speak for itself. Go to bed, and sleep deeply. No dreams."

She was glad to be back for the wedding in the Rectory on the 24th. It reminded her of Eleanor's wedding almost a year ago, especially since to her surprise Beth asked her to be her brides-maid. The 'small' wedding had expanded to between thirty and forty guests. Caroline came back on the Friday evening, so that she could help Mrs Dibble with the food preparation, while Agnes and Myrtle were flying round doing their best to smarten up the Rectory. She wondered if Mrs Dibble would launch into a lament about the cookery lectures, having heard all about the hullabaloo from her mother. When there was no word, she decided it would be prudent not to remind her, though she was fiercely on her side.

Unfortunately, Friday was the first day of a government food-economy initiative, bringing a moral dilemma over whether sausage rolls should be prepared for the Saturday.

"Meatless day, indeed," Mrs Dibble snorted. "We've been having them at the Rectory for the last year. Good job I showed the ladies how to make a tasty vegetable pie—" She broke off, suddenly tight-lipped, and Caroline hastily congratulated her on the cocoa-butter cakes, her latest idea to get round the butter shortage. (The Sharpes at Home Farm were having one of their periodic sulks and pretending all their spare went to the Dower House and the hospital.)

How odd to be preparing food for Philip's wedding. Philip had wanted to marry Caroline two years ago, and irrespective of that she hadn't much cared for Beth Parry at first. Now she liked her, and considered she would make an excellent wife for Philip.

"Nothing fancy," she had warned Caroline. "I won't wear my white doctor's coat, and no silks and satins for you." Beth's fair hair was usually held back in a bun, and she wore severe suits or skirts and blouses. For her wedding, however, she was planning to wear an afternoon dress with full and fashionably short shirt in dark green wool and a frothy sort of hat swathed in tulle in which Caroline suspected Janie Marden must have had a hand. A straightforward, no-nonsense girl, Janie had an amazingly skittish way with fashioning new hats out of old, and no one would look askance at a little frivolity on a wedding day.

It was cold in St Nicholas despite the paraffin heaters the verger had brought in, and Caroline was glad to get back to the comparative warmth of the Rectory. Among the guests was Timothy Marden, on leave from the RNAS at Dover, and having heard George was now in the RFC came over to her to enquire about his progress.

"He's still doing his service training at Upavon."

"He'll be a good flyer. I remember thinking that when I took him up at Dover."

Caroline grimaced. "Tell that to my parents. They're quite convinced he'll be shot down the first time he goes up."

He grinned. "I'm not dead yet."

She realised with horror what she'd unthinkingly said: "I'm so sorry, Tim. It was just a figure of speech."

"It's a fact, unfortunately."

"I keep pointing out to them you're safe and you've been in the force since before the war."

"Yes, but I'm not on the western front. Yet."

"Do you think you'll have to go?"

"We're caught both ways. If the Zeps and LVGs start their fun and games again soon, we'll be needed here, and since they all seem to like Dover, there'll be plenty of action. If not, we'll be sent to the Front. Dover's enough of a front for me. I'm no hero."

"When will they come again, do you think?" Caroline shivered. In the bad winter weather, they had at least been spared the horrors of the Zeppelins, although a few nights ago an aircraft had attacked shipping off Deal.

"Soon," Tim replied soberly. "Everything tends to start in March. Pray God, for the last time."

"George will have his 'wings' by then."

"Yes. Ah well, gather ye rosebuds while ye may, is my motto," Tim replied cheerfully. "Except that Philip's pinched the girl I fancied."

"There's always me," Caroline laughed.

"So there is," Tim said politely. "I'll ask for your hand in twenty years, if that's acceptable."

It was a joke, but she could have done without it. Caroline decided she'd retreat to the kitchen for ten minutes. Perhaps Mrs Dibble's familiar presence would cheer her up. When she got there, however, Mrs Dibble was absent, and Percy was humming an old music-hall song. Caroline identified it with little difficulty:

"Why am I always the bridesmaid, never the blushing bride . . . ?"

"Oh, *thank* you," she muttered, retreating hastily.

Margaret placed the warm scones carefully above the chafing dishes in the dining-room, and was so intent on her work it wasn't till she was about to leave that she realised she was not alone. Lady Buckford was seated at the table, whether waiting for scones or escaping the wedding party was not clear.

199

"Anything wrong, your ladyship?" Margaret managed to sound polite.

"I wished to see you, Mrs Dibble."

Margaret prepared for battle, hackles rising all over her.

"I've heard from the Board of Agriculture," Lady Buckford continued. "They want the courses to begin on Monday 26th March and they will be held in the Great Hall opposite, so I gather, the railway station. You can discuss with them the timing of the lectures, publicity, and everything else involved."

Margaret thought she'd heard wrong. "Me, madam? You mean Miss Lewis."

"I mean you, Mrs Dibble. On further reflection I decided I could not spare Miss Lewis and that, in any case, you were the more suitable candidate. One must consider the war effort, before all else. I informed the Board of Agriculture of my decision."

Margaret felt dizzy, a rush of blood to the head, her mother would have diagnosed. "Very well, your ladyship." Her voice came out deadpan, but inside her there was a war-dance of triumph, churning her up. "Thank you, your ladyship."

"Please do not thank me, Mrs Dibble. The subject is now, in that distressing modern slang, *na-poo'd*."

"Thank you, your ladyship," Margaret repeated clearly and loudly. She was in such a daze she almost forgot what she'd been meaning to say to Miss Caroline.

On her way back from the kitchen after her fruitless attempt at escape, Caroline met Mrs Dibble, who stopped her in a very determined manner. "I've been meaning to say, but it's not my place, Miss Caroline."

Muddled, Caroline asked, "What isn't?" Whatever it was she was delighted. "I'll come into the kitchen and you can tell me."

"Speaking this way," Mrs Dibble explained, once there. "I'm worried about Mrs Isabel."

"*Isabel?* I thought she was nicely settled at the cinema." On the other hand it suddenly struck her that Isabel had been rather quiet this weekend, and far from her usual bouncy self. "I expect she's worried about Mr Robert, Mrs Dibble. He'll be going overseas very soon."

"It's my belief," announced Mrs Dibble cryptically, "that's only part of it. Mind you, it's not my place." And she bustled back out of the kitchen with a plate of vegetable patties and the air of a job well done.

Highly puzzled, Caroline watched Isabel carefully when she rejoined the party. She had to admit that like everyone in the family, she had been so relieved that Isabel had found something to occupy herself, that she had all but dismissed her from her mind. Mrs Dibble was right. There *was* something odd: Isabel was helping hand round plates. The old Isabel would have sat down, expecting it all to be brought to her. No time like the present. As she could speak to her on her own, she would get to the bottom of it.

"You make rather a good waitress."

She'd put her foot in it, Caroline realised when Isabel flared up immediately.

"That's you all over, Caroline. You imagine you're the only one of us who can manage to lift a finger."

"No, I – Isabel, what *is* wrong? Are you worried about Robert?"

Isabel dropped her eyes. "Yes," she maintained defiantly. "He's getting near the end of his balloon training at Roehampton and that means he'll be sent overseas for observation duties over the western front. He'll be up in one of those terribly dangerous Dragon things."

"Drachen," Caroline corrected.

"Oh yes, you know all about the war too, don't you? Well, let me tell you—"

"Isabel!" Caroline interrupted, pained, and Isabel apologised after a fashion.

"Anyway, he'll be floating over the Front, it's ten times more dangerous than George going up in an aeroplane. Mother and Father are perpetually worried about him, but no one worries about Robert other than me."

"Oh Isabel." Caroline put her arm round her. "I've been very blind. I'm so sorry."

"I feel completely on my own here," Isabel went on. "I don't even feel the Rectory's home any more, all Mother and Father can do is talk about how Felicia, George, Phoebe and you have gone away."

"But that means they value you even more."

"I don't think so," Isabel replied quietly. "But I'm going to show them they're wrong."

"You're doing splendidly at the cinema – didn't I see you'd got *The Light That Failed* and *Captain Scott of the Antarctic* in the programme? *And* that film on the *Ark Royal* so that Mrs Grendel could see the ship her son's on. That was kind of you."

"Yes, but that's work. It's here I want to be loved."

Isabel glared at her, and the contrast of her expression with her sentiments made it hard not to giggle. Somehow Caroline managed it, for Isabel was Isabel, and always would be, bless her. Daniel then came up to talk to her sister, and, greatly relieved since Isabel had immediately cheered up, Caroline slipped away. It wasn't for some time that she herself got a chance to talk to him, and then only because he sought her out. An odd kind of loyalty to Luke had made the idea of chatting on her old familiar terms with Daniel awkward to contemplate.

"How did Philip manage to slip through your clutches?" was Daniel's opening gambit, which promptly restored her to her old terms with him.

"He had a very narrow escape," she agreed. "I was proposing to gobble him up next Christmas. How's the job going, Daniel?"

"That's what I came to tell you. I suppose we can't very well retire up to the priest-hole – it might be misconstrued. But I can talk to you, the only one save Father, seeing we're all in the same business. Have you heard the news from our department?"

"No. Do tell. Let's go into the morning-room. We'll be on our own there."

He led the way, and immediately the door was closed, burst out: "We've had a coup at last, and it looks as if it may bring the USA into the war. Have you heard of a fellow called Zimmermann?"

"Of course. He's the German Foreign Minister."

"He was unwise enough to suggest in a coded telegram to their ambassador in Mexico that if Mexico threw in its lot with Germany, and the new unrestricted submarine 'sink everything' policy brought America into the war, Germany would give it a nice blank cheque to annex Texas, Arizona and New Mexico."

"What? But that's—"

"Rash to say the least. I thought you might have heard about it, since it was your lot got the code for us."

"What? I had no idea." So that was what the flap she had sensed in the new year had been about.

"It was the French and Belgian sections, actually. They set up a scheme to pinch the German diplomatic code from the rue de la Loi in Brussels. It's worked, and when we sent a decrypt through to the US Government it had a fairly explosive effect. That, coupled with the Kaiser's brilliant idea 'let's sink everything' including any US cargo ships, plus another decrypt by us of a telegram from Bernsdorff, asking Berlin for cash to bribe some members of Congress, has probably silenced the 'Keep American Neutral' faction over there. It can't be long now they've broken off diplomatic relations."

"Daniel, that's a wonderful achievement."

"Pretty good, wasn't it?" Daniel looked relaxed, and proud. "I'm going out to GHQ France next week," he continued. "Not quite the great travel I intended, but something at any rate. Maybe I'll try for Mesopotamia next."

"Will you see Felicia?" Caroline just couldn't keep the question back.

"No, Madam Interrogator, I shall not."

" 'Shall' sounds as though it's been a hard decision."

"You wouldn't expect it to be easy, would you?"

"I don't know, Daniel. I don't know what's wrong between you. All I know is that I'm sure Felicia still loves you, and yet you're letting Luke push in front of you."

"He's a good bloke," Daniel began, edging towards the door.

"So are you."

"You mean well, Caroline," he replied lightly, "but sometimes you are as dim as darling Isabel. Now, shall we go to toast the happy couple?"

She had asked for the rebuff she received, but she still smarted at it. It was all such a waste. With war raging on, people should take happiness when it was offered. 'Awake, my Little ones, and fill the Cup . . .' The quotation from *Omar Khayyám* reminded her of Yves, and as though she had yelped aloud with pain, Daniel asked casually as he limped across the hall: "Seen any more of that Belgian fellow, Henri's friend?"

"No. Not recently."

"He came in to see the pater while I was with him a week or two ago. Nice chap, if a little poker-faced."

Yves had been in London, not La Panne, and he couldn't even be bothered to come down to Folkestone to see her.

Folkestone seemed bleaker than ever as Caroline arrived at the town railway station, looked round in vain for a cab, decided the chances of a bus at this time on a Sunday night were non-existent, picked up her suitcase and began to walk back home, wishing she had timed her journey earlier to arrive in the daylight. As it was, she had to grope her way through complete darkness, and the thought of her landlady's supper awaiting her compared with the wonders Mrs Dibble produced on a wartime diet depressed her even further. She considered going to one of the Belgian clubs, but couldn't face it. Suppose Yves were there? The embarrassment and hurt would be terrible. She would have to put up with her fellow lodgers and be jovial at the Mad Hatter's tea party. It was almost worth going to bed hungry. As she replaced her key in her handbag in the hallway, she could hear the usual crowd gathering in the small parlour. She was back. There was someone else too – a guest was sometimes permitted under very special circumstances. Then . . . who *was* that? Someone in a uniform—

Surely it couldn't be. It *was*.

"Phoebe!" she cried in delight, dropping her suitcase and rushing in to shock her fellow lodgers with a display of sisterly emotion as she threw her arms round her. "Oh, if only you knew how glad I am to see you. And uniform too. How posh."

"That's good," Phoebe laughed. "I'm here for a month or so to drill."

"Drill? Where? What with? Where are you staying?"

"Nothing but the best. They've cleared the Hotel Metropole for us. We're an early draft for the new Women's Army."

Twelve

T alk about peas rattling round in a pod. That was the Rectory nowadays. Margaret Dibble put aside two of the knives for Percy to tighten up the handles. It was that Myrtle's fault. She would keep leaving them soaking in hot water, and goodness knows whether Mabel Thorn still stocked resin and sulphur in the ironmongers to repair them with. Mrs T had let the shop slide what with both Jamie and Len away in the forces, although Len wouldn't be marching home with a medal, Margaret was quite sure about that. You couldn't afford to let things slide, she decided, or you'd find yourself on so greasy a slope you'd never get up it again. There was nothing like cooking for taking your mind off things. The best physicians were Dr Diet, Dr Quiet and Dr Merryman. She couldn't do much about the last, with Mr George away, and Dr Quiet was here unbidden, but she could cosset Dr Diet.

Lady Gwendolen, the Rector's sister-in-law, had come up for a visit from Wiltshire, where she had moved to escape the Dover bombs, but no sooner had she arrived in Sussex than the Germans started their antics again. It wasn't a Zep, it was a floatplane but the bombs it dropped on Broadstairs must have felt the same. Then on 16th March, the Zeps had another go at Dover and Ashford, though this time they were driven off. That had decided it. Lady Gwendolen had scuttled back to Wiltshire.

Here in the Rectory life went on, Zeps or no Zeps, but it wasn't the same. Nor was Ashden, with those soldiers at The Towers. They were all officers, but that didn't stop them eyeing up the village girls. Not that some of them needed eyeing up; they stood around on Bankside in their Sunday best, waiting for them to come strolling down Station Road, and Ruth Horner had given up flashing her torch at the back row of the picture palace. The village lads when home on leave were more careful, being known here, but those Towers lot were out for a lark.

"Don't tell Father," Mrs Isabel had said, alarmed, when Margaret mentioned it.

She wouldn't. Poor Rector had enough on his mind, and the Rectory was a gloomier place this new year with Miss Phoebe and Master George gone, and probably both going overseas. She didn't know whether she wanted it to be all quiet out there on the Front, so Fred and Joe would keep safe, or whether she wanted another offensive to cut this war short and drive the Germans back to Germany. Ah well, it wasn't her decision, thanks be.

She had to laugh as she thought of what Fred had said when he came home on leave just before he went overseas; there wasn't much to laugh about, and so she had told Percy afterwards to give him a good chuckle. 'Drive the Germans back?' Fred had repeated, puzzled. 'Why don't we make 'em walk?'

She hadn't heard a word from or about him, save what Joe had told her. Of course he couldn't write much more than his name, but you'd think *someone* would have dropped a line. Rector had said at least that was good news; if he was ill or wounded, she would have heard. So there it was: her two sons over there and Master George, Miss Felicia and soon Miss Phoebe. If it wasn't for Lizzie and the baby she wouldn't know what to do with herself. She hardly ever saw Muriel for now she too was busy working, taking in clothes for mending; once a month she'd bring the children over. Lizzie was turning out grand, though, and they were getting on ever so well. Not that she approved of the way she was bringing that baby up, off the breast already, but she managed to button her mouth up most of the time.

Two days later the Rectory had another visitor. Master George came home unexpectedly, full of the joys of spring – if there were any joys this cold spring; he was going overseas; he'd got his wings.

"I'm flying off, Mrs D," he'd shouted, seeing her in the garden. "I'm an angel."

"I'll believe that when I see it," she retorted.

All that business in January over Miss Burrows seemed to have been forgotten, and the Rector and Mrs Lilley were overjoyed to see him. She cooked his favourite rabbit fricassee, for all they were nearly out of onions and eggs were like gold dust.

The next morning he swept into the kitchen, growling, arms outstretched, dipping and rising. "Watch me, Mrs Dibble. I'm an SE5. Look out, von Richthofen, here I come."

She'd laughed. It was just like when he was a child, and he wasn't much more in fact. Eighteen wasn't grown-up to her mind, though plenty younger were at the Front. The papers were full of the marvellous things these aeroplanes could do nowadays, but she couldn't help noticing there were a lot of RFC officers in the Roll of Honour.

"I'm going to 56 Squadron, Mrs Dibble, what do you think of that? Guess who's in it – Alfred Ball."

"Who?"

"You must have read about him. He's shot down at least thirty German planes to that von Richthofen's twenty; he's got *three* DSOs and an MC. He's commander of 56's A Flight. I hope he takes me. I'm joining them next week, and the squadron's due to fly out to France in April. I hope it's not all over by then. That's *weeks* away."

He zoomed round the kitchen again, managing to sweep the carrots and potatoes off the table in the process.

"Just you take care of yourself, Master George," Margaret

said sharply as he scrabbled to pick them up again. "None of your pranks up in the air – you're there to keep the Germans away, not show off. And you mind you find all those spuds – there's a shortage, you know."

"Yes, Mrs Dibble."

"Will you be anywhere near Fred? My Joe said he was on the Somme, and I can't help being worried." This was understanding the case. She hadn't slept a wink the night after she read that.

"There's no shortage of spuds out there, Mrs D. He'll still be busy on those, don't you worry. Someone has to peel them."

"Yes." She wasn't convinced. Weren't they recruiting girls like Miss Phoebe now for canteen work?

Master George stayed two days and then went back to join his new squadron. Everything became quiet again in the Rectory, and she tried to be extra cheerful herself for Mrs Lilley's sake.

"I've got a nice piece of lamb for family dinner, Mrs Lilley. Wally Bertram put it aside specially," she announced when she went into the morning-room for her daily 'orders'. Not that she was given (or accepted) orders nowadays; it was more a discussion of what was available.

"Now it's just the three of us again, and Lady Buckford, of course," Mrs Lilley said practically, "there's little point in your cooking two separate meals, one for us and one for yourselves. It's much more economical of time and food to cook just the one dish. And just the two courses."

"But what about the Rector's cheese?" Margaret was appalled. "He can't do without that."

Mrs Lilley didn't reply. She had been opening her post, was staring at one letter, something official, it looked like.

"It's this new Women's Land Army they're recruiting for. They want the WWAC to establish hostels and training facilities in East Grinstead. Oh, I wish Caroline were here. And they want to know how many we can absorb."

"Here in the Rectory, madam?" Margaret tried not to sound horrified. She thought of the war effort; then she thought of her Tunbridge Wells training school beginning in a few days, and kept her fingers crossed the answer was no. It wouldn't do to put such an un-Christian thought up to the Lord.

"No, but I have a feeling," Mrs Lilley said gloomily, "that the farmers aren't going to like this. They've accepted the idea of the village women being paid for helping out, but female foreigners coming in, as they'll call them, could be a different matter."

"What about soldiers?"

"The new Food Production Department at the Board of Agriculture is in charge of organising their labour. The lack of skilled ploughmen amongst them is the problem, so they're opening ploughing schools for them, but by the time they're trained it will be too late for us. We could apply for prisoners of war, of course, but—"

"Germans? Working on *our* food?" Margaret was outraged. Yorkshire was one thing, but not Germans. They might poison the livestock or crops.

"It works very well, I understand," Mrs Lilley said placatingly. "In fact, um . . . um – that's to say, our area has applied for a batch. If we're accepted, we get seventy-five prisoners and about half that number of guards for them."

"We're billeting them all in the Rectory, are we?" Margaret asked grimly.

"There'd be a specially built camp in the forest."

"Oh, the *forest*." There were enough soldiers already in Ashden Forest to make sure none of the Germans was set loose on decent village girls.

"That will take some time to set up, so it's a question of how many Land Army girls we need in the meantime."

"And where they'll be living?"

"We must take a couple. I'll have to speak to my husband."

"What about The Towers, Mrs Lilley?"

Elizabeth shook her head. "The Army has only just moved in. They'll need to get the land cultivated, but they won't want a group of young women billeted with them. Or rather," she corrected herself, "they may *want* them, but it isn't perhaps advisable."

"I'll ask my Lizzie if she's any ideas."

Tunbridge Wells was creeping up in Margaret's list of worries. The first lecture was next Monday, and after all the fuss she couldn't confess that she wanted to back out. She'd been over to the Great Hall which was nice and handy for the railway station, but it hadn't been as straightforward as she had expected. She had to make decisions on equipment, stores and special ingredients. It wasn't going to be a question of popping down to Mrs Lettice's provisions shop, but of ordering from the unknown. Worst of all, they'd informed her at the Hall they'd installed one of those new-fangled electric stoves. They looked like gas, and she didn't like to admit she'd never used an electric one, so she nodded wisely instead. Then she'd tackled the shops. John Brown's bakeries were very helpful, and so was the dear old Maypole. The butcher was not.

"Of course," she'd said to him, "I do understand. Mind you, it's a pity. I was going to put on the posters that you supplied the food, and ask you to do a talk on meat shortages. "I'll ask that new provisions store with the good butchery department in Mount Pleasant. Sainsbury's, it's called."

The butcher had rapidly changed his mind, but she went to Sainsbury's anyway. Butchers were only men, and men were like children. You had to let them know where authority lay.

On Monday morning Percy took her up to the station in Dr Marden's trap. She clutched her small bag containing her favourite kitchen knife and one or two other things she couldn't do without, and hummed fiercely to tell the Lord He was her shepherd. Lady Buckford, to her surprise, had said she couldn't manage the journey, and so Lord Banning was coming to introduce the talk. What would a man know about house-keeping? It would get her off to a good start, however. She had wondered, ever since that Christmas they'd spent here together, if Miss Tilly – when she came home – would marry him. He needed a good woman about the house, though she doubted whether Miss Tilly quite fitted this description. She had been more interested in hunger strikes than in organizing good meals for a man. Still, now that women over thirty looked likely to get the vote, there would be no more of this suffragette nonsense.

Women over thirty . . . for the first time Margaret realised this included her. *She* would have the vote. So would Percy for the first time, since he hadn't been able to have his say in the country's running before, not being a house-owner. She began to feel proud. Miss Tilly had been fighting for *her*, and women who had the vote need not be scared about cooking demonstrations in Tunbridge Wells.

Her voice was never going to carry. Her tiny squawk in this vast hall? Now it was filled with 700 expectant faces, its enormous size terrified her.

"I can personally vouch," she heard Lord Banning concluding, "for the delicious results of anything cooked by Mrs Dibble's hands – or, rather, her cooker."

She'd been eyeing this brightly polished stove, trying to get its measure. A Tricity it was called, with a radiant coil boiling plate. That she could manage, and the oven looked all right. It had a temperature button arrangement, which she'd never used before. She took a deep breath.

"We all know there's a butter shortage, so I'm going to show you what you can do with cocoa butter as a tasty substitute . . ."

She never thought she'd see the day when that nasty cocoa butter had to be mixed with cottonseed oil just to bake a few cakes or make a pie. Nevertheless, she popped the scones on the top shelf in the oven, just as though she'd been cooking electric all her life, and a reassuring blast of warm air hit her.

"And while they're baking, here's an idea for something to spread on your bread." It wasn't at all bad in Margaret's view; even the Rector had approved this mixture of cocoa butter, cornflour, syrup and mashed potato, and in this cold weather it kept for a week if you were lucky.

"Next week," she glared at her audience for they seemed to be getting restless after a while, "we'll be doing scraps and saving on eggs. It beats me how the hens know about the Kaiser, but—"

The smell! She'd been so intent on melting and mixing the blessed butter, she'd forgotten the cakes – no, she hadn't. They weren't due to be ready for another five minutes. She rushed to the oven all the same and a column of blue smoke shot up as she opened the door. Inside was a tray of little black circles. *At her very first lecture*! Centuries of iron Sussex discipline came to her aid, sending the panic back where it came from.

Margaret turned round, strode to the front of the platform where they had all gathered for the demonstration and flourished the tin so they could all see. "Nothing wrong with burnt cakes," she informed them severely. "Look at King Alfred. He burnt cakes and he still did a good job for England's war effort."

The sniggers turned into a roar of laughter.

"All the same," Margaret grinned, "don't you try to do it like that. It's not everyone can manage it."

The next day Lizzie came up with the answer, just as Margaret was in the middle of telling her for the fourth time about the way to handle big audiences.

"I've had an idea, Ma."

"You're no cook, my girl."

"About these Land Army girls," her daughter explained patiently. "We'll ask all the farmers to board them themselves. The Sharpes have room now Joey's not there, and they were asking for more help, and so was Seb Grendel; and Mrs Lilley was saying the numbers from the village are falling now."

214

"More babies what with menfolk on leave."

"Ma, I'm surprised at you." Lizzie giggled. "It's not only that, anyway, it's the unmarried ones going into munitions and this Women's Army Auxiliary Corps they're recruiting for. And Jenny Bertram was saying she's off to join the Forage Corps. They're looking for girls for the army camp at King's Standing. If the Rectory takes the lead . . ." Lizzie continued nonchalantly.

"Of course," Margaret gulped valiantly. "I'll speak to Mrs Lilley."

She put off this unwelcome task in favour of going to see whether Nanny Oates could put a few from the ones she sent to Tunbridge Wells. With the spring coming on and eggs being a little more plentiful, she'd tell them about preserving them in fresh-slaked limewater so they'd last through next winter, even if the war didn't. They were a luxury food now, according to the Food Controller, owing to only a quarter of their content having food value, thus making them expensive for what they gave you. To her mind, he was talking rubbish. There was nothing like a good egg – all of it.

Although they had not seen eye to eye when she lived in the Rectory, Margaret was now on better terms with Nanny Oates; especially since eggs had been scarce.

She put on her coat and hat, and marched purposefully up Bankside, where she was surprised to find the door shut, for Nanny didn't go out now and had all her shopping delivered. It was nearly dinnertime too, and the Rector hadn't said anything about her going away. She peered in the windows, but there was no sign of Nanny.

She'd been full of life yesterday, even pottering about her garden now. Worried, Margaret went round to the back to see if she could get in through the kitchen, but that was locked too. She debated what to do next. Fetch the Rector? Ask one of the neighbours? Fetch Joe Ifield, the village policeman? The Rector, she decided.

Five minutes later she was back, accompanied by the Rector and Agnes, as the most agile of them if they had to climb in a window, but the Rector managed to force the scullery door open. There was still no sign of Nanny, and Margaret braced herself. "I'll go upstairs."

"I'll go," the Rector said firmly, to her relief.

He disappeared up the staircase to the two small bedrooms upstairs, and they listened to his footsteps hurrying across the ceiling above them. A moment or two later he appeared again. "Agnes," he called gently. "Go to fetch Dr Marden, will you?"

As Agnes ran out, Margaret gathered her strength. She was needed up there, so up she went.

Nanny Oates had had a stroke. Dr Marden had come and said it would do more harm than good to move her immediately, and someone should sit with her to see what movement started to come back. At the moment she couldn't speak more than a gabble of words, and couldn't move her left side at all. Margaret had offered to stay, but Mrs Lilley had refused to let her, and gone over herself, having made arrangements for Mrs Hay, the midwife, to relieve her and stay overnight. Mrs Lilley returned just in time for dinner, and Mrs Isabel had come over from the cinema as usual. Margaret was keeping on eye on Myrtle serving the soup and was witness to a most surprising conversation.

"Can't she come here?" Mrs Isabel enquired, shocked at the news about Nanny.

"Dr Marden thinks it best not to move her for the moment. We'll have to find someone for tomorrow and tomorrow night. I'll do it if necessary."

"No, I'll do it," Mrs Isabel had said suddenly. You could have knocked Margaret down with a feather. "I could move in there and we'd just find relief for the times when I'm working."

"It means staying there until she's well enough to be moved." Mrs Lilley was very doubtful, and rightly, in Margaret's view.

"And there's only that cold tap, darling. Where would you sleep? The second bedroom is little more than a cupboard."

"I'll manage." Mrs Isabel had that obstinate look on her face.

She'd never cope, of course, Margaret thought. Mrs Isabel liked her comforts, and as well as the one tap, Nanny only had an outside earth closet.

"Isabel dear," her mother pointed out gently, "Nanny can't turn herself, and she'd need help with *everything.*"

"We've got that old commode chair. I'll clean that up, and if I need help, I'll . . . I'll . . . get Ben Brock's wife to help. The Norrington Arms is only a few doors along."

The doubt still showed on Mrs Lilley's face for Mrs Isabel burst out: "You don't think I can, do you, Mother? Or you, Father. You're keeping very quiet. You don't think I can do *anything*, but I can. I'll show you."

"But the cooking—" Mrs Lilley began helplessly, and this time Margaret spoke out.

"I can manage that, Mrs Lilley. I'll send Myrtle over with it, three times a day."

"That's very good of you," Mrs Isabel replied. "I'm not a very good cook."

She was no cook at all, in Margaret's opinion, but this time Mrs Isabel stuck to her word and stayed for two weeks with Nanny Oates. Nanny got some movement back in her arms and legs, even getting on her feet with Isabel and a strong stick supporting her, and a few words came back to her. All the same, it was a great worry for the Rector, and though Mrs Isabel said she'd stay on, he wouldn't let her. Instead, the Rector had come to see her, Margaret. She had known what he was going to ask immediately: "About Nanny, Mrs Dibble—"

"We'll manage, Rector. Bring her here."

He looked amazed at her speedy acquiescence, but she squared up her shoulders. If Mrs Isabel could do it, so could she.

"I could ask Lady Gwendolen—"

Margaret pooh-poohed this immediately. "What would Nanny Oates do in Wiltshire or Dover, Rector? Here's where she lives."

But where, was the problem, she'd realised after he'd gone. And after where would follow how and who. It was all very well doing your Christian duty, but the glow always came first and the hard work followed.

The evening post brought a forces letter with a strange handwriting. It couldn't be Fred, for he couldn't write. But it was in a way, for someone had written for him.

Dear Mrs Dibble,
Fred wants to tell you we're [the next few words had been blacked out by the censor] and he won't be on potatoes no longer. Yours sincerely, Archie.

Now what did that mean? Why did everything have to happen together? *We're* must mean they were moving somewhere else. Not on potatoes. What did that mean? It could mean anything from Fred having been put on peeling carrots to going in the trenches. Margaret decided not to show the letter to Percy, he'd be upset. Then she decided she would. After all, *she* was upset, and what were husbands for?

Thirteen

W ould this winter never end? It would soon be May and
there was little sign of spring yet. Caroline missed the
Ashdown Forest, where the birdsong, flowers and trees gave
more hints of changing seasons than the clifftops of Kent. Even
the birds were keeping their heads down in this cold weather,
and she envied them. Sometimes she could picture life at the
Rectory so clearly, it seemed as though she had just to walk
through a door and there she would be. Perhaps she was seeing
an idealised Rectory, not the real beehive it was. Beehive wasn't
the right word, however, for bees worked for a common cause,
whereas increasingly the Rectory seemed to house as many
different causes as there were people. When she had last visited
home for a weekend, two weeks ago, her mother was deep in the
worries of planning to increase village food production, now
that the Kaiser's submarine campaign of unrestricted warfare
was biting deep, and her task was made more difficult with the
long hard winter slowing down the usual pattern of growth.
The Board of Agriculture's 'Plough-up Britain' campaign was
all very well, but it needed organisation.

Caroline had been amused to hear that the very day the act
came into force, an officer from The Towers had visited her
mother, anxious to be co-operative. The two Land Army girls
lodged at the Rectory had promptly been allotted to The
Towers estate for belated hop-cultivation. After a few false
starts, including a certain amount of misunderstanding by some
of the soldiers detailed to work with them as to the girls' role

219

there, it was at last getting into shape. With the help of advice from Lizzie and one or two old hands from the village, the hops were already planted, stringing complete, and dressing in progress. There was markedly more interest among the co-opted soldiers in producing a hop harvest than fields of potatoes.

It was all splendid work, but what had happened to the Rectory, the serene hub of the village? With strangers in and out all day long, it reminded Caroline of her own office, and she acknowledged her nose was out of joint.

"When this war ends, our old ways will return," her father assured her. The mere sight of the two Land Army girls at dinner had convinced her otherwise, however. Unlike Miss Burrows, who had, cuckoo in the nest or not, fitted in to the Rectory, these two had a self-assured awareness of their role in Ashden, and to them it was definitely not home.

Caroline had promptly nicknamed them Chalk and Cheese. Chalk was a stalwart fisherman's daughter from Grimsby, Cheese a squire's daughter from Gloucestershire, shy and at first, so her mother told her, utterly bemused at finding herself in a Sussex rectory. Chalk had promptly clapped Cheese under her protective wing, especially when there were soldiers about, and with some initial difficulty over baths, all was now running smoothly. One of them had seen no need of the facility, the other had over-indulged. Only if Lady Buckford appeared would Chalk promptly cede the role of Indian chief to Cheese.

Lady Buckford, once assured she would not have to sit (yet) at the same table as her former nanny, had begun to appear regularly in the dining-room, and Caroline suspected she enjoyed the diversion of the two La-Las, as Father called them since he could never remember their names.

Nanny had been allotted Aunt Tilly's room with her permission since it overlooked the driveway and her chair could be pulled close to the window to give her a view almost as lively as she'd had on Bankside. She had recovered more feeling, and was able to hobble round her room with the help of two sticks and an anxious eye. Her speech, thanks chiefly to Isabel who spent many hours encouraging her, was also returning little by little. Would she return to Bankside? Caroline had asked, but no one knew the answer.

Her mother still missed Phoebe and George. Phoebe was at the end of her drilling training in Folkestone which Caroline had often watched from the office window with great amusement. Who would have thought that smart khaki-clad young lady was the slapdash Phoebe to whom sewing on a button ranked bottom in her list of abilities? She had grown annoyed when Caroline laughed at the drilling.

"I'm trained to drive motor cars, not march," she said crossly.

"It's the discipline," Caroline pointed out sweetly.

"You try it," Phoebe had replied vehemently. "Only a few days, and I'll be overseas. The first contingent left at the end of March, and now it's my turn. Oh, the bliss."

"Where to?" Bliss wasn't the word Caroline would have used.

"I won't tell you what I've applied for because I haven't heard yet and it's bad luck."

"Father says there's no such thing."

"Father isn't in the Women's Army Auxiliary Corps." That's what the new organisation would be called, even if despite the recruitment and training in progress, the Army authorities were still arguing over the details of setting it up.

Robert too had now gone overseas and Isabel had been very depressed when Caroline had last seen her. He'd had an unexpected forty-eight hour leave, and then been rushed off to France, where reinforcements were urgently needed for observation balloons on the Front at Arras where the new British offensive had begun, with what really seemed like success this time. Caroline had been vastly relieved that it was not Ypres, though most of their information from Belgium earlier in the year had pointed to that. It was another sign that

221

more immediate results could be gained for St Omer by observation over the Front.

She had been growing uneasy about her work in Folkestone, and had discussed it with James Swan, but always Luke brushed aside any such debate. In March the Germans had unbelievably begun to retreat to the Siegfried Line in the St Quentin area, and the office had buzzed with speculation as to whether they were heading back to Germany, or re-positioning for a new offensive by strengthening their line. They had burned everything in a fifteen-kilometre-wide area in front of the line, and forced the population east with them. The indications they received in Folkestone that they were planning to attack had turned out to be false, though understandable in the circumstances. Somehow the Germans had got wind that Arras was where the British would strike, and were strengthening their defence.

Going into the bureau was both relief and torture. She knew she was involved in an important job which filled her daily life and gave her companionship, but it rammed home that Yves was no longer there. Now she knew he was in this country, it was obvious he still came to Folkestone to visit the Belgian section if not their own, yet she had heard no word of him. She devoured the *Franco-Belge* every week, for her French was now up to it, but she never saw his name.

Early in April, Daniel had come down to Folkestone to crow over the good news that his predictions over the Zimmermann telegram were right. Just in the nick of time, with the uncertain position on the Russian front now the Tsar had abdicated, America had declared war.

"I feel as though I'm responsible for it all by myself," he boasted.

"You are," she assured him earnestly, hunting through her stew to see if she could track down any meat. So much for *casserole au printemps*. Vegetable stew or not, she was delighted to be out with Daniel for she seldom went out in the evenings now. Suppose she met Yves at one of the Belgian clubs, and he was forced to display politeness towards her? She knew this was cowardly; if women were to claim their new place in society, they had to accept the bad as well as the good. Fathers could no longer protect their daughters' aching hearts by demanding an honourable return of recalcitrant lovers. She may have the vote when she was thirty, but she wouldn't have Yves. Just at the moment, it didn't seem much compensation.

On 23rd April Luke took her to the cinema to see *Intolerance*, the new American film directed by D. W. Griffith set in Biblical times but oh, how relevant to today. It did not exactly cheer her up, and as they picked their way back to Sandgate Road, stumbling in the dark over kerbstones, she decided to tackle Luke head-on about her concern in the office. She was forestalled by Luke's announcing:

"I've managed to persuade Lissy to come to Paris for two days in May."

"You have remarkable powers of persuasion. She doesn't like Paris."

"I didn't realise she knew it."

"She was at school there at Grandmother's insistence for six unhappy months until Father came over to rescue her. She was so shy."

"That's very interesting. Do you recognise the same woman now?"

"No, but I understand the same woman. Does that make sense?"

"Caroline, you always make sense. When we're related—"

"If," she corrected politely.

"Silence, woman. On the other hand, ignore that last order. You said you didn't know why Daniel won't marry her. Do you ever hazard a guess?"

She hesitated. "Yes. Something to do with his injuries."

"And if we're right, which would you say was the best life for Felicia – with me and a family, or with Daniel, whom she loves."

"I don't know. I don't understand. I don't presume to know how men think, how my own sister thinks, nothing," she answered vehemently.

"Then let us discuss work like two patriotic souls doing their bit for their country."

Caroline grasped the opportunity he had unwittingly given her. "Have you noticed, Luke, there's something odd about the intelligence we're getting?"

"In what way?"

Was it her imagination or did Luke's voice suddenly sound detached?

"None of it seems to turn out right although it fits in with the current situation. Does that sound silly?" she added uncertainly, for he said nothing when she paused. "For instance," she continued, "in March, our intelligence pointed to an attack by Prince Rupprecht's Command in the north, which seemed to be confirmed by those crack troops arriving in Belgium from Romania – yet nothing happened, except that our resources may have been deflected from their prime need at Arras. Yet it's not false information, because those German troops could easily have been sent down to Arras when the Germans realised the offensive was there and not on the Belgian front. Since we've no links in northern France, we wouldn't know.

"And, again," she added, when he did not reply, "it's obvious the enemy is concentrating on defending the Siegfried line when our intelligence suggested all these extra divisions were being moved up to Sixth Army—"

"It's always easier with hindsight to realise why troops were sent to any one place," Luke interrupted lightly. He began to whistle 'Oh, oh what a lovely war' which irritated her intensely.

"This isn't a vague observation," she said impatiently. "I can pinpoint the source. It's the information collected by Olivier Fabre that—"

He stopped her with a sharp, "Caroline, that's enough."

His lack of interest puzzled her. "But surely if I have suspicions I'm right to report them to you. And look at the reports he brought from the network last week. One was supposed to be from Raoul Mishaert, but he usually uses a mapping pen. This was typed."

"Caroline, please hold on to your hat."

At last she understood. "You know."

"Take great care, Caroline. Forget everything about Olivier Fabre. Go on thinking if you must, but never, never suggest what you've just told me in your digests, or let it influence you in any way. Clear?"

"Yes, but—"

"Didn't your father ever tell you there are no buts in the Kingdom of Heaven?"

She managed to laugh. "You'd fit well into our family."

"That's the nicest compliment you've ever paid me. Come to that, it's the only one."

All very well, she ruminated when she was back in her room, but how did Yves fit into this? Yves had been with Olivier Fabre in Ashden at Christmas together with Henri and, apparently independently, Luke. Now Yves had disappeared, and she had had suspicions about Olivier Fabre's loyalty. All sorts of wild, fanciful thoughts raced through her mind: was Yves himself compromised in his work? Did he too now believe that Belgium's best chance of economic survival might lie with Germany? No. Even the foggy thinking of late evening rejected this. She had to trust her own judgement, and her love for Yves had grown out of respect for his integrity; she was not being swayed by emotion.

Then a worse fear arose. If Fabre was a German plant, had Yves discovered this fact, and Fabre murdered him? She told herself this nightmare would disappear with the coming of the day, but sleep did not come for some long while.

Today she had received a letter from home, sending on a recent letter from George to her parents and then passed on to her (thank you, little brother) full of jolly talk of how much he enjoyed the flying in France, and the glorious deeds of 56 Squadron and the famous Albert Ball. The squadron had been in France for only a week when he wrote the letter but at least it gave the reassurance that he was still alive. And so were Felicia and Tilly, but for how much longer? Luke guessed Haig would make an all-out attack to win the war, after the success of Arras. And where else could it be than Ypres?

The following evening was Phoebe's last in Folkestone, and Caroline dined with her at the Metropole with her – if dine was the word with army rations. Privacy was impossible sitting on long tables and surrounded by a muddy sea of khaki, but afterwards they managed to find a quiet spot to talk.

Despite the drab effect of the khaki on a face meant for bright colours, Phoebe sparkled in a way Caroline hadn't seen since Harry's death. "I can tell you what I'm going to do now," she said, bubbling with enthusiasm. "I didn't think the War Office would confirm it till I got to France, but they have. I'm going to be one of the drivers for Lena Ashwell's concert parties, and other entertainers. I'll be attached to St Omer, but picking up at Calais and Boulogne, and taking the singers round the bases."

"Oh, Phoebe, what a splendid job."

"You mean you're glad I'm not going to be sitting in a front-line trench like Felicia," Phoebe retorted percipiently.

"Perhaps a little of that. Two of you there would be very hard for us all."

"It was actually George who arranged it for me."

"How on earth did he manage that?"

"He has all sorts of chums now in London through his cartoons. Funny, isn't it – all the fuss that Father made about them, and now he's almost as famous as Bairnsfather. Anyway, he met Lena Ashwell, who told him all about her problems now the men from the Motor Transport Section were necessary for front-line work, and went to see Sir John, who shunted him to the right person at the War Office. He suggested they use some of the newly trained WAACs. It may mean driving army transport wagons, and I'll have to get used to driving on the wrong side of the road, but won't it be fun?"

"Yes," Caroline agreed instantly. There would be time enough for Phoebe to discover the other side of the war. The famous actress Lena Ashwell had been a suffragette and just like Aunt Tilly, when war came, she put suffrage to one side to concentrate on what she could do for the troops.

Phoebe laughed. "Poor Father. Not only George, but now here's me and Isabel linked with the entertainment business."

"Not so poor Father. I would think he'll be pleased. After all, he wanted to go on the stage himself, but followed the Church instead."

"I never knew that," Phoebe exclaimed. "How strange, yet I suppose, judging by his sermons, he'd have been a good actor."

"A touch of the Henry Irvings about him, isn't there?"

"More than that of Dan Leno, I agree."

"Unfair. Think of the Family Coach at Christmas."

Unfortunately, Caroline thought about it herself – and was promptly reminded of Yves. Phoebe too, for she asked: "What's happened to that nice Belgian officer who brought stars to your eyes at Christmas, Caroline?"

Caroline stared down at the cocoa dregs. "He brought too many. I haven't seen him since, but for one brief visit."

"That's very odd. Was he posted away?"

Caroline decided she could not talk about it. Instead, she turned the attack. "Do you realise, Phoebe, this is the first straight talk we've had in years?"

"That's because for the first time you're not speaking to me as a little sister. Because I'm wearing a uniform, you realise I'm grown up now and age doesn't matter any longer."

"Provided you still show me some respect," Caroline agreed. "Will you like being overseas, do you think?"

Her sister looked surprised. "Yes. You know how I've always wanted to get away. That's why I was so upset when war came and I couldn't go to school in Paris. It wasn't the school I cared about; I just wanted to get away from Ashden."

"But why? Don't you like the village?" Caroline was astounded. How could any of them not have deep feelings for it?

Phoebe considered. "It was the Rectory I wanted to leave. I felt like an ugly duckling, and I knew I'd always feel like that unless I got away. And now at last I have."

"You look like the loveliest ugly duckling I've ever seen," Caroline joked, despite her concern. How could you grow up with someone and have so little idea of what they were feeling? Phoebe had always been a problem, but how often had she stopped to ask herself why?

"You were always jolly nice to me, Caroline, but from the lofty height of Elder Sister. I couldn't talk to George, Felicia scared me and Isabel – well, Isabel is Isabel."

"Not any more. She's changing."

"Because of that business with Reggie?"

"You knew about that?" Caroline was horrified. She had thought it buried, a secret between herself and Isabel.

"I had a lot of time to see what was going on. You wouldn't have been happy with him, Caroline – Isabel or no Isabel, Lady Hunney or no Lady Hunney."

"Suppose I'd said that about Harry?"

Phoebe shot a look at her. "He and I didn't have time to find that out."

"And you were very young."

"I was eighteen. That was another reason I needed to get away. There was Isabel married to Rich Robert, there was you engaged to Rally-Round-the-Flag Reggie, Felicia firmly wedded in heart to Daniel – and my love didn't seem like any of yours. Meeting Harry was like—" she sought for words—"coming home out of a heavy storm on a dark night. I'd been battling to get out of the storm for years. I suppose that's why I teased Christopher Denis so much. I feel rather sorry about that now."

"You went very quiet about that time," Caroline remembered.

"They don't tell you at home or in books about the bad side of what's between men and women. I had a scare," she said jerkily.

"You'd better tell me," Caroline said quietly.

"Len Thorn—"

"*What*? Phoebe, he didn't—"

"No, but nearly. I got away. But a lot of it was my fault. It plunged me into that storm though."

"But it's over since you met Harry."

"Almost. He showed me what love really was."

"There's a path between Harry and the dark storm. You'll find it, Phoebe."

"If I do, it's thanks to Harry. I'll never forget him. Never. War is so unfair. Like," she gave Caroline a mischievous look, "you and your captain."

Caroline laughed at having the tables turned. "He's gone and I doubt if I'll see him again."

"What would Father have said if you had married a Roman Catholic – he is, isn't he? – and went to live in Belgium?"

"He'd say, 'At last I've got rid of you'."

"You're not playing fair, Caroline. I told you what I felt about Harry – you owe it to me to be honest too, or I'll accuse you of elder sisterdom."

Caroline was caught. She had to talk about it. "It's probably only wounded vanity. It changed so suddenly. Up to Christmas, Yves was just there, I looked forward to seeing him but I didn't ask myself why; somehow I just accepted he was part of me. Does that sound stupid?"

"No. I'm envious. I didn't have long enough with Harry to do that."

"Then at Christmas, we kissed and everything changed. He

seemed – I seemed – to be a different person. He came to the Rectory on the day after Boxing Day, and it was as if we shared some wonderful secret; he didn't even kiss me again, only once as he left. I thought this was a brave new world I'd glimpsed. If it was, Mr Wells' time machine dumped me firmly back into 1917. I haven't seen Yves since he called to say goodbye at the office a few days later. I feel as if half of me had been ripped away and left me limping along with half a life. Stupid, I know. I have work, I have my darling family. Perhaps I was grasping at straws after Reggie's death, and someday I'll meet someone else far more suitable."

"That's what I tell myself too. It doesn't help one bit, does it?"

"No," Caroline agreed gratefully.

"To God with heart and cheerful voice . . ." Margaret's cheerful voice was in fine fettle this morning, even though Myrtle was using the now Komo Handy Mop ('dust laughs at ordinary brooms') like a scrubbing brush. He deserved a spring hymn in May, even though everybody in the pea-pod was forgetting they were all under the same pod roof. Mrs Lilley was spending more and more time on her job again, not because she wanted to but because she had to, so the Government said. Margaret was beginning to see herself as the hub of the Rectory, holding the whole wheel together and making it turn, and she was proud of it. *And* she was doing a war job in Tunbridge Wells too. Her talks were popular and she had to organise more classes. The telephone was always ringing nowadays, and all too often it was for her. The ladies always needed to know about something or other. The Rector had joked about paying for another line once the war was over.

Meanwhile, His Majesty had pointed out by royal proclamation that the way to achieve this was to save bread. They had meatless days, potatoless days, now breadless days. No flour to be used in pastry, and every household to reduce their consumption of bread by at least one quarter.

Miss Caroline had a face as long as a fiddle when she came home last week. Missing Miss Phoebe probably. Margaret had gone so far as to ask her what was wrong, to which she had announced gloomily that she felt like the waste crust on that new propaganda poster, the bit left over.

"I am a slice of bread," she intoned dismally. "I measure three inches by two and a half and my thickness is half an inch. Alas, I am wasted every day."

Bread or no bread, spring weather was here, and life was looking brighter at last. Fred must be all right or she'd have heard. The Tommies were on the march in France; one more push, so Percy said, and those Germans would be running back home with their tails between their legs. There was hope in the air.

It was Friday, 25th May. In Folkestone, Caroline read her mother's latest letter three times. Oh, to be in Ashden now that spring was here. There the blackbird would be singing in the tree outside her window, and daffodils would have given way to tulips, forget-me-nots and bluebells. Everyone said the war was as good as over, now the Americans were in it, and she hadn't had a spot or toothache for a month. She put on the spring hat she'd treated herself to, and set off to work.

Fourteen

S un was a marvellous thing, even though her mother always
tut-tutted, warning her about its dangers. Caroline never
took the advice seriously, although looking at her mother's still
perfect complexion, perhaps she should. In a belated attack of
conscience, she pulled the brim of the new hat a little further
over her forehead.

As she emerged on to the front to turn towards the office, a
whiff of the sea caught her nostrils. Since the Leas was
unusually free of tramping columns of khaki, it was easy to
imagine that old-fashioned bathing machines still lined the
town beach, one end of which was allotted to gentlemen, the
other to lady bathers; and that beyond that, safe from dis-
approving eyes, white tents adorned another beach on which
both male and female daringly consorted in decorous costumes.
If she were to stroll up to the Metropole, would Madame de
Pompadour, as Caroline called the doyenne of Folkestone
society, be presiding over tea and delicate *petits fours*, or would
the familiar sea of khaki meet her eyes?

In fact Caroline was now part of the khaki brigade. The
Government had decided that since they had graciously allowed women into the uniformed services, all women working
for them should be in uniform. Caroline loathed khaki since
khaki loathed her, but there was a certain pleasure in not only
feeling but looking like part of the war effort. Nobody seemed
sure, but perhaps she was even a WAAC herself. She had
certainly received a visit from administrative staff of the new

corps, detailed to hand out uniforms to all fry, grander and lesser. She was the proud possessor of khaki skirt, brown boots, khaki jacket, wide-brimmed hat. The rest of the paraphernalia, like thick knickers, she was expected to provide herself, or so Phoebe had told her with an earnest and straight face before she left. Her jacket didn't fit; although it was supposed to be a thirty-four chest-measurement, it felt more like a sleeping bag, and now the sun was shining at last, she often abandoned it in the office and worked in her own blouse.

The few flowers on the cliffside this year were last year's tulips, which looked as if they were apologising for their presence in these times when every bit of spare land should be ploughed up for spring vegetables. She was glad to see them, for spring was a strange season: it should make one feel better, but sometimes it did not; it summoned you to achievement, whether you could cope with it or not. In George's last letter he had written of his camp, which they had managed to discover through Sir John was at Vert Galant near Amiens. He had been listening to the birds chirping on the airfield, just as if he were at the Rectory. Only he wasn't, and no amount of cheering talk could disguise it from his family. Two years ago, getting any letter from George was an event; now he was away himself, he too was obviously thinking of home, sending them special cartoons. It made them laugh, but they were undeceived.

Caroline had been impressed to see from a copy of the parish magazine, now produced by Beatrice Ryde, that Father had had a change of heart. Once George's cartoons were deemed too strong for Ashden; now he insisted, according to Mother, that one was put in every month – even those to do with the war. Gone were the days when Father could hope to exclude war from its columns, for the bereavement notices and memorial service reports had taken the place of many of the staple reports of the festivals and events that had hitherto formed the ritual of the Rectory and church year. Father had tried to struggle on with them, but against ever greater odds. Who was to organise them? Who to attend? And why bother when there were greater priorities on people's time? Rogation had come and gone with no mention of beating the parish bounds this year. The flower show would no longer be a bone of contention, for there were no flowers. It was a vegetable show alone. Moreover, Mrs Dibble was to be one of the three judges in her new role as Government authority on use of food. She had gone quite pink when Father had asked her, and muttered that the show was for the gentry. She didn't refuse, however.

Caroline hurried into the bureau at nine o'clock, determined to enjoy every minute of this spring day, even work. Luke was normally in before her, but today there was no sign of him, although one or two of her fellow clerks had arrived. When, fifteen minutes later, he did appear, he came not through the front door but down the stairs.

"Meeting," he explained briefly, "in Captain Cameron's room." Instead of putting the usual heap of reports and digests before her, he asked, "Can you run over to the French bureau, Caroline? I can't do it today, and someone has to represent us. They like you."

"Only because I'm female," she pointed out. "They'd like the fat lady from the circus."

She had been wanting to see the new batch of reports from Olivier Fabre, and she disliked the French bureau. Polite, and indeed over polite, though they were, the exclusively male staff seemed more interested in what lay under her uniform than what she had brought in her hand, and there were always pressing invitations – sometimes literally – to dinner and when that was refused, luncheon.

"They're having their GHQ liaison chap there today, and need a representative from this office present in case he has any questions."

She thought she understood. After the British success at Arras and the disastrous French attack last month, there must be urgent talks in progress. No one could even guess what would happen on the Russian front now Kerensky had taken control, but that made it all too probable that any new western offensive would be speedy and in the Ypres sector, in order to try to regain the Belgian ports.

When Caroline arrived at the meeting, the spoken French was too fast for her much of the time, but she was proud of being able to answer – in French – all but one of the few questions they addressed to her (while watching her indulgently as though surprised to hear a woman talk at all of such masculine matters). It took all day, and luncheon – although markedly superior to the sandwich she usually eat on the seafront – was brought in. By the time she was free to go it was gone five-thirty, and she galloped back to report to Luke, before dashing down to the shops in the town centre. She had arranged to go out that evening to the cinema with a friend and had promised her landlady she'd buy her some vegetables and meat before she did so. Mrs Clark did not trust food delivered now; few did, for the delivery boys were merely filling in time before they were called up; it wasn't a career like it used to be, according to Mrs Clark. They'd dump the stuff in the gutter if they felt like it, and that's all it was fit for half the time, even if you queued. On the whole, running her errands was preferable to receiving the orders, Caroline decided.

"Luke, the French are talking about unreliable networks," she probed gently. "Talk about it tomorrow?"

"Just keep your bright ideas under that ghastly brown hat of yours just a little longer, sweetheart." He grinned maddeningly and she considered whether to ignore the insult or hit him. Ignore it. She rushed upstairs to the first floor where the grand bathroom and water closet of the former house lay, used them, wondered briefly whether the ornate bath on its pretty little legs was ever used nowadays, unbolted the door and dashed out to hurry downstairs and pick up her jacket. She pitchforked herself straight into a group of officers descending from Captain Cameron's upper sanctum. "I'm sorry—" She broke off.

236

It was Yves.

He looked as appalled as she, though he could hardly have been surprised to see her. That was why she'd been sent out of the way, she realised with sinking heart. He'd been there all day, and asked Luke to get rid of her so that he should not be embarrassed by her presence. Well, *he wouldn't be.*

"Please excuse me," she said stiffly, bowed her head in brief acknowledgement of Captain Cameron, and hurtled down the stairs.

Through her confusion, she heard Yves shout something out, then footsteps coming down after her, but she did not look back. She seized her jacket and hat, crammed them on as she ran to the door, opened it, and escaped into the blessed outside world. She shut the door behind her, and it did not open again. She gulped in the sea air to steady her and reminded herself it was her own fault: she had been foolish in thinking that because he had kissed her, he felt about her as she did about him. She had been wrong, that was all. His work was taking him away, and he had dismissed her from his mind. If she took this calmly, her heart as well as her brain would see that was so, and she could proceed with her own life.

Automatically she turned towards the Sandgate Road, then, remembering the dratted shopping, hurried back towards the town centre. She needed some cottons, for mending – Oh, Agnes, where are you? – so she'd go all the way to Tontine Street where she could pop into Gosnold's drapery emporium, go to the best greengrocer, the wonderful Messrs Stokes, that nice Mr Hall the pork butcher, and pick up a copy of *Picture-goer* to indulge herself. She'd be finished in fifteen minutes with luck, and back home in half an hour at most. Then she could pull herself together to get over the shock she'd had.

How could all these people be carrying on life so normally? A woman screaming at a toddler, a Tommy with his arm round a girl, a milk-roundsman, an evening-paper seller. To them it was just another evening, to her it was Friday, 25th May, and the death of her hopes. No use telling herself she was lucky to be here and not in the trenches, where life was counted in hours not years, where friends made one day were memories the next. Just at the moment she wished she were anyone but Caroline Lilley.

She squinted up in the sky, hearing the sound of a low aeroplane engine as she reached the Slope. With all the RFC camps around, they were so frequent nowadays that no one else bothered to look up, but she gave it a friendly wave on George's behalf. Then someone else did look up, and said something to his companion, who looked up too. Odd. She felt faintly uneasy until the sound of explosions in the distance relaxed her.

How stupid. It was only gun practice. Nothing had been wrong at all. Nevertheless she quickened her step, and turned up Harbour Street. More explosions, nearer, louder. A woman screamed. A man shouted: "It's the Fleet. The whole bloody Hun fleet's in the harbour." But it wasn't to the harbour she looked. It was up into the blue sky she'd so admired that morning.

Everyone was gazing up now, and it wasn't just one place, it was a whole formation roaring towards them. "God bless the RFC," someone shouted. Someone cheered. The aircraft were almost overhead, and splitting up, fanning out. Then fear gripped her, stifled her, as a man yelled out: "They're fucking Huns!"

Almost instantly she was swallowed up in deafening noise all around her; her own scream and those of the people around her were indistinguishable, each in their own isolated pockets of terror, surrounded by a wall of thunder. The ground beneath her was shaking, and she was cannoned into a fruit barrow, rocking at her side. Ahead of her in Tontine Street an enormous pall of smoke and dust was rising, and the noise went on. Around her, many people were instinctively rushing for shelter, but she managed to stay still by gripping the barrow. Why court danger in buildings that might be on the point of collapse?

238

Further off the bombs were obviously still falling. She was choking on the debris falling all around her. When the noise stopped, there was an eerie silence, more frightening than anything that preceded it. Around her she could see people crouched in doorways, or lying on the ground where they had thrown themselves. And, ahead of them, where the first bomb had fallen, lay what?

The terrible memory of the night of the Gaiety bomb rose up to engulf her, the torn-off limbs, the mutilated torsos, the blood, and worse. And she must face it again; she was trained in first aid.

Her legs refused to work. Why couldn't she force them to propel her towards the carnage that must lie ahead? She wanted to go, she had to go, but she couldn't move. She found herself crouching on the ground, hugging her knees, rocking to and fro, cowering in fear, moaning. The horror swelled up inside her, and burst out in one uncontrollable angry cry.

"Not again! Dear God, not again!"

Then arms seized her from behind, forced her to her feet, and held her close.

"Caroline, *cara mia, cara mia,*" nothing else, just that repeated over and over as he stroked her hair and soothed her, dust and debris still floating down. She could hear nothing else save the sound of bells, church bells, fire-engine bells – what did it matter? Nothing mattered.

"Not again," she sobbed once more into Yves' shoulder.

"Never again, *never*. Are you hurt?"

Was she hurt? Something must have hit her hard for there was blood all down one arm, but she didn't seem otherwise injured. So that meant—

"I can't," she whispered. "I can't go into *that*."

"You must, *cara*, with me. We both must. Only for a little while."

"With you?"

"Yes."

239

Tears that she was too weak to control streamed down her face, she stumbled on, his arm round her, stopping at doorways to see if there were injured, until they reached Tontine Street. He glanced at her anxiously.

"Stay here, *cara*, I will go."

"I'm coming." Somehow she found the strength. If Felicia could do it, so could she – now Yves was there. He put out a hand to steady her, and she fixed her gaze on it. She couldn't let go of his hands again.

And so they entered Tontine Street.

Where was the greengrocers? That huge shop was only a pile of timber. The front of Gosnold's opposite had vanished. The butcher's shop a little further along was on the point of collapse, and many others. And where were the hundreds of shoppers, chiefly women and children, who would have been here filling the shops and thronging the streets? She forced herself to look ahead of her. They were dead, dying or injured. Parts of bodies lay mixed with timber, brick and stone. Those who had sheltered in shop doorways lay heaped together, dead and covered with rubble, hands, feet, baskets sticking out to reveal their presence. Colour, save for red, had vanished in a mound of grey. The red was blood and—

Stop, she told her heaving stomach. She could only cope if she took one tiny step at a time. She had to deal with what was in front of her at the moment. Yves had gone now and she must work alone. At her feet was a woman lying on her back, bleeding heavily and with a beam of wood across her. She felt calmer, for she knew what to do. She took a deep breath and began.

Two hours later she slammed the doors of the last ambulance shut on the last casualty, brought out of the wreckage of Stokes. The fire brigade had left some time ago after dealing with a fractured gas main, and telling them that bombs had fallen all over Folkestone, Cheriton, Lympne and Hythe. There was little talk, for everyone was preoccupied with rescue work. Later would come the reckoning. Mr Stokes had been killed, and now his fourteen-year-old son was being brought out, not likely to live, the ambulance men had told her. The butcher, that nice man – no, she would not think about it. This was but one evening, she told herself. Felicia coped every day.

She looked round, but there seemed nothing more for her to do. Now it was over, great waves of nausea hit her, starting somewhere deep in her stomach, forcing their way up, were repelled but at last conquered. She staggered over to what had been a shop doorway, leaned over and brought up all her sickness, revulsion and fear, coughing and retching. When at last she stood shakily upright, Yves was at her side again. She said nothing for there was nothing to say, nothing to do except to walk away from the stench of fear. Yves was cut and bleeding, covered in dirt. He looked at her with tired dark eyes. "Come," he said, and led her back along Harbour Street.

The streets were crowded as everyone came out with their own whispered stories of carnage and bereavements, but she could still say nothing. On the harbour front, he stopped at a fountain which miraculously still spouted water.

"Drink," he said, and she bent over the spout feeling the cool liquid dribble into the inferno of her nightmare. Then he wiped her mouth with the only clean spot on his handkerchief.

"Where are we going?" she asked.

"Home."

"No!" Caroline stood still. Not Sandgate Road, even if the house still stood. Perhaps it too was gutted, and Mrs Clark one of the bodies lying in the mortuary. And if it were unscathed, she could not face the ghoulish chatter – or was it that she could not face the loneliness of herself?

"My home," Yves corrected.

"Belgium?" Her brain seemed to be dulled to the point of stupidity.

"Hythe. If I still have a house there. The fire chief said

241

nineteen bombs fell there. Luke said you had gone to the town. When I heard the bomb, I—" He broke off. "My car is up on the Leas. Can you walk that far?"

"Yes." Provided it was out in the air and not in the town. It was almost dark now, and their progress was therefore even slower.

He lived in Hythe, he had said. It didn't make sense to her, nothing made sense any more with her ears still partly blocked by the aftermath of the explosions; everything seemed distant and unreal.

Unquestioningly she climbed up into the staff car, unable to cope with what was happening to her, or why Yves was still with her. The whole town seemed to be milling about on the Leas, a peaceful beehive had turned into an angry wasps' nest of civilians and soldiers. She thought she ought to make an effort to speak.

"Shouldn't you be with your Belgian friends? Aren't there things you should do?" Things? What did she mean? Her words fell into a deep pool of silence.

Then he replied: "There is work for me here to do that is more important."

He drove the car at a snail's pace to avoid congregating people as well as because of the dimmed headlights. What was the point of dimming them now? she wondered. The enemy had done its bit for tonight, surely. Not even the Germans would dare come back again; the whole of the Royal Flying Corps would be up to meet them. Rules were rules, of course. For some reason this struck her as very, very funny, and she began to laugh. Then she was unable to stop.

Yves halted the car on the Sandgate seafront, and the sound of the crashing waves seemed a Wagnerian background for her laughter. He pulled her out of the car and down onto the shingle beach, she could feel the stones through her boots, and that seemed funny too. He turned her into the night wind, which was cool and sharp, so that it blew hard against her face, bringing the spray with it. He held her until sobs followed the laughter, then held her closer until she could feel the thump of his heart.

Calm brought weariness and Caroline only dimly remembered jumping down from the car, and his leading her into a stone cottage somewhere at the back of the town near the church of St Nicholas. That too had been hit, judging by the group of people in the churchyard, although the church still seemed solid enough and she was glad. The safety of St Nicholas Hythe was a good portent for St Nicholas in Ashden.

The cottage was not large, and Yves brought her into the first of the two rooms downstairs. She took in nothing of her surroundings, save that they spoke of their former resident, not Yves. The photographs, the pictures, and the commemoration china displayed looked English.

"I have no Mrs Dibble," Yves apologised, "and my batman is in London, so for food you are at my mercy."

He drew across the curtains before switching on the gas light. His face looked grey in the flickering lights; there were streaks of dirt on his jaw and bloodstains on his uniform.

"I couldn't eat."

"Water first, for your stomach, and then soup before you sleep."

She did not have the strength to protest further, and sat down at the small gate-leg dining table when he returned with a tray, two bowls of soup and bread.

"This is waterzooi soup, left over from the vegetables and water the chicken was boiled in."

She found this puzzling. "What a coincidence. Did you guess I was coming?"

"No. I am too lazy to cook anything else now. It is always waterzooi soup."

She managed a real smile at that. The soup with tiny bits of chicken as well as the soft vegetables slid into her stomach surprisingly easily.

"Yves—" she began, but he interrupted her.

"No. You need sleep, *cara*." He took her by the hand when she had finished. "I will show you the privy as you call it, then I will show you the scullery with the washing basin which the owner of this house calls the bathroom. And then I will show you the bedroom."

She saw nothing odd in this; it seemed quite natural that he should be leading her up the narrow cottage staircase to the two bedrooms. He pushed open the door to the larger one. "That is where you will sleep," he said gently. "And I will sleep where my batman usually rests."

She stood still. "I can't."

He misunderstood. "You need have no fear. I will not—"

"No." She brushed this impatiently aside. Couldn't he understand? "Not *alone*. Not tonight." When the eyes closed nightmares would begin, the smell, the sight of charred broken bodies would rush back and Tontine Street engulf her.

He was silent for a moment, his arm still round her. "Very well," he said at last, "I will stay with you, but you will sleep, *cara*, we will both sleep, and no nightmares will come. That is understood?"

He was waiting for her when she came upstairs again. She had had to force herself even to visit the privy, and then to wash at least her face and clean her teeth with the powder and brush he must have put there for her while he was in the kitchen. But that was all. She wanted to strip off all her clothes to help eradicate the memories of the evening, but she was too tired to do so, and he led her into the bedroom, sitting her on the edge of the bed.

"Wait," he commanded. When he returned from his own ablutions, he took off her jacket, her boots and then her stockings as if undressing a doll. He loosened the waistband of her skirt and unfastened the two top buttons of her blouse.

"No more," he said. "Nor I either."

She watched as his boots joined hers on the floor, and his

244

tunic was laid by her jacket. Then he turned to her and took her in his arms. He still smelt of smoke, she could see dust in his hair, and knew that he smelt and saw the same on her. So they were together, and her eyes closed.

But the nightmares still came.

Her own cry awoke her in the early hours of the morning, and she sat bolt upright in the dark, her brain reacting slowly to what had happened and where she was. Then it came back. *Yves* was here.

"*Cara*, they are bad dreams, that is all."

His voice came out of the dark. She struggled to make sense, to divide the reality from that of her sleep. One thought seemed to crystallise all her terrors, and she wept it out to him.

"I never bought the meat."

"*Quoi?*" He sat up and put his arm round her, and she realised the ridiculous thing she had said. Yet she had to explain, for it seemed very important to do so.

"That's why I went, to get my landlady's meat and vegetables."

"You have probably saved them from a horrible fate if I remember your landlady's cooking rightly. Now, sleep, if you please. For my sake."

She couldn't. If she did, she knew the other memories would flood back again, and lay half-awake, half-asleep. She was in the Rectory kitchen. Mrs Dibble had no food and it was her fault. "Vegetable stew," she muttered.

"Sleep, *ma petite*, sleep."

"I can't."

"Then I shall light first a candle and then the gas to wake us up properly, and we will try again, in half an hour."

She sat up gratefully and the nightmares began to inch away as the gas hissed gently over their heads. Yves looked flushed, his hair and clothes dishevelled and she was aware she must look even worse. She didn't care, even that she was keeping him from sleep.

"What are you thinking about?" he asked politely. He swung his legs to the floor, came round to her and sat by her side, shifting after he had managed to find the exact spot where her left leg lay.

"How strange life is, I suppose. I began this morning cheering myself up because it was a beautiful spring day, and this evening here I am sleeping in your arms."

"And that," he took her hands, "makes you happy or unhappy?"

"It just seems right."

He stood up abruptly and moved away, his back to her. What had she said that wasn't obvious? She didn't care, for what was the point of holding anything back now?

"Why did you go, Yves?" she burst out. "Why do you call me *cara* when you hurt me so much? And why call me *cara* anyway? It's Italian, you're Belgian. It isn't fair. Why—" She stopped. There were so many whys, but only one that mattered. Why weren't you here?

At first she thought he would not answer, but he did. "My elder sister is married to an Italian naval officer, and I know and love the language. Why did I go away? That too is simple. Because we men are not so good at these matters as women. We act instead of speaking, imagining that explains all, but it explains nothing. I went away because I loved you. And because of that I thought of you as *cara*, not Caroline."

She seized on the one word. "Loved? You no longer do?"

He was at her side again and she in his arms. "Love, of course I love you still. Why else did I go away? My English is not so good that I never make mistakes in mere verbs. Past and present is the same; I love you, Caroline. I had loved you even before the first time I met you formally at Ashdown Park. I loved you, then, I went on loving you, and I will go on loving you. Is that enough verbs, *cara mia*?" He rocked her to and fro in his arms, grasping her so tight he was hurting her. "And then at Christmas I kissed you. I should not have done that."

246

"Why not?" Oh, the wasted months of misunderstanding.

"Because I wanted to make love to you so much I knew if I stayed it would happen."

"But that's what I wanted – *want*," she cried. "Please." She lay back trying to draw his body onto hers, but he resisted. His head was buried in her breast, but he would come no further.

"No." His voice was muffled.

"But why?" The pain was too great. So far, so much, so little.

"Because I can't marry you, much as I want to."

Her arms dropped away, and he sat up. "Why not?" she asked dully. "Because you're a Roman Catholic and I'm Protestant?"

"No. Yes. Caroline, you wanted to know about my family." His hands were clenched hard. "I told you the truth, but not all the truth. I am married."

She began to shiver again, though the night was warm, wanting to push this away and pretend it wasn't happening. "Why didn't you tell me?"

"Because for the first time for many years I had found some happiness and didn't want to lose it. Then I saw that was selfish and went away."

"You're not happy with your wife?"

When she woke up tomorrow, perhaps this whole terrible evening would prove to have been a dream, and she would be in her own single bed at her lodgings. Or back at the Rectory. Oh, for the Rectory's comforting arms.

"Do you wish to know the whole story?"

"Yes." However hard to bear.

"Very well. Annette-Marie was the daughter of a neighbouring estate owner. Our families were both Roman Catholic, both with army connections, and similar in age. She is now twenty-seven, five years younger than me. It is a familiar tale. We played together as children, our parents were eager that we should marry. Too eager, for I was full of romantic and headstrong ideas and refused. I fell in love with a dancer. It was a dream, and it died like all dreams do. She would not marry me, for I was not rich enough. We lived together, she was unfaithful and laughed when I protested. Beauty such as hers should be shared, she told me. I went back home and found that Annette-Marie had waited for me. She comforted me, bolstered up my male esteem, and eventually in gratitude I married her."

"Without loving her?"

"I believed I did. I thought that old ways, old customs, understanding hearts, added up to love."

"But you weren't happy."

"No. The dancer wanted riches, Annette-Marie wanted shelter and protection. I gave them to her, but she gave nothing to me."

"No children?" She managed to get the word out.

"No. She gave *nothing*. The marriage was never consummated."

He spoke so matter-of-factly she did not at first realise what he'd said. When she did, she reached out to take his hand. "Why, Yves?" she asked quietly. "Did she not want children?"

"No. She didn't want me. She has—" he hesitated "—a great fear of love."

"And nothing can be done?" She meant to help his wife, but he misunderstood.

"I am bound to her. My Church does not believe in divorce, and I, alas, do believe in honour. I could not put her through the pain of seeking an annulment, after what she did for me when I most needed it, nor after what she is undoubtedly suffering as my wife in German-held Belgium. Now, do you see, Caroline, why I went away?"

"Yes."

"I have brought pain to you, when I thought by leaving so quickly I could avoid doing so, that two light kisses would be easily forgotten."

"They are not."

She put her arms round him, and he relaxed towards her. She

248

tried so hard to think at this worst of times. In the end it was not difficult, for she already knew.

"It doesn't matter, Yves. I want to be yours anyway."

"No. Tomorrow I must go, *cara*."

"Then tonight. Can't we have that together?" she cried, unable to believe he could mean it.

"No," he said harshly.

"But—"

"I would never find the strength to leave you again," he interrupted. "And I have to return to London. Luke tells me you have realised there is something wrong with the intelligence you are receiving from Captain Cameron's networks. You are right, and that is another reason I must go."

"Won't I see you again?"

"I could not bear it, Caroline. We men are not so strong."

"If you won't love me, will you stay with me until the morning?"

"Yes."

Seeing how his hands trembled as he turned out the gas, she made a supreme effort to help him, surmounting her own pain. "But I don't want waterzooi for breakfast."

Fifteen

C aroline had leapt at the idea of the annual tennis match when her mother diffidently suggested it. It could not be so harrowing as last year, and she would not be sorry to leave Folkestone for two days. The townspeople and military authorities were both still recovering from the catastrophe of 25th May, and like many others every time she went into the town centre, she found herself constantly looking up to see whether the sky was criss-crossed with unfamiliar aeroplane formations; every aeroplane that passed over brought a sigh of relief. On 5th June it had been Sheerness's turn, and eleven days ago Margate and London.

They were all Gotha raids, the new German aeroplane which had taken them unawares in May. No wonder no one had recognised them. They would now. The word Gotha had replaced Zeppelin in the language of fear. The toll in London had been 162 killed and 432 injured. Sixteen of the dead had been young children in a school at Poplar, and this had added to the nightmares which still besieged her. The Zeppelins hadn't given up, however. Three days after the London raid they were back.

Rumours were still flying back and forth about the scale of the horror in Folkestone, but it seemed over ninety were dead and nearly two hundred injured. The coroner's inquest held the day after the raid had been highly emotional, and grief had united the town ever since. Caroline had not been able to bear to visit Tontine Street, where the greatest loss of life had been, since that day. Mr Hall, the friendly pork butcher had died, so had Mr Stokes and his son, and Mr Gosnold. She had known none of these men well, but they had been part of her daily life. Now war had plucked them away. Just as it had Reggie, just as it had Yves.

Perhaps the tennis match would give her a breathing space to think calmly. Her mother was waving a letter, when Caroline walked in, after an agonisingly slow and crowded train journey from Folkestone to the Wells. "We've heard from George," she cried jubilantly. It was 22nd June and they had had no letters since late in May. Her mother promptly burst into tears. "He's still writing about the death of Albert Ball and about how marvellous the other fellows are. Nothing about himself, save that he's having a 'topping time'."

"That's good news," Caroline said firmly.

"Yes. Oh, what a splendid day, and Phoebe wrote yesterday to say she had driven Harry Lauder to a camp concert, and weren't these music-hall stars fun? Your father pulled a face but he could hardly say he would prefer her to do Felicia's job, could he? So everything's wonderful, and you're home too, and now we can enjoy the tennis match," Elizabeth finished happily.

She *would* enjoy it, Caroline vowed. No matter that for the first time she felt like a visitor to the Rectory, for no longer could all her problems and worries be poured out to her parents or sisters. What had happened between her and Yves was battened down within her. No one could help save she herself. And she would. If the rest of her life had to be spent without Yves, then she might as well start getting used to the fact. Enjoying the tennis match was a tiny but important start.

Isabel, to Caroline's surprise, was in charge. Her sister's interest in tennis before the war had been minimal, but now she was enthusiastically organising the whole afternoon. Perhaps it was because of her *rapprochement* with the absent Robert, Caroline thought hopefully, pushing out of her mind the unworthy suspicion that Isabel must meet a lot of the officers from The Towers at the picture palace. She hardly recognised her sister. She was looking happy, far from the moody Isabel of last winter. Furthermore, her interest in high fashion seemed to have lessened, and instead of the ornate creations she had worn for the last two years, regardless of economy, she was in serviceable plain green linen.

"Have you heard from Robert, Isabel?" In April he had joined No. 25 Balloon Section in Flanders, and as Caroline had feared, the new offensive was clearly about to start at Ypres. On the 7th, there had been a massive strike to throw the Germans off the Messines Ridge, preceded by the greatest bombardment yet and the explosion of massive mines set under the ridge by months of tunnelling work. Felicia had written as soon as she could, and described the great black cloud on top of the red columns of flame that shot into the sky. The earth was shaking for miles around, and they had treated hundreds of dazed soldiers incapable of rational action. 'They say there's no such thing as shell-shock; they should have been at Messines Ridge.'

The Ridge had been taken, however, and when the main offensive began, it would be with much greater hope than had seemed possible earlier this year.

And what then if Belgium were freed? Caroline had heard nothing from Yves, nor had she expected to. They had parted, and she would never see him again, but that did not stop her worrying about him. Again her secret dread returned that he was in occupied Belgium, perhaps he had even managed to evade arrest and visit his wife – the knife twisted in the wound.

"I've drawn you, Caroline."

Philip strolled up looking pleased, though he had little cause to, she pointed out. She was not good at tennis, although not quite so bad as Isabel. Isabel had had no difficulty finding players this year, both female and male, since The Towers' officers were only too happy to oblige. Unfortunately one was called away this morning, and Percy Dibble had been the only solution, to Caroline's amusement. He looked very unhappy indeed – and she was even more amused when she found he'd drawn Isabel as a partner.

"Agnes, you mind what you're doing with that butter. Save on bread, save on fats. Spread thin, my girl."

There was no rancour in Margaret's voice, she felt as proud as a turkey-cock getting all this organised. She might not have Miss Caroline at her beck and call like she used to, or Miss Phoebe and Master George rushing through the kitchen like express trains, but life went on, and new faces were taking their place. Elizabeth Agnes was sitting on a stool at the table, 'helping' to whip cream. Myrtle was laying out the cutlery on the garden tables. Agnes was busy with the sandwiches. Everything was all right. When the war ended, Lizzie would still have her baby, even if it would have two fathers; Joe and Muriel would be popping in with their kiddies and Fred would be whistling around doing the lamps or out in his workshop, happy as the day is long. Having the tennis party was like lighting a candle in the window to tell them the Rectory was keeping the flag flying. She'd do her best to give as good a tea as she used to, despite the Kaiser sinking ships like he was drowning flies, and then they'd all come marching home safe and sound. What were a few meatless days, or potatoless days? What was rationing if it happened, come to that? She could put up with it all.

Myrtle came in; she said it was to find a few more spoons, but really she was agog to impart her news. "Those Land Army ladies says the Government's bought Castle Tillow."

"Prime Minister going to live there, is he?" If looks could kill, Myrtle would fall down dead. Didn't she ever think before she spoke? Agnes wouldn't want to be reminded of Castle Tillow with what she'd been through.

Myrtle shook her head. "It's going to be a hostel for the Land Army girls."

"Well, I never did." Then seeing Agnes was quiet, Margaret said to her: "There's no such thing as ghosts. Cleaned out, dried out, and made all nice for the girls will be a good thing."

"Yes," Agnes agreed. "But I'm not going back there."

"You'd better not, Agnes. The Rectory would come to a full stop."

Agnes blushed, pleased at the compliment, especially considering where it came from.

Two hours later Margaret surveyed her finished handiwork. It looked, she was forced to admit, a sorry sight compared with what she could remember at the beginning of the war, but she cheered herself it was a feast by today's standards. Dried fruit had to be dropped into cakes like milestones. Eleven ships had been sunk in a week and one of them must have been carrying her currants.

Caroline, having as usual been knocked out of the first round (together with Isabel and Percy, to his evident relief), sprawled on the grass, listening to the familiar and reassuring pit-pat of the balls. Caroline had executed the best backhand of her life today, and that was cheering. She felt an odd woman out here, for strangers outnumbered friends and family, and to her relief there had been no talk of the usual dance this evening. She'd go over to sit with Nanny Oates later, to give Isabel a rest. Nanny had wanted to go back home, but it had proved impossible to find someone to care for her full time, and she was annoyed at having to remain at the Rectory. She was regaining speech, but still could not look after herself.

Isabel flopped down beside her.

"It's a success, isn't it?" she asked, delighted with herself.

"Yes, thanks to you," Caroline obediently and truthfully replied.

Isabel glowed. "If only Robert were here."

"He'd be proud of you."

"I wish he'd come home on leave."

255

"It's rather soon. In the autumn perhaps."

"I want a baby."

"*What?*"

Isabel giggled. "Robert didn't want a baby while the war was on, and made sure we didn't have one. But I'm tired of waiting. I'm going to tell him so next time. After all, I shall be twenty-nine next January."

"Hardly a doddering crone yet."

"No," Isabel replied happily. "I'm still beautiful, aren't I?"

"It all went very nicely, I thought, didn't you, Margaret?" Agnes announced with satisfaction. She didn't often call her that; it must be relief it was all over. She was looking very well, Margaret thought. Must be her Jamie coming home on leave in May. Then she realised!

"Agnes Thorn, are you expecting?" she asked severely.

Agnes blushed. "I may be. I didn't want to tell anyone till I knew."

Margaret sighed. "Well I never. What we're going to do, I don't know. The less people there are in this Rectory, the more work it seems to take. Not that I'm not pleased, mark you. It's time that little miss had a brother or sister."

"I can work for ages yet," Agnes protested. "Of course, I couldn't expect Mrs Lilley to have another baby under the roof. I'll have to leave."

"Leave?" Margaret snorted. "No one leaves the Rectory. We'll have to talk it over when you're sure. And don't go lifting heavy weights like that, my girl," seeing Agnes carting a tray-load of heavy crockery into the scullery. "What do you think Percy's for?"

She finished the washing up with Myrtle, congratulating herself that everything had indeed gone well. She could do a demonstration one day on how to give parties in wartime. It would make a change from lecturing them about their waste bins and not peeling carrots and potatoes too thick. Percy hadn't done too bad; he'd even won one game with her eye on him and was quite proud of himself.

As Margaret put the last saucepan away, she remembered her post. She'd never opened it what with everything going on. Mr and Mrs Dibble it was addressed, which meant her. She was like one of them Roman emperors' food tasters, where joint post was concerned. It wasn't like the yellow telegram she dreaded day in and day out, and which everyone feared. She hadn't had one and Fred hadn't been in the casualty lists either. The Lord was looking after him, just as she'd prayed.

She opened the letter.

Caroline was glad she had taken Ahab with her to the forest, on the pretext that he needed exercise. The gardens were usually quite large enough for an ageing dog. She remembered that Yves had walked this way last year, and for much the same reasons – his own company in preference to that of strangers. Much of the forest had been taken over for army camps, but it was still possible to wander alone and take pleasure in its woods and heathland, now in full summer bloom.

It was a summer's evening meant for lovers, but she resolutely put this out of her mind. One path through life was to be closed for her; there were others, as many paths as there were in the forest, criss-crossing each other and interwoven. At the moment she was on the path she loved best, the Rectory path. That, at least, was what she tried to believe, but at times it was impossible as a flood of misery overwhelmed her and had to be fought off.

She returned just in time for supper. Once upon a time it was *de rigueur* to change – not into full evening dress unless they were going to Ashden Manor, but into something different and smarter than their daytime dress. It was no longer frowned upon, however, to come straight into dinner from one's daily work, if time did not permit changing, though her mother had told her with some glee of Father's reaction when last week

257

during the hay harvest Chalk and Cheese had come in to the dining-room in their smocks and *breeches*. He had been very polite and apologised to them for having adhered to the same time for dinner which had not allowed them time to change. They had accepted his apology, but not taken the hint. Two days later, she had been forced to have a more open word with them.

As Caroline went into the Rectory through the garden door, she almost collided with her mother. "Have you seen Mrs Dibble, Caroline? It's almost time for dinner and Agnes is coping alone. Nothing seems to have been done and Percy hasn't seen her anywhere. She's not in her room, not in the kitchen or the servants' hall, and nowhere in the house. It's most worrying."

"Gone to the village stores?" Caroline suggested.

"Not according to Agnes."

"Has Percy searched the gardens?" Caroline asked practically. "Perhaps she's tripped over in the vegetable garden and hurt herself."

"I think Percy went there. He's gone down to the village in case anyone's seen her there."

"I'll have another look here."

Caroline pushed Ahab back into the house and ran down to the vegetable gardens. There was no sign of Mrs Dibble. Perhaps she was visiting her old store? This was a tin-lined trunk hidden half-buried behind the potting shed. It was supposed to have been emptied years ago (when Father discovered she had been hoarding), but Caroline had noticed it still received the odd surreptitious visit. Mrs Dibble wasn't there.

There was no sign of her in the gardens, nor in the tiny walled garden which was 'hers'. Caroline thought hard, then walked over to Fred's workshop where she often used to find Felicia in days gone by, working companionably with Fred. Through the window she saw with a jerk of alarm that Mrs Dibble was indeed in there, but sitting quite motionless.

She opened the door gently. "Are you feeling all right, Mrs

Dibble?" Silly question. One look at her and anyone could see she was not all right.

Mrs Dibble raised her head and the look on her face appalled Caroline. "He's dead."

"Who?" Caroline asked gently, as terrifying possibilities raced through her head.

"Fred. Died on active service, they said in their letter."

"Letter? You would have received a telegram, surely. Are you sure you're not mistaken?"

"No mistake, Miss Caroline. It's from the War Office. Private Frederick Dibble, 11th Battalion, Northumberland Fusiliers, of the Rectory Ashden, is dead. No regrets. Nothing about Christian burial. He's gone. So thank you, Mrs Dibble, for looking after him for twenty-two years, but the worms can have him now."

Miss Caroline had said to wait there while she fetched Rector, but what was the use? Fred was dead, and he couldn't bring him back like he was Lazarus. So she might just as well get on with dinner. Everyone would be waiting, Margaret supposed vaguely. They couldn't do without her, she'd have to make an effort. Yet as she started walking back to the kitchen, it seemed there was lead in her belly, making it difficult to breathe save in gasps and impossible to walk. He was dead, no 'sorry, he was a brave young man, and you were right all the time, Mrs Dibble, we should never have sent him out there'.

Bitterness ate away at her. How would that Haig like it if his wife had a letter just saying 'died on active service'? It could mean anything from a German bullet in the trenches to a row in the cookhouse over whose turn it was to peel the spuds. Fred was dead either way. She felt as if he'd been torn from her womb all over again, only this time they'd thrown him on the dust heap, not put him into her arms, all chubby red cheeks and great soft brown eyes. What was the use of singing to the Lord every day, if He let this happen? How could she go on living in the Rectory, where she'd believed God was looking after them all, when He had let this happen to Fred? She tried hard to reprove herself for those blasphemous thoughts and think of the Lord's loving arms sweeping Fred up with Him to Heaven, but all she could think of was that film about the Somme where there wasn't a loving arm in sight, save a Tommy's own mates.

Margaret saw the Rector running down the garden path towards her. She wondered why, and then realised he must be coming to speak to her. She couldn't bear it, she couldn't. Yet there was Percy to think of. And dinner.

"It's kind of you, Rector, but I can manage," she shot out before he could say a word. "Dinner will be a few minutes late."

"Agnes is looking after dinner, Caroline has gone to fetch Lizzie, and I have telephoned the Hartfield pub to send a message to Muriel. Mrs Dibble, my wife, Caroline and myself want to be with you and Percy this evening, unless you prefer to be alone. You must tell me if so."

"Much appreciated, Rector," she tried again, "but prayers—"

"No prayers this evening, Mrs Dibble. That will take time for you. We can mourn Fred in silence as well as words if you prefer it."

"How can we mourn, Rector, when he never ought to have been sent?" The agony began to spill out.

"Bitterness is a shield against grief, Mrs Dibble, but let the grief come first. When you and Percy decide you are ready, today, tomorrow, a month or two's time, we will all go out to carve Fred's name on the tree."

"The tree? He liked carving animals with wood, *making* things, Rector, not gouging lumps out of living bark." She should have been grateful, but she wasn't. What was the point?

"He has given his life just as the others have whose initials are there. Would you have his name omitted?"

"Mayhap you're right, Rector. We'll see. Percy and me will decide."

*   *   *

The death of Fred Dibble cast a deep shadow not only over the Rectory but one which Caroline took with her, back to Folkestone. She was overwhelmed by the sadness of it all, the way that war had its own momentum and swept everybody with it, uncaring of individuals.

Percy had persuaded Mrs Dibble that Fred was just like any other fallen hero, and on the Sunday evening everyone in the Rectory had gone down to the tree, watched by, it seemed, the whole village now the word had spread. Even two or three officers from The Towers were there, having heard, Caroline presumed, from Isabel at church yesterday morning. The initials had been carved, a prayer had been said, and Mrs Dibble had marched bitterly back to face the rest of her life.

Caroline could not analyse why she should feel so low over Fred, to the point where Luke asked her what was wrong with her. She had managed to disguise her deep heartache over Yves so well. At least she could talk about Fred to Luke, and she did so, explaining what made his death even sadder than the shock at losing someone who had lived in the Rectory almost as long as she had.

"Felicia was very fond of him. They shared a lot."

"What, for instance?" Luke demanded. He always fastened on to any detail of Felicia's likes and dislikes that Caroline let slip.

"She used to help him nurse wounded birds and animals, and would sit and watch him when he carved wooden animals in his workshop."

"So that's where she got it from."

"I never thought of that," Caroline said with surprise. "I suppose you could say Fred was responsible for what she's doing now."

"I'm sure she would," Luke said, unusually seriously for him.

"Poor Mrs Dibble. His kit arrived back. Everything. A carved fox he'd done out there, the picture of him with his parents picnicking in the Forest with him hanging head down out of the tree laughing. That upset her even more than the letter, although that was harsh enough, just 'Died on active service'. No, we regret—"

"What did it say?" Luke interrupted.

She repeated it. "Why?"

"Nothing."

He was lying. On the Sunday he asked her to come for a walk, and she accepted gratefully, for the weekends were the hardest to bear now Yves had gone for ever. It was a blow therefore when he began:

"I have some bad news for you, Caroline. For *you*. No one else, save perhaps your father, but certainly not the Dibbles. Is that understood?"

"Yes." The afternoon looked ordinary enough, the Leas swarming with people out for a walk, soldiers, civilians, toddlers. How could there be yet more bad news?

"I'm afraid your poor Fred wasn't killed in action, Caroline," Luke was unusually gentle.

"In a brawl?"

"No. You've heard of what the soldiers call shell-shock?"

"Of course."

"Those words you mentioned from the letter your housekeeper received sounded ominous to me. There's been some talk in Whitehall about their callousness. That's why they rang a bell. So I made it my business to find out more, and I did. Fred was in the front-line trenches at the time of the big Messines bombardment last month. You showed me Lissy's letter, and that from what I gather was understating the case as regards the effect it had on our soldiers, let alone on Fred. They were wandering around out of their wits, and many haven't recovered. So Fred did the sensible thing as he saw it. He turned round and began to walk home."

Tears stung her eyes, and the sea breeze whipped at her cheeks. She began to shiver.

"The Army saw it as desertion in the face of the enemy.

Caroline dear, I'm afraid Fred was found, court-martialled and shot."

"*Shot?*" she cried incredulously. "By his own side?"

"Like quite a few other cases of desertion or apparent cowardice, and done, as with Admiral Byng, *pour encourager les autres.*"

"Shot," she repeated disbelievingly. How could such a thing be? He sat beside her on the grass, talking to her, but her disbelief remained. "Imprisoned, yes, but *shot?*"

"Many in the Army share your views, Caroline. I do myself. One soldier refused to carry out the sentence against Fred."

"And was he court-martialled for disobedience to orders?" she asked bitterly.

"No."

That evening Caroline summoned up enough strength to telephone her father. She had, she said, some information to give him, and would return home tomorrow. There had been a pause. "Is this about Fred?"

"Yes."

"I know what you have to tell me, Caroline. Don't distress yourself. I telephoned Sir John."

"The *tree*, Father. What if the Dibbles discover what really happened to Fred? Mrs Dibble was doubtful about it anyway, so what would you say to her then?"

"I shall tell them the truth. That Sir John gave me the news five hours before we added Fred's initials to the tree, and that I carved them because I believed they should be there."

Sixteen

L uke had told her he was going to Paris again. With those
few words, Caroline saw her path forward. She needed
time to think it through, however, and her lodgings were not the
right place for meditation. His casual statement had brought to
a head her concerns over the work she was doing – or, rather,
not doing, for agents' reports now made little sense in terms of
an overall pattern; they were far fewer in number and, it seemed
to her, of little relevance. Of what use was it to know that the
Germans had increased the number of civilian trains leaving
Brussels from the handful they had graciously permitted after
they first occupied the city to thirty-four, compared with the
pre-war figure of 292? And yet again the information that ten
additional divisions were moving through Ghent had correctly
pointed to a German attack on the bridgehead by the Yser, but
why had the enemy not followed it up if their strength was now
as indicated in their agents' reports? And were the divisions
noted passing through on the Menin line really because the
Germans were also about to attack at Ypres?

Caroline strolled down towards the harbour after work,
choosing a seat where on this mid-July evening she could see
not only the military transport ships, but the open sea, the other
side of which was the rest of the world. Much of it war-torn, but
one day it would revert to individual cultures, ideologies and
heritages. Much of it was ruled by Britain. It was a world of
which she knew nothing save from books, newspapers and
magazines, written by those brought up, as she had been, to

265

take pride in Britain's achievements in her empire; they reflected the native cultures with maternalistic indulgence. She began to see why Daniel was so set on travel; one could see for oneself, not be told by others.

Luke had told her he was going to Paris again. Next Tuesday, for a meeting on Wednesday. On Wednesday, 25th July Caroline Lilley would be twenty-five. She would have been in this world for a quarter of a century, and she had only just begun to understand what she wanted from it and to give to it. All around her walked people with a purpose in life. Soldiers marching to France, office workers and housewives hurrying to the shops, mothers with children. What had she achieved and where was she going? Behind her lay the Rectory, her parents, her brother and sisters, and her love for Ashden. Only two years ago she had assumed she would stay in Ashden for ever, even though she had also acknowledged a restlessness in her that made her impatient to know what lay outside. After she had realised she was in love with Reggie, she had discounted that. Reggie meant Ashden, but tenderly, she must lay them both aside. How could she take up the reins of her former life, sitting on village committees, editing the parish magazine (if she were cruel enough to wrest it away from Beatrice Ryde) and helping her mother run the house?

How could she now marry someone from Ashden or Tunbridge Wells and begin her own family? Even if she could do it, she did not want to.

Isabel of course would remain in Ashden, have children and lead the life she'd always wanted. Admired by everyone. Of all of them, there was no need to worry about Isabel. What would Felicia do? Marry Daniel and live near Ashden, marry Luke and travel far away, or not marry at all and find a vocation somewhere that was unlikely to be Sussex? Phoebe? After what her sister had told her, there seemed little chance of her returning to the Rectory. George? It was painful even to think of him, knowing the terrifying low survival rate among pilots.

He *would* survive, she told herself. And he would go to Oxford, or remain in the Royal Flying Corps, or even take up journalism with his now famous cartoons.

And lastly came Miss Caroline Lilley, spinster of Ashden parish, and twenty-five next Wednesday. Ashden's door was now closed behind her; in front of her was another closed door, slammed by the man she loved; as if that wasn't enough, the only other exit from her no man's land was a tiny door marked 'work', and it too appeared to be closing. She was trapped, and she had precious little ammunition to fight her way out. She had only one tiny bullet with which to blast her way through to the future and she must act immediately before any chance of doing so was whisked away for good. Tomorrow morning she would shoot that bullet – at Luke. *Luke was going to Paris.*

"Good morning, Luke."

He glanced up from his morning post, surprised out of his usual working mask of detached offhandedness, perhaps by the cheerfulness of Caroline's voice.

"May I have a private word with you?" she asked brightly.

"You can come with me as bodyguard while I take some stuff down to the harbour for GHQ, but it had better be important."

It was raining, but she didn't care a jot. In fact she was pleased, for under an umbrella there would be little escape for Captain Luke Dequessy.

"What is it then?" he asked, as he set off at a fast pace – deliberately, she suspected.

"I want to know why you are going to Paris."

He stopped abruptly. "I told you it had to be important. Why the blazes do you think I'm going? To have a slap-up meal at the Ritz? It's for a meeting of course."

"That's what I thought. And that's exactly how you blackmailed Felicia into coming down to Paris in May, isn't it? You told her that GHQ wanted to hear her first-hand report on conditions round Ypres at a joint allied meeting." She waited, it

267

seemed interminably, for his reply. It was a wild guess on her part, and she crossed her mental fingers that the fact wasn't obvious.

At last he replied, "Perhaps," and strode quickly on again.

"I thought it a little strange that Felicia should suddenly have left her post, even if it were a quiet time, just to cavort around Paris. It isn't like her." She was almost running to keep up with him.

"She enjoyed it," he said more amicably.

"As I shall."

That took the wind out of his sails. He stopped again. "I beg your pardon?"

"I said as I shall, when you take me with you next week."

"What for?" He managed a fair impression of his cheerful banter. "I hadn't realised you felt so affectionate towards me."

She was on safer ground now and laughed. "I'm not planning to seduce you. Your honour is quite safe. I want to come because I'm assuming – guessing – Yves will be there."

"Ah. Would Yves want to see you?"

"No."

"Then you can't."

"Would you accept that for an answer if it were you asking Felicia?"

"No."

"Would you want Felicia to know how you inveigled her down to Paris on false pretences? After all, you might wish to play the same trick again."

"Drat you, little rector's daughter," he replied crossly. "She's coming next week."

It was all working out splendidly, and even better she'd see Felicia, which seemed to place the crown of approval on her plan. "That's wonderful. We can share a room to save Mr Lloyd George money." A thought struck her uneasily. "Is that all right?"

A heavy sigh. "Yes, Miss Elder Sister, it is all right. I may not have been brought up in a rectory, but I do love Lissy and that means thinking of her best interests. Mind you," he added more cheerfully, "I don't give much for her chances the minute war ends and she says she'll marry me."

That weekend she remained in Folkestone, for Luke meanly made her work two extra days to make up for those she would spend in France, and part of them, he told her, could be spent thinking up a damned good story to cover her presence in Paris. She regretted not being at home because on the Saturday she received a letter from her mother with distressing news. The Dibbles had discovered the truth about how Fred had died. Her mother thought that they heard from Joe who had assumed they knew. The Rectory was full of renewed sadness and, what was worse, the whole village now knew the truth about how he died, because Muriel had made the first telephone call of her life in order to speak to her parents-in-law and did not realise that the postmistress who ran the exchange might be listening. However it happened, trouble had followed. Len Thorn had been home on leave, and eager to take revenge on the Rectory for its disapproval of him, had stirred up trouble over the tree.

'It looked as though the village feud would erupt with a vengeance as Mutters suddenly decided that Fred was worthy of inclusion. Your father soon put an end to the brawling. He listed all the good things Fred had done in his life, and suggested they compare that with what they had achieved. Then he flourished the knife he uses to carve with and asked who would be stepping forward first to obliterate Fred's initials. No one did, so he thrust it at Len Thorn. He refused to take it, because his fellow Thorns had been beginning to nod their heads as Father talked; Len growled something about a war wound in that hand. Caroline, you would have laughed. Beth Ryde stepped forward most solicitously to say she would cure this wound free of charge. He shouted at her that he'd soldier on, thank you very much, and even his relations sniggered.

'Mrs Dibble remains very quiet, however, and wanted to give up her classes. I explained this would be giving in as though she – and Fred—had something to be ashamed of, so she decided to continue. "Life don't stop, does it?" she said. I think it has for her, however. We haven't heard a hymn since Fred's death, and even your father misses it. How cruel life can be, Caroline.'

Squashed between Tommies, of whose language she could hardly decipher a word, Caroline hung over the ship's rail watching the khaki uniforms streaming on board, and every sort of supplies from food to armaments being loaded. She'd seen them before from the harbourside; now she was travelling in the same ship, surrounded by singing, shouting and cheering troops, though they had little enough to rejoice about, and they must by now be well aware of the fact.

"Lifebelt, Caroline." Luke struggled through to her just as the steamer funnel let off a great hoot behind her, and she saw that everyone was wrestling with them. She tried to put it on herself, but Luke had to help her in the end. To him it was routine; to her it was an unpleasant reminder that though they were heading for Paris and not the Front, they still had to cross the Channel safely. A destroyer was to escort them on either side, as a deterrent to German submarines to whom they were a tempting target. Aeroplanes were circling above them watching for any sign that a submarine was creeping up on them. It would be a short trip, but a hazardous one.

An hour and a half later, however, they docked safely at Boulogne, passing a hospital ship on its way back to England. Despite the red cross painted on it, it needed just as much guarding nowadays as the transports, for submarines were blind to any distinction in these terrible times.

Boulogne, to her disappointment, looked much like Folkestone, chalk cliffs, harbour, khaki, and stores everywhere ready to be distributed to their different destinations. Motor transport lined up for the officers and trains awaited the men. Half an hour later their train slowly steamed out, and as the smoke billowed outside the window, excitement began to replace her sense of anti-climax. She was travelling to Paris. Towards Yves.

The reason this meeting was so important, Luke had explained, was because General Pershing, in command of the American troops, had set up his HQ in the rue de Constantine in Paris, to organise the training of his troops before involving them in action. It was a difficult situation for the entente powers not only needed their early participation, but were aware of the resentment at all service levels that American troops would not be fighting until next year.

"But I thought GHQ were planning an offensive to finish the war *this* year." Caroline was dismayed.

"Quite. Thanks, General Pershing, is the general reaction. Our officers will tell our troops we can win the war with the coming offensive, yet their superior officers are planning for fighting on into 1918." Luke had explained that the Paris meeting would in practice be several meetings. General Pershing would not be interested in the views of Captain Dequessy, nor, he delicately implied, those of Miss Lilley. "He's at GHQ with Field Marshal Haig for four days, anyway, so these are joint intelligence meetings. Pershing's intelligence chief Major Noland will be there, and John Charteris, who is Haig's, and the French and Belgian chiefs too, plus Yves as personal liaison officer to King Albert." At a lower level, Noland's representative (there were only two of them in the section at present), would be listening to the Allied Bureau intelligence appraisals, which is where Luke came in.

"And Felicia?" Caroline asked meekly.

"Lissy will deliver a special report on morale," he replied promptly. "German and British."

"Why *do* you call her Lissy?" she asked. "You know me well enough to tell me now."

"My mother's name is Alicia. When I was a toddler, I decided that was a much prettier name than 'mother' so I practised calling her that but couldn't get it right. Mr Freud would like this story, wouldn't he? Lying half-conscious when Felicia and Tilly hauled me in, I called out for my mother – you see why I didn't want to tell you – and Felicia naturally thought I was calling for her. Don't disillusion her, will you?"

"I think you underrate her," Caroline said. "She wouldn't mind a scrap. Does Felicia know I'm coming?" she asked him now, as the train approached what was obviously Paris.

"Yes."

"Does Yves?"

"No. I'm too fond of my scalp to tell him."

"Thank you, Luke."

There on the right, in the distance, was a white dome which she immediately knew must be the Basilica of Sacré Coeur on the hill of Montmartre. She was here at last, and aware that happiness lay within her reach. Butterflies fluttered in her stomach, but there was no going back now.

As they walked out of the station to find their transport, she could smell food from the surrounding cafés and restaurants. Foreign food. How Mrs Dibble would sniff in disapproval. To Caroline it smelled excitingly different, and she tucked the Rectory back in her heart, where it would be kept secure.

Motor transport had been laid on to meet them and they rattled over the pavé roadways out to Versailles where the meetings were to take place. How nice it would be if God could provide one further coincidence and make the driver Phoebe. He didn't; it was a woman though, a sign that all able-bodied men were at the Front here too. Her excitement, tinged with nervousness, mounted as they drove, at Luke's special request, along the Champs Elysées, before weaving their way through the Paris suburbs to Versailles. Now she knew she was in France. The familiar sight of an English high street, each shop proudly displaying its owner's name was replaced by *boulan-*

gerie, charcuterie, chevaline – *horse*meat? she wondered, startled. Wait till she told Mrs Dibble about that.

"This is the Boulevard de la Reine," Luke told her as they drove through Versailles. "You're going in like Queen Marie-Antoinette."

"Let's hope I don't end up like her," Caroline retorted, catching her breath at the first sight of the château. "It's enormous. And beautiful. We're not staying in it, are we?"

"No. We're going to the Trianon Palace Hotel. The sanitary installations are somewhat more advanced there, so the French army wisely requisitioned it for their top-brass meetings."

Caroline had had only one brush so far with French plumbing. The water closet had provided plenty of water but precious little else. Merely two stone footsteps to step on over a hole and a flush that enthusiastically cleaned your feet, boots and, if you weren't careful, your skirt too. She was all in favour of the Trianon Palace – especially when she saw it. In its position at the far corner of the boulevard, it overlooked the château park and indeed looked grand enough to be a château in its own right. So was her bedroom; Felicia in her formal VAD uniform which she never wore at the Front since it was too impractical, looked a severe and small figure amidst this white and gilt elegance.

"Caroline." She ran across to embrace her. "I couldn't believe it when Luke said you were coming too. Isn't he kind?"

"Yes," agreed Caroline. If only Felicia knew! "I'm here to do a job of course, just like you." She had obeyed Luke, and now almost believed that *was* the only reason she was here.

A shadow crossed Felicia's face. "I didn't like coming away, because I'm sure the fighting is going to break out again in force any day now. All that persuaded me is that GHQ know when it's going to start and they wouldn't have wanted me to come here if it was to happen while I was away. Would they?"

"No," Caroline agreed guiltily.

"I did wonder why you were coming," Felicia confessed.

"Last time I was here, I talked to Captain Rosier. He told me all about his Christmas at the Rectory. I felt as though I'd been there with him. I like him very much, don't you?"

"Yes," muttered Caroline through clenched teeth.

Felicia looked at her thoughtfully. "He reminds me of Daniel."

"Why?" Caroline was startled.

"I'm not sure I can explain, but I'll try. Both of them try to rule their hearts with their heads, and to most people they succeed all too well. Those of us who love them know how hard it is."

"How would you like a pillow fight, dear sister?"

Yves did not appear at dinner, which increased Caroline's nervousness. She felt lost amid this sea of top-brass uniforms, and she was doubly glad that Felicia was present too. Yves' name was not even mentioned and she could not bring herself to ask Luke where he was. Instead she forced herself to join in Felicia's and Luke's banter, though feeling decidedly *de trop*.

In the morning she felt calmer, which was just as well. How, she asked herself, as her stomach kicked, could one khaki-clad figure stand out so arrestingly in a room full of uniforms? Yves was standing by one of the windows talking, and as the jolt of recognition shot through her, he glanced over and she saw his face freeze in shock. (Thank you, Luke, for not warning him.) Seeing his discomposure, she immediately felt more confident, and she bowed her head slightly to acknowledge him. Then she joined Felicia and Luke at the breakfast table. The worst was over.

"Caroline." He looked older, and the scar on his cheek seemed to stand out more prominently. "Miss Lilley." He bowed to Felicia. "May I join you?"

Luke waved to the spare chair as waiters (French army version) bustled around, bringing out steaming jugs of coffee and what looked like bread and jam together with new-moon shaped pastries.

"Croissants," Felicia informed her knowledgeably. "You can tell the top brass are here. We wouldn't get them otherwise."

"I am delighted to see you, Caroline." (There didn't seem very much delight in Yves' voice, however.) "May I ask, Captain Dequessy, why Miss Lilley is here?" he asked mildly.

"I will tell you myself, Yves." Caroline decided to rescue Luke from the guillotine. "Captain Dequessy will tell you that for many months I have been concerned there was something wrong with the reports we were receiving in Folkestone through Monsieur Fabre. I am a junior member of the section and naturally cannot therefore be taken into its confidence as to the exact situation with the Belgian networks, but nevertheless it seems to me that Monsieur Fabre is undoubtedly working for the enemy. Perhaps the Germans persuaded him to do so after the capture of our mail bag from the ferry last year. It occurred to me that were I to attend the meeting on intelligence this morning, ostensibly as a WAAC taking notes of the proceedings, I could then relay any information you wished from the section in casual conversation with Monsieur Fabre. False information of course. He might suspect Captain Dequessy; he would never suspect me."

There was a stunned silence as she finished, which Felicia eventually broke. "Face the wall, my darling, while the gentlemen go by," she quoted. "Have some stale bread – and do tell Mrs Dibble about *that*."

Luke and Yves seemed to be conferring without words, for Yves gave a slight nod, before Luke said, "That seems an excellent plan. If you agree, Captain Rosier, I'll go ahead."

If you agree? Caroline was puzzled. Why was Yves so involved still in the affairs of the British section? Yves looked uncertain now, and she congratulated herself that she had convinced him of the integrity of her visit. The second step was over.

The next was more difficult. He did not attend the meeting

she was at, and at luncheon he was sitting far away from her with the Belgian army intelligence chief. There would be another meeting tomorrow morning, but this afternoon was free for private discussions. And that was exactly what she intended to have. The time had come to stop dissembling, and for this she had to involve Luke, knowing he would be only too happy to escape with Felicia.

She waited in the hotel lobby with trepidation, keyed up. At last Yves came down the staircase, looking round for Luke whom he'd expected to meet. When his eyes fell on her, he obviously realised immediately that no Luke would be found. He came over to her, and from the look of anger on his face she decided to speak first.

"Luke told me you had intended to spend the afternoon at St Cyr, the military school."

"He was correct. We had matters to discuss."

"I thought you might prefer—" she would *not* be put off by his forbidding expression "—a walk in the gardens of Versailles. I know that everything of value has been removed from the house, but the gardens are still beautiful, and I would like to see the Trianons and *le petit hameau*."

"I am sure your sister would be better company – ah, I suppose Luke too has matters of more importance than mere war on his mind."

"Yes, and he is right. Yves, I came here only to tell you two things, and when I have told you, I will leave you – if you wish – in peace."

"Peace?" He raised an eyebrow. "That, my Latin master would point out, is a *non sequitur*."

It was another glimmer of humanity, and she held her breath as he seemed undecided. Several painful long seconds later, he made up his mind. "Come then, we will play make-believe for the afternoon."

"Like Marie-Antoinette dressing as a shepherdess in her *petit hameau*?"

"Yes. We too must have our means of escape."

They walked into the gardens by the porte de la Reine. The château was closed for all its portable splendours had been taken away for safety when the war swept perilously close to Paris, but nothing could affect those magnificent gardens, even though they were badly in need of love and attention. On this sunny afternoon, however, the avenues and statuary and fountains gleamed out their splendour, even if the water was not cascading from them.

"Shall we go to the *petit hameau* – and the Petit Trianon? I've always wanted to see it since I read the book by Miss Moberly and Miss Jourdain about their experiences there." Half of her wanted to plunge right in, the other half knew she needed time to get used to being with him again.

"What exciting adventures occurred to them?"

"In August 1901 they saw Marie-Antoinette on the lawn. Not to mention several of her courtiers and estate workers."

"What imaginative ladies."

"They're not. That's why they're taken seriously. They are principal and vice-principal at an Oxford college."

"Too much of *le bon vin* on a summer afternoon?"

"They *both* saw the ghosts. They lost their way, just as we might do, walking along these paths, and were directed to the Petit Trianon by oddly dressed men they took to be gardeners. As they approached the house from the rear, having passed several houses that had long since disappeared, the queen was on the lawn, sketching. It was the anniversary of the day the queen was on trial, pleading for her life, and the theory is that she fixed her thoughts on happier days at her *petit hameau* and the Petit Trianon, and the ladies somehow tapped into her images which were imprinted on the atmosphere."

"And these ladies run an Oxford college, you say?"

Caroline laughed, and he said immediately, "You are happy, *cara*, despite what has occurred between us?" He took her hand and there was a mist in her eyes.

"I am happy to see you, because of what occurred. I see no ghosts from the past, Yves. I see us, now."

He took her into his arms, and kissed her. "Tell me your two things, *cara*, and then we shall talk politely of Versailles and its splendours, take coffee at the restaurant in the gardens, and nothing more. You know, my dearest, if you speak of now, that is what must happen."

She took a deep breath. "The first thing I want to tell you is that Fred Dibble is dead."

He looked at her in surprise. "Dibble, that is the name of your housekeeper, yes? But who is Fred? Her husband?"

"Her younger son. You never met him. He was twenty-two and simple-minded."

"That is very sad, for you were obviously fond of him. But I do not see what this has to do with us."

"It has everything to do with us, Yves. Fred was conscripted, and the best that Father and Dr Marden could manage was to get him allotted to home-service duties only. Then came the Somme and men were needed, so they forgot about home-service and sent him abroad. When they found he wasn't up to trench work, they put him to work in the cookhouse. Then in May the battalion was moved up the line at Ypres to be ready for the offensive, and as women are now replacing the soldiers in cookhouse jobs, they could send him to the trenches. He was in the bombardment at Messines Ridge. He ran away afterwards to come back home, but he was found, court-martialled and shot for desertion."

An exclamation of breath. "Caroline, I am very sorry. This is terrible for his family and yours."

"That's not all —"

"Tell me, *cara*."

"Don't call me that, Yves, not till I've finished. And then only if you wish to. If you don't, I'll understand."

His hand tightened on hers. "Fred's name was carved on our local tree on the list of fallen heroes," she continued, "and then the truth emerged about his death. Some in the village wanted the name removed, by carving a large white patch to obliterate them. My father refused to let that happen, but the Dibbles are deeply, and irrevocably, hurt. What has it to do with us? Because much cruelty comes about when there is no time for justice; it steamrollers over everything and everyone. The only way to beat it is not to give in to the sorrows it places on us, but to snatch each joy as it flies. After seeing Fred's initials on that tree I believe his death is so terrible that we must fight the war by strengthening ourselves with what happiness we can."

There was a silence. "And the second thing?" he asked quietly.

"The second is very simple. It is the 25th July, 1917."

"And its significance?"

"It's my birthday."

Taken by surprise again, he began to laugh. He tried to draw her close again but she stopped him. "No, Yves, not till I have finished. I'm twenty-five years old today, and life stretches out before me like this long avenue. I want to walk down it with you, and if that is impossible, I want to walk as far as possible at your side."

"We discussed it, Caroline, and I told you why we cannot do so," he said quietly.

"Then we must discuss it again. At Easter in 1914 I was listening to the blackbird singing in the tree outside my window in Ashden, and knew I wanted something more than it could offer but not what it was. Now I do. It's you, Yves, whether for a day, a month, a year, or for ever. I want to be with you, share your life with you as far as that's possible, and be happy with you. That's all I can do for Fred."

His hand was trembling in hers, as she quoted gently: "The Bird of Time has but a little way to flutter/And the Bird is on the wing."

"Is that why you gave me the *Rubáiyát* last Christmas?"

"No, but I don't think Omar Khayyám would have hesitated over what I'm asking."

"Life is not a poem, my beloved."

"If we don't try to make it one, there is no point to it. Yves, all I ask is that we love each other while we can. When the war ends you will return to your wife. I accept that."

"Do you think I could accept what you are offering and then *leave* you?" He flushed angrily.

"Yes, because we would be sharing the same pain. I've had a long time to think this out, Yves. We must control our lives, if war is not to win."

"Very well. Now I have two things to ask you, Caroline. First, do you know what it was that I was to discuss with Luke this afternoon?"

She shook her head.

"I had taken a selfish decision – as it seemed to me," he continued. "Seeing you again this morning, I knew I would not have the strength to cut myself off from you completely again. There must surely be some way that Captain Rosier could work with you, even though Yves Rosier is not free to love you. Then you announced your excuse for being here – and do not blush, it was an excellent excuse no matter that I realised it was not the only reason for your presence. Have you heard of The White Lady, La Dame Blanche?"

"No."

"Good. It's the new name for the remnants of Captain Cameron's network in Belgium, which had broken down because of Olivier Fabre. We knew there was a traitor somewhere, but weren't sure it was him. That was why Sir John invited him at Christmas, and why Henri and Luke were also present. In fact there were two traitors, and Fabre was one of them. We have been disregarding his reports, which were faked, and feeding him information to take back to the Germans. A dangerous game, and one we must now stop."

"If only George was here," she couldn't resist saying. "He always wanted to catch a spy."

"Your brother? *Cara*, I am glad he is not."

"So am I. I couldn't tell you how much I love you, then."

She heard a sharp intake of breath, then his arm was round her. "As I love you, *cara*, and if we were alone as we were that night, I would show you how much."

"Life *is* a poem, then." She was deeply content. "Christ, that my love were in my arms/And I in my bed again," she quoted. "A schoolteacher once changed the And to Or. That is not the same thing, is it?"

"No, *cara*, it is not. So let me tell you the rest of my story instead, since it will be part of our future. The new leaders of La Dame Blanche, who are fortunately unknown to Fabre, have offered their services to rebuild the organisation, provided the British Secret Service backs them from Holland."

Caroline tried to concentrate. "That's Captain Landau, isn't it, in Rotterdam?"

"Yes, I have great faith in the plan, and I shall liaise between Captain Landau, British GHQ Montreuil, and London, and King Albert and his intelligence staff. Luke is coming to join me to liaise between Folkestone and London. We will need an assistant, and I was going to suggest selfishly to him that it should be you, in the hope he would agree."

"He'd better." Caroline was dizzy, overwhelmed with joy.

"Now I must come to the second matter. *Cara*, now you know that we may still be loving companions, please consider whether it is wise to let me love you as a man loves a woman, knowing what will happen when the war ends?"

"Wise? I can't answer that. But I want it, oh yes, so much."

They sat in the Café de la Flottille by the Grand Canal, watching the sparrows peck at crumbs and Parisians enjoy the sunshine just as though there were no such thing as war. Yves ordered wine, remarking that coffee seemed inadequate for a birthday.

"How jealous Percy would be," she laughed.

"He is a lover?"

"No. He's our *sommelier!*"

"The Rectory has hidden depths."

"It has one cellar which usually holds the six bottles of wine Uncle Charles sends us each Christmas, one inch of medicinal brandy, and Percy's home-made wine for the tennis-match punch."

"I remember." He took her hand across the table. "Caroline, I should tell your parents."

"No," she replied instantly, for she had half expected this. "It would hurt them. Yves, I know my own mind."

"Then let us begin to walk up that long avenue, *cara.*" He was looking at her with love in his eyes.

"I shall ask you to kiss me once more, as I did at Christmas."

"And I shall obey."

She was deliriously happy. Joy was bubbling out of her like champagne. She was Caroline Lilley, she loved and was loved, she was twenty-five and she had come home at last.